KU-009-528

The Secret Voices

The Secret Voices

MJ White

hera

First published in the United Kingdom in 2022 by

Hera Books
Unit 9 (Canelo), 5th Floor
Cargo Works, 1-2 Hatfields
London, SE1 9PG
United Kingdom

Copyright © MJ White 2022

The moral right of MJ White to be identified as the creator of this work has been asserted in accordance with the Copyright, Designs and Patents Act, 1988.

All rights reserved. No part of this publication may be reproduced or transmitted in any form or by any means, electronic or mechanical, including photocopy, recording, or any information storage and retrieval system, without permission in writing from the publisher.

A CIP catalogue record for this book is available from the British Library.

Print ISBN 978 1 80032 965 2
Ebook ISBN 978 1 912973 87 3

This book is a work of fiction. Names, characters, businesses, organizations, places and events are either the product of the author's imagination or are used fictitiously. Any resemblance to actual persons, living or dead, events or locales is entirely coincidental.

Look for more great books at www.herabooks.com

Printed and bound in Great Britain by Clays Ltd, Elcograf S.p.A.

I

For Dad

Who never doubted I could do this.

I think you'd be chuffed.

xxx

'You can never lose anything that really belongs to you,
and you can't keep that which belongs to someone else.'

Edgar Cayce (1877–1945)

Prologue

Hannah

They lied.

They said I only had to wait a while and then I could go home. They said it would be fun to play hide-and-seek till then.

But it isn't fun anymore.

The Small Space was meant to be the best place to hide. I was so pleased with myself for squeezing through the little doorway into it because They said I couldn't do it. But now it's getting dark and cold. And my legs hurt from curling up to fit.

There are shadows creeping across the white walls. They look like monsters. I'm scared they might be real.

They said They'd keep me safe.

They said, 'It's okay, Hannah. You know you can trust me.'

They *lied*.

Twenty-Four Hours Earlier

Chapter One

Hannah

Hannah Perry gazed up at the photographs of houses filling the estate agent's window near the Meatcross. The glass was still peppered with raindrops from the storm that had raged all morning, but she didn't mind them. In the brand-new sunshine bravely peeking out between the clouds they sparkled like diamonds. And besides, this was her favourite shop window in the whole of St Just.

Her friends at St Bart's Primary School would think she was weird if they knew, but Hannah loved the House Shop. She would imagine what it would be like to live in each one; how it would feel to run around the gardens and eat meals in the shiny kitchens, and most importantly, which room she would have as a bedroom. *Her* bedroom – a whole room she could call her own. Not like the cramped room she shared with her two younger sisters, all of them fighting for space in the too-small single bed. She dreamed of a bedroom with a wardrobe where she could hang her clothes, instead of them being piled up by the side of the bed so deep that you had to step on them like wobbling fabric stepping stones; and a chest of drawers with fronts and handles that worked, not the collapsing shell she shared with her sisters. Nothing was safe in the bedroom at home: no secrets could be hidden. Lily and Ruby got their sticky fingers into everything and Hannah's belongings were the first they tried to grab.

In the glossy house photos Hannah saw rooms with single beds and lush carpets (she'd forgotten what colour the carpet in her room was underneath the sea of clothes), matching curtains and duvet covers, princess paintings on the walls and fairy lights around the headboards. She saw living rooms free of clutter and piles of dirty crockery, kitchens big enough to put a table in and gardens bigger than the whole of her house put together. Some houses overlooked the sea;

others had enough space for paddocks and stables. Even the smallest houses seemed like palaces compared with her home.

Hannah dreamed of running through the pretty gardens and stripy lime-green lawns with her dream dog – a golden retriever like Mrs Adamson's from the end of their road. More than anything in the world, Hannah wanted a dog. She would even give up the dream of having her own bedroom if it meant she could have a dog. She'd already chosen a name for it – Amber – and dreamt of taking her for long walks. Amber would have a pink collar and lead like the one she had just seen in the pet shop and she would fetch sticks and balls and roll over when Hannah told her to.

Mum said dogs carried diseases. Hannah thought Mum should look at the diseases growing in their house, in the mouldy plate stacks and dirty bathroom sink and the spots of black creeping slowly up the corners of each room. Those were worse than any disease a dog could carry. Mrs Adamson's dog Beauty had puppies last Christmas and Hannah had begged Mum and Shaun for one. She never asked for *anything*, she'd reminded them, not even when her school jumper got holes under the arms. She thought Shaun might say yes – he was still making it up to Mum after the last time he'd made her cry – but he'd refused to budge. On Christmas Day she got a colouring book. A horrible, stupid colouring book about cars that still had a torn charity shop price sticker on its cover. There wasn't even a dog picture in it.

That was why Hannah loved the centre of St Just. She could pass the pet shop in St Bart's Street – the road that led to her school – turn into the High Street and follow it all the way down towards the park she crossed to get back to her estate. The High Street had the new sweet shop with its pink-and-white striped awning and jars of sweets in the window like a rainbow of coloured sugar, then the newsagent's with its racks of shiny magazines showing famous singers and actors, and three doors down was the House Shop. From there, she could pass the *Argus* newspaper offices, which usually had paintings in the window from a local school, then the charity shop with its ever-changing displays and the small Co-op supermarket, where there was often a dog tethered outside that she could say hello to.

And today, her favourite walk home was even more exciting. Despite the earlier storm the High Street was now decked out with pastel-coloured balloons and streamers, the Easter Market in full swing. She had gone to school for the last half-day of spring term and

6

walked halfway home at lunchtime with her friend Ava. Ava's mum wanted to go all the way home, but Hannah said she was meeting her mum at the Easter Market. It was just a little lie, but worth it to be in this happy place for a while. She didn't want to be away from school for two weeks, not like her classmates. Being at home wasn't the treat for her that it was for her friends. If it were up to her she would be camping out in her school's library, feeling safe, surrounded by shelves of comforting books. Hannah didn't want to be at home, not in the daytime. Not when Mum was at work and it was just her and Shaun while Ruby and Lily were at the childminder's house. Hannah *never* wanted to be on her own with Shaun.

He said he was going to be home early today. That's why Hannah wanted to take as long as she could to walk back. She remembered the Bad Thing and her tummy wobbled. Shaun was going to be so angry when he found out. Angry Shaun was worse than the scariest monster from her books, because closed pages couldn't lock him inside.

She shook her head, shaking the thought as far away as she could. *I'm a good girl. Miss Mills says so.*

In her schoolbag was the certificate Miss Mills gave her at the end of term class awards. *Most Helpful Person* in big gold shiny letters. She said Hannah was her Star Helper. Mum would be pleased when she saw it. So she deserved a treat for being good. And besides, it was okay to go to the market because Mum said the St Just markets were special. One for Easter, one for St George's Day, one near Bonfire Night and the Christmas Market.

The Easter Market was fun with all the stalls covered in bunting – pale green, pale pink and pale blue – and fluffy toy chicks everywhere. Some of the stallholders were giving out free chocolate, too. And even though Mum would say she couldn't have any and Shaun would be angry if he found out, Hannah took some of the foil-wrapped chocolate eggs and miniature chocolate bunnies, pushing them right down to the bottom of the front zip pocket of her schoolbag, way beneath the half-full packs of tissues, scrunched-up empty crisp packets and her old pencil case shaped like Peppa Pig, which she still loved, even though she was nearly nine. She smiled as she gazed back at the perfect homes in the House Shop window. It was a nice feeling to know about the secret chocolate that only she knew was there.

A flash of bright yellow balloons caught her eye, summoning her attention away from the photographs in the window. It would be okay to take a balloon home. Maybe they would let her have one for Lily and Ruby, too. Mum would be pleased. Free things were always good, Mum said. Forgetting the house shop – and what Shaun might say about being late again – she headed towards the smiling person holding them.

Chapter Two

Cora

On the edge of the beach, the wind whipped at her scarf, lifting it like a charmed snake above her shoulder. Here the wind was deafening, its harsh insistence obliterating all else. But this was how Cora Lael liked it: a single, all-conquering sound in her ears. As other people on the storm-battered promenade of the east-coast town hurried for cover, she remained motionless, comforted by the buffeting blows beating against her chest.

Charcoal clouds shrouded the seafront with dank dreariness, sheets of diagonal precipitation lashing in from the lead-grey sea, forced inland by icy March winds. Felixstowe in mid-summer was a draw to visitors, the town's bustling centre, pier, vanilla fudge-coloured sand and shingle beach beautiful and welcoming. But today, as the spring storm raged, the town seemed to cower beneath the bleakness. Cora had lived here only a few months, but already it felt like home. Perhaps when the summer came she would leave the town to its busyness – seek refuge in a quieter, wilder place, away from the bustle and the noise. For today, Felixstowe was the perfect place to be.

'Cora!'

A voice by her ear made her jump and she turned to see the flustered face of her friend, cheeks red from the wind's assault.

'Didn't you hear me? I've been calling you right across the prom.'

'I'm sorry, Liz. The wind's so strong.' A rush of adrenaline followed her words. She couldn't hide her smile.

'You're telling me. It's *awful*! What are you doing out here, anyway? I thought we said we'd meet at Al's.' She pointed over her shoulder with her thumb as if hitching a lift and Cora followed its direction towards the small, whitewashed building across the road from the promenade. Its windows were steamed up, glowing yellow against the shades of grey of the car park, clouds and rain.

'We did. I finished early at work, so I thought I'd come straight here and take a walk.'

'Only you would think that was a good idea in this weather.' Liz pulled a crumpled tissue from her coat sleeve and dabbed at her nose. 'Most sane people would have waited in the car.' She swore as the wind snatched the tissue from her hands and carried it away.

As it blew past Cora's face, she flinched.

I don't understand you.

She swallowed the old familiar retch of emotion, blinking quickly in case Liz caught her reaction. But her friend was too preoccupied with searching her pockets for another tissue to notice. Cora closed her eyes and willed the unwanted voice away.

'We should get inside, out of this weather,' Liz said. 'Cora?'

Steadying her breath, Cora linked arms with her friend. 'Yes, of course we should. Sorry.'

Liz laughed, but her eyes didn't. 'Don't apologise. I've known you long enough to be used to your weirdness.'

That was what she'd always called it, from the day Cora's ability first manifested when they were both sixteen. She'd been helping Liz and her mother get a charity jumble sale ready in the Methodist Church hall in St Just, the small village she'd grown up in. As teens, she and Liz were regularly roped into the community fundraising efforts by Liz's mum and they were no strangers to tackling large bin bags of old clothes and bric-a-brac. But this day was different. The moment the first bag of donated items was tipped out onto the waiting trestle tables, everything changed.

Even today, the memory of that moment caused bile to rise in Cora's throat. The intrusion was so sudden, so all-consuming – a cacophony of voices rushing in as if a crowd had laid siege to the church hall. Each garment seemed to yell at her in a different voice, countless memories, emotions and screamed opinions vying for her attention. Liz and her mother could only watch in dumbstruck horror as Cora sank to the floor screaming, her fists slammed against her ears no barrier to the sound.

In that moment, the world as Cora knew it changed. The voices, which appeared often and without warning, forced her to seek sanctuary in quieter places, driving unbreachable distance between her and everyone else.

At first there had been assessments – visits to doctors and psychiatrists, ever more senior figures brought in to puzzle over her condition. She wondered if she might be losing her mind, the hushed whispers of her parents' voices rising from her father's discarded newspaper in the kitchen and her mother's empty coffee cup revealing their fear that she was mentally ill. Cora kept diaries, noting down exactly when the voices appeared, and spent hours answering questions in countless airless consulting rooms.

In the end, a chance remark in one such meeting led to a breakthrough. After rounds of the same questions – *do the voices talk to you? Do they ask you to harm yourself?* – she yelled out in sheer frustration: 'The voices aren't for me, don't you get it? I'm just overhearing them, like conversations in the street.' The consultant neurologist recalled a report he'd read in a medical journal about a young man in 1980s small-town America who had gained local notoriety as a mind reader. He would ask a volunteer to think of a word, a phrase or a song while holding a baseball which he would then repeat correctly back to them when they handed it to him. The neurologist had picked up a pen on his desk and handed it to Cora. The phrase 'Hello young lady' barked into her mind in his deep Southern Irish accent. From that day, Dr Brian Byrne became an ally, diagnosing Cora as an 'emotional synaesthete' and helping her to view it as an ability rather than a condition from which to be cured.

Dr Byrne discovered that the areas of Cora's brain linked to emotion and memory fired when she heard a voice from an object and came to the conclusion that the cognitive pathways were somehow linked together. Where a person with synaesthesia could perceive letters and numbers as colours, or experience words as taste, Cora could sense emotional echoes attached to objects, as real as if the emotions were her own.

This did much to bring Cora to terms with her ability but little to ease the experience of living with it. Other people didn't understand. How could they? Protecting herself was her only recourse. Friendships, relationships and acquaintances were pushed away in order for Cora to claw back some control. It hurt. But to be safe from the voices meant being apart from everybody else. Cora became an outsider by necessity, not choice.

Liz Allis had seen it all and had stuck around, which counted for a lot. It was more than other people had done over the years. And while

Cora had long since given up hope that Liz would become the kind of best friend she longed for, her willingness to be a friend at all came a close second.

Al's seafront café was thick with the aroma of all-day breakfast bacon and too-warm air, which hit Cora like a smothering blanket. Passing the first table strewn with discarded sugar packets and paper napkins soaked in a pool of spilt tea, Cora shivered.

Bored…

Don't want to be here…

Too full…

Frustrated…

Braced against the onslaught, Cora focused on her breath.

The sound can't hurt me. The words are waves breaking over my head.

She found a table at the back of the café, where the table had been recently cleaned and the seats were free of detritus. Slowing her movements in time with her breathing, she removed her coat and scarf, placed them on the back of her chair and gradually lifted her gaze to the busy interior of the café. Each act was a gentle, deliberate meditation, a mindfulness that quietly brushed the panic aside.

It's just sound. It can't hurt me. The voices are just echoes of the past.

Most of the time she was in control, developing strategies to cope with the constant intrusion of uninvited voices from her environment. At work she could compartmentalise the voices she heard from discarded objects, but here in the tiny, storm-beaten seafront café – far outside the comfort zone of her carefully ordered life – it was too easy to be ambushed by them.

'I got you a Chelsea Bun,' Liz stated, pushing a large, sticky pastry on a pale pink plate towards her. 'To prove to me you're eating.'

Cora sighed. 'I am eating, Liz. I eat like a horse.'

Liz cast a critical eye over her frame, so markedly different from the soft padded limbs of her own. 'A Shetland pony, maybe. And if you do eat normally then I hate you even more than you realise.'

Cora recalled the voice she'd heard on the edge of the beach when Liz's tissue blew past her, but pushed it away. 'Not this again. You look great.'

'That's kind of you, sweets. But I don't.' Liz flopped onto the plastic seat opposite and ripped open a packet of sugar. As she emptied it into her mug of coffee, Cora braced herself. There would be three of these in quick succession: three screwed-up packets discarded, three voices to hear.

'I'm thinking of ditching Slimming World…'

Like you even know what that is.

'…It isn't doing any good and I'm so hungry all the time…'

I should look like you.

'…I should just accept this is the shape I've been given.'

Bitch.

The words hit with physical force, the steamy interior of the café swaying slightly as Cora wrestled her breath under control.

She doesn't mean it, she repeated to herself, *it's just subliminal thought. Breathe through it…*

'That creepy bloke's in again,' Liz said, nodding not so subtly over her white mug. 'No – don't look, he'll see you.'

Cora turned back but she'd already seen the older man by the window with the watermarked beige anorak, nicotine-stained fingers and yellow-grey hair that looked as if it had been smeared with butter. 'Maybe he's just on his own and lonely,' she said, defensively. She'd heard his mournful voice rising from the detritus on his empty table as she'd passed last week – a single name in an anguished whisper: *Olivia.* Who was she? Wife? Daughter? Lost lover? Cora didn't know. 'He might just come here for company.'

Liz pulled a face. 'I don't want to be the kind of company he's looking for. He stands too close to you in the queue. Gives me the creeps.'

'There are lots of lonely people here,' Cora returned. It was true. Seaside towns drew lonely people like the discarded fast-food containers on Felixstowe's seafront drew ants. Cora had heard the mournful voices rising from the packaging littering the promenade; the stories only she could hear that lamented lost loves, broken homes and shattered dreams.

She wished she could help, but all she could do was listen to the echoes of other people's pain nobody else heard. Her ability gave her a window into other lives – a gift but also a curse. She carried their voices, their stories, in her mind.

It was why she had decided this year to push the boundaries of her gift, to study its potential in real time. Right now she heard brief snippets of memory and washes of emotion she experienced as tangibly as if they were her own. But what if she could push into the sound and discover more? It was a risk. But she was ready. For years she had accepted her ability as something to live with, at peace with its existence but never daring to explore what might be possible. But now she was choosing to pursue rather than be pursued. The voices had come to her: could she use them to make a difference?

Chapter Three

Minshull

Acting Detective Sergeant Rob Minshull typed his login details for the third time and sighed as the terminal flashed the same error message. You would think the joy of swapping letters on an Acting DS's keyboard would have worn off after a fortnight, but not, it seemed, in the CID office of South Suffolk Constabulary. The practical jokes had begun as soon as his promotion had been announced and showed no sign of abating. Salt in the sugar bowl he'd heaped a spoonful into his coffee from before spotting, files from his desk mysteriously appearing on top of shelves, balls of paper stuffed into the pockets of his suit jacket and the relentless assault on his keyboard were just the tip of the iceberg. Three months into his probation as DS felt like an age already – would he cope with three more?

It didn't help that things in CID were unusually quiet. A few burglaries, a spate of farm machinery thefts and a depressing number of ongoing domestic disputes were little compensation for the mountain of paperwork they inevitably accrued. Not like the fraud ring the team had smashed five months ago – the investigation Rob had instigated after he'd uncovered evidence of a local van hire company using the business as a front to launder money. The success of that case led to his sudden fast-tracking to DS despite only four years as a DC.

He'd resisted the promotion at first, concerned it might be too early in his career, but now all he wanted was to get started. Properly started, not scuffing his boots in the CID office waiting for something to happen.

'Try swapping the "T" and the "W", Minsh,' Detective Constable Dave Wheeler muttered as he delivered Minshull's morning tea. God bless Dave Wheeler and his legendary niceness. Not wishing to draw attention to his colleague's compassionate act, Minshull made a show of struggling for the next few minutes before exchanging the wayward letters and finally logging in.

It was standard procedure, of course. The mickey-taking and practical jokes were no worse than he'd done to other colleagues daring to move up the ranks. An 'acting' job title implied career progression but was more akin to the teacher leaving the classroom and appointing a student to be in charge. Minshull might be an *Acting* DS, but as far as his colleagues were concerned, he was still very much a DC. Only difference to them was that he'd stepped over an invisible line: not one of the superiors yet but no longer within the ranks of the detective constables. For the next few months, it was only going to get worse. But like so much in the force, this was a necessary rite of passage. You were unofficially judged as much by your ability to withstand grief as you were by your ability to do the job. Superiors gave it, too. Until the 'Acting' disappeared from his job title – or something more exciting arrived to distract his colleagues in CID – the jokes and jibes would continue.

The door to the small CID office crashed open and DC Les Evans blustered in, a box of cakes balanced precariously atop a stack of files. He looked like he'd been assaulted by a small typhoon, his thinning hair plastered to his flushed head and his suit jacket covered in dark patches of damp. His arrival was met with a cheer, responded to with a string of expletives. Minshull allowed himself a small smile. At least he hadn't had 'cakes' called on him lately. And as long as Les Evans found himself on the dodgy side of operations, he was safe from it for the foreseeable, too.

'Surely it's someone else's turn for cakes?' Les groaned, hefting the files and cake box onto the bombsite otherwise known as his desk.

'Shame for you this unit's turned in such a high efficiency rating lately,' Minshull replied, for a brief moment feeling the support of his colleagues. 'And until someone else slips up...'

Les pouted. 'They're crap cakes, anyway. Got them from the Happy Shopper on Broadbent Hill. Probably months over their sell-by date. See, the longer you lot have me doing this, the worse they'll get. Another week and I'll start making them myself. Then you'll be sorry.'

His protests were lost in the rush of bodies to the cake box.

Minshull stared at his tea. Dave Wheeler was a saint and always in early, but his tea-making abilities were about as impressive as Les Evans' baking skills. The insipid grey-brown beverage clung limply to the sides of his Ipswich Town mug. No change there.

The March storm was still throwing all its disgust at the windows of the small CID office as the clock above Minshull's desk struggled to make nine a.m.

Just let something happen, he pleaded with the invisible decision-makers in the universe. *I'd be happy with anything. Anything at all…*

The grey phone on his desk gave a sharp ring, making him jump. In the small kitchen area, the youngest DC in the team, Drew Ellis, dropped the mug he was washing, spraying the front of his suit trousers with soapy water.

Suppressing a grin, Minshull snatched up the receiver before it reached its third ring.

'Acting DS Minshull.'

'Sir, it's Bren Duffy from Control. We've got a report of a missing child, St Just area.'

'How long?'

'It was called in just after nine last night. Uniform have made initial checks with immediate family and friends, but no joy. It's being passed to you. Operation name Seraphine. I'm sending the details over.'

Minshull hated the inevitable rush of adrenaline as he opened the case notes from his email. A missing child was terrible, a nightmare no parent should ever endure, but it meant something happening, *finally*. Thanking the caller, he hung up. Wheeler, Ellis and Bennett were at his desk by the time he looked up.

'What we got, Sarge?'

'Missing child in St Just.' He watched a shadow pass over the smiles of his team. Only DC Evans, still at his desk, kept his grin. There was something strange about it, beyond concern for a missing kid. What was he missing? 'Give me half an hour to get this together and we'll have a briefing. Dave, can you let the guv'nor know?'

DC Wheeler nodded. 'Sarge.' As he approached DI Joel Anderson's office door, Minshull saw his colleague take a deep breath before he knocked…

Hannah

I wish I'd looked out of the window on the way here.

I keep thinking about it in the Small Space now. Mum says I should pay attention more. 'Head in the clouds,' she says about me. Maybe she's right.

But being in the clouds is better most of the time.

Like when Shaun gets angry.

Like when I hear Mum crying.

Like when I know it's only him and me in the house.

If I'd looked out of the car window I would know where I am. I don't think I'm going home tonight. I'm scared.

They can't keep me here, can They?

Mum will be worried. I'm always home before dark. And Ruby and Lily will have nobody to read them a story, or keep them quiet when Shaun's there.

I'm glad I held onto my bag. When I cuddle it, I feel a bit less scared.

But I wish I knew where They'd brought me…

Chapter Four

Cora

'Square. Cloud. Bright. Angry.'

'Good.'

'Nervous. Boat. Iron. Hidden.'

'Mm-hmm.' Professor Daniel Gold nodded as he marked his notes and dropped another ball of screwed up paper on the floor.

Cora swallowed her irritation, focusing on Daniel's inner voice that came from each dropped sheet. 'Bird. Effervescence. Neutral. Hot sex? Cute.'

'You're welcome.' He grinned over the rim of his glasses. 'Although you don't need the paper to tell you I'm thinking that.'

She smiled at his cheekiness and glanced at the clock – an hour had passed since they began the study session. No wonder her shoulders were stiff. She longed to be back at her uncluttered desk in the University of South Suffolk's Cognitive Psychology unit, getting on with her own research work instead of contributing to Daniel's. But this had been her idea, of course: her attempt to study her gift and offer the findings to Daniel's *Cognitive Divergence* study. That's what Daniel would say if she asked to leave so soon. It was good to spend time with him – especially as none of their colleagues knew they were together – but today her need for quiet and order was greater than usual.

The floor of Daniel's office was thick with paper balls, as if a sudden blizzard had fallen onto the dark grey carpet. They'd agreed the format beforehand: Daniel would drop each ball of paper while consciously thinking a word from a pre-determined series he had devised. Fifty rounds, four words and four discarded paper balls in each. Cora would say what she heard; Daniel would check each one from the list. Clinical, measured, quantifiable, but boring as hell. This wasn't what she'd had in mind when she'd told Daniel she wanted to test her ability. Volunteering to take part in Daniel's *Cognitive Divergence* study had seemed a perfect opportunity, but after a week of the same repetitive tests every morning she felt like a lab rat.

She eyed the video camera aimed at her. 'Actually, can we take a break?'

He frowned. 'There are still five rounds to do.'

'I need coffee. And a rest.' She rubbed at her temples, the dull ache that sat there refusing to be pacified. 'Plus I have a mountain of work to get back to.'

'But you've submitted your PhD thesis,' he argued.

'I still have my other work. We can't all be like you with only one research project at a time. We're run off our feet in Cog Psych as it is: spending every morning doing this has given me a backlog.'

'Well, okay…' Even his tone was irritating her this morning: *I'm disappointed, but if you have to stop, I'll let you…*

It didn't help that her conversation with Liz yesterday was still preying on her mind.

'Still hiding you when his students are around, is he?'

Cora had stiffened. She didn't need to hear Liz's inner thoughts to know her opinion of her and Daniel hiding their relationship from everyone else. Daniel had wanted it that way and in the beginning it had been fun. But now?

'He's really keen to get this research project published. It's going to make his name and put our university on the map. When that happens, he'll tell people.'

'That's big of him.' Liz had huffed into her mug. 'Has he even asked you if that's acceptable? Of course he hasn't. *Men*. Self-obsessed idiots…'

But Liz had been right, hadn't she? Daniel had practically jumped into a lab cupboard this morning when a group of his students had seen him talking to her. Eighteen months was a long time to pretend *not* to see someone…

He joined her out in the staff kitchen, the tension in his body sucking the air from the small room. Cora ignored him and poured coffee from the percolator jug. Her colleague Marie had made it this morning and it was thick, dark and packed with enough of a caffeine punch to floor a heavyweight boxer. Just what she needed.

'You don't seem happy.' Daniel nursed his empty mug like a comfort blanket. It was a statement, not a question, the little-boy-lost response to anything he didn't understand.

'I'm fine.'

'You're not. You've been jittery for the last few days. What's the matter?'

It was the invitation she'd hoped for, even if now the thought of taking it filled her with dread. Would he even understand?

'This study – these tasks – I don't feel I'm being stretched at all.'

'It isn't meant to stretch you. It's designed to quantify how your ability functions.'

'I know that. But I want to find out what I'm really capable of.'

'Which is the point of the study.'

He didn't understand, did he? For Daniel, the study was everything. He would never share her frustration because he hadn't spent his entire adult life being singled out for 'otherness'. For him, Cora's ability was a genetic rarity, an anomaly to be scrutinised and studied, picked apart and pinned down. For Cora, it was a reality she'd lived with since she was sixteen. Every discarded item she passed, every scrap of rubbish on the streets she walked: thousands upon thousands of uninvited unwelcome intrusions into her day.

'Daniel, these tests are boring.'

'They're *necessary*.'

'I don't expect you to understand. I just – I need something more. A challenge. Something to really test me.'

His hand was hesitant as it touched the small of her back. 'Which we will find, in time. But, baby, this study has to be what it is – you know that. We need to present this as unique research with quantitative results. Maybe when it's published we can dare to be braver. But right now the faculty is depending on us to make our mark. Dean Soper wants results.'

Cora stiffened at the mention of the soon-to-retire Dean of Faculty. Gordon Soper and Daniel had always been close but lately they met for long discussions most days. Dean Soper knew about Cora's ability, proclaiming her to be their secret weapon in Daniel's *Cognitive Divergence* study. There was talk of the Psychology Faculty – and in particular Daniel's groundbreaking Cognitive Psychology unit – being put on the map by this research. Since Dr Brian Byrne's initial paper on Emotional Synaesthesia prompted by his experience diagnosing Cora, no further studies had been conducted. The first, global, wide-scale study was exactly the research the university wanted to encourage. Money and prestige were at stake and Cora was key. But Gordon Soper couldn't know she was also seeing Daniel personally. Daniel had been firm on that. If Soper found out, it could jeopardise the integrity of the study because Daniel was nowhere near an objective assessor. Of course, it made sense. But it still felt as if their personal relationship was a dirty little secret that could spoil the party.

'Oh well, if Soper wants results.'

'You said this was what you wanted.'

'No, I said I wanted to stretch myself. You decided studying my ability as part of your project was the way to do it.'

Revealing her ability to Daniel had been a risk in the beginning. She'd been working in his department for two and a half years when they'd struck up a conversation one evening in the pub after work. The attraction was there from the beginning, of course, but that conversation changed everything. Daniel's complete acceptance of her emotional synaesthesia and his delight at discovering it added fuel to an already smouldering fire.

At the time their sudden progression from work colleagues to friends to lovers had been a thrill, a surprise neither was expecting. She still felt it, sometimes. But when he was being like this – so focused on the study that she wondered if he even saw her beyond it – it was hard to find the man she'd fallen in love with.

They drank coffee in overheated silence, the whirr of the strip-lights overhead taking the place of all the things Cora wanted to say. It had been a mistake entering into this project. Mixing their personal and professional lives was dangerous. Cora couldn't be objective: everything felt like Daniel dismissing who she was, what she wanted from life. And all of it being hidden from their colleagues just magni-fied how unfair it was.

'Perhaps we should stop now,' Daniel said. 'For today. We have the responses from the global respondents to go through. Maybe it will give you the chance to regroup.'

–

At her desk, a reassuringly tall wedge of papers in front of her, Cora could finally breathe. It helped that the *Cognitive Divergence* study had already identified thirty other people around the world who shared her ability. Like her, all of them had run the gamut of ill-informed diagnoses, from mental health issues to epilepsy, migraines and psychosis, but Cora drew strength from the possibility that this study may unlock for them the understanding she'd gained from Dr Byrne's diagnosis and the growing sense of purpose she'd discovered over the years. If Cora could discover ways to utilise her ability, others could, too.

Daniel's clinical tests were exhausting, though. Everything ached. It always did after an episode, but putting her ability under so much pressure magnified the effect. The closest comparison she could draw with how her body was affected when she used her ability was how she felt after a bad migraine: as if every muscle, every nerve ending, had been drained of power. All Cora really wanted to do was curl up beneath her desk and sleep until her strength returned. But tackling a mind-numbing stack of questionnaires would at least allow her bruised mind to relax a little as she read.

Cora's workspace suited her down to the ground. The tiny, sparsely furnished office with standard-issue pale grey walls and white tiled floor that squeaked under her rubber-soled work shoes was easy to control. It was tidy, free from mess – and mercifully free from unwanted noise. Her colleagues by and large preferred silent working to chat, leaving Cora free to focus in both body and mind. She liked working here. It felt safe. She liked working with Daniel, too, but since she'd handed in her final PhD thesis on methods to improve the link between attention and memory and they had begun his *Cognitive Divergence* study in earnest, the cracks were beginning to show.

Cora caught sight of her reflected image in the glass door of the document cabinet and wished her smile were still there.

Cora Lael, what do you want?

The day passed in blessed blandness, hours passing as she worked methodically through the surveys from emotional synaesthetes around the world. Being in their company, in the cool, measured calm of her office, was a welcome change from the high emotion of the morning.

'You still here?' Rory Jeffs, whose office adjoined Cora's, ducked his head around the door. He was what Cora's mother would call *jolly* – ruddy-cheeked, full-bearded and the owner of the sparkliest pair of hazel eyes Cora had ever seen. 'It's after six. The gang's heading over the road to The Crown for a bit of post-work lubrication. You game?'

'I'd love to, but…' Cora cast her gaze across her too-neat desk with its carefully stacked and categorised papers, knowing full well she'd finished all the work for the day half an hour ago.

'What? You have to arrange microscopic dust particles into tiny DNA double-helix models?'

Cora laughed. 'Maybe.'

Rory surveyed her for a moment, before edging into the room. Unlike other members of the research team, Rory immediately accepted Cora's desire for a clutter-free workspace without question. In addition to his innate generosity, Cora suspected he'd assumed she was a fellow OCD sufferer. His office was twice as controlled as hers, with a constant covering of disinfectant from the wipes and sprays stashed in the bottom drawer of his desk. The discarded cleaning wipes in his wastepaper basket often whispered to her as she passed his room: *Has to be cleaner!* It saddened her that Rory was bound by such commanding voices, when in every other respect he was as relaxed and happy as anyone she knew.

'Come on, mate. It's only a drink.'

'I know. It's – *tricky*…'

He nodded. 'You think I don't know? Have *you* tried flushing a pub loo with your foot? Just one drink, Cora. You can keep me company. We can avoid germ-riddled beer mats together – think of the fun that'll be!'

–

The rowdy cheer that went up when Rory presented Cora to their surprised colleagues in The Crown's back room made her smile.

'The Ice Queen of Cog Psych, here? In our humble kingdom of ale? Praise be!'

'In that case, Squire Antony, you can get me a drink,' Cora returned, loving the shock on Tony Frobisher's face and the rousing chorus of jeers that went up. 'Pear cider, thanks.'

'Smacked down by the quietest member of the team, Frobie! Gotta be a new low for you…'

'Nice one, Cora.'

A rush of warmth flooded her cheeks as Rory winked his appreciation of her response. The conversation moved away from her unexpected appearance to a topic far juicier.

In the corner of the pub a TV played rolling news, the sound off to accommodate the landlord's preferred Smooth FM radio feed. Cora used the scrolling banner across the bottom of the screen as a focus for her mind instead of the clamour of inner and outer voices around her. International stock market figures danced with sports headlines and the latest political scandals. And then, the newsreader's face was replaced by an outside broadcast. Cora squinted but she wasn't mistaken – the location was the Meatcross, the ancient stone cross at the market centre of St Just, the small Suffolk village she'd grown up in. She recognised the reporter, too – the editor and senior reporter of the local free paper, *The Argus*. The woman looked windswept and a little dazed in the glare of the TV lights. It was strange to see St Just on camera. Behind the familiar Easter Market stalls Cora had visited yesterday after seeing Liz, a bank of TV wagons had now assembled. She couldn't hear what the woman from *The Argus* was saying, but beneath her the red-and-white caption read:

CHILD MISSING IN SUFFOLK

Rory nudged her. 'Isn't that your neck of the woods?'

'It is. I grew up in St Just and Mum still lives in the village. I was only there yesterday.'

'Looks like the news trucks are rolling in. Missing kid, is it?'

Cora nodded. 'It happened before, a few years ago. A child was killed.'

Even though she didn't know the boy who died, she knew his name: Matthew Cooper. Everyone knew it: if you'd lived in St Just during the four horrible weeks he was missing it was branded on your memory. The village had been under constant attack from the swarms of journalists stalking the streets and the rest of the country drinking in each horrific new development as it appeared. The whole community was judged and found wanting in the national press: its police force were country bumpkins bumbling a case, its people badly educated, insular and unfeeling.

Cora remembered her father co-ordinating the volunteer search effort, arriving home hollow-eyed in the early hours of the morning, frustrated by the lack of success and branding himself a failure for not finding Matthew. If you lived in St Just, you took it personally.

And then, inevitably, the horror of the body being discovered; the graphically gruesome injuries the press shared in lurid detail; and worse, the knowledge that Matthew had been found in a car park you passed on your way to school or work every day. The monster responsible was never caught and for years St Just had cowered in the shadow of the knowledge that the murderer was still out there. It had carved a deep scar on to the community that never fully healed.

'Bloody hell, I remember that.'

'It was so awful. And then I heard Matthew's parents died a few years back. A car accident while they were on holiday in Spain. So they never got to see justice for their son.'

Rory winced. 'Tragic. I hope this one doesn't turn out like that.'

'Me too.'

'Oi, Lael, you heard anything about your PhD yet?' Marie Tordoff called, summoning Cora's attention from the TV screen.

'Not yet.'

Hugh Davis gave a grunt that for him meant anything from amusement to mild annoyance. 'And there was us lot hoping for an excuse for a piss-up. Remind me why we brought her again?'

'Jeffs needed a buddy for when we get too lairy,' Tony laughed, seeing Rory blush.

Rory snorted. 'You'll be buying the first round when she gets it, then, Davo?' A ripple of jeers passed around the table.

'Only if this place accepts payment in *groats*,' Marie sniggered. 'His wallet's such a rarely opened artefact I reckon the Archaeology department could conduct an entire study on it. Can you open a dig site in pleather?'

'*If* she gets it,' Hugh scoffed, folding an empty crisp packet into a ball and flicking it across the table.

Spending all that time with the Prof, it said in Hugh's voice as it skittered past Cora.

So much for Daniel keeping their relationship secret. Of course everyone knew. Which made his insistence on hiding it even more ridiculous. The official story was that Cora was acting as research assistant to Daniel for one section of the study and their long mornings spent in his office were to design tests for emotional stimulus synaesthesia, not to actually be doing them with Cora as first subject. But even Cora had to admit it looked like an elaborate ruse to spend time together. Had she been on the other side of Daniel's door, she would be suspicious, too.

'She'll ace it and then you'll have to grovel to *Dr Lael*, Davo,' Marie said, winking at Cora.

'Talking of grovelling, where is Prof Gold this evening?' Tony, recovered from the attack on his wallet from the latest round of drinks, grinned over his pint. 'Cora? Any ideas?'

'I wouldn't know,' she replied, her tone measured.

'Cosying up to Gordon Soper, hoping for his job, I reckon.'

'Nah, mate. Cosying up to some curvy undergrad more like. You know the Prof and a pretty face.' Hugh's comment was directed at everyone but clearly meant for Cora. 'And if he *is* with the Dean he's doubtless relieving old Soper of his fine whisky collection.'

'Out of everyone in Cog Psych, Dan's the one who'll be in line when Soper retires, you watch.'

'Twenty quid says he isn't interested.'

'Make it fifty and you're on.'

More snack packets were torn open, emptied and discarded as the researchers mulled over the possibility. Cora gripped the neck of her cider bottle as she breathed through the silent revelations none of her colleagues realised they'd let slip:

Bloody golden boy...

Total suck-up...

Overambitious tosser...

Cora let their conversation wash over her with the music and the voices as the silent pictures of her childhood home flickered on the television news.

Chapter Five

Anderson

Detective Inspector Joel Anderson glanced at the framed photograph of his wife on his desk and wished himself with her. Rosalyn would take one look at him and know exactly what his thoughts were. She would see the battle before he could give it a name. Beside the frame, greying coffee sat stagnant in his mug – the third left to go cold that morning. In this office there seemed to be an unwritten law that every hot beverage delivered to his desk must be interrupted until cold enough to be unpalatable. Perhaps he should start bringing in a flask. Better still, a hipflask. Judging by the direction Detective Chief Inspector Sue Taylor's 'little chat' was heading, alcohol was about to become necessary. He'd suspected it coming for a while; now, as he watched his superior officer talking from the seat on the other side of his desk, his worst fears became reality.

'Missing child cases are sensitive at best, but I don't have to tell you how much more so this is for us. We can't afford another media frenzy in South Suffolk, Joel.'

He kept his gaze steady, but behind his eyes he was a balled fist of fury. Seven years. *Seven years.* Would he never be allowed to forget? 'What are you suggesting?'

'I'm suggesting you work as SIO on this in name only.'

Was she serious? 'Excuse me?'

Detective Chief Inspector Taylor didn't flinch. 'Top brass are keen to push Rob Minshull. Fast-track him. This is the perfect opportunity.'

'But he's only been an Acting DS for three months…'

What's next, Sue? Promoting work experience kids to superintendent?

'And we hope to push him to DI within the year. He's just what this force needs. He's bright, ambitious…'

And the son of the force's most celebrated officer, Anderson finished in his head. *Because that's really what this is about, isn't it, Sue?* The great

John Minshull, former detective chief inspector of the South Suffolk Constabulary. A legend in the force. He'd presided over CID like a vulture for ten of Anderson's police years and was acknowledged by most as an absolute bastard. Nobody liked him, but nobody crossed him. Even the high-ups avoided conflict with him. In all honesty, Anderson had been surprised to find Minshull Jr so markedly different from his father. Rob Minshull was new breed in every sense: driven by a desire for justice over any consideration for politics or personal gain. Commendable, but a tough road to pursue in a force still characterised by the old-school ways designed to favour utter gits like his father. Poor sod seemed affable enough – and Anderson had to admit the kid's recent success had been impressive – but Rob Minshull was not DI material yet. Not by a long chalk.

'He's inexperienced,' he argued, pushing his luck. 'I prefer my detective sergeants to have a few years under their belts before I nudge them higher up the ranks.'

His superior observed him for a moment. 'I take your point. And ordinarily, I would agree. But this force has had enough negative press recently and we need a positive boost. Show the right image.'

'He looks prettier on the telly, I suppose.'

DCI Taylor's hawk-like eyes narrowed. Anderson pictured her as a circling predator, observing him like a tasty mouse. 'Jealousy doesn't suit you, Joel.'

'And there was I thinking it was one of my greatest charms.' Seeing the joke fall on stony ground, he held up his hands. 'I'm just wary of pressing him too hard too fast, Ma'am. He's a good kid. Give him time and he might be a great detective. But I need him doing his job, not constantly chasing promotion because you lot are dangling it over him. It won't sit well with the rest of the team, you know that. It could cause divisions in CID and I won't allow it. Regardless of what the media thinks, our ability to police effectively is all that matters to me. I have my team to think of.'

'As do I. So, Acting DS Minshull will head up the ground search, reporting to you as usual, but let him co-lead in briefings, take control of operations. Clear?'

She leaned forward in her seat and for a horrible moment Anderson thought she might reach across and pat his hand. As if he were a petulant child. *Maybe I am*, he thought. But if he was never going to be allowed to forget his mistake, how could he ever be anything else?

'Clear, Ma'am.'

Sue Taylor slapped her hands on the chair arms and stood – a morning's work well done, another operational box ticked. 'Excellent. Well, I'll leave you to it.'

As soon as his office door closed, Anderson slumped back into his seat. Poor kid goes missing and his superiors see it as a chance for media redemption. When he'd first joined the force he'd believed in justice above all else, like Rob Minshull. He'd believed victims came first. Now he wasn't so sure. It was bad enough that another child had disappeared in St Just without imagining the unbridled glee of his superiors about the PR potential of the story. It was *mucky*, as his father would have said. He didn't like it. He didn't like any of it.

Anderson groaned into his cold coffee. An SIO in name only – was this what he'd been reduced to? Twenty years of faithful CID service, countless cases successfully investigated, all forgotten because of one failure. A catastrophic failure he'd only made because of pressure from above for results. Seven years of fitful sleep; seven years of counselling that sapped his spirit; seven years of constant reminders that a child had died on his watch – did it all mean nothing to them?

And meanwhile, somewhere out there, a small, terrified child was lost.

I can't think about Sue Taylor and her cronies, he told himself. *What matters is the child.*

A smart rap at the door made him snap to attention, a habit formed by years in the force. 'Yes?'

DC Kate Bennett gave a fleeting smile as she entered the office. 'Guv, briefing's almost ready.'

'Ah. Good. I need to have a word with Minshull before we start.' He stood and scooped up his notes from the desk, then stopped. 'Look, Kate – about Rob getting the DS role…'

She smiled, but he saw his own irritation mirrored in her face. 'It's okay. I know it's not your call.'

'If it was, I'd have appointed *you* as Acting DS in the first place.'

'I appreciate that, sir.'

'Well – good.' Not knowing what else to say, Anderson followed his DC into the main office.

Hannah

Maybe God is angry with me.

Maybe that's why I'm here and not at home with Mum and Lily and Ruby.

Miss Mills said in assembly once that God loves everyone and never gets angry. Except the next week she told the story about Noah's Ark and he seemed pretty angry to want to make a big flood and kill everyone who wasn't in the boat. Maybe I did something like the people who Noah didn't put in the Ark. And, instead of making it rain on me, God put me in *this place*.

But what did I do?

I've been thinking about it a lot, squashed up in the Small Space in the dark. I told Ava's mum the lie about the market. Lies are bad. But I had a good reason for it. And anyway, I don't think God would mind me going because it was Easter and that's important to Him. But the only other thing I can think of is when I asked for the puppy. It was a long time ago, but Mum says what goes around comes around. So what if They've been waiting till now to punish me for asking? I wasn't happy with the Christmas present they gave me and I said so. Why did I say it out loud? If I'd just kept the words inside my head and hidden the colouring book under the piles of clothes in my bedroom, They would never have known.

But I said it. Out loud. And it must have made God angry because here I am now. When They come back, I'll say sorry. I'll promise never to ask for anything ever again and promise to be a good girl.

And then, maybe, I can go home.

Chapter Six

Minshull

'Where do you want these, Sarge?' DC Drew Ellis asked, the newly printed briefing papers shaking slightly in his hand.

Minshull remembered his own nerves the first time he'd attended a team briefing in his first CID posting. The team were being kind to the kid for the time being – 'Breaking him in gently,' Les Evans had grinned, which was more sinister than anything else he could have said – but how long that would last was anyone's guess.

'Put one on each chair, cheers.'

'Is it a big one, Sarge?'

'Looks like it.' Minshull recognised the contrary mix of thrill and fear in his young colleague's expression. It was what you got into the job for, but when it happened it wasn't just a juicy storyline in a TV cop drama, it was happening to real people in real time. Three weeks into his first CID posting, Ellis was about to experience his first major investigation. Missing child cases were the worst, whether you had kids or not. Someone's son or daughter was in danger, far from home, scared. And that was without the looming shadow of a previous case that still hung over South Suffolk CID. Refreshing his distant memory of the Cooper case that had played out before his move to CID, Minshull had finally understood the reason for the subdued air that now surrounded his team. Anderson had led that investigation – and taken the fall when it ended in tragedy. No wonder his colleagues were concerned. Minshull wondered if Ellis was aware of it, too. Given the young detective's wide eyes and flushed face, perhaps he was...

'Sarge.' DC Les Evans handed Minshull a fresh coffee, noticeably stronger than Dave Wheeler's meek offerings.

'Did you make this, Les?'

'Thought you'd need the caffeine.'

'Aw, mate, I didn't know you cared.' It was good to joke, even if Minshull was secretly touched by the unlikely gesture of solidarity.

'We stick together,' Evans said, his voice low. 'But tell anyone else I did this and it won't just be your keyboard keys being messed with.'

Minshull watched his colleague flop onto a chair and smiled. How bad must things be if Les Evans was handing out random acts of kindness?

One by one the CID team took their seats. Minshull shifted from one foot to the other at the head of the room. He'd been in many briefings, but the view from the front was alien to him. More so than it might have been, considering he'd only been made aware of his SIO nomination five minutes ago when Anderson summoned him to the corridor outside the CID office to deliver the bombshell.

'Thanks for the vote of confidence, Guv,' he'd managed, reeling but not wanting Anderson to see it.

'Not my decision. If it were up to me, you'd still be making tea as a DC. Personally, I think you need more experience.'

'I'll do a good job.'

Anderson had shrugged, his stare still heavy on Minshull. 'I've no doubt you will. I'm not standing in your way, son. I just wanted to put my cards on the table. I don't think you're ready, but DCI Taylor disagrees. So you have my support, but you've got to step up. This is no fraud ring. A child's life is in your hands. Be under no illusion, Minshull: one false step and I'll be on your sorry back like a ton of bricks. Clear?'

'Crystal, Guv.'

Stony silence filled the room now, every member of South Suffolk CID grave-faced as they watched Anderson walk slowly across the office to join them. He acknowledged them with a nod, but there was a prickliness about him that Minshull hadn't seen before.

'Right,' Anderson said, standing by a chair at the front of the room as if unsure whether to sit or not. 'I know you're all aware of the developing situation in St Just. Acting DS Minshull is taking the lead on this, assisted by me.' The slightest twitch of his eyebrows conveyed all he wanted his team to know about this. 'Rob, if you could run through what we have so far and then we'll discuss where we go from here.'

'Guv. Right, thanks everyone. Before we begin, I'd like to welcome our good friend PC Steph Lanehan.' He smiled at the uniformed officer sitting next to DC Dave Wheeler. A cheer went up from his colleagues and Minshull joined them in spirit. He was glad she was here. She'd been his first thought when DCI Taylor had called him about the team and Steph's superior had agreed to release her. Nobody knew St Just like Steph did. And everyone in the room had worked alongside her at some point in their police careers. She may yet prove to be the investigation's biggest asset.

'Happy to be here, Sarge,' she grinned back.

'Steph's joining us on secondment for the duration of this investigation and I'm glad to have her here. Welcome to the team, Steph.'

A murmur of agreement passed around the room, smiles fading as soon as they turned back to Minshull and the briefing began in earnest.

'Okay, this what we know so far: Hannah Perry, 8 years old, reported missing late yesterday evening by her grandmother and aunt. Lives in St Just, on the Parkhall Estate, and was last seen by her teacher leaving St Bart's Primary School on Thursday lunchtime, around 1.20p.m., with a school friend. She was due home around 2p.m., to be looked after by her mother's partner, but she never arrived. Initial door-to-doors are being carried out by uniform this morning and I've asked Sergeant Vic Bonham to concentrate first on immediate family members and friends, people Hannah knows well and may have gone to visit before heading home. What we know of Hannah is that she's considered a quiet, conscientious girl, liked by her friends and teachers. It's not in her nature to wander off. So far, nobody contacted has reported seeing Hannah at all.'

As Minshull spoke he could feel his superior's stare like a heat spot at his back. Nobody made eye contact with him, their stolen glances cast at Anderson. He knew why: he'd heard the whispers. It was too close for comfort for his boss. Similar aged child, similar circumstances of their disappearance, same village, seven years apart. Matthew Cooper's murderer had never been found. Could he have returned to St Just? It might not be the same person, Minshull told himself, but the expressions of the team disagreed. Everyone feared the worst. And not just for the child's safety – for the sanity of their superior.

'It pretty much broke Joel,' DC Wheeler had confided, as they'd finished setting up the room for the briefing once Minshull knew he was SIO and Anderson had disappeared back into his office. 'I mean proper breakdown, side-promotion; many of us didn't think he'd come back. Still being counselled for it now, I heard. No offence, Minsh, but it's why you've got SIO. DCI Taylor thinks Joel's a ticking time bomb.'

Knowing the truth made his colleagues' careful study of Anderson at every turn easier to accept, even if it felt their attention of their superior was a snub to him. He could lead this investigation and lead it well. He was ready – of course he was – but it felt unearned somehow, much like the hints from DCI Taylor that she expected him to progress further in the near future.

'You're promising, Minshull. You have great potential. Not to mention coming from a notable pedigree...'

She meant Dad. Always Dad. John Minshull, the great DCI, feared and respected in equal measure if what he'd been told all his life was correct. John Minshull, whose word was law regardless of your opinion. John Minshull, who couldn't, wouldn't ever be wrong...

'Do you want to add anything at this stage, Guv?' he asked Anderson, quick to push away his father's image from his mind. This was *his* job now. John Minshull was long retired, left a king only of the beige kingdom of the family home, barking edicts at the endless blur of daytime television in the too-warm living room.

'All sounds good to me. So, what's the plan?'

Minshull could tell the effort the question required – verbal confirmation to all in the room of Minshull's position in the investigation and the diminished position of Anderson.

'I think we need to divide our attention between the school, the route Hannah likely took and the streets surrounding her home.' He moved to a map of the village, pinned to the wall. 'According to the Family Liaison Officer who's been assigned to Hannah's mother at the family home, Hannah's usual route back from school – here – would be along St Bart's Street, turn right at the end and go up along the High Street, past the Meatcross, then along Chancel Lane and down the footpath behind St Just Church.' As his finger moved along the route, Minshull pictured the young girl from the photo attached to each briefing sheet, walking along the streets. 'Then across the rec ground and up here, to emerge on the Parkhall Estate on Alderman Close. Then it's two streets to her house here, on Hickson Road.'

He glanced at the smiling girl in her school photograph for a second before turning back to the room.

'The Easter Market in St Just runs Maundy Thursday and Good Friday. I'm getting some officers from Uniform down later this afternoon before they pack the market up this evening. Les, can you start calling businesses along the route from St Bart's Street, the High Street and Chancel Lane? Find out who has CCTV.'

'Sarge.'

'Thanks. Now, Hannah's school. It's Good Friday and ordinarily St Bart's Primary School would be closed, but I called the Head first thing and she has agreed to open for us. She will be there from 12 noon today, along with the school secretary and Hannah's teacher, a Miss Jennifer Mills. Kate and Drew, can you head over as soon as we're done and get their statements, please?'

'Sarge.' DC Bennett nodded, DC Ellis sitting to attention beside her.

'Great. Dave and Steph, if you could go to the Parkhall and start door-to-doors on Hickson Road and the two roads directly adjacent – Butterfield Avenue and Appleton Drive. Liaise with Sergeant Vic Bonham – she's down there already with her uniform team.'

'No probs, Sarge. We don't mind a mosey, do we, Steph?' Wheeler nudged his colleague.

'Mosey's about all your poor knees can handle these days, isn't it, Dave?' she returned, the moment of lightness a welcome break in the room.

Minshull let its glow linger before turning to Anderson. 'Anything more, Guv?'

Anderson's shoulders seemed strained against an invisible weight. 'We're up against it before we begin. It was reported late, hours past the usual for missing persons' reports for kids of Hannah's age. So we've already lost the golden window to find her. You all know the stakes. A missing child, regardless of the place or history, is not a situation we want to have. Even if—' He gave a cough, straightened a little under the pressure. 'It's just a missing child. That's enough. Let's find her.'

Chapter Seven

Bennett

St Bart's Primary School had the smell unique to school buildings. The ghosts of cooked dinners, laminated plastic and chalk permeated the place, even though DC Kate Bennett was fairly certain no chalk had been near it in thirty years. Beside her, DC Drew Ellis shifted uneasily in his seat, his too-long limbs ill-suited to standard issue waiting-room chairs.

'Bring back unhappy memories, does it?' Bennett grinned.

'Sitting outside the Head's office? Yeah.'

'I'm not surprised. Probably only two years since you left, right?'

Drew Ellis rolled his eyes to the bright strip-light overhead. 'I'm almost twenty-five, thanks.'

'*Almost?* Wow, okay, big boy.'

It was probably wearing thin on South Suffolk CID's youngest detective, Bennett knew. But that was no reason to let up now. Besides, before Drew had arrived, the baby-of-the-team jokes had all been aimed at her. She'd hated it, of course. But it was just one of those things – like the grief everyone was currently vesting on their new DS.

She smiled at her colleague and was about to offer some respite by changing the subject when the double doors to the staff area opened and a young woman strode in. With the kids officially out of school for Easter, the teacher was dressed casually, a striped Breton T-shirt over skinny jeans and purple Converse sneakers. Her hair was piled on top of her head in a messy bun, a pencil threaded artfully through the blonde strands. The effect made her look remarkably young.

'Hello, officers. Apologies for keeping you waiting. I'm Jennifer Mills, Hannah's teacher.'

Bennett stood quickly and Ellis struggled to do the same. 'I'm DC Kate Bennett and this is DC Drew Ellis. We'd like to ask some…'

'Questions about Hannah, I know. My classroom's a pit, I'm afraid. I'm rearranging it for next term, so there are desks, chairs and boxes everywhere. We can talk in the staffroom.'

Without waiting for a reply, she turned and headed for a room at the end of the small corridor.

Bennett and Ellis exchanged glances and hurried after her.

The staffroom was exactly what Bennett was expecting. A tiny kitchen sink and single worktop with a hot water urn and various labelled jars of teabags, coffee and sugar. The drainer beside the sink held a teetering stack of mugs, none of which matched. A grubby-looking red-and-white checked tea towel, folded into a long strip beside it, housed a chaotic pile of hastily washed teaspoons.

Around the room were placed identical low chairs that seemed unchanged since Bennett's own days at school, all in an uncertain shade of green. Some of the seats were tattier than others, threadbare corners revealing vivid yellow flashes of foam beneath. The whole place had an air of disquiet about it, as if ancient resentments had seeped into the fabric of the empty chairs like the age-old stains of coffee and tea.

Jennifer Mills appeared oblivious to it all, pointing to a corner set of three chairs and heading to the kitchen area to make tea she hadn't asked if they wanted.

Bennett and Ellis hid their amusement. It was a running joke in the CID team about which officers attracted the most unwanted tea. Kate always won – because *of course* women were hardwired to require tea on all occasions – followed by Drew Ellis on account of his baby face. As unwanted tea attractors went, Miss Mills had unwittingly hit the jackpot.

When the teacher joined them with drinks, Bennett saw the cracks in her sunny disposition. Her eyes appeared red as if she'd recently cried, her skin pale behind its rosy foundation.

'Have you found Hannah?' Her voice squeaked a little when she mentioned the child's name.

'We're doing everything we can,' Bennett smiled. 'How did she seem to you when you last saw her?'

'Fine. A bit subdued near the end of the morning, maybe, but Hannah often is.'

'She hadn't had any fights? Disagreements with her friends?'

Jennifer Mills shook her head. 'Hannah rarely does. She's one of those kids that gets on with everyone.'

'Did she mention any problems? Any concerns?'

'No.'

'Did she say what she had planned for the Easter holidays? I imagine all kids are just excited about all the chocolate they're going to get.'

The teacher gave a long, slow blink. 'Not all kids. Some of our children come from very poor homes.'

Bennett felt the rebuke like a kick.

'Why was she subdued?' Ellis was leaning forward now, his question delivered.

Excellent spot, Bennett thought; for a shy kid he was remarkably observant. Was Miss Mills implying Hannah might not have wanted to go home?

'Sorry?'

'You said Hannah is often subdued at the end of the day.'

Miss Mills' expression darkened. 'Well, are you surprised? I knew something like this would happen to that poor child.'

'How did you know?'

'Experience. You meet them over the years – the kids who break your heart. The ones you want to take home and keep safe.'

Ellis looked at Bennett but she nodded for him to continue, carefully watching the exchange between the teacher and her young colleague. 'Do you think she isn't safe at home?'

Bennett watched the teacher wind her anger back. 'She is with her mum. Ms Perry works hard for her family and is doing her best. She'd do anything for them. Her partner, on the other hand…'

Ellis consulted his notes. 'Shaun Collins?'

Bennett noted the way Jennifer Mills bristled at the name. 'He's the problem. But you flag it with social services, they trot out a few home visits and nothing ever changes.'

Bennett glanced at Ellis and stepped in. 'Do you think he could be a danger to Hannah?'

'Social services don't think so.'

'With respect, that's not what I asked.'

Miss Mills picked at a stray thread on the hem of her T-shirt. 'I see bruises Hannah can't explain. The way she becomes quieter the closer it gets to home time. How she flinches when anyone raises their voice. She's scared of him. That's what I think.'

Bennett took her time writing this down, making a note to flag the stepdad up with Minshull as soon as they were done here. While she wrote, Ellis took the helm again.

'Hannah's mum said that Hannah walked home from school on her own. Isn't that against school policy?'

Miss Mills frowned. 'She didn't leave alone.'

'Did Shaun Collins collect her?'

'No. Hannah left with Ava Guiney and her mother. She and Ava are friends.'

'Was this unusual?'

'No, it happens sometimes. Technically she's not related so we wouldn't usually allow it. But knowing Ms Perry's situation, we have an understanding: if Hannah's mum isn't here to collect her by the end of school, Ava's mum will walk her home. She lives on the same estate – Parkhall Estate, over at the north end of the village.'

'Do you have Mrs Guiney's number?'

'I can get it for you.' The teacher made to stand, then stopped and turned back. Her eyes glistened. 'I'm scared Hannah's been hurt. I've tried everything to help her and nobody ever listens. And now look what's happened. If anything happens to that child it will be because the system has massively let her down.'

–

Walking back to the pool car, Bennett glanced at her colleague. 'So what did you make of that?'

'She's no fan of the stepdad, that's for sure.'

'Run a check with social services when we get back. Find out the history of the complaints Jennifer Mills has made and what was done about them.'

'No worries.'

'And good spot with the subdued comment.'

'Ta.' Drew Ellis flushed red, his dopey grin appearing.

Ah, bless.

'Bet you got your "Observation" badge from Scouts.'

'I did, actually.'

'Last month, was it?'

'Get stuffed.'

Bennett chuckled as she dialled Minshull. That joke was never going to get old.

'What do you have, Kate?'

'Sarge, we've just talked to Hannah's teacher. She says Hannah was picked up from school by her friend's mum, a Mrs Guiney? I have her number. Should Drew and I head over?'

'Good work, both. Where does Mrs Guiney live?'

'On the Parkhall Estate, near to Hannah's home.'

Bennett could hear the muffled bark of DI Anderson behind Minshull and imagined Joel giving orders from the open doorway of his office. She couldn't make out the words, but the urgency was unmistakable. Everyone in CID knew what this meant for Anderson. It was why all of them were scared for him.

'Dave's over on the estate already with Steph. Call it over to him. I'm on my way to see Hannah's mother at their house. Head over and meet me there.'

Drew Ellis's eyes were wide when Bennett ended the call. 'Parkhall next? To talk to Mrs Guiney?'

'Dave and Steph are doing it. We're off to Hannah's house.' Seeing the young constable's disappointment, Bennett reached out and patted his arm. 'Don't worry, kid. If you're a good boy I'll buy you a bag of sweeties from the Co-op on the way.'

'Not likely. My mum said never to take sweets from mad old women.'

'Oh ha bloody ha.'

Chapter Eight

Wheeler

Dave Wheeler's feet hurt. His ankles hurt. His knees, which were still recovering from the battering he'd given them in the match last Sunday, hurt most of all. He was falling apart – not good for The Nag's Head United's only goalie. Walking door to door on a council estate where nobody wanted to speak to you wasn't helping either. Every step was an effort.

He glanced at PC Steph Lanehan. She'd walked as far as him, was half his height and only two years younger, but she was frustratingly fresh-faced and sprinting several paces ahead of him. How did she do that?

'You been working out, Steph?' he panted as they hurried across the estate to the address Kate Bennett had called over.

'No, why?'

'You're walking fast.'

She stopped and grinned up at him, not even a hint of pink in her cheeks to signal any effort. 'I got little legs, mate. Have to walk twice as quick to keep up with you.'

'You're leaving me for dust.'

'Well, I didn't like to say. You getting old, Dave?'

'I didn't think I was, but my knees disagree.' He grinned back at her. 'Lovely to have you on the team, Lanney.'

'Nice to be here. Even if I am escortin' your old knees around the Parkhall.'

Wheeler felt his spirits lift despite his complaining joints. 'When're you going to do your National Investigators Exam, eh? Join us proper. You'd ace them.'

'Maybe I like my uniform too much,' Steph shot back, injecting a little pace into her walk. It was an old conversation and not one that

Wheeler ever thought would be resolved. She'd be great in CID, but Steph had been a uniformed copper all her working life. Making a change now would be a big step.

They reached 24 Mirrin View and Wheeler rang the bell. Carefully tended hanging baskets surrounded the porch entrance and stone tubs of geraniums and lobelia stood sentry on the concrete step. The old pebbledash frontage of the former council house had been recently painted and new windows caught the early afternoon sun.

You could tell a lot about someone from their house, Wheeler reckoned. Meeting people on their home turf revealed so much more about them than anything they may tell you back at the station.

According to Kate Bennett, the woman they were here to meet could well have been the last person to see Hannah Perry before she disappeared. So, what happened? Did she take Hannah home, as arranged, or leave her somewhere? Or leave the girl with someone else? Might she know where Hannah was? Was the child hiding here, in this carefully presented house?

There was a clattering of keys and bolts, and the front door opened on a chain. Wheeler could just make out blue eyes and a mane of strawberry-blonde curls through the narrow gap.

'Hello?'

'Mrs Guiney? DC Wheeler and PC Lanehan from South Suffolk CID.'

'Wait a minute.' The chain slid back with a click to reveal a tall woman, her noticeably thin arms held protectively across her body. 'You'd better come in.'

Wheeler and Lanehan followed Mrs Guiney down a cream-painted hallway into a bright sitting room. Two armchairs and a matching settee vied for space, their arms and generous seat cushions almost touching.

'Would you like tea? Coffee?'

'We're good, thanks,' Wheeler answered quickly. In truth he'd have loved a cuppa, but it was getting on and they still had so much to do.

Mrs Guiney perched on the very edge of the farthest armchair. Wheeler indicated the sofa to Lanehan and took the nearest armchair for himself.

'Thanks for seeing us, Mrs Guiney.'

'Lara, please. Mrs Guiney makes me sound like my mother-in-law.' She didn't smile when she said this. Wheeler could only imagine why not.

'Lara. We've spoken to Miss Mills from St Bart's Primary and she informed us you collected Hannah from school yesterday?'

'I did.' Her eyes flicked between Wheeler and Lanehan. 'I know it isn't supposed to happen, but we have an understanding – to help Ashleigh.'

'How long have you had this – *understanding*?'

'For the last year.'

'And you started doing this because…?'

'Hannah is best friends with my daughter Ava. We live three roads away. It just made sense to offer.'

'And the school is aware of this arrangement?'

Lara Guiney shifted position. 'Miss Mills is. We both want to help Ashleigh. I mean, the hours that poor girl works to look after her family. Three kids, two of them under five, bills to pay and no help from that idiot she's with. Have you met her yet?'

'Not yet. My colleagues are talking to her now.'

'She's barely twenty-five but she looks like a ghost. She's a good mum and Hannah's a credit to her. It's no bother at all to get her home safe when Ashleigh's working.'

'Did you take Hannah all the way home?'

'I wanted to.' Lara Guiney's gaze dropped to her long, batik-printed skirt, the cluster of hammered silver bangles at her wrist jangling as she smoothed the fabric over her knee. 'I fully intended to…'

'But you didn't?'

Lara blinked at Steph Lanehan. 'Hannah said she was meeting Ashleigh at the Easter Market in the village.'

'So, did you take her to meet her mum?'

'No.'

Wheeler felt his gut tighten. 'Why not?'

'Hannah was insistent. She said I shouldn't worry, and it was fine to leave her.'

'She's eight years old,' Lanehan said, a swift verbal slap that shocked Lara into silence.

Wheeler ignored this and pressed on. 'And you believed Hannah?'

'I had no reason not to. She's a good girl. She always tells the truth.'

Wheeler could feel the disgust rising from his colleague and rushed to get another question in before Steph went for the kill. 'Did you check with Ms Perry that this was the case? Call her? Wait with Hannah until Ashleigh arrived?'

'No.'

'Did someone else arrive to take Hannah?'

'No.'

'So you left her in the village?' Steph broke in.

Lara Guiney's eyes flashed at Lanehan. 'Look, officer, it was the last day of term. Total chaos, with all the kids coming out and my two already squabbling. I had school bags, coats, things the kids had made and two warring siblings to referee...'

'But you have Ashleigh's mobile number?'

'Of course I do,' she snapped. 'But my phone was buried in my bag and I had no hands free to search for it. And Hannah was insistent.'

She was angry now and they were in danger of losing her goodwill. Wheeler stepped in fast to pour soothing oil on boiling waters. 'Where did you leave Hannah?'

'By the pet shop in St Bart's Street.'

'That was where Hannah said she was meeting Ashleigh?'

'No, she said Ashleigh had told her to wait for her at the Meatcross. Lots of people in St Just use it as a meeting point. Everyone knows that...'

'Then why didn't you take her there?'

Lara Guiney sighed, the fight leaving her. 'I've been asking myself that question over and over since she disappeared. I honestly thought she'd be okay. The Meatcross is only at the end of the High Street and it's always closed off to cars while the market is on. Hannah said her mum loved the Easter Market and they always went together. I thought, with so many people around, she'd be okay waiting by herself. If I'd known she was lying...'

'And you're certain Hannah turned into the High Street towards the market?' Lanehan's voice was calmer but edged with steel.

'I watched her wander from the pet shop round the corner into the High Street. The last I saw, she was headed for the Meatcross.'

'Okay, thanks. Do you have any idea where Hannah might have gone?'

Lara's shoulders dropped. 'None. I've asked around the estate and nobody knows where she is.'

That's more than we found out, Wheeler mused, the frustration from their morning door-to-doors returning. Recent years had seen more people view the police with suspicion. Everyone in the force felt it. It was only going to get worse, especially with this case. According to Steph, even more monolithic hulks of TV satellite trucks had been spotted rolling into St Just, the press pack swelling. The Cooper case was still fresh in the media's minds, and nobody in the village needed reminding of that. And once the inevitable fingers began pointing, who knew what fresh hell would be unleashed?

Lanehan stepped in. 'Your daughter is the same age as Hannah, isn't she?'

'My eldest, Ava. My youngest, Lizzie, is just turned six.'

'And do you let Ava go into St Just by herself?'

Lara Guiney's eyes narrowed. 'Never. She's too young.'

Wheeler could see where Lanehan was going but wasn't fast enough to stop the next question.

'So would you agree that leaving a vulnerable young girl on her own, in the middle of the village, in a marketplace surrounded by strangers – any one of whom could have taken her – was irresponsible?'

'Now, hang on—'

'What my colleague meant—' Wheeler jumped in, but Lara Guiney was already eyeballing Steph.

'Oh, I know what she meant. I am not the villain here, okay? I was just doing a favour for a friend. You want someone to point the finger at? Try Ashleigh's good-for-nothing boyfriend, Shaun. If he pulled his weight, Ashleigh wouldn't have to rely on acts of kindness from helpful people like *me*...'

–

'What the blazes was that?' Wheeler asked as they walked out onto the road, Lara Guiney's door slamming hard behind them.

'She was the last person we know who saw that poor kid alive and she thinks she can stand on her high horse and preach to us about kindness?'

'Steph, she made a mistake.'

Lanehan stopped walking and glared up at him. 'She could have cost that kid her life.'

'We don't know...'

'Oh, come off it, Dave! A kid missing, here, again? You only have to look at Joel Anderson to see what everyone's thinking. Whoever took Matthew Cooper – whoever suffocated him and slashed his poor body to bits – they could have Hannah right now. And *that woman*,' she jabbed a thumb back at number 24, 'might just have chucked her into his hands.'

Chapter Nine

Minshull

Hannah Perry's mother looked as if she hadn't slept for days. Minshull was careful to maintain a professional distance but couldn't help feeling sorry for her. Nobody should have to endure the relentlessly dragging terror of a child going missing. A weary-looking Family Liaison Officer was making tea and doing her best to entertain Ms Perry's other two children, who were as hollow-eyed as their mother but hyperactive with the unusual atmosphere and emotion that had invaded their home.

Upstairs, his team were conducting a careful investigation of the children's bedroom. DC Drew Ellis had whispered to Minshull five minutes ago that the bedroom was in a worse state than the ground floor rooms, a fact that didn't surprise him. You should never judge a person by the order of their home, but it was hard to avoid taking visual clues as he surveyed the cramped, messy living room of Hannah's house. Most of the furniture had seen better days. The armchairs and sofa had threadbare patches on the arms, the cushions squashed almost flat. An odd sideboard-slash-display unit shouldered the wall at a wonky angle, its glass doors hanging limply from their hinges without a hope of closing. Piles of washing were balanced on every flat surface and jumbled to the point where it was impossible to tell which garments were clean and which were dirty. The cheap laminate across the floor was buckled, as if attempting to escape the lounge, and the room smelled of stale cigarettes and overcooked food. It wasn't a house Minshull could imagine anyone feeling safe in.

'There you go, Ms Perry,' the FLO handed her a mug of tea. 'Acting DS Minshull is leading the search for Hannah and he wants to ask you a few questions, if that's all right? I can sit with you if you like.' She spoke to Hannah's mother like a child but as Minshull took a seat opposite the woman he could see why. She couldn't be much older than her early twenties and looked as lost emotionally as her absent daughter was physically.

She nodded, keeping her red-rimmed eyes firmly focused on the mug in her hands.

'Ms Perry, I know this is a terrible time for you, but I assure you we are doing everything we can to find Hannah.' Minshull wished his words could reassure the young woman more than they did. 'If you can, think back to yesterday morning when you last saw her. Did anything happen that might have upset Hannah? Was she arguing with her sisters, perhaps? Maybe worried about her last day of school?'

'She doesn't argue.' Ashleigh Perry's voice was a steel-edged whisper. 'My Han never does. She's a good girl. She is *always* a good girl.' She shook her head. 'She'd be more worried about missing her last day.'

Minshull frowned. 'Was there a possibility she'd miss it?'

'No, I mean, Han loves school – more'n any of us ever did. I reckon she'd live there permanent if they'd let her.'

Not surprising, when you see her house. Minshull kicked himself for even thinking that. It was the kind of thing his father would say. 'Who else was in the house on the day Hannah went missing?'

'Me, the girls and Shaun.'

'Shaun?'

'Shaun Collins, Sarge,' DC Kate Bennett said, passing Minshull a scribbled note. 'Ms Perry's partner.'

FLO says he's hardly been here since she arrived and Hannah's teacher has raised concerns about him with social services before, the note said. As he pocketed it, Minshull kept his expression steady.

'Is Mr Collins here?'

'He's off on a job. He does bits and bobs for a builder mate.'

'Has he been in contact with you much since Hannah went missing?'

'He texts. Calls when he can.'

'When he comes back, we might need to talk to him.'

Ashleigh's eyes met Minshull's, drifting back to the mug she appeared to be hiding behind. 'Of course.'

–

'Did you see that?' DC Bennett asked when they were outside on the cracked tarmac drive, watching the team milling in and out of the house. 'She flinched when you asked her about her bloke.'

'I did. Thanks for the note. Was Collins with Ashleigh Perry when she reported Hannah missing?'

Kate consulted her notebook. 'Don't think so. Hannah's grandmother and aunt were the ones who called it in. But looking at her mum, she probably wasn't in a fit state to talk to anyone last night.'

'All the same, you'd think a frantic mother and her concerned partner would be the first to raise the alarm,' Minshull said, his mind beginning to tick. 'No job is more important than your child disappearing. And if Hannah's teacher flagged a concern about him, it's worth pursuing. Run a background check on Collins, just in case. And check for any history with social services. Very odd that he isn't here when his stepkid's gone missing.'

'Sarge.' The lanky frame of DC Drew Ellis emerged from the front door and lolloped towards them. Minshull suppressed a smile. The new detective constable was as gangly as a teenager and still flushed beetroot-red when he spoke. Minshull had it on good authority that the newest member of the detective team was regularly ID'd in pubs, his youthful looks at odds with his almost twenty-five years. 'Nothing yet up there. Want us to remove anything?'

'Not unless it looks pertinent to the investigation. Just make a note of what you see.'

'It's a mess, I can see that.'

'So I understand.'

'I mean, three kids living in that? Shocking, it is.'

'We're not here to judge.'

'But what if that was why Hannah ran away? Can't have been much fun for her, sharing that cramped bedroom with the other two.'

'What makes you think she's run away?'

Drew blushed fiercely. 'Well, we don't know she hasn't.'

Minshull observed his colleague for a moment and then smiled. 'It's a good observation, Ellis. Keep them coming.'

'Bless,' Kate Bennett mocked as the young DC headed back into the house. 'If only we were all still as earnest as him, eh?'

Minshull didn't smile. 'If only.'

Back at his desk later, Minshull surveyed the startlingly sparse evidence his team had so far unearthed. Hardly any of Ashleigh Perry's neighbours wanted to talk to them and the few who had didn't recall anything helpful. Hannah's teacher said she'd been subdued but had left school quite happily with the schoolmate's mother. Lara Guiney insisted Hannah had been okay when she'd left her in the centre of St Just. Ashleigh Perry said her daughter was a shy child and would be unlikely to talk to a stranger. Minshull's sigh shivered the edges of the papers across his desk. They would have to conduct door-to-door enquiries on St Just High Street in the morning and check the list of businesses with CCTV Les Evans had compiled, to track Hannah's last known movements. Was any of it enough? Right now, in the crucial early stage of the investigation, they had nothing of any consequence.

In the meantime, uniform divisions were working with a group of local leaders and volunteer organisations to organise a search of the village and surrounding countryside, starting in the park Hannah often used as a cut-through to the Parkhall Estate. Searches had begun at midday and would continue into the night, recommencing at dawn tomorrow. If they found something it would help the investigation. Minshull had to hope they would.

'Sarge.' Les Evans' expansive face mooned at him from beside his desk. 'Could I have a word?'

'Sure. What's up?'

The portly DC settled his middle-aged spread on a nearby chair and Minshull heard its frame creak in protest. 'The girl's stepdad, Shaun Collins. Turns out he's a bit of a nasty character.'

'Oh?'

'Did time a few years back for aggravated burglary. Cautioned for suspected illegal money lending. DSS nabbed him for claiming incapacity benefit when he was doing cash-in-handers for a local courier three years ago. And five outstanding parking fines.'

Minshull considered this. 'Doesn't mean he had cause to harm his girlfriend's kid, though.'

'Maybe not. But his halo isn't exactly shining, either.'

'Right.' Minshull stared at the notes on his desk, his mind searching for a clear route forward. It was the only way he knew how to focus in the job: one step at a time, looking for a workable path to form beneath his feet. Think any further ahead and it was too easy to become overawed by the task or miss something important. Especially when at his core he suspected he was far from the best candidate to do it.

'We could bring him in?' DC Evans suggested, voicing Minshull's thoughts. 'Ask him to assist us with our enquiries, away from his missus. If he's got nothing to hide, why would he refuse?'

There could be a hundred and one reasons why he might – his current absence given the severity of the situation his family were facing among them – but it was a worth a shot. 'Right. Let's do it.' He saw the gleam in his colleague's eyes – the scent of new blood animating him – and was quick to intervene. 'But best if it's Dave and Kate.'

'What?'

'Face it, Les, you're hardly king of the softly-softly approach. We need Collins to assist us willingly.'

Les Evans adopted a pout a two-year-old would be proud of. 'I'd ask him nicely.'

'I think we both know what your definition of *nicely* is. Let Kate and Dave bring him in. I have a lovely pile of sex offenders for you to go through for me.'

'It stinks, Minsh.'

'If it helps, I'll get someone to bring you biscuits when they do the snack run later.'

'Lucky old me.'

Minshull watched his colleague slope away. There weren't many perks of his job, but denying DC Les Evans the chance to play 1970s bad cop was one of the exceptions. He considered the grey phone on his desk for a moment before lifting the receiver.

'Yes?' Anderson sounded impatient. But then, Anderson always did.

'Guv, we've had some information on Shaun Collins, Ashleigh Perry's partner. Could be useful. I'm bringing him in on a voluntary to assist.'

There was a pause on the other end of the phone call. Minshull could hear the rhythmic clicking of Anderson's tongue against his teeth – a habit he wasn't aware of but which his colleagues were only happy to imitate behind his back. 'Fine. Let me know as soon as he comes in.'

Did he approve? Minshull was surprised by his own question. Anderson could think what he wanted: this was Minshull's call. So why had he even considered what his superior's opinion would be? The thought unnerved him and, keen to surround himself with other people's conversation instead, he left his office in search of his team.

Hannah

It's daytime again. I can tell because there's a little spot of sunshine on the wall of the Small Space coming from the gap in the blue plastic across the window. I should be going home, but They said Mum was working today so she can't get me yet.

'Just stay there like a good girl. She'll come and get you soon.' That's what They said.

But I don't think she's coming at all.

It was scary in the night in the Small Space. The spot of sunlight is my new friend and I'm glad it's here. I put my hand on the cold wall and the gold spot is like a warm kiss on it. It makes me miss Mum. No matter how busy she is in the morning she always gives me a kiss.

I've been thinking a lot about why I'm here and I don't think it was because I didn't like my Christmas present. I think it's because of the Bad Thing. I hid it. Have They found it? Do They know?

Something is bothering me. If Mum's working, who is looking after Lily and Ruby? Julie the childminder has gone to her caravan in Wales for the holidays, so she can't look after them. Has Mum left them at home on their own? Are they in a Small Space too? My tummy feels nasty thinking that.

When They come back I'm going to say I have to go home, right away. Someone has to look after Lily and Ruby. Mum says I'm a good girl. I can help her if she's busy. Mum works hard and I should be at home playing with Lily and Ruby. I shouldn't be here.

I *shouldn't* be here...

–

Breakfast News Bulletin

'The search for a child who disappeared from a small Suffolk village two days ago is intensifying today.

'Eight-year-old Hannah Perry from St Just disappeared on the way home from school on the last day of term before the Easter holidays. We go live now to St Just in Suffolk where we're joined by Jan Martin, local reporter, who was one of the first to break the story. Jan, good morning.'

'Good morning, Elodie.'

'Thanks for joining us. Can you tell us the latest?'

'Indeed. It's early here in St Just, but the search effort restarted hours ago at first light, following a break overnight. Around fifty volunteers are working with police, combing the fields, roads and residential streets in the immediate area around the village, searching tirelessly for the missing girl.'

'I imagine everyone there is in shock.'

'They are, Elodie. There's a real sense of disbelief that this should happen and everyone I've spoken to is determined to find Hannah.'

'Have the police given any indication of why they think Hannah disappeared?'

'It's too early to say. I've spoken to those who know Hannah and by all accounts it's completely out of character for her to wander off. Fears for her safety are naturally growing. As for the police, officers leading the investigation are yet to make a formal statement, so until they do we simply won't know what their theories about the child's disappearance are.'

'Now, in a further dark twist, a child tragically died in similar circumstances in St Just, seven years ago. No one was ever convicted of Matthew Cooper's murder. How is the village dealing with the possibility that the killer may have struck again?'

'People are scared, understandably. But while there might be similarities, I must stress that the overwhelming feeling here in St Just is hope that Hannah will be found safe and well. That's what we're all focused on.'

'But they must be concerned? Especially given South Suffolk CID's failure to arrest anyone for Matthew Cooper's death?'

'Everyone just wants Hannah home, safe and well. And people in St Just trust the police to make that happen. I've heard that officers will be in the village later this morning, talking to local people and businesses to determine Hannah's last-known movements. Everyone I've spoken to just wants to help find her.'

'I'm sure they do. So what can people do to help?'

'Police are urging anyone who may have seen Hannah Perry, or know where she is, to call them. I believe the incident line number is on screen now. The first, vital hours of the search have passed, with what looks like little discernible progress. Anyone with information could really make a difference to this worrying case.'

'Jan Martin in St Just, thank you.'

Chapter Ten

Minshull

The CCTV image was dark and grainy, belying the daylight in which the pictures had been captured. The High Street was a blur of activity – the Chamber of Commerce's Easter Market in full flow. For several minutes the screen was filled with indeterminable figures milling around, the only distinguishing features their height and size. The silent pictures played out in ghostly monochrome ballet as Minshull and PC Lanehan hunched by the tiny screen in the cramped security guard's office above the Spar supermarket in the High Street.

Minshull glanced down at the frustratingly sparse notes in his notebook. Had Hannah even walked this way? Lara Guiney said she thought Hannah had walked around the corner from the pet shop in St Bart's Street onto the High Street where the market was taking place. Hannah had told her Ashleigh Perry was waiting for her at the Meatcross, but her mother had confirmed no such arrangement had been made.

'I told her to come straight home. Shaun said he was getting there early to watch her. She never asked about the Easter Market. If she had I would have told her we couldn't afford it this year.'

Had Hannah been deliberately disobedient and gone to the market anyway? Or did she have a reason not to go straight home? Might she have not wanted to be there with her mother's partner? Or had she arranged to meet someone else that neither her mother nor Mrs Guiney knew about?

If they could track her movements, they might have a chance of finding answers. *If.* Minshull was waiting for one thing to make sense. Just one, to start the ball rolling. In the fraud ring investigation one piece of evidence had led to another and another until they had what they needed. Missing child cases, he was quickly learning, were

57

nowhere near as compliant. A large knot was forming in the muscles across his back and he shifted a little on the too-small office chair. It didn't help that the market stalls that would have lined the High Street on Thursday were now gone. Uniform had talked to some stallholders yesterday afternoon but by the time they arrived in the High Street after being released from door-to-doors on the Parkhall Estate most of the market traders had packed and left. Minshull kicked himself – his first mistake. At the time all he'd thought of was the estate where Hannah lived, there being more possibility of her being close to home. Why hadn't he made the market a priority?

'Sarge.'

Minshull glanced across at Lanehan, who was tapping the screen with her ballpoint pen.

'There – can you see? Is that…?'

Squinting at the blurred image, Minshull's pulse kicked into gear. A small figure holding a backpack, wearing what looked like school uniform, was standing on the pavement gazing up at a shop window. As other figures moved around her she stood out from the haze of the moving bodies, which seemed to throw her small frame into sharper focus. A few moments passed, the white scrolling second counter on the bottom right of the screen marking the passing time. And then she turned away from the window, seemed to look at something ahead of her out of shot, then walked into the crowd and disappeared.

'Stop!' Minshull called out – and it was only when the security guard stared at him that he realised he was saying it more to the girl's shadowy figure than the screen operator. He shook off the cold chill laying waste to his spine. 'Can you rewind that?'

The guard did as he was told, the figures falling back into place until the girl was frozen in a single frame.

'That has to be her. What time do we have on that?'

'1.35p.m.,' the guard replied.

'Right. How long is she there for?'

The guard shifted the video forward in slow motion, the time counter clicking slowly on screen. Hannah spent a while looking at the window then looked suddenly to her left, swung her school backpack onto her shoulder and walked out of shot. Had someone called her? Or had something caught her attention? 'So, she leaves at 1.40p.m.'

Minshull made a note. 'Okay. Where is the next camera on the High Street?'

The guard shrugged. 'Kebab shop, I guess, just before Higgins Court. Chap who owns it had trouble with break-ins a few months back. Don't know if he even has it turned on, mind, but it might be worth asking.'

Minshull scribbled another line of notes and clapped his hand on the security guard's back. 'Jed, I owe you a beer next time you're in The Miller's. Any chance I could have a copy of that sequence?'

'No worries.' He grinned at Minshull. 'Nice to see you again, mate.'

Minshull smiled back at his former colleague. Back when he was a uniformed officer he'd worked with Jed Stuart for several years before the big man left. 'You too. See you swapped one uniform for another, then?'

Jed patted the black jacket he wore and laughed. 'You know me, Minsh. It's all about the outfit!'

Out on the rain-soaked High Street, Minshull paused to look at the window Hannah had stopped at. It was an estate agent displaying photographs of overpriced property on the Suffolk coast.

'Why would an eight-year-old be looking at this?'

'Sarge?'

'Not likely to be buying a house any time soon, is she?'

'Maybe she just liked to look.'

Minshull sniffed. 'Maybe. Bit weird, still. Make a note to ask Hannah's mum, yeah? See if Hannah did that a lot. Also, we need a plan of the market stalls from Thursday – give us an idea of what Hannah might have walked towards after she left here.'

PC Lanehan nodded. 'We can ask John Dean from the Chamber of Commerce. He organises the special markets as a favour to the Rotary Club who run them for charity.'

'Do you know where we can get hold of him?'

Lanehan grinned. 'I've his number in my phone. My sister dated him for a while and we still share a pint occasionally when Fred and me are out. He owns the hardware shop on Chancel Lane, over the other side of the Meatcross.'

Not for the first time that day, Minshull thanked the universe for the decision to second Steph Lanehan onto the team. 'God bless you and your local knowledge, Steph.'

'Like an oracle, I am,' she replied as they crossed the street towards their next port of call. 'I'd say you can cross my palm with silver to say thanks, but knowing CID budgets I'd be lucky to get a Hobnob with my cuppa.'

'Can't promise you a biscuit, sorry. Or tea. Reckon it's too early for a kebab?'

–

Eastern Promise kebab shop had seen better days, Minshull thought, as he waited in the faded black-and-white tiled interior while the young guy behind the counter disappeared into the kitchen to fetch his father.

'You ever had a kebab from here, Steph?'

Lanehan brushed raindrops from the brim of her hat. 'Once or twice. My Fred likes a kebab after the pub quiz at The Swan sometimes. Though he usually goes for the Magic Turk on Sheep Street.'

'Any good?'

'As good as they ever are. Kebab's a kebab.'

'Afternoon, officers.' The proprietor was smiling but his eyes darted between Minshull and Lanehan like a startled stag.

Minshull presented his warrant card. 'Acting Detective Sergeant Rob Minshull, South Suffolk CID, and this is PC Steph Lanehan. Mr?'

'Faisal. Ali-Akbar Faisal. How can I help?'

'I wonder if we might have a look at your CCTV from Thursday, Mr Faisal?'

'That girl, is it?'

It never failed to amaze Minshull how quickly news travelled in the small rural communities. A phenomenon fanned into flame by the rush of news coming from journalists already camped out in St Just. Only this morning he'd seen the local newspaper editor reporting from the village on national news. 'We need to look at footage taken on the first day of the Easter Market,' he replied, careful to maintain a steady expression. 'If you still have it?'

'Of course.' The kebab shop owner led the way up the back stairs from the shop into a cramped office in the flat above. Minshull noticed the way he bodily blocked a curtained-off area to the right of the desk where the CCTV screen and recording equipment was stored. That was odd. Squirrelling the thought away, Minshull followed Mr Faisal to the desk and took a seat by the monitor.

It took some time to locate the correct recording, but once it was playing Lanehan assumed her position by the screen, scrolling the footage forward to the time the young girl had been captured by the previous camera. Minshull leaned closer as the white counter marked the passing seconds. Bodies passed beneath the camera, mounted just above the sign over the kebab shop; people stopped to take mobile phone calls, chat to neighbours and peer at the stalls lining the street. 1.41p.m. and five seconds – ten – fifteen – twenty... No sign of her. Frowning, he watched the time counter tick a minute past, then five, then ten. Still the small figure didn't appear.

'She could have crossed the road?' Lanehan suggested, reading his mind.

'It's possible. But uniform told me the stalls were tightly packed right along the street with no gaps between them until the zebra crossing almost at the Meatcross – and we would have seen her on this camera if she'd gone that far to cross the road. Unless she ducked underneath the tables I don't think she would have left the pavement.' He scrutinised the screen. 'Take it back to 1.40p.m. Maybe the clocks on the two machines aren't in sync.'

He watched as the street scene switched into fast reverse, the figures retreating backwards. *Where was she?*

'What's between here and the Spar?'

'Estate agent's, two charity shops, a sweet shop, a newsagent's, the newspaper office, a butcher's and a dry cleaner's on the corner.'

'No driveways, small roads, empty units...?'

'No, Sarge. There's only Higgins Court but that's a dead end. The only way out of it is back out onto High Street.'

'Then where can she have gone?'

Steph shrugged. 'She must have crossed the road. Only explanation.'

'Barclays over the road has CCTV,' the kebab shop proprietor suggested, a little too keen to bundle the police officers back downstairs. 'Maybe they've caught her.'

'We'll check. Thanks, Mr Faisal.' Minshull turned in the doorway, clocking the flinch of the Turkish man. 'Actually, there was something I wanted to ask you. I don't suppose you saw a young girl between 1.40pm and 2pm on Thursday?'

A visible layer of sweat beaded across the man's top lip. 'Sorry. We didn't open on Thursday,' he shrugged, adding quickly: 'And we were in Doncaster at a family funeral.'

'Bit shifty, wasn't he?' Lanehan said, as they ducked out of the shop and continued along the High Street.

'Just a bit. But then I don't suppose Mr Faisal has many visits from police officers. Aside from off-duty PCs after Saturday night pub quizzes.'

'From what I can remember of the state of my Fred's guts the day after I'm not surprised.'

Minshull smiled at her comment, but questions crowded his mind. Where had Hannah gone? Had a stallholder let her pass under the stall? It didn't make sense that they would, with the market being so busy. Had a stallholder taken her? It was a possibility but why would they leave when the market was in full flow? She had turned from Emerson Estates' window and paused, as if she'd spotted someone or something that summoned her towards it. But who?

The kebab shop owner bothered him, too. Why was he so cagey about his whereabouts on Thursday? And why the body-blocking of the curtained-off area when they went upstairs?

Questions. It was all they had. And Hannah Perry was out there, alone, the precious time to find her being eaten by the circles they were moving in. Something had to break – and soon.

Chapter Eleven

Cora

'Stay at mine tonight?' Daniel grinned from the doorway to Cora's office, all boyish good looks and devilish intentions. He must have known everyone else had left for the day, to say it so loudly, Cora thought. She smiled, despite her better judgement.

'I can't. Sorry.'

His shoulders drooped and he shuffled into the room. 'But it's been a *week*. And you said you wanted to stay more often...'

'No, *you* said you wanted me to stay more often. I'd love to, just not tonight. I want to look in on Mum.'

Daniel made no attempt to hide his opinion. 'Again? You only saw her a couple of days ago.'

'She was supposed to phone me this morning about the shopping she needs but she hasn't. I've called her three times and she isn't answering her phone. I just need to check she's okay. Don't look at me like that. I'm all she has.'

'Well it's commendable. And bloody annoying. It's almost as if you'd never moved out of her house.'

'She hasn't done well since Dad died. I'm worried she might be retreating again.'

'But it's been four years...'

'They were childhood sweethearts. Married for forty-three years. He was Mum's life. And I'm sorry, but who are you to put time limits on my mother's grief?'

'That was insensitive, I'm sorry.' Daniel shook his head. 'I know she's had a tough time and you care about her, of course you do. But I don't think that's why you're going round. You're feeling guilty you moved out.'

'That's not fair.'

He held up his hands to signal defeat, taking a subconscious step back. 'Sorry. I'm being an arse because I want you all to myself. You do what you have to. I love you anyway.'

She smiled. 'You're amazing. And *so* supportive.'

'Yeah, yeah, tell me something I don't already know.'

—

The house was in darkness when Cora arrived, but this wasn't unusual when her mother was home. Steeling herself as she always did, standing on the threshold of her childhood home, Cora took a breath and let the air slowly leave her lungs, willing the old familiar tension to attach to the end of her exhalation like ribbons on a kite string. She knocked, knowing there would be no answer. There never was. She had long since abandoned hope of her mother hurrying to the door, but now it was a habit, a never-to-be-satisfied desire reduced to a mindless act.

This house had too much emotion. It was infused into every wall like the ghost of ancient cigarette smoke, impossible to avoid. It amplified every voice she was now braced to hear and magnified the absence of the one voice she longed to speak. She would have given anything to catch even a whisper of her father's words within these rooms. Four years without him felt like nothing when she was here. Moving out had made it worse, the distance she'd established between this place and her new home making the voices all the more debilitating when she returned.

As soon as she pushed open the front door, the voices hit her. She'd prepared herself, as she always did, but even so, the physical force of the rush of noise caused her to stumble back. She threw out a hand to steady herself on the balustrade at the bottom of the stairs, the flaking white paint gathering beneath her nails. In the dim orange glow of the streetlights shining in from the still-open front door, she could just make out the source of the voices still screaming in competition – boxes and black rubbish bags stuffed with bric-a-brac, lined up like a guard of honour along one side of the hallway in the nineteen-thirties semi. Once confined to the garage, Sheila Lael's collection had entered the house and was now seeping like a sinister oil slick into every room.

Cora employed the breathing technique she'd developed over the years, slowly, methodically blocking out each individual voice.

She first imagined each voice had a manual volume control, and then set about muting them, one by one. Each voice that faded strengthened her sense of control, made each onslaught a little less overwhelming. Control, Cora had learned, was a slow, methodical, mindful process. It eradicated her panic, soothed her mind. She'd come across a similar technique in a Yoga Nidra class at university designed to relax the mind and focus inwardly to enter into relaxation. Instead of acknowledging each voice and letting it pass, she silenced them, from those farthest away to the loudest beside her.

It was effective, but exhausting.

Cora pressed on, moving along the cluttered hallway as the shouts slowly fell under her control. A thin line of flickering blue light came into view beneath the sitting room door at the end of the hall, drawing her towards it.

Pushing open the door a fresh wave of voices tumbled towards her; noticeably weaker than those in the hall as the belongings were contained within clear plastic stacking boxes. They were arranged like semi-transparent skyscrapers around the sitting room, their coloured lids coded for a filing system only Sheila Lael understood. To Cora, the voices of the former owners sounded trapped behind plastic walls – muffled exclamations of disgust, reminiscence and disinterest jostling for her attention. The room smelled stale, as if the windows hadn't been opened for a long time; the carpet was mildly sticky under her feet.

Cora's mother had assumed her regular position on the sagging sage-green settee, the television entertaining itself in a corner of the room while Sheila's attention was taken by the white-blue command of her laptop screen. Sitting cross-legged in the centre of the three-seater, an oversized black hoodie dwarfing her petite frame, she looked far younger than her sixty years, her face pale and brow furrowed as she scrutinised the scrolling auction lots.

'Hey, Mum.'

'Mm?'

Cora leaned over the sofa and planted a soft kiss on the top of Sheila's head. 'It's me.'

Sheila looked up, dark grey hollows visible beneath her eyes as the laptop light receded. 'Oh, hello love. I'm just...' She rarely finished sentences these days, the urgency of her internet auction lots a constant pull for her mind.

'How's sales?' Cora nudged the unkempt ball of brown fluff known as her mother's cat, Walt, from the only chair in the sitting room not commandeered by eBay sales stock. She sank into its ancient seat and continued mentally muting voices.

'Mm, good tonight. Chap in Milwaukee is bidding on that royal family memorabilia I picked up last… Gonna cost him a fortune getting it across, but…' Her eyes drifted back to the screen. 'Sorry, I just need to – this bloke's being a pest…'

Without waiting for an invitation, Cora rose and picked her way through the shouting boxes to the kitchen. From the discarded fast-food bags and boxes heavy with Sheila's sighs littering the worktops it was clear her mother wasn't taking care of herself. At least if she made Sheila something resembling real food and a decent pot of tea, Cora could leave feeling a little easier about her mum's wellbeing.

She found a passable half-loaf of bread in the wooden bread bin, a carton of eggs in the mostly empty fridge and a new box of teabags in a cupboard, indicating that Sheila had at least remembered to buy essential items in between her home-delivered pizzas, Chinese food and curries. The comforting smell of toasting bread and freshly made tea filled the kitchen as Cora did her best to lessen the mountain of unwashed crockery piled high in the sink.

Once, way back in the sparse rosiness of Cora's childhood memories, Sheila had been the one fussing around her daughter and younger son Charlie, insisting on regular meals and a constant supply of tea. Toast soldiers and boiled eggs had been their special Sunday tea, while Cora's father worked an extra night shift at the grain store; talk of the week past and the week to come floating over regimented rows of crunchy brown rectangles dipped into glossy yellow, soft-boiled rivers. Cora remembered snapshots of that time: her feet swinging happily in bunny slippers high above the terracotta-tile vinyl of the kitchen floor; Charlie's eggy handprints on the vinyl tablecloth; their mother's then golden hair freed from its band and falling in damp curls onto her towelling robe – the only night of the week it was allowed to do so.

She peered back into the unearthly blue of the sitting room and, seeing Sheila engrossed, returned to the stove and put four eggs on to boil anyway. Her mother would never refuse food once it was prepared. She closed her eyes in the calm of the kitchen; the click of the toaster and the whistle of blue flame beneath a saucepan the only sounds Cora allowed into her mind.

It was always a bittersweet experience to return home. She loved her mum, but Sheila's increasing obsession with her auction lot reselling business was pulling her further away from everything she had once held dear. Her doctor had diagnosed severe depression following the death of Cora's father, Bill, and for a while the anti-depressants and regular counselling sessions he'd prescribed seemed to be helping. But in the last twelve months Sheila had begun to retreat back into the always-gloom of her home. She was more removed from Cora and the world now than she had been in the earliest days of grief after Bill Lael's passing.

It hadn't begun like this. At first, Sheila had started to buy and sell antiques and interesting items she found in vintage shops and fairs scattered across East Anglia. Cora had welcomed her mother's fledgling business because it seemed to give her a renewed purpose. The auctions she drove across Suffolk and Norfolk to attend revitalised her – within weeks she was sleeping better and looking less ghostly. Slowly, the house had filled with boxes of other people's cast-offs, each purchase reflecting Sheila's hope for the new stage of her life. With them came the inevitable rush of noise to Cora's ears but she endured the intrusion because her mother had looked so happy.

But a faulty clutch on Sheila's ageing car just before Easter last year had changed everything. While housebound waiting for a repair, a friend had introduced her to online auctions – and the rot began to set in. Soon, the round-the-clock thrill of bidding, winning and selling auction lots outweighed that of travelling to antique shops and auction houses, the adrenaline boost irresistible and far more addictive. Now the car sat resignedly on the drive outside 11 Butterfield Close, relegated to trips to the local supermarket, the tachometer never registering more than five miles for any journey.

'I'm going to make a million this way,' Sheila had assured her concerned family. 'The returns are immediate. And people on eBay hardly know what they're selling, half the time. But I'm different, see? I study the markets – I know exactly what I'm looking for. One day I'll find a diamond in the lots, I can feel it.'

Two years on, the diamond still eluded Sheila, the collectors' magazines and thick, encyclopaedic antiques guides stacked in listless piles around the edges of her beloved green sofa.

Cora longed to be able to talk to her about the changes she was seeing for the better as she managed her ability, but it felt wrong to speak of a new lease of life to a woman so set on destroying hers. She knew what it would once have meant to her mother to know her daughter was at last managing the condition that had plagued her for years. But would Sheila care now? It was too much to try to explain in the small window of attention span Sheila could commit to any conversation. And despite knowing all of this was an involuntary reaction to the grief, it was impossible for Cora not to take the inevitable drifting away of Sheila's attention as a snub. Far better to care for her mother's immediate needs than expect any of her own to be supplied.

Carrying the eggs, toast and tea through to the sitting room, Cora forced a smile.

'Mum – *Mum* – I made you some tea.'

'Hm?'

'Okay, I'm going to take this for ten minutes.' She caught the edge of the laptop and pulled it gently from hands that didn't want to relinquish it. 'Just ten minutes, Mum. You need a break and you need to eat.'

Knowing when she was beaten, Sheila grudgingly complied, wincing as she slowly unknotted her legs. 'You're a good girl, Cora. I always said that. Your dad...'

Cora turned away to move clutter from the coffee table, not wanting to see the tears in her mother's eyes. Even now they never spoke of their loss, raw as ever despite the passing years. It emerged instead in sentences left hanging like the suspended state their lives seemed left in.

'There. I made a bit more space for you.'

'Eggs! Oh, I love dippy eggs.' She bustled to the sofa's edge, a glimpse of the woman from Cora's memories flashing into the room.

'I know you do. Me too.'

'Have some with me?'

'I'm okay, thanks. I had something to eat before I came.'

'Then sit with me, at least. Can't have you standing up while I'm... Come on, I'll budge up. Here.' She patted the green Dralon next to her and Cora sat, the closeness at once soothing and a sharp reminder of how far away the two women really were from each other.

For a while, neither spoke, their eyes drifting to the television where a reporter was standing outside a high street estate agent.

> '...CCTV images captured the eight-year-old looking into this window before she then disappeared. Police are appealing for witnesses who might have seen Hannah during the Easter Market on Maundy Thursday...'

The camera cut away to a grainy image of a young girl in a school uniform, a backpack by her side, peering into the shop window as a police spokesman's voice continued the appeal.

'Anything the public can tell us about Hannah Perry's movements that day will be of great help to our investigation. The market would have been busy in St Just. We know that from CCTV images of the time of Hannah's last-known sighting. Obviously we are keen to find Hannah as soon as possible...'

'That's St Just again?' Sheila pointed at the screen where the reporter was reiterating the appeal.

'Yes. A little girl's gone missing.'

Sheila frowned. 'Oh no. Not again. Your poor dad would...'

Cora caught her mother's hand as her voice cracked. 'I know.'

'He blamed himself, you know.'

'What for?'

'He wanted to be the one that found the boy. With the searches. Everyone came out to help but your dad was the one leading it. He worked so hard... "Even if it's a body," he said. "Someone should take the kid home."'

Cora stared at her mother. 'I didn't know that.'

'I never told anyone. Your dad was so sensitive about it. Poor man. Your brother knew him a little – Matthew, the boy who died. Used to go up the golf range with his stepdad sometimes at weekends and Charlie would do putting with the kid while the stepdad did a round. I think that's why he went off...'

Cora's younger brother Charlie's anxiety had started to appear five years ago, prompting his sudden resignation from the insurance firm where he'd worked since leaving college and his decision to travel. Had the missing boy's murder brought that about?

'I think he's been happier since he started travelling.'

'I wish he'd call.'

'I know. I think he was heading for Guatemala this month.' Cora was careful to keep her opinion on her brother to herself. Charlie should phone their mum more, no matter where he was. He'd been living in Sydney for almost eleven months before his most recent expedition and had hardly called Sheila. As ever, it fell to Cora to care for her mother.

Sheila nodded at the TV screen. 'Poor kid.'

'Poor parents,' Cora replied, suddenly aware of how telling her reaction was. She glanced at her mother, who was gazing glassily at the screen again, munching toast. 'I hope they find her.'

'You've got to hope, haven't you? Let's hope she bunked off school with a friend. Your brother was forever doing that. Thinks I don't know, of course, so don't tell him otherwise.' She looked away from the television and twisted the eggcup on her plate. 'We always had eggs for Sunday tea, didn't we? While your dad was…'

'Yes, we did.'

'Have some, Cora love. I don't like eating on my own.'

'I'm fine, Mum. But you need to keep your strength up, with all of these hungry bidders keeping you busy round the clock.'

'It's looking up, Cor. I mean it. I think this week the business turned a corner. If I can get a few more Yanks bidding on my stuff I'll start making a profit.' She licked butter from her fingers as she chewed an egg-dipped toast sentry. 'That's why I can't be gone long because they… It's easy to be forgotten on there.'

Was that what fuelled her addiction? The fear of being left behind – as she had been when her husband died?

'They won't forget you, especially when you have items they want. Don't give me that look, either. You can survive for ten minutes in the real world, Mum. I promise you'll feel better for a break and a meal.'

The pale hand that grabbed Cora's wrist was birdlike, its sudden contact shocking. Hollowed-out eyes stared at her.

'I don't deserve you.'

The urge to cry churned her gut, burning in the back of her throat. Instead, Cora smiled, her heart breaking as it always did in this house. 'Shush. Eat your tea.'

–

She didn't go home. Not tonight. Seeing her mother so broken, so changed, tore at her soul. She already felt a traitor for leaving. Sheila Lael was an invisible tie keeping Cora in one place. The responsibility, once the flipside of belonging to the family, was now iron-heavy on her shoulders. Tonight she needed to feel she belonged – and there was one place she still felt safe, wanted. Loved.

Daniel's sleep-creased face broke into a smile when he found her on his doorstep and opened the door to let her in. Cora said nothing as she headed for his bedroom.

Chapter Twelve

Wheeler

The list from the Chamber of Commerce wasn't worth the paper it was written on. Turned out that to have a stall in the St Just Easter Market, all you had to do was pick a random name out of the ether and say it was you.

Wheeler had spent most of the afternoon yesterday trying to contact stallholders and listening to the voicemail message on market co-ordinator John Dean's phone. When he finally managed to talk to one trader, she suggested a different approach.

'Best get yourself down to the market tomorrow – the regular one in Chancel Lane? You'll find us all there. All us Sunday regulars had stalls at the Easter Market on Thursday and Friday. Always do. Johnny Dean gives us first dibs, see? There'd be a riot if he didn't. About the only good thing he does for us, to be honest.'

He'd arrived early as the market traders were setting up, vying for space with the monstrously large TV satellite trucks. After he'd assisted two uniformed officers to shift a large vehicle blocking a market pitch, Wheeler was finally able to start his enquiries.

Unfortunately for him, his problems were far from over.

'Tom Cawston? He's been dead three year, ann' 'e?'

'Right.' Wheeler sighed as he crossed yet another name off the useless page. 'Any idea who was working the stall opposite Emerson Estates at the Easter Market on Thursday?'

The red-cheeked man on the butcher's stall scratched his beard. 'Not a clue, bor. See, mine was booked both days. Most regulars were. But the stalls between me opposite the *Argus* offices and the next regular, Silas Beckwith, opposite the hospice charity shop, were all flibbertigibbets.' His face creased into a smirk when he saw Wheeler's confusion. 'One-offs. Out-of-towners mostly, dashing in with their organic, vegan, upcycled, conscientious overpriced shit for a day, whacking it on the trestles then legging it when it was gone.'

'Do you remember what they were selling at least? You being here all the time an' all?'

'All looked hokey to me. Smelly pots of lard, candles, beady things. You know the stuff.'

Great. The description could match about seventy per cent of the market stalls, going by the vague details Wheeler had been able to glean from the other market traders.

'You could ask Nance over on Parham Pies,' the butcher offered, inclining his neck to look at Wheeler's useless list. 'Nothing gets past her.'

'I will, thanks, sir.'

'She'll put you right.' The trader leaned over his stall to rearrange a pile of packed sausages. 'An' I should know. I married her once.'

Wheeler chuckled as he left the stall. Only in this part of the world…

–

It turned out the majority of the Easter Market stalls had been 'one-day jobs', and even some of the regular market traders who'd had pitches admitted their stalls had been staffed by casual workers who passed through the local markets like the shifting sands on Covehithe Beach. The lady on the pie stall sent Wheeler to a tiny woman who was barely visible over a mountain of hand-dyed wool skeins. She in turn directed him to a cheese stall that smelled like heaven on earth – so good that he could hardly concentrate on what the well-spoken trader was saying.

'…We've had words with Rotary and the Chamber about it,' the man intoned, while Wheeler tried not to ogle a rather lovely half-round of local Baron Bigod Brie. 'If you want a regular Sunday pitch you have to jump through all manner of administrative hoops, but they'll happily hand out one-day tables to just about anyone for their precious Easter Market. It brings down the quality of the market and that's not good for our customers.'

Wheeler forced his eyes away from the cheese. 'I see. So you don't know who might have had stalls R12 to R15?'

'Sorry. Too focused on the cheese, if you know what I mean.'

Wheeler knew only too well. 'It's lovely stuff.'

'Can I interest you in a piece?'

It was tempting, but from somewhere deep within he summoned the willpower to resist. 'Not on duty, sir, but I'll take a card if I may.'

'With pleasure.' The trader handed him a business card, then snapped his fingers. 'Hang on, Will might know!'

'Sorry, sir?'

'Will, my assistant. He's from here. One second...'

The trader ducked behind the broad canvas sign lashed across the back section of the stall. Wheeler waited, staring up at the striped awning to ignore the siren call of cheese. A moment later, the stall-holder returned, trailed by a pale-faced young man who couldn't be more than twenty.

'This detective wants to know who was working the stalls between here and Southwold Meats. Do you remember?'

The young man screwed up his eyes against the sun. 'Johnny Dean organised the one-dayers on this side so there was all sorts. Lots of the uptowners he knows that moved here from London. There was one doing organic stuff, veg boxes – didn't recognise them. But there was that chocolate stall – All That Glitters? It comes to all the special markets, usually for a day at a time. I don't know the woman that runs it 'cos she's never there. But I do remember thinking it odd that Neil Worley was working on it.'

'Why odd?' Wheeler asked, trying to work out why the name was familiar.

'Well, he's on the register, isn't he?'

'The register?'

Will pulled a face. 'Kiddy-fiddlin'. I knew they let him out of prison a few years back and he was meant to be all reformed, but I wouldn't have him on a stall that kiddies come to. Not right, that.'

Every nerve in Dave Wheeler's body began to fire. 'And you're sure he was working on Thursday?'

'The chocolate stall was only there on Thursday, so yeah. Bit of a showman, he was. Doing that balloon-modelling guff, trying to bring the little ones over. Probably learned that from the other paedos in jail. Made me go cold watching him. He was making yellow poodles to match the chocolate company logo.'

Heart thumping, Wheeler dialled Minshull as he hurried from the market, all thoughts of cheese long forgotten.

Hannah

The yellow balloon dog looks different now. Its nose has gone wrinkly and the twists where its legs join its body are floppy. It doesn't look friendly like it did. It feels wrong, too. When I pick it up, the balloon stuff is cold and sticks to my fingers like it's trying to suck me in.

I don't like it anymore.

I've pushed it under the dirty blanket in the corner of the Small Space so it can't see me. But I'm scared when it gets dark and cold and I need the blanket again, the dog will jump out. I don't want to think about that.

I thought it was a good idea to get one when I was at the Easter Market. They were giving them out to everyone for free, and Mum says free things are always good. It made me think of the puppy I asked for. I thought if I had a puppy made from just balloons nobody would mind. Not even Shaun.

They said Amber was a lovely name for her. They even put a seatbelt on her in the back of the car when I got in.

But that dog isn't *my* Amber.

That dog is a yellow monster. And it's just it and me in the Small Space.

When can I go home?

Chapter Thirteen

Minshull

'Sarge, one of the casual workers working Thursday on a stall in the area of the market we're looking at is on the register.'

'*Shit.* Who?'

'Neil Worley.'

'Hold on a minute, Dave...' From the corridor where he'd taken the call, Minshull ducked into the office where DC Evans was a lone figure behind a skyscraper of files. 'Les – have you come across a Neil Worley in your search?'

He could see the pique of interest from across the office floor. The DC scrabbled in a file and held up a page, triumphant. 'The very same.'

'What do we know about him?'

'Did six years for possessing indecent images of kids and attempted grooming of two young boys. Nothing since he was released two years ago.'

'Do we have an address?'

'Yes, Sarge.'

'Good.' He raised the phone back to his ear. 'Great work, Dave. Who are you with?'

'On my own right now.'

'Okay.' Ignoring the wild gesturing coming from his colleague in the office, Minshull headed back to his desk, mind racing into action. Les Evans was not the one to send to pick up Worley. This was their biggest lead yet: they had to handle it with utmost care. Kate Bennett and Drew Ellis were back on the Parkhall Estate following up some reports of people who'd claimed to see Hannah at the Easter Market and wouldn't be in till later. 'I'll send Steph in the pool car to come and meet you then I want you both to head straight over. With any luck, nobody you've spoken to in the market will think to warn Worley.'

76

'You're sending Dave?' Les Evans was incredulous when Minshull joined him in the office.

'He's nearest.'

'I'm the one trawling through sex offenders. I should be bringing him in.'

'I want you to find everything we have on Worley. Cautions, voluntary interviews, previous complaints, outstanding parking fines: anything. And then, if you do that, I *might* let you sit in on the interview.'

'That's big of you.'

That was it: he'd swallowed Les Evans' blatant lack of respect for too long. Les might not like it, but Minshull now outranked him – *acting* or not. He glared at the red-faced DC. 'Sorry, I didn't catch that?'

'Thank you, Sarge.' Shrinking back, DC Evans dropped his gaze to the open files on his desk.

It was a small victory, but he'd take it. 'You're welcome.'

–

Neil Worley was a short man, balding and quiet. Aside from a small angry scar on the right side of his neck he was completely unremarkable, the kind of person nobody noticed. But the wide, earnest stare and unflinching eye contact he maintained chilled Minshull. He'd seen people like him before and while he wouldn't allow any of his personal opinions to be on display in the interview room, he was glad to share it out in the corridor, talking to Wheeler and Lanehan who had brought Worley in.

'Charming character. What do you make of him?'

'Creepy git,' Lanehan said, arms folded tight across her body. 'Proper nasty.'

'How was he on the drive over?'

'Quiet. But *starey*…' Wheeler shook his head. 'I had to make myself look away from his reflection in the rear-view mirror while Steph was driving here because he wouldn't stop eyeballing us from the back seat. You don't want me in there, do you?'

Minshull had known Wheeler for many years and considered him a good friend outside of work. He knew that the only crack in Dave Wheeler's perennial fairness was dealing with child abusers. 'The moment I think of my two lovely boys at home, I lose all perspective,' he'd admitted once after a very uncharacteristic outburst during an interview. 'Anyone going after kiddies can rot in hell as far as I'm concerned, and I'm not afraid to say it.'

Minshull smiled. 'I wouldn't do that to you, Dave. You and Steph head back up to the office, okay? Grab something from the canteen first if you need to, I know it's been a long shift.'

'Cheers, Sarge.'

'Great work, both of you. It's appreciated.'

'Pleasure. Who's in with you then?' Wheeler asked, his brow furrowing when the thud of double doors sounded at the end of the corridor.

'Bastard all tucked in nicely, is he, Dave?'

Wheeler stared in shock as DC Evans walked towards them. 'You have got to be joking.'

'Just your regular scumbag welcoming committee,' Les Evans grinned, arms wide.

'Is that us welcoming you or you welcoming him?'

Minshull stepped between them. 'Thanks, Dave, Steph. I'll see you upstairs, yeah?' As they left, he turned to Evans. 'Right. Follow my lead. And *behave*.'

'Of course, boss. Don't I always?'

Not even beginning to answer that, Minshull opened the interview room door.

At the desk, Neil Worley looked up from neatly folded hands. 'Is this going to take long?'

'I hope not, Mr Worley. Thank you for coming in today.'

'I didn't have much say in the matter, but whatever.'

The small man's stare was intended to throw Minshull off, but it wouldn't work. Calmly, Minshull leaned across Les Evans and clicked on the tape. 'Interview commenced at 4.45 p.m. Acting DS Minshull and DC Evans present. Mr Worley, could you state your name for the tape, please?'

'Neil Anthony Worley.'

'Thank you. Mr Worley, where were you working on Thursday between the hours of nine a.m. and five p.m?'

'Officially, nowhere.'

Minshull sensed DC Evans' irritation as he shifted beside him. 'And unofficially?'

'Well, you know, don't you? Or else I wouldn't be here.'

'For the benefit of the tape…'

Worley's sigh was meticulously calculated to annoy, as sharp as fingernails dragged down a blackboard. 'I was working on the chocolate stall at St Just's Easter Market.'

'That's the All That Glitters stall?'

'Correct.'

'And how did you come by this work?'

'It was a favour owed to me by Johnny.' He nodded at the sheaf of papers in the file in front of Minshull. 'John Dean, from the Chamber of Commerce. He co-ordinates all the markets in St Just. He'd promised me a cash-in-hand job a while back that fell through. This was his way of making amends.'

'And were you asked about your record prior to you being given this work?'

'What do you think?'

'But the market has rules, presumably, about the people operating the stalls.'

'It was a cash job, no questions asked.' Worley's crow-like stare passed from Minshull to Evans and back again. 'Which, since your colleagues' intervention eight years ago, is pretty much the only work I can get.'

'Was Johnny Dean aware of your past conviction?'

'You'd have to ask him.'

'Or the owner of the chocolate stall? Particularly knowing children would be likely to visit?'

'They were unaware. I needed the money.'

'You contravened the conditions of your supervision order.'

'I didn't go near any kids.'

'Funny that,' DC Evans interjected. 'According to my colleague, one of the stallholders said you were making balloon animals to attract young children to the stand.'

The pale face reddened. 'There's no law against drumming up business.'

'For you or the stall?'

Minshull cleared his throat loudly and Les Evans fell silent.

'Did you see any children between 1.40p.m. and 2p.m?'

'Plenty. The schools kicked out at lunchtime... And before your troll here goes for me, everyone knew that. It wasn't my special interest.'

The words turned Minshull's blood cold. Pushing the reaction away, he slid a photo of Hannah towards Worley. It was a school photograph taken a year ago, the most recent picture Ashleigh Perry had of her eldest daughter. The proud smile and carefully worn uniform seemed so at odds with the fear of where she might be now. Did Worley know? Had he taken her?

'Did you see this girl?'

Worley blinked slowly and leaned a little towards the photo. 'I might have.' He pushed it away but Minshull slid it back.

'Did you see her?'

'I don't know. Lots of little girls came up to the stall. I couldn't say for certain.'

'Think carefully, please. Did you see Hannah Perry?'

Worley's eyes shot up. 'The missing girl?'

'Did she come to the stall? Did you make her a balloon animal? Did you talk to her, or offer her chocolate?'

'I didn't take her.'

'That's not what I asked. Did you see Hannah Perry at the stall on Thursday?'

Worley's hands were busy now, thick fingers working over cracked knuckles, over and over, as if trying to remove the accusations from his skin. 'I know what you're insinuating and I know why. And you are *not* pinning this on me. I didn't talk to the girl – or if I did, I don't remember. I have some control, officers. I have some personal rules. One of which is that I don't look when I'm working.'

He was rattled now, energy leaking out of him from his tapping foot beneath the desk to the working hands, to the words tumbling from him. Minshull took the advantage. 'Did you have any interaction with Hannah Perry?'

'I don't know, okay? But I didn't take her.'

'Why mention taking Hannah if you didn't do it? Why would you assume that was what we were asking?' Evans leaned forward a little, taunting him.

'Because it's always the assumption, isn't it? Do I need a solicitor? Because this doesn't feel like the nice little chat your colleague said it would be.'

Minshull kept his voice low and calm. 'You aren't under caution, Mr Worley. Of course, if you think you need representation...'

'I don't because I've done nothing wrong!' Worley slammed his fist on the desk, sending concentric ripples through the untouched paper cup of tea beside him. 'If you think I had anything to do with that child's disappearance you're mistaken. And I can prove it.'

'How?'

'Because I went straight from the market to The Swan that afternoon and I worked a shift there. It's why I left before the market closed at five p.m. Ask Marty Bingham, the landlord. He'll tell you. I left the stall at twenty past four and started my shift at the pub at half past four. And I worked through till nine forty-five. Then I went home in time for my curfew at ten – my mother can vouch for me all night after that.'

It was a dead end. One Minshull found himself grateful for, though it took them no closer to finding Hannah Perry. Because the thought of Hannah in the hands of a man like Worley was too awful to consider.

'Thank you,' he returned, keeping his tone steady. 'Is there anything else you'd like to tell us about that day?'

'Nothing about the day. But for your information,' he gave the photograph a sudden stab with a nicotine-stained finger, 'I wouldn't have been interested in her anyway. She'd be no use to me. I don't *do* girls, Detective.'

It was all Minshull could do to snatch Hannah's image to safety and end the interview.

Chapter Fourteen

Anderson

'You join me on this Easter Monday morning in St Just, where it's now four days since eight-year-old Hannah Perry was last seen. Substantial police and volunteer search efforts have so far proved fruitless. With every passing hour, fears are growing for this young girl. There are murmurs of disquiet in every corner of this small, unassuming Suffolk village. With no new developments and an embattled police investigation remaining tight-lipped, tonight the question is being asked here, as in the wider nation: Is Hannah Perry still alive?'

'With me is Jan Martin, editor and senior reporter of the local newspaper. Jan, what sense do you get of local people's reactions to this case?'

'People are scared, Mark. This is a close-knit community; a place where everyone knows everyone else and they are feeling Hannah's loss keenly. She is one of our own and we want her home.'

'Now, the police investigation has come under intense scrutiny in recent days. Many commentators are pointing to what they see as a local force overwhelmed. In a place where few serious crimes occur, do people in St Just still trust the police to find Hannah?'

'I know there's been criticism and maybe some of that is warranted, but I honestly believe South Suffolk CID are doing their best. They are working all hours to find Hannah, under impossible pressure from all sides. They're easy targets for everyone's fears about finding Hannah but they don't deserve the accusations of "bumbling". Detective Inspector Joel Anderson and his team are doing the best they can.'

'But St Just is a village divided.'

'Everyone wants Hannah home. We have that in common.'

'Bastards. Utter vicious bastards.'

Anderson only realised he'd given voice to his thoughts when he caught sight of the CID team's reaction. 'Forgive me.'

'No, they are,' Kate Bennett said, her wry smile exactly what Anderson needed today.

He'd already had DCI Taylor yelling at him first thing. *People expect results, Joel, what the hell is the team playing at?* All of it was *his* fault, of course. Being SIO in name only apparently meant you still copped the flak for everything even though the gig was no longer yours.

'At least we have Jan Martin,' Wheeler offered. 'She's been sticking up for us every time she's been on telly.'

'She's the only one.'

Privately, he appreciated it. Jan was a good friend of his wife and she'd lived the nightmare of Matthew Cooper's disappearance, too. Ros had encouraged them both to talk, months after the body was found, and to his surprise Anderson had discovered much in common with the journalist. She'd entered therapy too, she'd revealed, and Anderson had understood the struggle in her admission. They were both of a generation for whom trauma and mental health issues were taboo and seeking psychiatric help brought shame and suspicion. While they officially represented different sides, in person they shared a respect borne out of experience.

Perhaps Jan was better prepared for the media scrum this time. She certainly looked stronger in the news reports Anderson had seen. Wiser, less inclined to be led by news anchors with an agenda. Anderson watched with his team as Jan skilfully avoided three more attempts to be led by the interviewer, maintaining each time that the majority in St Just shared her support for the investigation. Bless her.

The report ended and Minshull turned off the television.

'Moving on. So to update you all – and you, Guv – we interviewed Neil Worley late afternoon yesterday and it's a dead end there. He has an alibi and can prove where he was for the whole of Thursday.'

'Has it been followed up?' Anderson barked, as if hope may still be alive with this fast-dying lead.

'I spoke to the landlord of the pub and Worley's mother before I left here last night,' Les Evans answered. 'Both confirmed his story.'

'Could he be working with someone? Take Hannah, pass her to them, return to work?' He knew it was a stretch, but when he'd heard a convicted child abuser had been working in the Easter Market and had likely met Hannah; it seemed a perfect link. With the investigation under such heavy media scrutiny it was imperative every possibility was checked.

'He's a loner,' Minshull replied. 'Even his conviction for indecent images wasn't linked to any group. Let's be relieved a man like Worley doesn't have Hannah.'

Anderson couldn't feel relief, only frustration. Their only decent lead was dead and all that Hannah Perry *not* being with a convicted paedophile meant was that she could be with a murderer instead. Matthew's murderer, still free after seven years. He didn't want to link the girl's disappearance with Matthew Cooper, but the similarities were alarming. Both St Just kids, both taken while in school uniform and carrying school bags, both living on the Parkhall Estate where many of St Just's poorest families resided.

'So what do we have?'

'We finally managed to track down Ashleigh Perry's partner, Shaun Collins yesterday evening. He's not been staying at the family home so it's been difficult to catch him. He's agreed to come in later this afternoon to assist us.'

'Fifty quid says he doesn't show,' Evans muttered from the back of the office, loud enough to be heard. Anderson saw Minshull's shoulders tense.

'We also need to know if anyone saw Hannah, in the market, in the estate agent's, or anywhere on the High Street from the beginning of the market to the Meatcross. The other three CCTV cameras we identified along the High Street turned up nothing, but the market was packed on Thursday. Someone must have seen Hannah. Les, I need you out during the next two hours, talking to everyone you can. Dave and Steph, if you can hang back, please, I've some stuff for you to do here.'

'Sarge.'

'I've got uniform on the ground at Parkhall and visiting the businesses beyond the Meatcross in St Just, in case she walked past there on her way home. Kate and Drew, where are you off to this morning?'

'The estate agent's – Emerson Estates? Their office was closed over the weekend but it's open today.'

'Great, that could be key. If they saw where Hannah went after she'd looked in their window, we'll have our next step. Thanks, everyone.'

Anderson watched the team disperse. None of them looked optimistic. He knew he didn't, either. He headed over to Minshull's desk, where his Acting DS was already seated, poring over case files for Shaun Collins.

'How are we really?' he asked.

The young man seemed to slump a little. 'We're getting there, Guv.'

'Where, exactly? You heard the news report: they know we have nothing.'

'I think the stepdad's a lead.' Minshull lifted a sheet from the file and offered it to Anderson. 'Look at this: he has previous for intimidation and violent behaviour and more than enough reason for someone to want retribution.'

'Go on.'

'If you want to get back at a bully, taking their kid is a pretty strong message.'

'You think this is revenge?'

Minshull shrugged. 'Or extortion. Holding the kid to ransom.'

'Could Collins afford it?'

'Your guess is as good as mine. But Hannah doesn't have any enemies. Ashleigh Perry doesn't appear to, either. If Shaun Collins does, that could make Hannah a potential target.'

Anderson considered this. Could Minshull be right? 'It's conceivable. Let me know as soon as Collins comes in.'

'Guv.'

In the stillness of his office, Anderson leant against the door and closed his eyes. Should you pray for an extortion attempt instead of a body? He hated himself for even considering the question. That news report had rattled him, dredging up every rancid ghost from before. This couldn't be a carbon copy case; it just couldn't. Not another on his watch.

He wouldn't let it.

Chapter Fifteen

Bennett

The air in the office of Emerson Estates was stifling and stank of old coffee and overzealous cleaning products. Kate Bennett swallowed against the dryness in her throat. She hated offices at the best of times but at least the CID office in Ipswich had windows that opened. She hated estate agents, too, but that was down to an excruciating house move she'd endured over the course of last year. Liars, the lot of them. She doubted any of the Emerson's employees would know the truth if it ran bollock-naked into the place.

She was smarting, too, from being sent back to the High Street door-to-doors. Dave Wheeler and Steph Lanehan had done most of the legwork so why weren't they here? Bennett wished again that DI Anderson had really been in charge of Op Seraph, instead of this name-only nonsense. There would be no fear of her getting the arse-end jobs if it were up to him.

It was scary to see him like that in the briefing, watching his whole body sag as the news report played out. Did people really blame the police already?

Rob Minshull was okay, she supposed, a decent enough copper. She'd liked him when they worked as DCs together. But she'd been in CID four years longer than he had and was two years his senior. If anyone was DS material it was her. Of course, she didn't have a famous dad – or a dick – and that seemed to be all that mattered. While she'd avoided talk of going up a grade until now, the snub still stung.

'Are you looking for something in the village?' the young woman with the too-tight ponytail and too-bright veneers trilled, rising from behind her desk. 'We've some great new properties, not yet listed...'

'DC Bennett, South Suffolk CID.' Bennett enjoyed the virtual slap of showing the estate agent her warrant card, watching the woman shrink back to her seat. 'And this is DC Ellis. We're investigating the disappearance of Hannah Perry. CCTV footage we gained from the Spar supermarket over the road suggests she was looking into your window on the day she went missing.'

Ellis stepped forward to offer the grainy CCTV printout to the young woman. 'Do you recognise her?'

'Hang on…' The estate agent tapped an acrylic nail on the photo and turned her head. 'Ted, isn't this the kid who's always looking at houses?'

An older colleague moved across the office to her desk, peering over her shoulder. 'Ah bless her, it is.'

'You've seen her before?'

'Yeah, regular as. Shame she isn't in the market to buy them, that'd be my commission for the year sorted.'

Bennett glanced at Ellis. 'Has she ever come in here?'

'Oh no. Just stands outside, lookin'. Never known a little 'un so fascinated by our window. You'd think we'd packed it with toys and sweets, the way she gazes in. Such a sweet little thing. Bit strange, but always smiley.'

'Did either of you see her last Thursday? The first day of the Easter Market. Somewhere around 1.40p.m?'

'I wasn't working Thursday,' the young woman, whose badge said *Hi, I'm Shanice*, replied. 'But Ted was.'

The male estate agent nodded. 'I remember seeing her, around that sort of time. I'd just come back from lunch and my colleague Adam had gone for his.'

'You were in here alone?'

'While he was off on his lunch, yeah. The boss doesn't work Thursdays so it was just me covering. That's what happens if you don't play golf.' He smile died on his lips as soon as it appeared. 'But yeah, I saw her.'

'How long was she there for?'

'It's never long. Five minutes, maybe?'

Ellis looked up from his notes. 'Did you see where she went?'

'Stall opposite had some poor sod dressed in a rabbit suit handing out free stuff to the kiddies – chocolate bunnies and chicks and that. I saw him give her some and when I looked next, she'd gone.'

'And you didn't see her again?'

'Sorry.'

Ellis tapped his notebook with his pen. 'Just a thought, but have you seen the news lately? There was even a report from outside here.'

The man reddened. 'Everyone saw it.'

'And you didn't recognise Hannah as the girl who looks in the window then? Or think to tell police?'

Silence fell in the office.

'It's just, you both seem really sure now.'

Bennett suppressed a smile. The more time she spent with Drew Ellis, the greater her respect for him became. He asked the questions nobody expected someone looking as gangly and awkward as him to ask, completely nailing the issues before anyone had a chance to think better of their reply.

'I am sure,' Ted returned, his voice low and his eyes somehow failing to connect with either of the detectives. 'I know she didn't come in here so I didn't reckon it was important.'

Ellis blinked. 'Not important to tell police searching for a vulnerable child in imminent danger?'

'I'm sorry, okay? I didn't want this office linked with *that*. Those journalists out there are nutters; they'll crucify anyone they think could have helped the kid. Head office has had this place on a warning of closure for a year – we can't afford the bad publicity.'

Ellis turned to Bennett. 'I don't have anything further to ask, do you?'

'No.' Bennett eyeballed Ted and Shanice as she took a card from her jacket pocket and handed it to them. 'But if you happen to remember anything else – *anything* at all – you call me immediately. Clear?'

Receiving two dumb nods in reply, she turned and swept out of the office, with Ellis hot on her heels.

It was a lead but not much of a lead, as most of their enquiries so far had been. They knew Hannah had looked into the window of Emerson Estates and that their suspicion that she crossed to another stall was now correct. But after that, the trail went cold. Did she make it to the Meatcross? Did she go down a different road entirely?

'That's good, isn't it?' Drew Ellis asked, once they were outside. 'Even though they didn't report it when they should have done. It still confirms she was here and that it's a regular thing.'

Bennett recognised that look of hope he wore. She'd worn it herself at the start of her career, but every year in CID had chipped more of it away. 'Sure. It just doesn't take us much further, that's all.'

'Who was the bunny?'

'Sorry?'

'Was Neil Worley dressed as a bunny when he was working on the stall? The guy Dave and Steph brought in?'

Bennett swung round and tried to picture where the Easter market stalls had been. Today the road was unusually quiet, a few scraps of litter blown into the gutters the only evidence the market had even been here. 'Good point. I think that was further along, but we need to check.'

Ellis gave a smirk. 'I call dibs on interrogating the Easter Bunny if we get to call him in. Maybe he'll tell us where he keeps the eggs.'

Bennett rolled her eyes. Drew displayed such flashes of brilliance only to remind everyone he was not long out of short trousers. And now he was pleased with himself for how he'd handled things in the estate agent's. It was going to be a long shift.

Chapter Sixteen

Minshull

Tap… Tap… Tap…

Minshull looked down and realised the sound was coming from his own pen as it hit the stack of notes on his desk. The decision to bring Shaun Collins in for informal interview had been an easy one to make and for his part Collins seemed amenable to the idea. The FLO at Hannah Perry's home had been surprised when he'd accepted, having argued with Minshull beforehand that Collins would be more likely to confess to his stepkid's abduction than show up for a voluntary interview, given his past history with police. The interview had been set for five p.m. and all of the team had raced back from their appointed enquiries to be here to witness it. Minshull suspected this had less to do with their eagerness to progress the case and more to do with an unofficial book on whether Collins would show at all.

Anderson had already stuck his head out of his office twice to ask if Collins had arrived yet. Minshull considered the latest cup of grey-beige beverage Dave Wheeler had delivered and decided against it. He glanced at the clock. Five fifteen.

A snigger sounded from Evans behind him and Minshull imagined his colleague's glee at winning the bet. Les Evans had already pegged Collins as a crook; nothing was going to change his opinion.

The door to the CID office opened and Drew Ellis hurried in. The team turned and Minshull sensed the anticipation level rise in the room.

'Well?'

'He's in.'

The news was met by a mix of groans and cheers as the sweepstake's victims and champions responded accordingly.

Buzzing, Minshull turned to DC Bennett. 'You want to sit in on this, Kate?'

'Love to.' She grinned at DC Evans as she passed his desk. 'Les can give me the twenty quid he owes me when I get back.'

They headed down the grey corridor that on Minshull's first day at the station had seemed endless. The faceless corporate corridors and rooms were a familiar part of police life but the ones here seemed a few degrees colder since his promotion.

'Is he a suspect, Sarge?'

'He isn't painting the best picture of himself so far,' Minshull replied, careful not to reveal too much. Beyond Collins' strange absences from the family home at such a critical time, and the concerns raised by Hannah's teacher with social services, he had no solid evidence. But his gut told him Hannah's stepfather had something to hide. What was it? 'Right now we just want him to talk, so he's a witness. According to Les Evans he has a history of being inside so the guy isn't likely to be our biggest fan. We need to stress to him how much we value his thoughts on this.'

'Flatter him?'

'In a word.'

'So he *is* a suspect?' Bennett's smile was a moment of solidarity at the right time. Minshull allowed his guard to lessen a little as he grinned back. He'd chosen the right person for this job.

They reached the door of Interview Room 2.

'Ready?'

Bennett nodded.

Shaun Collins was already seated in the interview room, a freshly made coffee in hand. He was shaven-headed, a striking tattoo of an eagle on one side of his neck and the edge of a cuff-style ink around his bicep visible beneath the sleeve of his faded England football shirt.

A friendly PC smiled and vacated the chair opposite as Minshull and Kate entered. Minshull took a second as he offered his hand to get a measure of the man. He appeared relaxed but his handshake revealed a slight shiver of nerves. That could be anything, of course. Police interview rooms were disconcerting at the best of times; after a stint at Her Majesty's Pleasure even more so. Still, while Hannah's stepfather didn't smile, he made easy eye contact, the blueing tattoo on the right side of his neck pulsing a little.

'Mr Collins, I appreciate you coming in,' Minshull said, taking his seat. 'Can I get you another drink before we start?'

'I'm good, ta.'

'Excellent. I asked to see you here rather than at your home because in the circumstances I felt it wise. Ms Perry has enough to deal with right now.'

'She's taken it bad.'

'I understand. Do you both have everything you need in terms of support from us?'

Collins shrugged. 'The woman you sent has been good to her. Put her mind at rest as much as anyone can.'

'I'm glad to hear it. PC Grove is one of our best family liaison officers. But if you or Ms Perry need anything else, please just let her know.'

Collins nodded and took a long, steady sip of coffee. Minshull waited until the cup was back on the teak-effect desk before he began.

'Okay. There are just a few things I wanted to go over with you. Obviously at this stage anything you can tell us could be instrumental in bringing Hannah safely home. We don't know your stepdaughter, so we need to gain as full a picture of her as we can from those that know and love her.'

His subtle stress on the word *love* didn't elicit any response from Shaun Collins. Noting this, he pressed on.

'Have you seen any differences in Hannah's behaviour recently? Has she changed her habits, been preoccupied or withdrawn?'

'No. I mean, Han's eight so, you know, she knows everything. But she's a good kid, does what her mum says, looks after her sisters.'

'Has she said anything about friends at school? Problems?'

'No.'

'We spoke to her teacher...' He consulted his notes, observing Collins' reaction in his peripheral vision. 'Miss Mills?'

A flicker of distaste registered. 'Yeah.'

'She mentioned Hannah had been a little quieter in recent weeks.'

'Pressure, ain't it? These days it's all about results and assessments. Kids are snowed under. Her teacher is the worst. Ash has been up the school about it before now, the amount of homework she saddles the kids with.'

Minshull sensed a raw nerve so deliberately didn't speak. True to form, Collins accepted the unspoken invitation and continued. 'New, she was, last term. Thinks she knows everything. Stuck up, if you ask me. Takes one look at Ash and me and it's alarm bells ringing.'

'You've met Miss Mills?'

'I've met her cronies who turned up to snoop around our house. That's enough.'

Minshull nodded. He'd read in the notes from Bennett and Ellis's interview with Hannah's teacher that a home visit had been requested and made, after Jennifer Mills had become concerned by remarks Hannah had made regarding her living arrangements, followed by two subsequent visits from a social worker to check Ashleigh Perry was coping. No action had been taken regarding Collins, despite Miss Mills' concerns.

Had he been in the teacher's position, would he have acted any differently? He could believe Ashleigh Perry was wrongly accused of not caring. To all intents and purposes, her kids appeared to be her lifeblood – the stark absence of her eldest slowly sapping vitality from her body. But Shaun Collins was another thing entirely. He was calm now, but Bennett said Miss Mills had spoken of bruises Hannah couldn't explain and the child's apparent reluctance to go home. Given his ambivalence to Hannah's disappearance, might he be capable of hurting her?

Collins had begun to relax in his chair and Minshull saw an opportunity. 'That must've been stressful.'

'Nobody wants to be called unfit. Made Ash sick, that.'

'And yourself?'

Collins gave a wry smile. 'Too late for me, innit? You know as well as I do that my opinion don't count for nothing. Once you've been inside, authorities don't see you. Just another drain on resources, me.' He considered his words for a moment. 'But Ash didn't deserve it. She's a good mum.'

'Could this tension between the school and yourselves have worried Hannah? Could she have picked up on Ms Perry's distress?'

'Maybe. Han's a sensitive kid.'

'Was she often late home from school?'

'No.' His brow creased. 'Sometimes. She likes school.'

Minshull saw Bennett's pen dip as she made notes. It was an interesting admission, not least because Hannah's teacher had noted the same thing:

Sometimes I think she doesn't want to go home. If she could live at school, she'd be happier...

Why would a young girl who reportedly loved her mother and sisters rather stay at school? Could her stepfather be a reason to avoid going home?

'How would you describe your relationship with Hannah?' Minshull asked, careful to keep his tone light.

Collins paused a second before he replied, cautious eyes studying Minshull. 'All right.'

'Would you say you were close?'

'We get on.'

'It says in my notes that you're a builder?'

Collins shrugged. 'Yeah, do a bit of everything really, mostly jobs for mates. Some electrics, some plastering, few roofing jobs if they come up.'

'All local?'

'Yeah. Don't like to travel too far.'

'How far would you say?'

'No more than five miles out. Lots of work around right now.'

Bennett was frantically taking notes beside him. Minshull changed tack. 'And how often do you look after Hannah and her sisters by yourself?'

Collins sniffed. 'Ruby and Lily only when I take them round to my mum's. Hannah, maybe once or twice a week, when Ash is working late.'

'And the two of you get on okay when you're in sole charge?'

'Han's a good kid. She knows to behave.'

Minshull nodded as he scanned the list of questions in his folder. 'I'm sorry but I need to ask this next question – we're asking everybody. Where were you on Thursday afternoon?'

'I had a building job over in Hale End most of the morning, then I came back to Ash's because Han was due back.'

'And you were in the house alone?'

'Yes.'

'And when Hannah didn't arrive? What did you do?'

For the first time, Collins appeared rattled. 'I know you think I should have called your lot then but honestly I just figured she'd gone home with that mate of hers from class and the mother. It happens sometimes. Or maybe they'd stopped at the market or something.'

'Did you call Mrs Guiney?'

'Don't have her number.'

'Did you call Ms Perry?'

'They won't let her take calls at the grain store when she's working.'

'Did you leave a message?'

'No.' He shifted a little, brows low over his stare.

'But she was due home…'

'I don't know, do I? Han goes off with friends sometimes. She knows her mum is back around five-thirty, so as long as she's home by the time Ash brings Ruby and Lily from the childminder it's okay.'

'What time did Ms Perry return home with the other children?'

'It was gone six. Childminder wouldn't stop yakking.'

Bennett tapped her pad with her pencil to indicate she had a question and Minshull nodded her in.

'Why was the call made so late to police?'

Collins gave a slow blink. 'We waited. To see if she came home.'

'Three hours after your partner came home? When Hannah had been due back at, what, two p.m.?'

'My mum and my sister came round. They wanted to check friends' houses first. So we waited till we knew Han wasn't there. Then Mum called you.'

–

'So he has an alibi,' Bennett said as they walked back to the CID office.

'Of sorts. He was still alone in the house for the time Hannah disappeared.'

'It just staggers me that they waited so long before reporting her missing.'

'It happens,' Minshull replied. 'People refuse to believe their loved one has vanished. They'll exhaust every other possibility before they call us.'

'I'll check with Maddie Grove, the FLO. See if his mum and sister can confirm what time they arrived.' Bennett nodded thanks as Minshull held open the corridor door for her. 'No love lost between him and the teacher, is there?'

Minshull laughed. 'That's an understatement. Collins reacted immediately when we mentioned school – the only thing he took the bait on. It's worth looking into.'

'I could talk to the other teachers, perhaps? See if anyone else mentions it?'

'Good idea. Find out if Hannah was in any after-school clubs, lunchtime groups. Did she get on with school friends? Could there be any tension there? Talk to anyone else who had regular contact with her.'

'No problem, Sarge.'

'How was the slimy toerag?' DC Evans looked up from a half-eaten pasty.

'Our *key witness* was very helpful,' Minshull replied.

'I'll bet he was. Nasty bit of work, that one.'

'Just because he was inside, Les…'

Blood vessels began to pepper the DC's cheeks as he glared at Bennett. 'No, Kate, not *just because he was inside*. Did you read his file? Well, I did. And I talked to the copper who arrested him first time around. Remembers him well – but then you don't tend to forget the bugger that broke your nose during arrest, do you?'

Minshull turned. 'Does the guv'nor know this?'

'He will do. I just got off the phone to Steve Clark at Cambridge CID. He was a beat officer here when Collins was nicked. Magistrate added GBH to the rap sheet because of the damage his nut did to Clark's face.'

Two versions of Hannah Perry's stepfather appeared in Minshull's mind, side by side: the chatty, salt-of-the-earth bloke from the Parkhall Estate versus the dangerously violent thug resisting arrest. Which incarnation had Hannah Perry seen? Was this why she didn't want to go home from school? Had Collins ever directed his anger towards her? His violence?

Whatever the truth, if they were to gain his trust Minshull knew he would have to tread carefully to keep Shaun Collins on the right side of his anger…

'Sarge? I said, what happens next with Collins?' Bennett was staring at him.

'We'll call him back in when we know more. In the meantime, we'll ask around the estate, see what the pervading feeling is about the family – Collins in particular. I think there's more to that situation than he's telling us.' Minshull looked over to Wheeler's desk. 'Dave, didn't you say Lara Guiney mentioned Collins was an issue?'

'She said he was a waste of space.'

'Did she say why?'

'Not in any great detail. Just that he didn't support Ms Perry with the home and the kids.'

'Call her again. Ask for specifics.'

'Do you think Hannah might just have run away?' Bennett asked, as Minshull turned back. 'I mean Collins isn't the kind of bloke you'd feel easy with as an adult, let alone if you were his stepkid. But what if she was scared of him and scared of spending the holidays in the house? Are we certain someone's taken her?'

Of course, she was right. Minshull could see the logic in it. But with the history of the Cooper murder and the circumstances worryingly aligning, it seemed an optimistic shot.

'She might. And we might yet discover she has,' he replied carefully. 'But given the previous case and the similarities, I think we have to consider the possibility that someone has Hannah. Drew, any news on our elusive Easter Bunny?'

Ellis brightened. 'I tracked him down. It was Neil Worley. He didn't want to admit it, but his mum confirmed he was wearing the costume. Said he had to leave the rabbit paw gloves off so he could make the balloon animals.'

Minshull shuddered. Animal suits unnerved him at the best of times, but the thought of the evil contained within such an innocent-looking suit turned his stomach.

'Right. Good work.'

As the team returned to their desks, Minshull considered the next move. Something didn't sit right with him about Collins. And he couldn't shake the feeling that someone had Hannah – that she hadn't just run away to avoid spending time with her stepfather. But were the two connected? And if so, how?

Hannah

It's getting colder now. I stopped being able to feel my toes a while ago.

There's a sandwich on a plate nearby but I'm scared it might have poison in it. There are mice in the Small Space – I've seen their little brown poos near my feet and when it's dark I can hear a horrible scratching behind the wall I'm squashed up by. I lie like a statue at night. I don't want to breathe or move because the mice might come and bite me. I *hate* mice.

Mrs Hartley from next door once said that mice are more scared of you than you are of them. But right now, I am the most scared I have ever been in my life. And if a mouse scurried into the Small Space, it would *know*. And it might not be more scared of me then. It might be hungrier than I am, too.

So I shut my eyes as tight as I can and I hum very quietly. It tickles the back of my throat and it's more of a rumble than a sound, but it helps a bit. I make my mind think of the noise more than any other sound and it stops me thinking about the mice quite so much. The scared feeling keeps trying to stop the hum, but every time it does I push it back down my throat again.

This is all I know for hours and hours: the cold and the hum and stopping the scared feeling winning.

It's all I can think about…

Chapter Seventeen

Minshull

One glance at his colleagues working around the CID office on Tuesday morning confirmed the mood. Minshull could see the weight heavy on shoulders; feel the prickle of irritation just below the surface. Already Les Evans had snapped Dave Wheeler's head off for no reason. Everyone felt the pressure. Everyone knew the odds were stacking up against them. Speculation was building in the media, packs of jostling journalists now present outside South Suffolk Police HQ as well as laying siege to the Parkhall Estate and the centre of St Just.

And still no sign of Hannah.

Minshull felt it more than most. The responsibility. He'd wanted to be further along than this, have more potential lines of enquiry to pursue. Instead, it felt like he was treading water, at the mercy of whoever had taken Hannah Perry. It felt like the investigation was waiting for the abductor's next move. They had no more CCTV images of Hannah and no clear theory about where she might have gone between the image of her captured by Emerson Estates that the Spar supermarket camera had captured and the next two on Eastern Promise and Barclays Bank that failed to show her at all. Neil Worley had seemed a perfect fit, but he had been ruled out. Residents on the Parkhall Estate had seen nothing – and when pressed clammed up entirely. Whether this was from fear of what had happened to Matthew Cooper, or fear of betraying trusts within the estate, Minshull couldn't say.

This was nothing like the fraud investigation he'd so successfully led, where evidence slowly formed a chain leading to the perpetrators. But a life wasn't at stake there, just money and reputations. Minshull wanted to give more to the team who were working so hard for him, to Joel Anderson more than anyone. His superior was already displaying dangerous signs of strain – Minshull saw it in every raised voice, every dark silence, in the way Anderson stalked the periphery of each conversation like a desperate phantom.

After Minshull's interview with Shaun Collins yesterday, he'd made the decision to focus on Hannah's stepfather. Minshull's gut told him Shaun Collins was a key player. This morning the thrust of the investigation had shifted to focus on him. His past convictions were being studied, contacts were being gone through, questions were being asked about his past activities and what influence they might bear on Hannah's disappearance. Bennett had spoken again to Hannah's teacher by phone, delving deeper into the concerns and allegations she had raised. On the Parkhall Estate the door-to-door interviews now included strategic mentions of Collins' name. And the decision had been made to hold a press conference where Ashleigh Perry would make a public appeal for Hannah to come home, while two police psychologists sat among the crowd of journalists specifically tasked with watching Shaun Collins and gathered family members.

The more they found out about him, the worse it looked for his stepdaughter. Hannah's teacher said the child visibly recoiled when asked about him. Neighbours clammed up when his name was mentioned. And then there was his previous record. Illegal money-lending, intimidation, a charge of GBH that only failed in court due to the judge ruling some evidence inadmissible – not to mention several call-outs last year for domestic incidents at the house he shared with Hannah's mother. Put together, it didn't exactly qualify Collins for Father of the Year. Either he was involved, or someone he'd bullied was out for payback...

'Sarge.'

Minshull looked up from the list of Shaun Collins' previous convictions and allegations to see DC Wheeler's ashen expression. For the most cheerful member of the CID team, this could only mean trouble. 'What is it, Dave?'

Wheeler was grabbing protective gloves from the drawer in his desk as Minshull approached. 'Development in Op Seraph.' He looked up at Minshull and his face said it all. 'We've had a delivery.'

Without a word, the entire team moved as one to Wheeler's desk and a heavy silence settled over the CID office. Minshull could feel the collected dread of his colleagues as they watched Wheeler carefully opening a brown paper bag, the padded envelope it had arrived in already placed inside a clear plastic evidence bag. With gloved hands he shook out the contents and a small velvet-covered child's headband fell onto the desk. Bennett swore under her breath as Wheeler turned it around. Across the top of the headband a name had been stitched in bright rainbow coloured threads:

HANNAH

'There's a note, too.' Wheeler's tone was flat. Unfolding a single sheet of paper, he spread it on the desk.

HANNAH SENT THIS.

'Is that it?' Minshull asked, but the faces of his colleagues revealed more than anyone was saying.

Evans, stripped of his usual attitude, stared hollowly back. 'It's happening again. That *bastard* is doing it again.'

'Who?'

'Cooper case,' Wheeler said, simply.

Shit. The press had been mentioning it for days but in the CID office it was conspicuously absent from conversations, as if any mention might bring it into being.

'It was like this?'

'It was exactly like this.'

Cold, sick dread seeped through Minshull's body. 'Someone needs to tell the guv.'

Wheeler was already on his feet. 'I'll do it, Sarge. I was there last time.'

'Thanks, Dave.'

Watching him go, he turned to the others. 'Right. We need to bring up everything from that investigation. I'll contact Hannah's mother and ask her to identify this. And then we need to get it to forensics.' His heart sank as the dark reality bit. Was Hannah alive when the kidnapper had taken this?

What if they were already too late?

Hannah

I *hate* Them.

They hurt me when They did that.

I said 'No!' – loud, like Mum taught me. I said, 'It's *mine!*' But They didn't listen.

They didn't listen at all.

Nobody has a headband like mine. Auntie Siobhan sewed my name on it in rainbow colours because she said rainbows always make you happy. Now *They* have my rainbow. It hurts in my heart that I don't have it anymore.

My head hurts where They pulled my hair. Some came out when They took my headband. I saw the strands hanging from it when They snatched it away.

Why did They take it? Why didn't They stop when I said no?

If They try to take anything else, I'll scream. I'll scream louder than anything.

Next time They won't win.

Chapter Eighteen

Anderson

Anderson glared at his computer – as if this action could make the inanimate object retract the news report it had just delivered to the screen.

> The search for Hannah Perry is continuing today, despite growing unrest among people living in the small Suffolk village she disappeared from last week. While community leaders in St Just have been quick to defend the investigation being led by South Suffolk Police, many local people have said they don't trust the police to find the eight-year-old.
>
> 'We're scared,' Alison Kenton, 38, told The Sentinel. 'I have a daughter the same age as Hannah. It's the Easter holidays when kids should be playing outside but I just don't feel I can let her out of my sight.'
>
> The same fear has been expressed across the village, with many locals who publicly support the police operation now privately voicing their doubts. 'Nobody trusts them. They never caught Matthew's killer,' said Colin Staunton, 52, referring to the ten-year-old abducted and murdered in the village seven years ago. 'If they'd arrested him, Hannah Perry would be safe.'
>
> South Suffolk Police have not responded to The Sentinel's request for comment. The investigation continues.

Anderson flung his pen across the desk, where it bounced off the framed photograph of his wife. He imagined Rosalyn's calming voice and wished again that she weren't hundreds of miles away nursing her invalid mother. Today he needed her more than ever.

As he retrieved his pen, a knock came at the door.

'Come in.'

The moment Dave Wheeler appeared, Anderson knew. He'd seen that expression before – worn by a younger version of his friend and DC.

'Guv. There's been a development in Op Seraph.'

'Sit down, Dave.'

Apology was etched into Wheeler's face. 'I wanted to be the one to tell you. I'm sorry, Joel.'

No.

Not again.

Not now...

'Tell me what?'

Let me be wrong. Let it be something else.

'We've had a delivery. Allegedly from Hannah Perry's abductor.'

Already every nerve was twisting, but the question was unavoidable. 'Go on.'

'I opened it. We have a child's headband allegedly belonging to Hannah. Judging by the note, the tone, the method of delivery...' He let out a long sigh that seemed to suck the air from the room. 'It's the same as before. Too similar to be a coincidence. It's almost identical to Matthew Cooper's deliveries.'

Anderson shuddered.

Cooper.

For seven years he had dreaded the mention of that name. He'd prayed he'd never hear it again.

'Are you certain this—' He paused, his mouth inexplicably dry. '—*delivery* is genuine?'

Wheeler nodded, his eyes now firmly fixed on Anderson's. 'It was listed by Ashleigh Perry as one of the items of clothing Hannah was wearing on the day she disappeared. Her aunt made it for her – there's no way it could be anyone else's.'

Anderson was quiet, his mind racing with thoughts he had hoped never to consider again. Seven years ago, a ten-year-old boy went missing during a school field trip. At first it was believed Matthew Cooper had bunked off with friends, but when he failed to come home after twelve hours, the alarm was raised. Initially Anderson treated it as a case of a runaway: there had been indications from the family of the boy's troubled relationship with his mother's live-in boyfriend. There had been a significant argument prior to Matthew's disappearance – it was well known among the family's neighbours that he and the boyfriend clashed regularly.

Anderson assumed the boy would be found safe, that he was hiding out with friends, making his mother sweat for a few days. Everything about Matthew Cooper's reported character suggested this to be the case. But then South Suffolk Constabulary received an anonymous package claiming to be from the boy's abductor. In it was the school shirt Matthew had been wearing on the day he disappeared and a note saying Matthew had sent it. No ransom demand, no further details. In the days that followed more packages arrived, each delivered to police stations within a twenty-mile radius of Matthew's home. Items from the boy's schoolbag, one of his socks and the jumper he had been wearing the last time his mother saw him were all returned, each with a note giving no further clues to the kidnapper's identity or the location of the boy.

After a week, the press got hold of the story. A local paper, *The St Just Argus*, broke the news and within hours the village was teeming with blood-hungry journalists. At first the reports were largely sympathetic, painting the local force in a favourable light – so much so that Anderson was persuaded by his superiors and the force's press office to provide *The Argus* with an exclusive interview, to highlight aspects of Matthew's disappearance in order to jog the public's memory for any useful information, but also to reward the paper for its support.

And now the journalists are returning to St Just...

As days had turned to weeks, the vultures began baying for more salacious details. Neighbours were courted for less-than-favourable tales of the boy's family, the finger of blame aimed squarely at the mother's boyfriend who, it transpired, had served time inside for aggravated burglary and was known in the area for his hot-headedness. Anderson tested this line of enquiry only to confirm the boyfriend's firm alibi that he had been working at a local pub, where over fifty regulars corroborated his presence. And then, one national newspaper switched its attack to the police investigation – and all hell descended.

Anderson's integrity was called into question when an instance from his beat officer days was brought to light. He had been found innocent of all charges back then but the fact of the investigation was fuel for the media's fire. His officers were portrayed as country bumpkins, bumbling a case that should, in the media's condemnatory opinion, have been solved weeks beforehand. Votes of no confidence were unanimously declared and the high-ups became twitchy.

A final package arrived, this time with a ransom demand for one hundred thousand pounds. Panicked, Anderson's superiors demanded greater action and Anderson, keen to prove them and his critics wrong, stepped up the investigation by issuing a police statement that sent a clear message to Matthew's abductor: *We will not negotiate. Our officers are closing in. We need Matthew now and we're coming to find him.* It was a move that, ultimately, was to prove a catastrophic mistake.

A day later, the packages stopped. So did the demands. And then, a body was discovered, stashed behind shrubs in the car park of the local Co-op supermarket. It had been stripped naked, stabbed multiple times and stuffed into a clear plastic shroud. Gaffer-taped to ten-year-old Matthew Cooper's slashed chest was a note bearing words that, to this day, Anderson couldn't think about without being assaulted by a million regrets:

TOO LATE.

YOU MADE ME DO IT.

HIS BLOOD IS ON YOUR HANDS.

'Are you sure?' he asked Wheeler now, as if he might be able to change the truth. As if it was that easy.

'We have every right to believe so, Guv. I'm sorry. So sorry, Joel.'

Anderson's blood went cold.

Chapter Nineteen

Cora

'Boat... Aeroplane... Dog... Lightning...'

'Mm-hmm.' Daniel continued screwing up sheets of paper and dropping them. His head was bowed, eyes focused on the task, ticking boxes as he went.

It was a process identical to every other session of the study so far, no longer alien to Cora although every bit as monotonous. But this morning the voices were muted, as if shrouded in thick wool. Cora closed her eyes, summoning them to the centre of her mind. But that space was crowded, other voices clamouring for attention. Voices not connected with the study or the endless, mindless list of unconnected words.

...the search for eight-year-old Hannah Perry appears to have taken a sinister turn...

'Sand... Fox... Newspaper...'

...Hannah's belongings returned to police...

'Newspaper...'

'You said that. First mistake in two weeks.' Daniel gave an irritated sigh and made a show of screwing up another ball of paper. It dropped with a voice so distant Cora couldn't make out the word.

'News...'

The news report she'd heard on the radio driving into work played now on repeat, fragmented excerpts rushing back at her like an incoming tide.

'You missed it. Again... *Cora.*'

Disorientated, Cora's attention returned to the brightly lit office. 'Sorry?'

'This is a pointless exercise if you don't focus.'

'I was. I'm trying to...'

Daniel threw the clipboard onto his desk with completely unnecessary force, a petty, man-child tantrum he should have been better than. 'I can't understand why you aren't over the moon after getting *that*.'

Cora glanced at the letter on the desk beside her, confirmation that her PhD submission had been successful and she was now officially Dr Lael. It should have meant everything, but other concerns had pushed it aside.

'What is wrong with you this morning? You've been miles away since you came in.'

He didn't deserve an explanation, demanding it like that. But Cora needed to talk, had to provide an outlet for her dangerously overcrowded mind.

'Have you heard the news? About the missing girl?'

Clearly this wasn't what Daniel expected to hear, his next volley rendered invalid by her words. 'Which girl?'

'In St Just? It's been all over the news for days, Dan. Don't you watch the news?'

'Not if I can help it. I didn't think you did, either.'

'I couldn't escape this.' Every mention of St Just jarred her, bringing memories, emotions and history she didn't want to relive. 'Look, I'll show you.' She pulled her phone from her pocket and found the BBC news report she'd heard the audio of in the car:

> 'Breaking news from Suffolk where the search for eight-year-old Hannah Perry appears to have taken a sinister turn. We cross live to St Just – where Hannah went missing last Thursday – and our reporter Tom Neale. Tom, what's the latest?'
>
> 'Elodie, we are getting reports from a source close to the investigation that police have begun to receive items from Hannah's school bag, reportedly sent by her abductors. Now, at this point we don't know the details of what exactly has been sent, or whether ransom demands have been attached to them, but this is a significant development and a chilling mirror of the previous missing child case that happened here, seven years ago. I know many viewers will remember that tragic case, when ten-year-old Matthew Cooper's body was dumped after a string

of his belongings were sent to police. That case remains unsolved and fears that the killer could strike again appear to have been confirmed by the news today.'

'Tom, have the police said anything about this?'

'Obviously this has only just happened and we've had no formal statement from South Suffolk CID, who were largely blamed for Matthew Cooper's death. We have been informed that a press conference is imminent, so we are waiting for confirmation of when that is likely to take place.'

'And what's been the reaction in St Just?'

'People are terrified. Angry. They want answers and they want Hannah found alive. Now, more than ever, all eyes are on the police, with many here calling for the investigation to be passed to another, larger force. There are rumours that both The Met Police and West Mercia Police are on standby to intervene. Mistakes simply can't be made this time. Nobody here wants a repeat of the tragedy of Matthew Cooper...'

Cora looked up as the report ended. 'You see?'

'No, sorry. What does this have to do with you?'

Frustration pushed Cora to her feet. '*Everything*. I was born in St Just. I lived through that whole nightmare. My brother knew Matthew – everyone did. I saw what it did to people I loved, people I'd grown up alongside. The fear. The suspicion. The lies levelled at us by the media that tore the village to shreds. I saw what it did to my dad...' Her voice cracked but she pressed on. She couldn't stop the words now even if she wanted to. 'Dad led the search. He half-killed himself by going out at all hours, refusing to stop even when the police said finding Matthew was unlikely. And then there were reports of Matthew's belongings arriving with demands, the police not knowing whether this meant he was alive or dead. When his body was found, it broke us all.'

The fight had gone from Daniel. He reached out and his fingers closed around hers, a warm and steady anchor in the torrent of recollection. 'That sounds horrific.'

'It was. It still is. I just remember thinking back then that someone like me might have *heard* something – when the police couldn't. Clues to where he was, indicators of how he was feeling, something that could have given them an advantage.'

'In the returned belongings?'

Cora nodded. 'But I wasn't pushing my ability then. I was too scared to face it. It haunted me for a long time – this news brought it all back. Only now I'm not helpless, am I? Now I have a choice.'

'What are you thinking?'

She leaned against the wall beside him, her hand drifting from his. 'If it's like last time, that child might not have long left. If she's alive at all. There have been no arrests, no details of the investigation – I think that might mean the police don't have anything to go on. And I know this is going to sound ridiculous, but I can't stop thinking about it: I think I could help them.'

Daniel recoiled a little. 'I can't see how…'

'If Hannah is alive, if she's *still* alive, her voice will be in her belongings. Strong – really strong. And even if she isn't, if her death is recent, I would still hear the voice for a while.'

'Would you? How do you know that?'

'Because of Dad.' Cora swallowed hard against the memory. 'When he died, for the first few days it was as if he'd left his voice behind in the house. I could hear him everywhere, as loud as if he were standing next to me. But then, it started to fade. It happened so gradually, the volume slowly decreasing day by day. I had to focus harder to hear him – I'd turn off the TV, the radio, move other things he hadn't touched out of the way, just to be able to hold onto the sound. To hold onto him. And then, two weeks after we lost him, I lost his voice.'

It still hurt. It would have been far better if Bill Lael's belongings had been silenced at the moment of his death. Losing his voice was like losing him again, only this time it was final, devastating.

'Oh baby…'

Cora held up her hands. His sympathy was kind but she didn't need comforting now. Her own thoughts demanded a voice. 'So I would know. Whether she was alive or dead. She went missing last Thursday, so it's within the time when her voice would be present. But if they've killed her, that window is shrinking.'

'What are you suggesting? That you could help the police?'

Cora could hardly believe what she heard herself saying, but the conviction wouldn't leave her. 'Yes. And soon.'

Daniel didn't say anything. Cora waited, the wall cool against her spine. Inside, everything was racing. She knew she was right, but was she ready? Would the police even accept her help? It was a relief to have it all said, but now the urgency assumed the place where her frustration had been. What if she could make the difference? What if Hannah's life depended on her?

When Daniel spoke again, Cora recognised his tone. It was the same voice he'd used when considering his pitch for the *Cognitive Divergence* study: cool, measured, strategic. 'We would have to play it carefully. Approach from a wholly scientific perspective. You would be seconded to the investigation as an expert advisor. We'd need the Dean's approval to offer your services at no cost to the investigation – I suspect that would be their initial concern and the first hurdle we'd have to clear.'

He was pacing the floor now, his mind so clearly at work that Cora could almost hear the electrical impulses.

'Would Gordon agree?'

'I don't see why not. It wouldn't be extra money for him to find, just a commitment to continue paying your salary while you were released to assist the police. And it would be a killer touch for the study. I think he'd go for it. Nobody has ever studied your condition before, but more than that, nobody has ever deliberately placed your ability in an uncontrolled environment. It could lift our work to a global stage. Gordon Soper's wanted that level of recognition for years and he hasn't long to achieve it with his retirement due.'

What did Daniel really think? Did he support Cora or was this a cerebral challenge he felt compelled to crack? Did he even think her capable of helping to find the child? Cora couldn't say. What mattered was that he'd heard her, *really* heard her this time.

'So what do we do?'

'I'll go and talk to the Dean now. Immediately.'

'And if he agrees?'

Daniel's eyes met hers – and in them she saw the determination she'd hoped for. 'I'll contact the police.'

Chapter Twenty

Minshull

Minshull jabbed a finger at the screen, his rage so all-encompassing that he could barely squeeze air into his lungs to speak. 'I don't care how the press got hold of this, I want to know *who* told them?'

All eyes met his apart from one pair.

'Les.'

Now the DC looked up. 'What?'

'Know anything about this?'

His face flushed. 'No, I bloody well don't! Typical that you blame me when I've just been doing my job...'

Minshull raised himself to his full height, voice chillingly quiet. 'Excuse me?'

Watching Les Evans hastily stuff away his anger like contraband should have been a reward. But it wasn't. Nothing would make this better – it was a huge blow to the investigation. Any hope of gaining an advantage over Cora's abductor was gone. This was what they wanted: publicity. Notoriety. It was what they'd been driven by last time. *Last time*. Minshull hadn't been in the CID office when Matthew Cooper was missing, but now he felt the child's accusing spectre hanging over everything.

'It wasn't me, Sarge.'

Had Anderson seen it? He'd been holed up in a meeting with DCI Sue Taylor for the last two hours, which might just have kept the news from reaching him. Regardless, Minshull knew precious little time existed for damage limitation.

'Nothing that happens in this room is repeated *anywhere*, do I make myself clear?'

'Sarge.' The chorus was resigned more than decisive. Did they respect him enough yet to comply?

'Good. We have little enough in our favour as it is. Ashleigh Perry has confirmed the headband belongs to Hannah, made by her aunt. The DNA check on strands of hair found on the headband will confirm it. But that's all we've got. We don't know if Hannah was alive when it was taken from her, but we press on as though she's still out there. Whoever has Hannah craves attention. They want notoriety – they will feed off it. Now the media has the story they'll be playing right into the bastard's hands. So we find new avenues, new lines of enquiry while their attention is focused on this. We redouble our efforts, revisit every lead. We pull out everything we have from the Matthew Cooper case and re-examine every line of investigation from it, whether it was pursued at the time or not. Someone has to know something…'

A crash at the far end of the CID office made the whole team turn. Minshull's heart sank. DI Joel Anderson entered the room like a man possessed, kicking a chair out of the way as he made for the team.

'*Who was it?*'

'Guv, we've already—'

'Do you not think we aren't on our bloody knees already? We have *nothing*. And that child is still out there. I told you to protect everything that happens in here. Were none of you listening? Do you think you know better than me? Or *him*?'

Minshull bore the dismissal, despite its sting. Now wasn't the time to raise it. 'Closed shop from now, Guv. We're all agreed.'

A little of the fire vanished from Anderson's chest, but his stare remained wild on them. 'I *want* her *found.*' There was no mistaking his words, every syllable a low, guttural growl.

'Guv.' This time the response was muted not by uncertain respect but by fear. Minshull caught Wheeler's eye and saw his own concern magnified. This could never happen again, not on Minshull's watch. He watched his superior stalk to his office, felt the slam of the door at the centre of his chest.

Anderson was too close to breaking. This was on him now.

My case. My responsibility.

It was all on him.

Chapter Twenty-One

Anderson

He wasn't going to speak to him.

When the email arrived from a professor at the University of South Suffolk, Anderson assumed it was a glory-seeker, someone suggesting they were eminently better qualified to solve the case than he was. You got them all the time, especially when cases attracted media attention: fake confessions, sightings from the other side of the country – or other countries entirely, conspiracy theorists, rubberneckers. People drawn to horror and scandal. People for whom gruesome details fuelled fantasy. Wasters of police time, space and frankly, in Anderson's opinion, air.

But Professor Daniel Gold wasn't deterred by the standard issue *thanks but no thanks* reply. After the email came a phone call, missed by Anderson as it came during a meeting with DCI Taylor. Then two more messages taken by the team and left on Anderson's desk. Annoyed, Anderson had returned the call, mainly to tell the persistent professor where to get off.

But somehow that call had become *this*.

Observing the surprisingly young, eloquent and sickeningly handsome man relaxing in the high-backed armchair across the table from him, Anderson wondered again how he'd ended up here. The pub they were meeting in, a high-end gastro job in the middle of nowhere with better furniture than Joel Anderson had in his house, was warm and soothing after the day he'd had. An endless shift of dead ends and detours had left him exhausted, not helped by having to dodge the dogged press pack now permanently camped at the entrance to police headquarters on his way out of the building. And worse, the only evidence his team had was Hannah Perry's headband, which gave no clue about whether she was alive or dead. Anderson had presided over it all, witnessing the team's dejection and weariness, trying not to notice the toll it was taking on his young acting DS. They had given so much with little to show for it and he feared they would soon reach breaking point.

It was happening again: his worst nightmare. And he was powerless to stop it.

Maybe it was the intense, gnawing ache of fear, growing by the hour, that had led Anderson here. His missed his wife, away in Ilkley caring for her mother after a fall. Rosalyn would have told him to ask for help. She would have insisted.

Ros would have pushed him here, if she knew.

Maybe he'd tell her later. Or perhaps he'd purposely forget. He didn't need her worrying about him way up north, even though he knew she would be.

It was supposed to be an informal conversation, far enough away from anyone who might be listening. But it had already become a pint and dinner, Anderson finding the promise of steak and ale pie he didn't have to defrost from the stash Ros had left in their freezer too alluring to resist.

'I'm curious, why did you agree to meet me?' Professor Gold asked, pushing aside his empty plate. 'After so many missed calls, I assumed I wouldn't hear from you.'

Pub pie and beer churned in Anderson's gut. He took another swig to force it all back down. 'I thought I'd better hear what you had to say.'

'Because of the case?'

'Because of your offer. I admit it made little sense. We have staff psychologists. Why would we need another?'

'Fair point.' The professor nodded. 'But Dr Lael has abilities your staff psychologists don't have.'

'Such as?'

'Let's just say her area of expertise links directly with the methods Hannah Perry's abductor is now utilising. And Matthew Cooper's killer seven years ago.'

That was a kick to the guts. While Daniel Gold took a slow sip of beer, Anderson wrestled control back. 'So you contacted me because you saw the news yesterday?'

'Dr Lael saw it. She's keen to help.'

'And how does the good doctor believe she can do that?' He was mocking now, his only defence against rising panic that had returned – panic he'd fooled himself was dealt with. It had taken him to the brink last time. If he had to face it again…

'Cora has a unique ability that informs her work. I've been working with her for two and a half years and I can vouch for the accuracy of it.'

Anderson's body was now alert. 'How accurate?'

'In the tests we've been doing for our latest study, one hundred per cent.'

That couldn't be right, could it? Even the most skilled professionals Anderson had worked with over the years wouldn't dare claim one hundred per cent effectiveness. 'Forgive me, I find that hard to believe.'

'I would too, had I not encountered Cora's ability. It's so rare that we have only identified thirty people worldwide who possess it.'

'When you say "ability", what do you mean?'

The professor took a breath. Was he nervous? 'Cora can hear emotional echoes from discarded items. Subconscious thought, tangible emotion, from the moment it left the person the item belonged to.'

Anderson's snort caused a woman at a neighbouring table to turn and stare. 'This is a joke. I'm sorry, Professor, but you are wasting my time.' Incensed, he began to stand.

But Daniel Gold didn't flinch. 'It's really quite fascinating. The closest known condition we can link it to is synaesthesia, only in Cora's case signals in her brain trigger emotion, not the senses. She's an emotional synaesthete, if you will.'

Halfway to his feet, Anderson halted. 'This is a real thing?'

'Oh, it's real. The university has international funding for a major study of this condition. It's of worldwide importance, revealing cognitive divergence we previously haven't encountered.' He watched Anderson resume his seat. 'Cora hears these emotional echoes as sound. Tangible sound, as if each item carries the voice of its previous owner.'

Hope, that had taken sudden residence in Anderson's chest, faded a little. 'The item we received wasn't discarded. It was taken.'

'If Cora is right, she could sense stronger emotion – hear a louder voice – from something forcibly removed.' His voice dipped. 'Or taken from a deceased person.'

'And if she's wrong?'

'Then you've lost nothing on your current position.'

Anderson's back cracked as it hit the backrest of his chair. Could he believe any of this? How would he even clear it with his superiors? 'We have no budget for this. We're stretched as it is; I've had to fight for the resources we already have.'

'It would be the university's contribution to the investigation,' the professor smiled. 'All we ask is that we can include general, non-sensitive details of Dr Lael's work for you when we publish the study in eighteen months' time.'

That would appeal to Sue Taylor at least. Whether those above her would agree was another thing. Whatever the ethical considerations of involving an untested expert in the investigation, one fact was irrefutable: they needed an advantage. Something they didn't have last time. Anderson would not, *could not* lose another child.

Dr Cora Lael might be an asset the monster who'd taken Hannah hadn't bargained for. Or she might be the snake oil seller that could bring the investigation crashing down – taking the reputation of South Suffolk Constabulary and Anderson himself along with it – if word ever got out of her involvement. But could he take the risk of losing the advantage she might offer them? Anderson was torn. But he also knew the stakes of *not* pursuing every possible avenue to find a missing child. Right now, they had precious little in their favour and time was against them: anything that might give his team an advantage mattered.

'Tell Dr Lael to stand by,' he said, his mind set. 'Let me set the wheels in motion.'

–

'A consultant?' DCI Sue Taylor's eyes narrowed.

Anderson didn't even blink. 'A specialist. Dr Lael comes highly recommended.'

'By whom?'

'Daniel Gold, Professor of the Cognitive Psychology department at the University of South Suffolk. They're world leaders in psychology and behaviour.'

'And will they be sending us an invoice?'

Money. Why did everything have to be governed by money? It should have annoyed Anderson, but not this morning. He savoured the information that would wipe that sanctimonious smirk off the DCI's face before he let it fly.

'Actually, her services have been offered free of charge on behalf of the university. To assist us in Op Seraph.'

'And Dr Lael is aware of this?'

I don't care if she is or not, Joel wanted to say. *She's free – isn't that enough?* 'She has agreed to assist us with the investigation. For Hannah.' That was the killer line, any last vestige of Sue Taylor's all-powerful budget considerations obliterated. Philanthropy was a beautiful thing…

'And how does she propose to assist the investigation?'

'By advising on the psychology of our perpetrator.'

'We have staff psychologists. They will be at the press conference tomorrow, watching Mr Collins.'

'And we are grateful for their expertise. But they can't offer the specific insight that Dr Lael can.'

Sue Taylor eyeballed him from the other side of her desk. 'Psychic, is she?'

You have no idea… 'She has specialist skills we can use. Skills we didn't have last time.'

Anderson thought he caught the smallest flicker in his superior's expression. Nobody wanted to link Hannah's disappearance with the Cooper case, but the arrival of Hannah's headband now made it a necessity. While he had borne the weight of the Cooper case failure, Sue Taylor had felt its kick in the resulting headlines and damning internal enquiry that challenged her precious force's image.

'I don't know, Joel. It's risky bringing in a civilian at this stage of the investigation.'

'We need help, ma'am. Serious help. We are at breaking point with no discernible advantage over Hannah's abductor since news of the returned belonging leaked to the press. Dr Lael could give us the edge we've been missing. You have to see how that could work?'

'I can see how it could fail.'

'Yes, well, you and me both.'

She was quiet for a long time, reading the proposal Anderson had typed up last night in preparation.

He thought of the small headband in its evidence bag, lying ominously on Rob Minshull's desk, the mountain of hope that now rested on the shoulders of a completely unknown party. It had been years since he'd gambled on anything, but this felt like the surest bet he could place. *If* she agreed.

But if she didn't…

'Fine. But I retain the right to veto this decision the moment I deem it detrimental. Understood?'

Hurrying from the DCI's office, Anderson placed the call to the number he'd had on standby on his phone.

'Dr Lael? It's Detective Inspector Joel Anderson from South Suffolk CID. Apologies for calling so early but could you come in this morning, please? For nine a.m., if you can. We need you.'

Chapter Twenty-Two

Minshull

It was *insane*.

Was DI Anderson out to undermine him? Had he finally lost the plot?

Staring at his superior officer, Minshull tried his best to conceal his true reaction.

Anderson prowled his office like a jaguar, eyes keen on him, and Minshull suspected much more was going on behind his professional scrutiny than his superior officer would admit.

'Dr Lael will merely be assisting us,' he continued. 'I'm not suggesting her input will be anything other than an experiment.'

'With respect, Guv, this isn't the time for experiments,' Minshull returned. *Just let me do my job, you bastard.*

'It's been six days, Minshull. The press are already all over us. What exactly do we have other than a child's hair accessory and a deliberately vague note?'

'We're pursuing several lines of investigation. Shaun Collins, for one. I think there is more there to discover. We'll watch him during the press conference tomorrow. And we've made a start on combing the Cooper files for anything that was missed last time—' Seeing his superior flinch, Minshull corrected himself. 'I mean, anything we couldn't have known before.'

'That's at best circumstantial, at worst pissing into the wind. We have no time, Rob. Before that headband arrived, we could assume this wasn't the same as Matthew; now we know it is. It's started already and I don't know how long we have. Do you have a better solution?'

Minshull glared at the stubborn grey office carpet and said nothing. He hated to admit it, but Anderson was right. What did they have? Not enough to find Hannah or arrest her captor. 'No.'

'Precisely.' Anderson folded his arms. 'So you will meet Dr Lael at nine a.m. today. And you *will* take this seriously.'

'But a *psychic*, sir? How do we know she's not a time-wasting loony?'

'She isn't a psychic. She has – abilities that may or may not shed light on the current situation surrounding Hannah's abduction.'

'How, exactly?'

Anderson's sigh was long and heavy. Minshull sensed an impending storm. 'She may be able to surmise whether or not Hannah is still alive.'

This was crazy. Anderson had a point to prove – everyone knew it – but to deliberately sabotage Minshull's first investigation as SIO simply to satisfy his own ego was unacceptable. Minshull wasn't going to let him ruin everything. Not without a fight. 'So she *is* a psychic? Don't you see how this could seriously scupper our current lines of investigation? Give us decent time to find Hannah before you start wheeling in the fruitcakes, please, Guv…'

'Enough, Minshull! It's been arranged. I have DCI Taylor's personal endorsement. You will meet Dr Lael at nine this morning. You will comply with this appointment. And you will allow her to do her work.' He took one step closer to him, a tiny movement imbued with all the threat of an elephant stampede. 'And if I hear even a whisper that you aren't, I'll have your scalp. Clear?'

Minshull stood to attention, every fibre of his being hating his superior whose face had begun to blur with that of his own father. 'Yes, Guv.'

Chapter Twenty-Three

Cora

Come on. You can do this.

Her hands still resting on the steering wheel, the reassuring hum of the engine long since replaced by an uneasy stillness, Cora gazed up at the nondescript concrete building across the car park. She had arrived early but now wished she hadn't: there was too much time to think before she had to enter South Suffolk Constabulary's headquarters. Too long to talk herself out of it.

What if her theory was false? What if she heard nothing?

She longed to talk to someone about what she was doing, but Daniel had told her it was to remain confidential. She'd even considered phoning her mum last night, safe in the knowledge that Sheila Lael wouldn't remember enough of their conversation afterwards to tell anyone – not that she had anyone to tell, of course.

She glanced at the orange display on the dashboard.

8.50 a.m.

Close enough.

Taking a breath, she opened the door.

A small group of people were camped out by the entrance of the building, placards leaning against a pile of rucksacks on the stone steps, but they were too preoccupied by one of their number handing out takeaway coffee cups to block her path. Safely past them, she entered the building.

A tired-looking woman behind shatterproof glass at the reception desk handed her a pass and directed her to a row of blue plastic chairs to wait for DI Joel Anderson. All she had was Anderson's name as a contact and the memory of his gruff Scottish voice; beyond that she didn't know anything about him. Daniel's memory of the conversation with the detective inspector appeared sketchy at best, which didn't help Cora's nerves as she perched uncomfortably on the creaking plastic seat. The waiting area was starkly furnished – regulation blue vinyl tiles matching the chairs, and grey walls that smelled of disinfectant. Mercifully for Cora, its clinical emptiness made it free of any object voices that might affect her. Taking a moment to use her breathing exercises, she closed her eyes and focused on the movement of air through her nostrils: cooler in, warmer out.

'Dr Lael?'

She started and looked up. A tall, broad-shouldered man in a dark grey suit was standing beside her, a broad smile not quite meeting his grey eyes. Scrambling to her feet, she accepted his formal handshake.

'Good morning. Sorry – I was just…'

'Breathing exercises, eh?' This time his eyes registered the smile. 'Do them myself, from time to time. My wife's a yoga devotee.' His accent lilted across the words and Cora tried to place it. Glasgow, perhaps?

'It helps me focus.' Why did she need to explain herself? Cora wished her nerves weren't as visible as she'd made them.

For a moment they fell silent, hands awkwardly joined, before the man chuckled and let go. 'I didn't introduce myself. DI Joel Anderson – Joel, please.' He hesitated.

'Dr Cora Lael,' she replied, new title strange on her lips, as if she were still trying it on for size. 'Cora.'

'Excellent, Dr Lael. Shall we?'

Cora followed the detective inspector through a set of double doors and up several flights of concrete stairs that reminded her of the faded secondary school she'd attended. Anderson's strides were long and confident, making Cora feel as if she were scurrying to keep up with him. They climbed towards the third floor, Anderson speaking as quickly as he moved.

'I know you must be very busy, so we appreciate your time. I can assure you that your involvement with this investigation will remain strictly confidential. Despite the fervent press interest, we are carefully controlling information that reaches the media. You have my personal word on that.'

'Thank you. I—'

'We'll head to my office first and then I'll introduce you to Acting DS Minshull, who is leading the case. This way…'

Cora's head was awash with information: the policeman's words, the unrelenting sameness of her new surroundings, the questions she wanted to ask but didn't know how. Already she was questioning the wisdom of being here. But once they were in the slightly more comfortable surroundings of Anderson's office, the smell of coffee and recently applied polish replacing the hospital-like tang of industrial cleaner, she found space to think. All of her senses were on high alert: she needed to calm down and focus.

Anderson seemed to be giving her a potted history of the South Suffolk Constabulary, pacing a little self-consciously around his modest office. Was this a sign of nerves? Cora did her best to smile and nod in appropriate places while she tuned his words out of her mind, shifting her focus back to her breath.

Nerves aside, she was here now and she had a job to do. For the first time in her life, somebody else's welfare depended upon her ability. This was the opportunity she'd craved, the chance to discover what she could really achieve.

'Coffee?' Anderson handed her a mug without waiting for her reply.

'Thank you.'

'I expect you have questions about the case?'

'Yes, I do. I understand a girl is missing and that something of hers has been sent to you – I know that much from the news.'

Anderson let out a sigh and leant against his desk. 'That's pretty much the sum of it. The note we received with Hannah's belonging gave no indication of where she is, whether she's alive or not or what the person who has her wants. Talking to Professor Gold, I can see how your...' He appeared to be picking his way through a minefield of unsuitable terms. '... *input* might be beneficial to us at this stage.'

'I want to help in any way I can.'

'I appreciate that. This might be daunting, I understand, but what you are doing is incredibly important. Anything you can tell us, any light you can shed at all on Hannah's disappearance or how her possession was taken from her will be invaluable. Perhaps, if you can bear that in mind, the task will seem a little less intimidating.'

A knock sounded at Anderson's door, quickly followed by a smiling man who nodded his acknowledgement of Cora before speaking. 'Guv, Acting DS Minshull is ready.'

Anderson's relief was palpable. 'Excellent,' he barked, a little too brightly. 'Send him in please, DC Wheeler.'

The door opened fully and a young man entered. He was dressed formally in suit and tie, his dark hair close cropped at the sides, longer and wavier on top. There was a weariness about him, at odds with his careful appearance, the toll of the investigation contained within every dark shadow, muscle and line on his face. Aware she was staring, Cora stood, suddenly self-conscious.

'Acting DS Rob Minshull, may I present Dr Cora Lael.'

The young detective's smile left his face as soon as it had appeared. His stare was sharp, making Cora instinctively shrink back. She withdrew her outstretched hand when he didn't take it. Grey-green eyes observed her from beneath dark brows.

'Good to meet you. DI Anderson's told me a lot about you.'

Without warning, Cora was hit by an urge to laugh. This was more awkward than any first date she'd ever been on and would have been utterly ridiculous, had it not been for the seriousness of the occasion. She bit the inside of her cheek to maintain composure. The detective's eyes narrowed as if seeing something he didn't approve of.

Anderson, looking between the two of them, jumped in. 'Excellent. So, Acting DS Minshull, I suggest Dr Lael accompanies you to meet the rest of the team. And then, we can begin.'

The emphasis on his last word fell heavy as lead on Cora's shoulders, her amusement vanishing. Minshull turned without reply and walked out, clearly expecting Cora to follow. She glanced helplessly at Anderson whose encouraging smile did nothing to allay the sense of dread creeping over her. Steeling herself, she slung her bag across her shoulders and scurried out after the detective.

'It's just down here,' Minshull said over his shoulder as they walked.

'Are there many people in your team?' Cora asked, keen to make conversation.

'Five of us in CID, usually, plus DI Anderson leading. We have a uniformed officer, PC Steph Lanehan, working with us on this case. Some of the team are out on calls this morning, but you'll meet them all in due course.'

At the end of the corridor, Minshull stopped suddenly, turning back to Cora. 'I have to say, with respect, that I'm not sure you can help us. My superior disagrees. I just want to ask you, before we even go in there, will you be honest with me? If you don't – *get* anything, please don't pretend you do. We don't have time for things that might take our attention from the job.'

Cora stared at him, not quite believing what she'd heard. 'Do you think I'd be here if I didn't think I could help?'

'No, but—'

'With the greatest respect, Acting DS Minshull, I'm more than able to assist you. I'm here for the little girl's sake.'

And not yours, she added silently.

This wasn't a promising start and Minshull's distrust did nothing to encourage her. She had no intention of being branded a time-waster now – by him or anyone else.

'Forgive me. We're just under a lot of pressure.' He shook his head and for a brief moment Cora saw behind the flint exterior. 'Look, let's start again, yeah? We'll meet the team, I'll get you up to speed on where we are with the investigation and then I'll ask you to inspect the object we believe to be Hannah's. Is that okay?'

Cora nodded, still bristling from their exchange.

With the swiftest of smiles, Acting DS Minshull opened the door to the CID office. The chatter in the large, open-plan space faded as they entered, but for Cora the shouts of discarded paper, takeaway food packets and screwed-up paper cups in the rubbish bins beneath each desk continued to compete for attention.

Breathe through it… she repeated in her mind. It didn't help that she was nervous, or that the people in the room followed her every step. Pressured situations always made it harder for her to control the voices. Why hadn't she thought of this before? She'd been so certain she could help, but she'd forgotten what wearing her difference in public could be like. The looks. The distrust. The dismissal. Walking into the CID office was walking into classrooms, social situations and workplaces all over again. All eyes on her. Nowhere to hide.

The detective team turned to watch as Minshull stopped in the middle of the room. What were they thinking of her? Did they think she was a weirdo, too?

'Right, everyone, I'd like to introduce you to Dr Cora Lael. DI Anderson has enlisted her skills for the investigation and she has very kindly agreed to assist us. For the foreseeable future, she will be part of this team, so I hope you'll all make her welcome.'

Like you did? Cora thought, working hard to wear her smile.

This received a mumbled response from the gathered detectives. It wasn't the most rapturous of welcomes, but it would have to do. Cora didn't need them to like her in order to function here. Sometimes, being an outsider had its benefits: this way she could do what she had to and leave without anyone having the power to hurt her.

'Great. As you were,' Minshull nodded at the team and turned to Cora as the room resumed its activity. 'Ready?'

Not certain she was, Cora followed him across the office.

'So, what are you, some kind of medium?' he asked, the directness of his question little surprise considering his less-than-effusive welcome.

'No.' She looked down at the grey liquid masquerading as coffee in her paper cup. 'My brain has a neurological divergence. It allows me to sense the emotions of someone from the objects they discard.'

His laugh was sudden and unbridled. 'You're joking?'

'No.' Cora hated the look on his face – the mockery of someone blessed with ordinariness. Like so many people before him. 'I don't expect you to understand.'

'Look, no offence, but personally, I think my boss is out of his mind bringing you in.'

He drained his cup and threw it into the wire wastepaper basket by her feet. Cora shuddered as a voice shouted and a shot of emotion hit her square on.

'*Angry*,' she repeated under her breath.

'Sorry?' His smirk had abandoned him now.

She wasn't going to explain. He might expect her to perform like a freak show curiosity but she had no intention of obliging. 'What do I need to know about the missing girl?'

He observed her for a moment, his eyes drifting away to the discarded paper cup. 'Hannah Perry, eight years old. Reported missing last Thursday by her grandmother and aunt after she failed to return from school.'

'What do you know about her?'

'Other than the basic facts, not a lot. My team have been interviewing her friends, family, teachers – anyone who knows her. As it stands, we're getting a pretty standard picture – a pleasant, quiet girl, lots of friends, popular with her teachers.'

'So it's definitely out of character for her to disappear?'

He heaved a heavy sigh, as if Cora's question confirmed his worst suspicions of her. 'It's never "in character" for any missing person to disappear.'

She ignored his tone. Obviously they weren't going to get on. Keen to do what she came for and get out as soon as possible, she took a notebook from her handbag. Might as well look prepared even if in truth she was floundering. 'So how can I help?'

'That's the question I've been asking myself since you arrived.' He must have caught her expression because instantly he relented. 'Forgive me. It's not been the easiest of weeks. You're here because this is not a standard missing person case. We think – we strongly suspect – that Hannah is still alive. But we can't say for certain. And we don't know where she is, or who has her. We suspected from the start that she had been taken by someone but the recent delivery of one of Hannah's belongings has confirmed this beyond reasonable doubt.'

Minshull walked over to an enormous whiteboard covered in multi-coloured scrawl – scraps of information weaving around photographs, sections of Ordnance Survey maps and newspaper cuttings. Cora's mind raced as she approached, taking it all in, blocking out the familiar buzz of voices that rumbled thunderously over the actual din of the room.

Minshull tapped his finger against a photo of a smiling young girl in a school uniform in the centre of the board. 'This is Hannah. Whoever took her likes playing games.' Reaching into a box on the desk nearest the whiteboard, he pulled out a clear plastic evidence bag containing a velvet headband, the name 'Hannah' embroidered on it in rainbow threads. 'This is the item that was sent to us. Her mother has confirmed it belongs to Hannah.' He pulled another evidence bag from the box. Inside, a single scrap of paper bore three words: *Hannah sent this*. 'This note was attached. Nothing more.' He shook his head. 'Seems he wants to play hide-and-seek with us.'

Cora's stomach lurched. 'Is that what happened last time?'

Minshull stared at her. 'You've been reading the news.'

'No. I grew up in St Just. Everyone knows about Matthew. That's why I wanted to help.'

'I didn't know that.' A pause, then: another crack in the wall. 'We need to know whether Hannah is alive or not.' He passed the evidence bag to her. 'If you can get a sense of anything that would indicate this either way, it will significantly alter our approach to this investigation. Take all the time you need.'

'Now?'

'Please.'

Suddenly, the worry of hearing nothing was superseded by the fear of Hannah's voice emerging from the headband. If she heard nothing, she could be released from the cynical detective's stare, which had unnerved her since she'd arrived. She may be dismissed as a nutter, but at least she could walk away.

Everything she had prepared for rested in her hands. A child's life may rest there, too. Cora looked down and the enormity of the moment almost stole her feet from under her.

This was a mistake. I'm not ready.

But the evidence bag was in her hands, Minshull's eyes on her. It was too late to rethink this.

Fingers clumsy against the plastic, she slowly opened the bag.

As soon as she did, it came: a young girl's voice, shrill and terrified, a physical shock of intense fear:

GIVE IT BACK!

IT'S MINE!

A surge of bile rose from her stomach and she swallowed just in time, a sticky-cold shiver following its downward progress. Minshull was staring at her again, his mouth dropped involuntarily open.

Cora looked away.

'She's alive.'

Chapter Twenty-Four

Cora

All the detectives looked up as one. The room hushed.

Minshull's breath quickened beneath his shirt, the knot of his tie moving up and down in time. 'Are you certain?'

'Absolutely.'

'How do you know?'

Cora closed her eyes, the memory of the voice still raw. 'She protested when it was taken from her. Her voice was so loud. If she was dead it would have been quieter, or I wouldn't have heard it at all.'

Hannah's cries still resounded in her mind as Cora handed the bag back.

'What did you... What happened?'

'I heard her scream.'

'Audibly?'

'Yes. As loud as if she were right next to us.'

'Did she say anything?'

'...*Give it back! It's mine!*' As she repeated the words the memory of Hannah's voice merged with the sound of her own. An inextricable link. An inescapable calling.

'And you're certain of this?'

'As certain as I can be.'

Minshull lowered his voice, his question not one for the CID team to overhear. 'How did she sound?'

'Scared. But defiant. She screamed it.'

Now the room echoed with bated questions. Glancing at his colleagues, Acting DS Minshull caught Cora's elbow and hurried her out of the room. Cora couldn't read his response but sensed a change in the air between them as they moved.

In silence they passed along grey corridors and back down the concrete stairs until Minshull pushed open a heavy set of dark wood doors and they emerged into bright street sunlight that stung Cora's eyes.

'Where are we going?'

'Out of earshot,' he muttered, picking up pace.

Turning right at the end of the police station car park, Cora and the detective headed into the noise of the high street, continuing past shops, pubs and people until they stopped outside a bland-looking café, its windows half-barred by thick iron mesh, half-obscured by slimy steam.

'In here.'

A balding man with a ketchup-red face behind the counter seemed to know the detective, nodding at him as he approached. At a loss for what else to do, Cora sat shakily at a table by an overwatered yucca plant, forcing the tremors of Hannah's voice to the farthest reaches of her mind.

'*Waste of time,*' grumbled a voice beside her and she looked down to see the grease-stained pages of a badly folded tabloid, discarded amid a slick of grey-brown tea on the red melamine table. She blinked away the image of the tattooed neck of its former owner as she moved the item to the next table and huddled against the wall.

'I wasn't sure what you drank, so this will be a disappointment in any case,' Minshull smiled briefly as he placed an off-white mug of murky brown liquid in front of her. 'Allegedly, it's coffee.' He reached into his pocket and slung a few packets of brown sugar onto the table.

'*Angry,*' his voice shuddered from the tumbling packets. Cora shrugged it away. She didn't need her skill to tell her that – one look at his expression confirmed it.

'Thanks.'

'You're welcome. Look, Ms Lael, I'm sorry if I…'

'It's *Doctor.*' Point made, she sat back. 'But please, call me Cora. Dr Lael is too formal.'

'Cora, then.' He extended his hand. 'I'm Rob – although when my colleagues are around, it's best we stick to formalities.'

Cora shook his hand and was surprised by its warmth.

'I wanted to apologise for how I was in there. As I'm sure you can appreciate, this is a tense time for all of us and I can't be seen to be grasping at straws this early on.'

'Which is what my involvement amounts to, I suppose?'

His expression didn't alter but he picked up a teaspoon which danced between his fingers. A tell, if ever she'd seen one. 'Other people could see it that way. We've never used someone with your *ability* before. Honestly, I thought DI Anderson was joking when he suggested it. Other divisions have consulted alternative experts in the past and it's always proved a source of great frustration to them and hilarity to us. I never thought we would rely on anything except standard procedure. This is all a little – *left-field*.'

'I can see that.' She couldn't blame him for thinking that way. Had she encountered someone with her ability, not experiencing it herself, would she have reacted any differently?

'And you say you actually *heard* Hannah's voice?' the detective asked. 'Not the thought of a voice but an actual, audible sound?'

'Yes. That's how I always hear it. As real as if the person is speaking next to me.'

'Wow.' He risked a grin. 'Surely you could make some money out of that? Be the Derren Brown of lost property?'

Cora blinked back, unsmiling. Her mother had made the same comment many times and Cora had lost count of how many misplaced items she'd been summoned to retrieve from their cluttered family home. 'Derren Brown studies human response and manipulates it. He doesn't have an ability like mine.'

'Okay, okay. I was joking. I'm sorry – *again*.'

Aware her own nerves were on show, Cora relented. 'It's fine. I've heard it all before. People joke about things they don't feel comfortable around. I get that. You don't understand what I can do. But it isn't a party trick; it's something in my brain that I never asked for but I have to live with. Permanently.' She attempted a smile. 'You can walk away from this weirdness today. I have to take it home.'

'I didn't call you weird.'

'You didn't have to.' She glanced at the teaspoon he was still fiddling with.

Minshull dropped it like a chastened dog.

'So what did you hear in my office?' His question didn't miss a beat.

Embarrassed, she looked away. 'I – I don't…'

'It's okay. I'm interested. Tell me.'

Would he understand? The ground beneath them was uncertain enough – could she trust him with the truth?

'Please?'

'Okay. You're angry.'

The detective buckled slightly, as if winded by an invisible opponent's jab. 'Say again?'

'You're angry. Intensely so. I heard it and felt it, physically. That only happens when emotions are extreme.'

Minshull sat back, folded arms a stronghold across his creaseless shirt. 'You could have guessed that. Stressful environment, pressures of a new case...'

'...Having to baby-sit some nut-job your superiors have forced upon you.'

His eyes widened. 'Now hang on, I never said...'

'Only I think it's more than that. Nothing to do with work.'

He was shrinking so far from her he was practically at the next table. Cora had seen this countless times before and if she'd been the kind of person to get a kick out of having power over others she could have enjoyed the cruelty of it. But she wasn't that person; instead, Rob Minshull's reaction only served to further drive a wedge between them. She hated seeing the fear in his eyes – the first real sign of emotion he'd shown – now screaming louder at her than anything his discarded belongings could have revealed.

'Forget it. I'm probably wrong.'

'But you can't be wrong, can you? Not if this – *thing* – you have is real.' He forced himself to sit upright. 'I shouldn't have asked.' Keeping his eyes occupied by a low survey of the sticky table top, he twisted his mug a little. 'Uncanny, though. Even if it was a guess, it was a good one.'

Words stalled between them, caught in the muggy air of the café. Cora wished she'd avoided his question. It was clear what Rob Minshull thought of her and now he had a cast iron reason to distrust her.

She wished herself back in Daniel's office, the steady drop of paper balls on the grey carpet, the only words in her head those from the list they had agreed. *This* – this was too complicated. She'd been right about being able to hear the child's voice but in her haste to push her gift she'd forgotten everything else. The awkwardness of its presence around others. The feeling of always being on the outside. The suspicion and fear levelled at her. Everything she'd worked so hard to distance herself from.

When Minshull spoke again, however, his tone was different. Calmer. Softer, even. 'I need you to be completely honest with me. I'm saying this off the record, obviously, but there are people in CID who want to see you and your ability fail. I don't know how long you'll be needed, but for the time being, your insight is all we have to go on. Until our other lines of enquiry pick up something worthwhile, what you hear is vital to this investigation. Can I count on you?'

She didn't want to say it, but if she was the only person to have heard Hannah's voice, what choice did she have? Hannah's possession had spoken to Cora: it was her responsibility to keep listening.

'Yes, you can.'

Chapter Twenty-Five

Minshull

The police station canteen was busy when Minshull returned from escorting Cora Lael to her car, but he found a space near the wall where he could mull everything over without interruption. Around him, the happy banter and vociferous grumbles of his colleagues continued, an unrelenting white noise he was grateful for. It was impossible to find a quiet corner in the CID office, so he had learned to allow the constant din of conversation to swell around him, allowing space for his mind to work. It was better than silence, most of the time.

He didn't want to go back to CID yet. First, he needed to think.

Anderson would be stalking the corridors already, awaiting his return, and would demand Minshull's reaction to the newest member of the investigation. Before that happened, Minshull had to work out what his reaction was. In truth, he didn't know. He'd spent the best part of the morning with the quietly spoken, diminutive woman, but found himself juggling more questions than he'd harboured prior to her arrival. How was that even possible?

Had Dr Lael really heard Hannah's voice?

Her reaction had unnerved him, not to mention the handful of his team who had seen it before he'd rushed Cora from the office. He knew he would be fielding questions from them, too, when he returned to his desk. And then there was *that thing* she'd said in the café. It was probably just a lucky guess, as he'd suspected. But could she have heard something he hadn't wanted her to know?

Was Cora Lael deluded? He had to consider the possibility, to cover his back if nothing else. Whatever Anderson and the eminent quack who'd recommended her said, if she proved to be mentally unstable she could jeopardise the entire investigation. With all that was resting on a satisfactory outcome for the case, Minshull couldn't afford to make mistakes. Cora certainly appeared to believe what she'd told him. But was that any real indicator of the truth?

Before their conversation in the greasy spoon café he'd thought her prickly, remote. He'd expected a quasi-spiritual charlatan, a snake oil pedlar. Cora Lael was none of those things. There was fire in her – carefully guarded but ready to spark to her aid. There was honesty, too; and sadness. When she'd repeated the word she said she'd heard from him, she seemed almost resigned.

He was surprised to discover that he wanted to trust her. Despite the rock-solid defences she peered out from behind, something about Cora struck a chord within him. She didn't want the extraordinary gift she claimed to have. If she were a charlatan, surely she would have taken every opportunity to proudly state her claim? But Cora hadn't done that. In fact, she wore her ability like clothes that were too large and too heavy. That was intriguing.

He recognised it because it mirrored how he felt as the newest DS in South Suffolk CID. Everyone thought they knew Rob Minshull's game, but they were wrong. He wanted to do his job, to be the best he could be, but the ominous presence of his father's shadow refused to leave him. It was true that he'd joined the force to try to appease John Minshull, but once there, he'd found his own love of police work and the desire to pursue it. His way: not his father's. Yet even as the career progression he'd worked for was beginning, all his colleagues saw was John Minshull's legacy pushing him up the ranks. He was being judged by that measure every day. He felt it in the CID team – and Anderson, too – heightened now that bodies were weary and nerves frayed. In his darkest moments, Minshull had begun to doubt he would ever be viewed on his own terms.

You're only here because of him.

Must be nice to have a famous dad.

You'll be like me one day, son. Just like me. You're a Minshull, cut from the same cloth. All you need to do is toughen up…

In his office and again in the café opposite the police station, Cora Lael had stared at Minshull as though she'd seen his secret fear. That was the scariest thing of all.

He *was* angry. She'd been right.

So what if Cora Lael was right about Hannah? If she had heard the child's voice, Minshull's investigation had just discovered a key advantage. It wouldn't carry weight in a court of law, of course, but it could prove vital to the case. If this was as they'd feared and Matthew Cooper's abductor now had Hannah Perry, there would be more deliveries until a ransom note arrived. If the team believed Cora, it could motivate them to believe they could change the outcome of the abductor's game this time and push them harder to find the evidence that still eluded them – much more than any pep talk he or Anderson could give.

If they believed Cora.

It was a risk, but what choice did he have?

He stared down at the table, where a scattering of salt from a discarded packet spread across its surface. Tiny white balls rolled across the blue vinyl as he breathed. Les Evans and Kate Bennett would take some convincing. Drew Ellis was bright and likely to be persuaded by reasonable logic. Of all the team, Dave Wheeler was probably his best bet for an immediate ally. If Wheeler's open, respectful manner towards Cora that morning was anything to go by, Minshull might have the beginnings of a plan. It was well known in the station that Dave Wheeler was oil on troubled waters, treading the delicate line between having the respect of his superiors and being one of the lads.

Minshull allowed his shoulders to relax a little as a way forward began to present itself. He would talk to Wheeler first; find out what he thought of it all and then, provided everything was good, unleash the charm offensive on the rest of the team.

He still wasn't certain of Cora Lael, but he knew enough to make up his mind.

He was going to trust her.

Hannah

I try to notice everything in the Small Space to stop me thinking about the mice. I make a list in my head and think each word slowly. I'm too frightened to say them out loud. I don't want Them to hear. So I *think* my list again:

Too small.

Dark.

Cold.

Rain hitting the cracked glass like the sound from a big drum.

The drip that hits the back of my neck, no matter how much I crouch away from it.

A blanket that's too small to cover me.

The scary balloon dog hiding under it.

A locked door.

Not enough room to stretch out my legs. They ache. The skin on my knees is scuffed white and going blue.

I don't like the last thing on my think-list. But it's in the Small Space as much as the blanket or the drips of rain or the cold, so I have to think it:

The Fear.

The Fear has made me cry until no more tears come out. I'm too scared to eat, so all that fills my tummy is The Fear, tumbling around inside it. The Fear is cold and feels like someone is twisting me. And it gets stronger when I think that the door might open any time and the shouting will start again…

The Fear comes from the person I trusted. From the person who said, 'It's okay. I'll take you home.' They brought me here and left me in the Small Space with the mice and the rain and the huge, sick-cold, jaggedy Fear.

They said They'd take me home. But this *isn't* home.

I don't think I'll ever see my home again.

Chapter Twenty-Six

Cora

The yell that dragged Cora awake echoed around her darkened bedroom. Several moments passed before she realised she had made it. The sound was replaced in her ears by the quickened beat of her heart, the breath fast and rasping in her throat, which stung from her scream. Beads of cold sweat clung to her brow and traced the line of her spine. Her familiar surroundings were oddly alien, as if she'd suddenly been transported there from another place.

The dryness of her mouth made her throw back the bed sheets and stumble her way onto the darkened landing, down the stairs to her kitchen. Beyond the kitchen window a full, bright moon painted the garden in shades of monochrome greys against a clear, black sky. Moonlight danced in the stream of water from the sink tap, circling the rim of the glass she held beneath it. In the kitchen coolness her breathing eased, her heartbeat receding from her ears. But another sound remained stubbornly present.

Her voice.

The voice of the missing child.

Cora had dreamed of her: a tiny, terrified figure in an unfamiliar place. She had heard Hannah's cries for help over and over; then the repetition of her insistence that whoever was holding her give back her belongings:

It's mine! Give it back!

She shuddered. The chill of the kitchen floor tiles seemed to be seeping through her bare feet straight into the marrow of her bones. Her glass filled, she grabbed the kettle and filled that, too, leaving it bubbling towards a boil as she moved to the living room.

Easing into an armchair, she pulled a blanket from the back of it and tucked the woven wool around herself, reaching out to snap on the standard lamp beside the chair. The lamp's small glow sent some of the demons scurrying from the shadows of the room. Cora closed her eyes and took a mouthful of water.

She hardly ever dreamed. She certainly didn't find herself scared awake by them.

Long before her father died, her mother had been a firm believer in the potential of dreams to reveal important truths. Sheila had kept a well-thumbed book of dream interpretations on her bedside table and took great pleasure in deciphering the dreams of her family members and friends. Bill Lael was forever teasing her about it, concocting preposterous dreams he'd allegedly had just to see her find a meaning. What did her mother believe in now? Had her fascination with dreams been swept into the void of widowhood, along with everything else from her former life?

Cora had been affected by voices she'd heard before, but not like this. The memory of the scared little girl's voice remained viscerally fresh; eighteen hours since she'd heard it in the police station. It was more than a vivid recollection. Hannah Perry's voice was haunting her.

She'd played it down when she'd called Daniel from the police headquarters car park, still shaken by the events of the morning. Should she tell him everything? He'd need to know soon, for the study. But should she tell him about the dream? The voice?

It was far too early to call him now. A glance at the clock above the mantelpiece confirmed that. 3.49 a.m. was no time to make an emotional phone call to Daniel Gold, however much he would love the opportunity to rescue her. She had pushed to be part of the police investigation – she had to deal with the consequences. If she was ever going to discover what she was capable of, it had to be on her own terms.

She hadn't anticipated *this*, though.

The stretch of night between now and daylight seemed endlessly lonely and the memory of Hannah's voice refused to leave her. Knowing that she'd lost any last hope of sleep, Cora switched the television on and allowed the ever-scrolling images and text of a news channel to distract her mind.

Chapter Twenty-Seven

Minshull

'It's a *joke*.'

'It's a development. First we've had, Les.'

'Tell that to the CPS, Dave. They'll laugh us out of the bloody room.'

Minshull heard the whispers, present this morning after a muted reception to his briefing yesterday. He'd reported what Cora had heard, seeing nothing but slyly exchanged glances and a silence too heavy to ignore. Whatever the team's misgivings, Cora Lael *had* proved useful. And she had achieved more than the rest of them: for all their bluster, none of their enquiries had turned up anything to prove Hannah Perry was still alive.

He still wasn't certain of any of it. But he wasn't about to let his team ride roughshod over their only advantage.

'Care to share your thoughts?' he asked, the sharpness of his question causing his colleagues to snap to attention. 'No?'

'You're all right, Sarge,' DC Evans smirked.

'Don't give me that. If you've a problem with Dr Lael, I want to know.'

Ellis gave a loud sigh. 'You have to see it from our point of view. We're all busting a gut to find the kid and then the guv'nor brings in a… Well, she isn't a proper expert, is she?'

Minshull stared at his team. 'And you all agree with Les?'

'No…' Wheeler began, but Bennett stepped in.

'Actually, I think I do.'

Oh Kate, not you as well.

Minshull thought he'd found an ally in his colleague in recent days. So much for that comfort. 'Why?'

Bennett lowered her voice. 'We're worried, Minsh. All of us are. We know what Anderson went through before and none of us want it repeated. That kind of experience, it changes you. And not for the best. It would be easy to lose focus.'

'He isn't losing focus.'

'Oh leave it out, Sarge. He's so wound up he's practically twitching...'

'Whatever you may think, Les – whatever anyone else thinks – DI Anderson is committed to finding Hannah Perry. I trust him.' Minshull stared down his colleagues, praying his superior couldn't hear his vote of confidence. It was one thing to be quietly supportive, quite another to do it out loud.

'But that kind of commitment can cause mistakes...'

'And he has the press conference this afternoon. Have you seen all the online stuff? They're already ripping him apart. That's got to hurt after last time.'

'I see.' Minshull surveyed the team, each one averting their eyes as his gaze fell on them. 'And you all think this?'

Bennett shook her head. 'We're just worried.'

'I know. I understand where this is coming from, believe me.'

'But, Sarge, that woman...' Drew Ellis said. 'The way she reacted yesterday was just *odd*. We can't be building foundations on freaks and con-artists like her...'

'She's a doctor of psychology, isn't she?' The soft tones of DC Wheeler silenced the rest of the team, who turned to look at him. It wasn't often Dave Wheeler went against his colleagues, but Minshull could see the flush of resolve across his face. 'If she heard something, I believe her. So does Minsh – the sarge. And you all forget I was closest to him last time. I *saw* what it did to Joel. I know what he's been through since. If we'd had even the smallest reassurance Matthew Cooper was alive, things might have been handled differently.'

It was time to ask. Minshull had avoided the question because it reinforced the fact that he was the only one of the team who had not been there during the Cooper investigation – apart from Drew Ellis. Now, his need to know overrode his desire to be counted among them.

'How was it handled last time?'

'You've read the files.'

'I'm not asking about the files. I'm asking how it happened in here.'

As one, the team dropped their heads.

'Anyone? Les? Dave?'

'Joel made a statement.'

'What kind of statement?'

Wheeler raised his eyes. 'Wasn't his idea. The high-ups were pushing hard for results – I mean, four weeks with nothing, the press going nuts. And then the ransom note – well, you can imagine.'

'It was his call…' Evans began, his mouth snapping shut at the sight of Wheeler's uncharacteristic glare.

'It was out of his hands, Les, and you know it.'

'What was the statement?' Already Minshull could feel the weight of it bearing down on the assembled detectives.

'To the press. On live TV. "*We aren't interested in games. We won't negotiate. It stops now. It's time for Matthew to come home.*"…' Wheeler rubbed the back of his neck, as if the memory stung him there, his colleagues around him appearing to shrink into their seats. 'Ten hours later, we found the body. And the note. "*Too late. You made me do it. His blood is on your hands.*"'

'*Shit.*' It was out before Minshull could summon it back.

'Exactly. Everyone blamed us. Matthew's family, the village, everybody who'd searched night and day to find him. And the top brass stood back while Joel copped the lot. That's why we're worried. He made that statement because he was desperate, because his hand was forced. It can't happen again.'

'It won't happen again,' Minshull replied, resolve burning.

'So you say.' Les Evans scoffed. 'But this time it's our backsides on the line. And I don't want to be crucified because we listened to a nutter.'

'This isn't up for discussion,' Minshull said quickly, watching his team scurry back to their desks as Anderson's door opened. 'Op Seraph briefing in ten minutes, please. I want everything we have so far.' He nodded at his superior.

'And cheer up, please,' Anderson barked, unaware of the mutiny he'd interrupted. 'We've just edged ahead in the game. This is a good thing.'

Chapter Twenty-Eight

Anderson

Members of the press were gathering nosily as officers buzzed about making last-minute preparations for the press conference. There had been some confusion over the number of seats and tables required for the line-up on the stage and three uniformed officers were fussing over the layout as journalists snapped opportunistic images of the lack of organisation. By tomorrow morning the 'Bumbling South Suffolk Police in Action' headlines would already be out there, a thinly veiled accusation that the investigation was in jeopardy if its officers couldn't even handle furniture arrangement.

Anderson surveyed the scene from the half-parted double doors with incredulity, wishing for the hundredth time that day that he hadn't quit smoking. It had been a promise to Rosalyn he fully intended to keep – not least because of the discovery last year of an ominous shadow in his right lung. That health scare had sent his wife into overdrive: removing anything unhealthy (and, therefore, remotely worth eating) from their food cupboards and insisting Joel join a gym. Smoking had been first on her hit list and he had agreed, more because of guilt for putting her through such worry than because he actually wanted to quit. The shadow had proved benign and while he had to admit he felt healthier than he had in years, it didn't mean he didn't miss the comfort smoking used to afford him. He half-wondered if he could blag a cheeky smoke from one of his colleagues, just for today.

'Ready to go, Guv?' With irritating brightness, DC Wheeler appeared at his side.

'Not really. I hate these things.' He eyed the pack of hyenas, jostling for the best seats, their phones and notebooks primed for action. 'Bastards, the lot of them. Look! They're loving it.'

'Thought you might need this.' Wheeler handed him a large takeout coffee cup from the canteen. 'Picked it up on the way over.'

Anderson could have kissed his colleague. 'You read my mind, Dave. From the bottom of my heart, I thank you.'

'No worries, Guv. Can't be easy facing that lot.'

Anderson grimaced. 'Let's just say it's not what I joined the force for.'

A primly dressed media liaison officer with a deep frown much older than the rest of her face hurried across the stage to them, shielding her eyes from the glare of the TV crews' lights with her clipboard. 'DI Anderson? Five minutes then you're up. Okay?'

Anderson didn't reply, only nodding as he downed the hot, strong coffee.

She pressed on. 'I've told them we want no questions on current developments. That'll keep them under control.'

Anderson was touched by her misplaced faith in members of the media. 'Oh well, that's comforting to know.'

She cast him an uncertain smile and scurried back into the room.

Wheeler sniggered. 'Bloody clueless. She's not long been in the job, has she? How long d'you reckon she'll last?'

'If it's anything like the last three, I give her six months, tops. Are the body-language bods in place?'

Wheeler peered into the room. 'Yup. Beardy bloke with the red tie on the right; woman in green top, second row back on the left. You really think Shaun Collins is a contender?'

Anderson shrugged. 'Minshull thinks so. Nasty piece of work, by all accounts.'

'Not a nice thing to say about a colleague, sir,' Wheeler smirked.

'Ha bloody ha.' He tried his best to give Wheeler an admonishing look, but deep down Anderson appreciated the joke. Wheeler, along with a select few colleagues, knew Anderson's true feelings about his sideways promotion. It was never spoken of, but comments like this helped to send the message. Those officers put themselves in Anderson's shoes and knew how they'd feel. Acting DS Minshull wasn't a bastard, of course, but sometimes it helped to think he was. Anderson straightened his suit jacket. 'Better go and stare off the jackals, eh?'

'Break a leg, sir.'

Knowing my luck I probably will.

This morning he had felt hope for the first time. He had an advantage. Dr Lael said Hannah was alive and he believed her. When the next of Hannah's possessions turned up, she may well tell them more. Because there would be another. There was no doubt in his mind: this was Matthew's murderer, back to try again.

Would he be watching from wherever he was? Was he thinking he'd already won?

Waiting to be announced, Anderson looked across the roomful of hacks. A few he recognised – Maggie Jones from the *Suffolk Herald*, Jan Martin from the tiny *St Just Argus*, the aged Frank Sommersby from BBC Look East, who should, by rights, have been put out to pasture years ago. Behind the usual suspects were others he didn't know: bland-faced Fleet Street hacks, marked out from the local press contingent by their expensive jackets, hi-tech gadgets and the unmistakable discomfort with which they fidgeted in the unforgiving blue plastic chairs. Bit of a comedown from the plush hotels used for Met press conferences in London, Anderson mused. When they stepped off the train in Ipswich this morning they must've thought they'd landed on another planet.

From the other side of the room, the jittery media liaison officer waved frantically at him. Behind her, Anderson could see Hannah Perry's mother – ghost-faced and hollow-eyed – and, kicking at the regulation grey carpet with grubby trainers, Shaun Collins. He didn't look particularly nervous, but people handled pressure in different ways. Anderson didn't like the look of him; his copper's gut still very much in action even if the rest of him was mostly relegated behind a desk these days. Collins seemed to exude defiance in the way most blokes exuded sweat, the angry veins in his scrawny neck as blue as the eagle tattoo inked there. He didn't look like a man in abject terror at the thought of his stepdaughter being snatched away.

The evidence arriving daily from the team's searches surrounding Collins' known associates and recent history suggested he didn't care about much else than himself. Uniformed officers had managed to fit a tracking device to his van yesterday: the log of his movements away from the house would be known soon. While his mother and sister had confirmed his alibi for his absence from the house on days immediately following Hannah's disappearance, Anderson knew Minshull suspected more was happening that they had yet to uncover. Maybe the body language experts in the room would cast more light on his behaviour.

'Ready for your close-up, Guv?' Dave Wheeler's grin was good-natured and Anderson silently thanked him for the vote of confidence.

'If they start chucking rotten fruit, rescue me, okay?' Anderson grimaced, before walking to his seat to a barrage of flashbulbs, as Hannah's family arrived from the other side of the room. Today, he needed all the allies he could get; judging by the faces greeting his arrival at the press conference table, he had precious few in the room.

Staring resolutely ahead, he spoke to confirm his name and the status of the investigation. 'Good afternoon ladies and gentlemen. I am Detective Inspector Joel Anderson of South Suffolk CID, and I am leading this investigation. Hannah Perry, eight years old, from St Just, went missing seven days ago, sometime between half past one and two o'clock on the afternoon of Thursday 27th March. She was on her way home from school and was seen by several local people as she walked along the High Street, through the village's Easter Market, reportedly heading for the Meatcross, where she had told a friend she would be meeting her mother. She never arrived there. CCTV footage stills of Hannah's last-known sighting will be distributed to you all following this press conference. We are here this afternoon primarily to appeal to anyone who may have seen Hannah, or have further information on her current location. There will be an opportunity for questions soon, but first the parents of Hannah Perry wish to read a short statement. I firmly request the room receives this politely and *without interruption.*'

Anderson nodded at Hannah's mother who didn't quite manage to meet his eye, her head burying down behind a creased sheet of lined paper.

'Hannah is a good girl and she is not in trouble. We love her and we just want her back home with us...' Ashleigh Perry's voice cracked and the flashbulbs intensified in reply.

Anderson kept his eye on Shaun Collins, who had one arm around his partner's shoulders, pale eyes staring pointedly down the lenses of forty cameras. What would the body-language experts be gleaning from Hannah's stepfather's response? Making a note to request their report as soon as the conference ended, he turned his attention back to the broken young woman battling her way through a standard script. It was the last thing any parent should have to do and he knew all of his colleagues were united in their dislike of parental appeals. But they were necessary. Today's press conference was little more than a carefully staged theatre in which to observe those closest to the missing child, who, sad as it was, were statistically more likely to know what had happened to Hannah Perry than anyone else in the room.

'…So if you have any information at all, please call the police. Help us bring Hannah home.' Ashleigh Perry dropped the paper as she covered her face, providing the perfect front-page money shot for tomorrow's edition of every damn rag in the room.

'I believe we have some questions from the floor?' the media liaison officer squeaked into the microphone.

As Anderson had predicted, questions surged towards him.

'Clive Mordaunt, *Daily Signal*. Is it fair to say South Suffolk Constabulary has made no significant progress to date in finding Hannah or identifying her abductors?'

Anderson kept his expression and voice steady. 'I don't think that's fair at all. We have a specialist team working around the clock to find Hannah…'

'Jo Gordon, *Daily Call*. In that case, how would you respond to Hannah's step-aunt, Siobhan Collins, who told us she blames police incompetency for endangering her niece's life?'

Along the table from Anderson, a hard-faced woman flanking Ashleigh Perry, lifted her chin in grim defiance.

Great. Another development the press pack knew before him. He'd wondered why Hannah's step-aunt had avoided conversation with him when the family had arrived earlier. *Bloody woman probably cares more about the shiny new cash in her bank account than the child she just sold down the river…*

The nervous media liaison officer attempted to jump into the fray but was beaten back by the torrent of questions shouted from the floor. Paling, she gave Anderson an apologetic shrug and shrank back into her chair.

'I'm not in a position to comment on that matter directly.'

'Alexis Alcott-Green, *The Epoch*. Is it wise, given South Suffolk Constabulary's previous mishandling of a high-profile missing child case, for the force to be investigating Hannah's disappearance now?'

Bastards. Anderson had been waiting for that. Discarding official protocol, he held up his hands to silence the room. 'Look, I understand Hannah's family's anguish at this time. Every one of my officers does. You think we don't lose sleep every night because we haven't found her yet? I have my team working double-shifts; many of them volunteering to do it because they want Hannah found and safely returned to her parents…'

A hand rose in the middle of the room and Anderson squinted against the bright TV lights to identify its owner. 'Yes?'

'Maggie Jones, *Suffolk Herald*. With respect, DI Anderson, this is all very noble of your officers and I'm sure I speak for the county when I say how much their dedication is valued. But do we even know that the missing girl is still alive?'

'No further questions!' the media liaison officer squeaked.

Ignoring her, Anderson leaned closer to the microphone. It was highly unprofessional and likely to warrant a bollocking from DCI Taylor, but he was damned if this bloodthirsty mob was going to accuse his team and write their *bumbling police* headlines again. Minshull had witnessed Cora Lael's reaction to Hannah's headband yesterday morning: he'd told Anderson he believed her. Was it enough to suggest they had more? With so little else to go on, it *had* to be enough. 'I can confirm that we have strong evidence to suggest Hannah Perry is alive.'

DC Wheeler was gawping at him from the side of the stage and he could only imagine the look on DCI Taylor's face as she watched the live feed of the press conference from the comfort of her well-appointed office. But Anderson didn't care. Let the media bastards chew over that tasty morsel for a while…

As the room erupted in a frenzy of flashbulbs and yelled questions, he rose slowly and walked out.

Almost immediately his mobile phone began to buzz angrily in his pocket. Seeing the caller ID, Anderson grinned grimly and answered the call.

'How did I do, Ma'am?'

DCI Taylor's tone was incandescent. 'What. The. *Hell* do you think you're doing?'

'Telling the truth, Ma'am.'

'We don't even know that *is* the truth!'

Anderson smiled into the phone. Maybe it was the masochistic streak in his nature, but he couldn't help but enjoy his superior's fury. 'Maybe not. But my team witnessed Dr Lael's reaction to the evidence and I believe it was genuine. Right now, there's beggar all else to go on.'

'It's irresponsible, Joel, not to mention completely reprehensible!'

'What choice did I have? We had to give them something to get them off our backs. The more they try to dig, the cockier the bastard who has Hannah will get.' He cast a careful glance around him to ensure nobody was in earshot and hissed through gritted teeth. 'You know what happened last time. We pushed too hard and we lost him. I will not lose another child on my watch. If it keeps the pack off our backs for a few days, so be it.'

There was a pause and he imagined Sue Taylor pacing her office. 'Fine. But I swear, Joel, if this comes back to bite us I'll expect your resignation.'

'I wouldn't expect anything less from you, Ma'am.' He ended the call, bristling from the exchange. Typical Sue Taylor to be calling the shots from the safety of her own position! She could bleat all she liked about the reputation of the force, but *he* was the one at the coalface with what remained of his career hanging by a thread. If things went wrong she would emerge unscathed, every inch the strong, decisive leader, leaving him as the scapegoat carrying the constabulary's sins off the nearest cliff.

He turned as Wheeler arrived by his side. 'Well, Dave, how did I do?'

'Shocking,' Wheeler said, his kind humour not quite meeting his eyes. 'I reckon you'll make front page tomorrow.'

They pushed through the double doors, leaving the buzz of journalist chatter in their wake. 'I hope they got my good side in the photos,' Anderson joked, ignoring the heaviness in the pit of his stomach. 'My fans will be so disappointed if they didn't.'

Chapter Twenty-Nine

Minshull

Minshull gathered with his team around the small flat-screen monitor, watching the live stream of the press conference on Sky News. He could feel the tension among his colleagues as tangibly as if they were pressed against him and he knew what each of them was thinking. No officer ever wanted a press conference to happen, either for the family involved or the investigation. It was a nerve-racking game of cat-and-mouse with the press, the threat of giving too much away always present. As much as the police were watching the family for clues, the journalists were scrutinising everyone on the top table for anything they might conjure a story out of. Nobody could relax in those situations.

'They're killing him,' Evans said, as DI Anderson's pale face filled the screen, stony and grim. 'Poor git.'

Bennett nursed her mug of coffee like a shield. 'It was always going to happen, though. Too many similarities with the Cooper case for that pack of piranhas not to clock it. And now they know about the package we've got, it's a hundred times worse. Anderson must be bricking it.'

Minshull said nothing, secretly agreeing with the comments of his team. It was horrific to watch – the shouts, the accusations, the barrage of flashes. Horrific enough without everything Anderson had endured last time. Could he do that? Face such hostility and maintain his composure? Would that be him one day, answering questions?

Minshull turned his attention back to the screen – just as Anderson's words caused a chorus of groans to ring out from his colleagues.

'No way! He did *not* just say that!'
'What the hell is he thinking?'
'Sue Taylor will go ape!'

'That's *Detective Chief Inspector* Taylor you're referring to...' Minshull cut in, his heart beginning to crash in his chest. Why would Anderson say such a thing, when they had no evidence but Cora's testimony to go on?

'Sarge, he can't say that. Can he?'

'He just did.'

'That puts us seriously up the creek. The press will be all over us.'

Minshull turned to his team, thinking on his feet as much as they were but determined not to let them know. 'Then it's up to us to make sure they don't find out about Dr Lael's involvement. I need all of you to agree. We protect our advantage at all costs. Understand?'

–

When Anderson returned, he wordlessly acknowledged the team before disappearing into his office, not to be seen again for the rest of the afternoon. Minshull and the CID team kept their heads down, nobody willing to repeat the morning's showdown. Door-to-door enquiries were proving fruitless, and even Hannah's teacher had become suddenly reluctant to discuss the family further. Minshull wondered if Shaun Collins – or the not-so-friendly members of his family – might have had a hand in that.

Hannah's aunt's tabloid interview appeared on the *Daily Call* website just before the end of Minshull's shift – and it wasn't pretty reading.

> 'I worry for the child,' Siobhan Collins, 51, told our correspondent. 'The police should be spending their time searching for our Han instead of dragging my brother in to ask questions. They got a kid killed last time it happened in St Just. I couldn't bear it if they murdered Han, too. She might not be Shaun's flesh and blood, but we love her like she is. We just want her home.'
>
> The small Suffolk village of St Just is no stranger to macabre killings. Seven years ago, Matthew Cooper, 10, was brutally murdered following a four-week disappearance. His body was discovered naked, with knife injuries and a note blaming police for his death. Sources close to the investigation have expressed concern that

Hannah Perry's disappearance may be linked to the Cooper murder. Chillingly, a week since she disappeared during an Easter Market in the town, there have been no reported sightings of Hannah. Nobody at South Suffolk CID was available for comment this morning...

Minshull had intended to head straight home, mentally exhausted by the developments of the past twenty-four hours. But as he drove away from work, he had a sudden urge for a pint. St Just was only a small detour from his route home. The press conference and news story laid heavily on his mind. What did people in the village really think of the investigation? Were they as angry as the news reports made out?

If he went for a pint now, dressed in his civvies, he had a chance of finding out. Nobody knew he was involved yet, having only seen DI Anderson's ugly mug on the news. Confident in his anonymity, Minshull headed for the small half-timbered pub at the end of the High Street.

He declined the offer of the food menu, despite the insistent growl from his stomach, choosing a spot by the bar to savour his pint of ale. It was a filthy night – icy cold rain falling at a steep angle, fine enough to seep inside your coat collar and soak your back – and Minshull was in no hurry to go back out in it. The chatter around him was mostly of the local football team's chances in the FA Cup and a row brewing between farmers in the area and the local authority that was trying to commandeer land to build a new estate.

After almost an hour, Minshull allowed himself to relax. Nobody here recognised him and there seemed little appetite for discussing the missing girl.

A lanky, bedraggled young man shuffled up to the bar, rainwater dripping from his dreadlocked ginger hair onto the polished wood.

'Lovely weather for it,' he grimaced at Minshull.

Minshull smiled into his pint, not wanting a conversation buddy this evening.

'I've just finished for the night,' the man continued. 'Bloody nightmare at our gaff.' When Minshull didn't respond, he pressed on. 'At the *Argus*, you know? Local kid that's missing – it's all gone nuts. Spent most of the day telling those bastards from the nationals to back off our turf. I'll be glad when they've gone. Taking over the village like they have.'

'Leave the nice man alone, Lloyd,' said the barmaid, leaning across the pumps to pick up three empty glasses. 'Don't mind him, sir. Local office boy thinks he's Clark Kent.'

'*Junior reporter*,' the young man returned. 'And actually, Auntie Mar, a little bit of family support wouldn't go amiss.'

The barmaid chuckled. 'I used to change your bum, bor. Your shit don't impress me.'

'You get all sorts in here.' A deep voice made Minshull turn, to find a familiar face on his left. Jed Stuart, the security guard from the Spar supermarket whose CCTV had caught Hannah, loomed large over the bar. Minshull had played rugby with him years ago, back when both of them were in uniform, and had seen the jovial man-mountain terrify many a local team. On any other night his company would have been welcome. But not tonight. 'Thought you wouldn't want to venture here, off duty.'

'Fancied a pint of Abbot,' Minshull replied, his smile tight. 'They don't do it near me.'

'Oh, now you make a good point there, Rob. Marie, my love, I'll have one of those and another for the detective sergeant? Reckon you need it, mate, searching for that poor kid all day.'

Minshull's heart sank. 'Actually, I'm just about to...'

'You're a copper on the missing kid case?'

He turned slowly back to the young man on his right. So much for not being recognised. 'And you don't miss a trick.'

The young man shrugged, the damp patches on his jacket shoulders dancing as he did so. 'S'quite easy when you do the job I do. Being an investigative reporter...'

Minshull's glass met the bar with a little more force than necessary. He'd had enough today and this latest development did nothing to lift his mood. 'Sorry, should I know you?'

'Probably not.' A damp hand was cursorily wiped across the rain-splattered jacket before being offered to Minshull, who didn't accept. 'Lloyd Price. From the *Argus*.'

'I thought the editor pretty much ran things there.'

The smallest twitch of irritation registered on Lloyd's brow. 'Yeah, I get that a lot. I've actually worked there four years this summer.'

'Work experience, wasn't it, Lloyd?' Marie grinned from behind the bar, eliciting the scowl of her nephew.

'How did you know that?'

'Your mum told me. She tells everyone.'

'Great.'

'Aw, Lloydy, she's very proud of you. Shows us all your big reports in the paper and everything.'

'Leave him be, Mar,' the landlord chuckled beside her. 'Proper big grown-up reporter he is. 'Specially now his editor's busy with all the TV interviews.'

'Cheers, Andy. Jan has appointed me in charge of the news desk. She trusts me. Only this morning she said—'

'You got any leads on that poor kiddie yet, then?' the landlord cut across him, nodding at Minshull, who had been about to quietly remove himself from the conversation. The buzz around him faded a little, the swing of eyes to his shoulder unmistakable.

'We're working through them.' He drained his pint, hoping it was enough to end further questioning.

'Glad to hear it. Put *that* in your paper, Lloyd. Our coppers need all the support they can get. Especially after last time...'

'Just like last time, I heard. Care to make a comment on the item Hannah's captor sent you?' Lloyd Price shot back, a filthy smirk contorting his face.

It was definitely time to leave.

As he drove through the darkened streets of St Just, Minshull tried to shake the irritation the young reporter had conjured in him. He hadn't liked Lloyd Price's stare, or the half-smile he wore.

Too quick to judge, that's your problem, his father's voice whispered in his mind.

'That's rich coming from you,' Minshull said aloud, glad he was driving alone.

Chapter Thirty

Anderson

He'd persuaded Sue Taylor he was in control. He'd shrugged off Dave Wheeler's concern. In the pub, at the end of the longest day he could remember for years, he'd made wry jokes about being the Next Big Thing on TV, making the landlord laugh. And when he called his wife on the slow walk home, he'd told Ros he was fine.

Lies. Every single one.

That night, as the endless dark hours rose like cage bars around his bed to banish any hope of sleep, truth came to find him.

Dr Lael had been a godsend at the time she'd arrived, a masterstroke nobody saw coming. Through her he'd found renewed hope: Hannah was alive and waiting to be found. When he'd dropped the bombshell at the press conference it had seemed his moment of triumph. He'd witnessed the shockwave passing from the top table to the assembled members of the media.

But he'd forgotten Hannah's family, still at the table. And Ashleigh Perry, who he later learned had required medical attention when she'd collapsed leaving the room. How had he missed them?

Now, the fear and the dread held at bay so successfully today, rushed back at him like a furious tide. And this time, with nobody else to deflect it with his lies, it struck him head on.

He'd played his biggest hand too soon.

And now the bastard who had Hannah knew. More than that, Anderson's overwhelming need to gain advantage over the pack of hungry hacks in that room had given Hannah's captor exactly what they wanted. Exposure. A platform. Reason to keep going.

There was no doubt in Anderson's mind now that this was the same person who'd snatched Matthew Cooper. He wanted notoriety, like he'd enjoyed last time, and Anderson had just handed it to him on a plate.

At 2.15 a.m. he gave up trying to sleep. There was only one place he wanted to be.

'Bit of a late one, sir,' Chris Wilmot the night sergeant remarked, looking at his watch as Anderson passed him in the ground floor corridor on his way to the stairs. 'Or is it early?'

'Who knows?' Anderson grunted, his brief nod in lieu of a smile.

'I just made a pot of coffee in the office if you're in need? Proper stuff, not that vile powder they've foisted on us.' Wilmot's gaze took in Anderson's unkempt appearance. 'Or I could lend you a flask to take up with you?'

'That's kind of you, cheers.'

Wilmot seemed relieved as he hurried into his office to fill the flask. Anderson couldn't tell whether this was because he'd accepted Chris's offer of coffee or because it gave Wilmot an excuse to escape his company.

The CID office was dark when Anderson opened the door. The dim white glow of emergency lights filled the room with ghostly colour. But the ghosts pursuing Anderson didn't disappear when the main lights were switched on. Ragged and hideous, they hovered above him as he saw what he was looking for, silently matched his steps across the room to the pile of file boxes stacked beside Minshull's desk, and gathered above them with accusing, empty eyes.

The Cooper files.

Operation Engel – the official title of the investigation Anderson had hoped he'd never see again.

The top box was open; Wheeler and Evans had already begun the painstaking work of revisiting each file. Was the answer even in there? Op Engel had been full of holes, frustrating gaps in their investigation that were never filled. Had they interviewed Matthew's murderer, now Hannah's abductor, only to let him go? Had he even been a suspect? Seven years vanished in a breath as Anderson leafed through the files in the open box.

One by one, he carried the boxes into his office, the weight of each one made infinitely heavier by the memory of his mistakes. Carrying them felt like penance. Anderson had avoided the issue while Minshull and the team were watching: now, alone, his eyes brimmed with tears.

This is my responsibility. My mistake to atone.

A wall of all he'd thought he'd lain to rest now hemmed him in. Sinking into his chair, he heaved a stack of files onto his desk, poured Chris Wilmot's coffee into his mug, and started to read.

'Guv?'

A voice shuddered through the dark woollen cocoon he felt himself surrounded by. A sound so distant it seemed to come from miles above him slowly became the gravel of his own voice, before retreating into the void once more.

'Guv...' He felt a pressure on his body now, detached from him somehow. Then, 'Joel. Wake up, mate. Have you been here all night?'

Anderson blinked against the woollen shroud, lifting the weight of his head to discover he'd been lying with his brow nestled in the crook of his arm, his favourite blue jumper he couldn't remember putting on finally emerging through the blur as he blinked his eyes.

Strips of pink-gold light illuminated his office, fractured vertically by the blinds at the window. Anderson followed their bright progression across the carpet, his heart sinking as he saw pile upon pile of half-opened case files stacked across the entire space.

'Dave? What time is it?'

Wheeler's kind face was etched with concern. 'Gone six. The rest of them will be in by seven. I can make your excuses if you need to go home...'

'No!' Anderson started to stand, stopping as his back jarred. Clamping a hand to it, he shook his head. 'I can't leave.'

'With respect, mate, you can't stay. Not looking like that.'

'Like what?'

'Put it this way, Joel, you look like shit and smell twice as bad.'

Panic gripped Anderson, so quickly he had no time to conceal it. 'But the team... Minshull... they can't see me like this.'

Wheeler raised his eyes to the strip-lights and promptly left the room.

Anderson dropped back into his chair, head in hands. How bad must it be if even Dave Wheeler wouldn't help him? He rubbed his eyes, slamming the heel of his hand against his forehead. Why had he let himself fall asleep? Now the team would arrive and they would *know*. Added to his performance yesterday and the whispered conversations in the CID office that quickly hushed the moment he walked in, it would be impossible to pretend he was on top of things. And if word got back to Chief Inspector Taylor...

The thud of an object hitting the desk inches from his arm made him jump back, only to find a light grey wash bag now resting beside his elbow.

'Use the shower at the end of the corridor,' Wheeler said from the doorway. 'And chuck us your shirt on the way.'

Anderson stared. 'My shirt?'

With a resigned air only a friend of twenty years could possess, Wheeler held up a small, compact travel iron. 'You get rid of the stink, I'll get rid of the creases.'

'Dave, I don't know what to…'

'Then don't. Get a soddin' move on.'

'Okay. Cheers. And if anyone comes in?'

'We say you went for a run before work. Your shirt got creased in your rucksack.'

'Right.' Anderson frowned, still not sure if this was real or a fever dream. 'Which rucksack?'

Wheeler shook his head, the beginnings of a smile appearing. 'The one in my locker.'

'Shit, mate. I—'

'No time. It's safe with me.'

The two men observed one another, enough said in the silence between them. Finally, Wheeler gestured at the door to the corridor, where any moment the CID team would arrive.

'Go!'

Chapter Thirty-One

Minshull

'Sarge. Someone asking for you at the front desk,' Dave Wheeler said, his grimace a welcome sign of solidarity. People demanding to see detectives by name were never a good thing. It usually involved shouting or a lot of wasted time.

It had been a strange morning. All of the team were engaged in the so far fruitless task of revisiting the Cooper case files. But the energy in the room was odd, as if something was being held back. It prickled Minshull's spine. He didn't like it.

A walk to the front desk was the last thing he needed.

With one last glance at the list of Hannah Perry's school friends on his computer screen, he grabbed his suit jacket from the back of his chair and followed Wheeler down the corridor.

'Who's asking?'

'Young chap. Not seen him before.'

'Any idea what he wants?'

'Wouldn't tell the duty officer. Saving all the good stuff just for you.' His laugh echoed through the adjoining corridor as he headed towards the canteen. Minshull shrugged on his jacket and descended the stairs two at a time. It had better not be some idiot riled up by Siobhan Collins' increasingly vitriolic tabloid interviews. He had too much to think about today without irate members of the public chasing grievances.

Pauline Wilks, duty desk officer, glowered as he entered the reception. Red-faced, she jabbed an angry finger towards a row of blue plastic chairs opposite. 'He's over there. Proper clever dick, an' all.'

Pauline's calmness in the face of whatever the people of Ipswich chucked her way was legendary. She'd encountered every horror from drunks to violent outbursts, top-decibel rows to projectile vomit, but this was the first time Minshull had seen her any less than cool and unimpressed.

'Acting DS Minshull,' he said, offering his hand as the visitor turned. *Great.* The last person he wanted to talk to today. 'Ah, Mr Price, isn't it?'

Lloyd Price made a point of not returning Minshull's handshake, that annoying half-smile still present. Minshull wondered how long it had been since the inevitable teenage acne had finally vacated Price's chin. Judging by the visible pocking that dotted his jaw line, not much more than a year.

'Finally. I've waited nearly forty-five minutes to see you.'

'My apologies. I wasn't aware you'd arranged an appointment.'

'I wasn't aware I needed one.'

So, he was going to be one of *those*, was he? Not a surprise after his little monologue in the pub last night. Minshull turned his expression to stone. *Sorry, sunshine. Not going to happen.* 'How can I help?'

'Not here. In your office.'

'My office?' That was a joke. A desk in a room of six, where not even your keyboard was safe from colleagues' tricks.

'I have something.' The young reporter patted his jacket and Minshull saw the edge of a padded envelope underneath. 'I think you'll want to see this.'

It was enough to change Minshull's mind. 'Follow me.'

He made straight for Anderson's unoccupied office, not wanting the rest of the team to see yet. Added to this, if the *Argus*'s junior reporter believed all detective sergeants had their own offices, best not to disabuse him of the theory. TV cop dramas had a lot to answer for – but in this instance it might just work in Minshull's favour.

He glanced at the clock as they entered, calculating how long he could present the office as his. Anderson's meeting with Detective Chief Inspector Taylor and the two body language experts from yesterday's press conference would likely occupy the best part of an hour. The team had seen precious little of Anderson this morning, although Minshull had noticed Wheeler making several visits, and when the detective inspector had left for his meeting, Dave had been hot on his heels. Anderson had been gone a while: maybe Sue Taylor was still reading him the riot act over his stunt at the press conference yesterday. Either way, there wasn't much time to take advantage of Anderson's office. Perhaps if he was quick, he could deal with Lloyd

Price and be out before his boss even noticed. Despite Anderson's absence, he chose not to occupy his chair, instead perching on the edge of the desk nearest the reporter.

'Nice office.'

'Thanks. You have something for me?'

Lloyd still held his jacket protectively across his chest. 'Depends. Do you have something for me, Acting DS Minshull?'

Fantastic. Pauline Wilks had been right about this one. 'With respect, my colleagues and I are in the middle of a major investigation. I don't have time for games. So either hand it over or leave.'

He watched the futile attempts of his visitor to wait it out, correctly judging the reporter's eagerness to share information. Journalists were all the same. Cocky as hell, but ultimately unwilling to lose their shot at a story. Lloyd Price may have the swagger and gob of a seasoned hack, but he didn't yet possess the bollocks to carry it off. 'I thought you should see this.' An A4 Jiffy bag was pulled from inside his jacket. 'It arrived in the office this morning, addressed to the paper.'

'And?'

'There's an item inside. With Hannah Perry's nametag on it.'

Now Minshull was listening, every nerve to attention. 'Have you touched it?'

'Of course I touched it. I didn't know what it was until I opened the envelope. There's a note, too. You might want to read it.'

Fetching a clear evidence bag from Anderson's drawer, Minshull spread it across the opened end of the envelope, tipping it over so that the school tie and accompanying sheet of paper slid inside the bag. Sealing it, he held up the bag to read the note. It had been typed as before, but the tone was unmistakable:

> Hannah sent this.
>
> Quite the performance at the press conference.
>
> Are you enjoying our game yet?

The tie looked tiny in the evidence bag: too small for the magnitude of its meaning. If Hannah was wearing her school uniform, the tie might have been around her neck when it was removed. Had it been snatched, like her headband had been? Worse, had it been used to subdue the child before it was sent?

And what was the significance of this parcel arriving at the *Argus* offices, not South Suffolk Police HQ? The note mentioned the press conference and Anderson's outburst – had it caused Hannah's captor to change tack?

Minshull's thoughts turned immediately to Cora Lael. Would she be able sense Hannah's voice with this? And would she know if it had been taken from a conscious child?

'Well?'

'Thank you for bringing this in.'

'I knew you'd want to see it.'

'Thank your editor, too. I know how you could use this. I'm glad you appreciate the importance of keeping this *strictly* confidential.'

The journalist seemed to deflate a little. 'But—'

'A child's life is at stake. I'm glad you understand the severity of threat. As does your editor.'

'My editor doesn't know,' Lloyd spluttered, his mouth jamming shut to prevent the escape of any more.

Finally, the truth without smart-arse remarks. 'Doesn't she?'

'It arrived this morning, addressed to the news desk. I brought the post in and it was top of the pile. I just opened it and... Jan doesn't know.'

'So you thought you'd get first dibs on the story?'

'It was sent to us! Maybe whoever has Hannah thinks we have a better chance of finding her than your lot.'

The little *git*... 'Maybe we have found who has Hannah.' Minshull tapped the evidence bag. 'And maybe that's you.'

'I brought the package in. Why would I do that if I had the kid?'

'For attention. For *the game.*'

'That's ridiculous.'

'I have the evidence – and *your* fingerprints – right here.'

Lloyd's head dropped. 'Mm.'

'Sorry, I didn't catch that?'

'It wasn't me.'

'Didn't think it was. Even you wouldn't be that stupid to bring your own evidence to the police. Now we have it, you're free to go.'

'You have to give us *something*! Every other publication is out for your blood. Only the *Argus* has your back.'

'A stance you don't agree with.'

Lloyd shrugged. 'If it was up to me I'd be doing the same as the rest of them. But Jan's all about supporting you.'

'Then I have your word that none of this gets back to other, not-so-sympathetic news outlets.' It was a statement, not a question. 'Because if anyone so much as breathes one word I'll know where it came from.'

The junior reporter stuck out his chin but his voice was devoid of defiance. 'Sure. Whatever.'

'And if more packages arrive, you will call me. Immediately.'

'Okay.'

Minshull sat back, his work done. 'Thank you for your co-operation, sir. It's much appreciated.'

With a certain sense of victory, he escorted the deflated youth back downstairs to the front door and watched him walk away.

'Nasty little scrote, that,' Pauline Wilks said behind him.

Minshull turned. 'Indeed.'

'I hope you kicked his scrawny arse to the kerb?'

In a manner of speaking, Minshull thought. 'I think I brought him down a peg or two.' Nodding his thanks to the surly desk sergeant, he headed back upstairs.

Maybe Lloyd Price was just an opportunist, but something about his swagger – and willingness to go behind his employer's back – made Minshull feel uneasy. Was it really just a lucky break? Receiving a parcel meant his fingerprints would naturally be on it, but what if it was more than that? A perfect alibi to cover his tracks?

He'd mocked him for the very thing, but was Lloyd Price now a suspect?

Anderson looked up as Minshull entered his office, his expression darkening the moment he saw the padded envelope he carried.

'Development, Guv,' he stated, a sting of breathlessness in his throat and the buzz of adrenaline at his neck. 'Another delivery.'

'Right.' Anderson picked up the phone. 'Let's call Dr Lael in. And don't tell the team until she's seen it.'

Chapter Thirty-Two

Cora

After another disturbed night, Cora sat nursing a coffee at her small kitchen table. The dreams were becoming darker and longer each time they occurred, the plaintive cries of the child sounding through walls of brick, iron and, in the last dream, shards of barbed wire perilously close to her skin. Daylight was a blessed relief and had brought a precious few hours of sleep, but exhaustion still pulled at her body and mind.

With the official story Daniel had circulated at the university being that she was away on jury duty, she had a whole day to herself. She half-considered taking her coffee back to bed, but her mind was restless from her overnight ordeal. One question had threaded through her dreams: where could Hannah have gone? On her first visit to South Suffolk CID, Minshull had shown her the CCTV evidence they'd gathered of Hannah's last known movements. But where did she go after that? What could have caught her attention to pull her away from the sound and colour of the Easter Market?

When Daniel called first thing this morning, Cora had tried to talk about it, but he had quickly tired of the subject, preferring instead to discuss the meal he intended to cook for her tonight. With nobody else to consult, she decided to take the initiative.

An hour later, Cora left her car in the car park just off St Bart's Street and walked into the heart of St Just. Around the Meatcross groups of people congregated, their expensive North Face padded jackets and extra-large coffee cups marking them out from the locals, who observed them from a safe distance with quiet suspicion. Satellite trucks jostled for parking space and the air was filled with unfamiliar accents from the incoming journalists and the rubbish they discarded.

I'm late…

Hate this…

He's just a loser…

So bored of this pit…

Cora kept her head down and walked quickly through the wall of noise.

Don't let any voice catch your attention… Keep going…

What would Daniel make of her being here? Maybe she would tell him, maybe she wouldn't. He'd said he didn't mind when she'd declined his offer of staying over last night, although his attitude this morning was at odds with that. He didn't seem interested in the specifics of the investigation, only in Cora's own emotional experience.

'What matters is that you're in control here. Keep telling yourself that. You're part of the investigation as an expert witness, not on trial for your abilities.'

But was she?

Around her the detritus of other people's lives yelled up at her, the whole spectrum of emotions skidding around her feet. She was used to the sensation now, no longer floored by the sudden intrusions, but recently she'd been more aware of them than ever, as if consciously listening to Hannah's disembodied voice for the police heightened her sense of all the others.

There was something else – not formed enough to be discernible yet, more like a subtle change in the air around her. It was almost as if her gift was growing, evolving, hinting at the promise of something deeper just over the horizon…

She shook the feeling away and quickly headed towards the Meatcross. This was the route Minshull said Hannah had taken on the day she went missing. Cora tried to imagine the wind-buffeted grey street transformed by bright early spring light – a day filled with hope and laughter, before the little girl's nightmare had begun.

The High Street was quiet today but Cora remembered enough of the busyness of the Easter Market to mentally populate the road with crowds of St Just residents and visitors. Where she'd embraced a storm coming off the sea in Felixstowe before travelling to St Just that day, the change in weather in the small village, thirty miles inland had been remarkable. She pictured it now – the sunlight illuminating everything, red and white striped awnings and pastel-shaded bunting shivering gently in the warm Easter breeze; balloons bobbing from every streetlight and soaring into the pale blue sky from careless owners' hands. Where today the only smells were damp tarmac and the tang of exhaust fumes, Cora imagined the scent of hot pork sandwiches and freshly cooked doughnuts, cheeses and cakes and chutneys from the artisan food market and the sweet tingle of candy floss sugar. Crowd noise and real voices audible where today the ghosts of internal monologues swirled past her, carried by invisible eddies of wind.

What would it have looked like to a child?

On her way here earlier, she had secretly hoped for an audible glimpse of Hannah. But that seemed ridiculous now she was walking the length of the High Street. From the description Ashleigh Perry had given of her daughter, it was unlikely she would have relinquished anything, let alone anything that may still be present in the pavement dander. She had heard for herself the vehement fight in the young girl's voice as her headband was taken from her. That wasn't the attitude of a child willing to discard anything she owned.

Reaching Emerson Estates, Cora paused to look in the window. She shuddered, knowing she was replaying Hannah's exact movements. Closing her eyes, she imagined the missing girl standing beside her. What was she looking at that day? Minshull said it made no sense and he was right. What attraction could rows of house photographs hold for an eight-year-old?

'Looking to move?'

The voice was loud beside her. Cora started and opened her eyes. Smiling at her was a middle-aged woman she vaguely recognised.

'Thinking about it,' she replied, hoping to prolong the conversation enough for the woman to offer some clue about who she was. 'You?'

The woman shrugged. 'Never hurts to look.'

Where do I know you from?

The question irritated Cora. Was she a mature student at the university college? Someone she knew from her childhood? A friend of the family? A former neighbour?

'Well, if you're considering a move to St Just I'd recommend picking up a copy of the *Argus*.' Finally taking pity on Cora, her smile broadened. ''Course, I would say that, being the editor.'

Light suddenly dawned and Cora realised it was the woman she'd seen interviewed about Hannah's disappearance on several local and national news reports. 'Sorry, I should have known who you were.'

'Don't worry, you wouldn't be the first to miss me. Provincial newspapers don't tend to make you a household name.' She held out her hand and it was warm when Cora shook it. 'Jan Martin.'

'Cora Lael,' she replied, wondering too late if she should have admitted her real name, given her involvement with the police.

'Lael – that's an unusual name. Although…' Jan tapped a finger to her temple which, added to her slightly dishevelled appearance, instantly made Cora think of watching *Columbo* with her parents on childhood Saturday afternoons. 'I know I've heard it before. *Lael…*'

Momentarily distracted, Cora found herself amused by the bright-eyed woman with her wild, grey, frizzy hair and slightly baggy over-coat, battling her memory over Cora's surname. Then she clicked her fingers, beaming with triumph. 'Bill Lael, former town councillor.'

Cora's heart contracted as Jan began listing all the interactions she'd had with Cora's father over the ten years he'd served the local community. It made sense that the editor of the *St Just Argus* would have encountered him. Bill Lael had been a tireless campaigner for the people he was elected to serve. Her mum would later blame his public role as partly responsible for his speedy demise.

'I even wrote his obituary,' Jan said, stopping short as realisation finally dawned. '…"*Survived by his wife and two children…*" Oh. You're Bill's daughter.'

'It was a lovely piece,' Cora lied. At the time the newspaper's tribute to her father had been an anathema to her: conclusive proof that he had gone. Her mother hadn't read it either, sadly nodding when friends and neighbours quoted extracts in an attempt to say something meaningful in the vacuum of their loss.

'Thanks. Hard to write, but I was pleased with it. Your dad was a real local hero. How's your mum now?'

It was an impertinent question, but Cora found comfort in someone else caring about her mother. She'd borne the burden alone for too long. 'Good.' Another lie, but far easier than the truth.

'Does she ever come to the St Just WI? I go sometimes. She'd like it.'

'I don't think Mum would be into it.'

'Well, she'd be most welcome. I'd be happy to take her if she didn't fancy going by herself. It can be daunting, I know, especially in a small place like this.'

'I'll mention it to her.'

'Do that. Look, here's my number.' She handed Cora a creased rectangle of card from the deep recesses of her mackintosh pocket. 'Tell her to give me a call if she'd like to come. Any time. You too, if you'd like?'

'No offence, but it isn't really my scene. I'll give this to Mum, though,' she promised. 'Thank you.'

Jan smiled. 'Good. I'd better get going – the office is a bit barmy with this police case.'

Suddenly very aware of her words, Cora kept her expression steady. 'Nasty business,' she said, hoping it sounded like idle gossip. 'Poor kid.'

Jan's smile faded just a little. Cora imagined it was a double-edged sword for a journalist: human empathy with the missing child battling the huge adrenaline rush of a national news story right on her doorstep. She'd seen reporters on the national news wearing the same half-smile of concern reporting from scenes of massacres, terrorist atrocities and war zones. 'It's a strain on everyone,' she replied. 'I imagine for the police also.'

Cora's breath caught. Did Jan know she was assisting the police investigation? It was time to leave.

'I don't envy them the task.' She held up the card. 'Thanks for this.'

The full beam of Jan's smile returned. 'No problem. Get your mum to call me, yeah? Be good to see her. I was very fond of your dad.'

Cora watched the woman leave, her head a muddle. Mentions of her father always blindsided her, even now. And last night's unsettled dreams had exhausted her. Dark clouds were building over St Just, the white-painted buildings thrown into stark contrast against the stormy sky. Cora shivered and pressed on. She was almost at the end of the street when her mobile rang. Seeing the caller ID, she answered immediately.

'Hi Dr Lael, it's Joel Anderson. I'm afraid we need your help again. Could you come in this afternoon, please?'

Cora turned on her heels. 'I'm on my way.'

Chapter Thirty-Three

Minshull

The school tie was curled up in the evidence bag, as if protecting itself from an unseen adversary. The thought made Minshull uneasy. He looked up at Cora Lael's ashen face and considered how much worse a prospect it was for her. Her eyes were fixed on the bag's contents as he held it towards her, the pronounced rise and fall of the scarf around her neck betraying her nerves.

'When did it come?' she asked, a slight tremor in her voice.

'It arrived at the *Argus* offices in St Just and was brought here this morning by one of its reporters.'

Cora looked up from the school tie. 'The newspaper offices? I was near them when you called me today.'

'You went to the *Argus*?'

'No, I just went for a walk in the village. I bumped into the editor by the estate agent, though – Jan?'

'You didn't say anything about...?'

'No. Of course not. We talked about my dad. He led the search for Matthew.'

'I-I didn't know that.' Was that why she'd been keen to assist Op Seraph? Trying to find another missing child in St Just, where her father had searched before? 'I'm sorry.'

She observed him for a moment, the fear from seconds ago replaced by something else Minshull couldn't read. 'Why are you sorry?'

Because I should have known, his mind answered. Surprised, he nodded at the evidence bag in her hands. 'Are you okay to proceed?'

'Yes.'

Minshull looked over to Anderson, who was watching them both from behind his desk, fingers steepled together, the tips of them turning white with tension. 'Okay, Guv?'

'Go ahead.'

He watched her take a breath, her shoulders squaring with resolve as she accepted the evidence bag. And then the jerk of her body as she opened the zip-lock fastening, as if gut-punched by a ghost. She shut her eyes tight as she listened; when she opened them again she blinked back tears, fingers fumbling as she struggled to close the bag.

Minshull reached across to take it from her, the move feeling more like an attempt to comfort her than retrieve the evidence. He noticed how cold her fingers felt beneath his before he withdrew his hand. Suddenly self-conscious, he looked to his right, where Anderson was watching him, one eyebrow raised.

Wheeler, who had been standing guard in the doorway of Anderson's office, sprinted across the carpet to guide Cora onto a chair. They waited for her to gather herself, the room lapsing into awkward silence. Cora breathed heavily for a while, then slowly folded her pale hands in her lap and raised her head.

'She didn't want to let it go. I think it was yanked from her neck – she said, "You're hurting me!".'

'Did you hear anything else? Any echoes in the room? Any other sounds.'

'Sorry. Just her voice.'

'That's okay, I just wondered.' Minshull nodded at Wheeler, handing him the bag. 'Get this tested for fibres. It's possible some of her hair or skin cells came away when it was removed.' He kept his voice low, not wanting to add to the visible distress of his now key witness. 'Dr Lael, can I get you a drink?'

'Coffee please,' she answered.

Minshull ducked into the CID office where the eyes of his team were immediately on him. Of course they had all known what was happening the moment Cora had been led in to Anderson's office.

'Could we get some coffee for Dr Lael, please?'

'Sure, Sarge.' Bennett hopped off the desk and made for the kettle. Evans, who had been standing beside her, took the hint and sidled back to his own desk. Minshull inhaled slowly against the knots of tension in his neck and headed back into Anderson's office.

'Coffee's on its way, Dr Lael. And DC Bennett is making it, so you've a hope of it being recognisable as coffee. How are you doing?'

'I'm okay.'

'And you're certain of what you heard?'

She stared at him.

'I'm sorry, but I have to ask.'

Her expression softened a little. 'I am. This must have been taken from her very recently. Her voice had a presence I didn't hear before.'

'How recently, would you say?'

Cora considered his question. 'A few hours at most.'

'Do you think Hannah Perry is still alive?'

'She was at the moment the tie was taken.'

'Great work, Dr Lael. Thank you. One more thing,' Minshull leaned across Anderson's desk and picked up the note that had accompanied Hannah's tie. He'd thought of something: if Cora could hear Hannah's voice from her belongings, could she hear the person who'd snatched her in the note to police? When Cora had listened to Hannah's headband, her response had been so strong that nobody had thought to let her listen to the note that had accompanied it.

It had been placed in an identical clear evidence bag. 'Could you take a look at this please? In was in the same package.'

Frowning a little, she accepted the bag. When she opened it, her frown deepened.

Minshull watched.

'I'm sorry, I...' she faltered.

'What can you hear?'

She looked at him. 'Nothing.'

'But you heard a scream from the tie? Why the difference? Surely an abductor's thoughts would be attached to a note? Especially if they are enjoying the game as much as they seem to be?'

'Well, Hannah's voice was strongest because her tie was forcibly removed. An act like that is always going to give a stronger voice to an object.'

'And a note wouldn't?'

Cora sighed and Minshull imagined her giving the same patient response to everyone who asked. 'Not necessarily. If it's a handwritten note I can often hear snippets of voice in the loops and curls of the pen. Like the sound has been embossed into the paper alongside the ink. If it's a printed one I may get some sense of voice but most of the time it's from the person who posted it, which is not always the one who typed it. But if it's neither of those and the person writing or typing or folding it did so wearing gloves, the sound can't attach. I may feel emotion, but most of the time I can't hear words.'

It seemed plausible and certainly Cora delivered the explanation with sincerity. 'So it's down to physical touch? A person has to have touched the item in some way for the emotional memory to attach?'

Cora beamed. 'Yes, exactly. Like an emotional fingerprint. So my guess would be that whoever made that note – whoever has Hannah – wore gloves when they put the package together. Does that help?'

Bewildered but sold, Minshull nodded. Then a thought occurred. Taking the Jiffy bag from Anderson's desk, he handed it to Cora. 'Can you hear anything from this?'

She accepted it and her eyes defocused as she listened. 'It's very faint. I can't make out any words, just the murmur of a man's voice and a rustling of paper. It's muddled – sorry.'

'You said a murmur – what sort of murmur?'

She frowned as if willing the right words to appear. 'Muffled, like it was covered by something thick. A blanket or – a coat?'

Minshull stared at her. 'Like it had been concealed under a jacket? A padded jacket?'

She immediately brightened. 'Exactly!'

Had she heard Lloyd Price's muffled inner thoughts? And had the voice come from the journey to the police station or the journey from wherever Hannah was being held? It seemed preposterous that the conniving young journalist was hiding Hannah but Cora's sense of a voice that could be his was intriguing.

Or what if it was another man's voice? A man closer to Hannah, who knew how to cover his tracks? The report from the body language experts at the press conference had noted Shaun Collins' guarded stance, which could have been attributed to nerves in such a highly charged atmosphere, but they also observed something else: defiance and pride. The way he had eyeballed every journalist, head held high, back straight. Almost as if goading them on. Almost like a challenge…

–

An hour later Minshull sat down in the canteen with an uninspiring beef sandwich and a mug of thick coffee as Bennett joined him. She'd opted for the ham salad, which didn't look any more enticing. Limp lettuce leaves hung dejectedly over the edge of the plastic bowl, as if accepting defeat after hours of reaching for freedom.

'What do you think, Sarge?' Bennett tucked into her meal with little regard for its appearance. A ten-hour shift tended to remove fussiness when it came to food. 'Is she legit?'

'I think so.' *I hope so.* 'What did you make of her?'

'I don't know. When I saw her reaction to the first package it was – weird. Made me think of those batty TV mediums on *Most Haunted*.' She grinned, mid-mouthful. 'It was strange, wasn't it? As if whatever she heard knocked her sideways.'

'Mmm.'

'So what happened with the note?'

Minshull nodded. 'Oh, you heard about that.'

'Dave said. I think he figured it was okay to mention it seeing as we'd all guessed why Dr Lael was there. How come she heard no sound from it? Presumably whoever made it was thinking stuff at the time?'

'Not if they were wearing gloves. The voices she hears are like fingerprints we find. Someone has to have touched an object for it to carry their thoughts. If someone wears gloves, no prints. Physical or otherwise.'

'And you buy that?'

'Don't you?'

'It's a bit odd, you have to admit. I meant to ask, does she have any – um – professional qualifications?' Her question was carefully phrased but Minshull knew exactly where it had come from. CID team gossip was about as subtle as a loud hailer.

'She's a doctor of psychology and works at the University of South Suffolk. Why? Les Evans calling her a con-artist again?'

Bennett shrugged. 'Les is a dick sometimes.'

'Only *sometimes*?' The joke felt good after so many hours absent of humour. He faced her and decided to ask her opinion on an idea he'd been mulling over all morning. 'I've been wondering if we should invite Dr Lael to Hannah's house. See if she hears anything there.'

Bennett observed him over the top of the coffee cup. 'The house is full of Hannah's stuff. How could Dr Lael hear anything specific?'

'Not just Hannah.'

'Who, then? Her mum? Her stepfather.' Her eyes widened. 'Collins?'

'Maybe,' Minshull shrugged, but even as he gave voice to his idea he could see how it might muddy the waters. 'Although if what the

174

FLO at the Perry house tells us is anything to go by, he isn't around much.'

'I can see why you think it might work.' Bennett appeared to be picking her words with care. 'But it's risky. The moment you take Dr Lael there you're letting the family know she's involved. And how do you explain it? Siobhan Collins is already circling like a vulture – can you imagine the havoc she'd cause if she told the press about that? We'd be pilloried for it.'

Minshull nodded. 'You're right. Forget I mentioned it.'

'Already forgotten, Sarge. So, where next?'

Minshull brushed half-stale breadcrumbs from his hands. 'See what comes back from forensics, keep sifting through the Op Engel files. Wait for updates on Collins' movements. According to the FLO he's been staying at his mum's since we brought him in. We need to know where else he's going. And I have to speak to him and Ashleigh Perry again. They need to know about the tie.'

'I don't envy you that task.'

Minshull didn't either.

Hannah

My neck stings. My fingers, too, where I hung onto my tie. Stinging hot, like when I touched the oven door at home and Nanna Collins had to hold my fingers under the tap until they went cold again.

When They took my tie, They screamed at me. Their face was so close to mine I thought They might bite my nose, like Lily used to do when she was a baby. I stopped shouting then. It was like They reached into my mouth and took all of the words away.

When I close my eyes now, I can still see Their angry face right in my face. It's like my mind took a photo and it won't stop showing me.

They don't want me to make a noise. They want me to give Them my things. But They aren't taking my bag. Or any more of my clothes.

Next time, I'll bite.

Chapter Thirty-Four

Minshull

Minshull folded his arms and looked at the growing collection of photographs and sticky notes on the CID office's large whiteboard. Beside the smiling school photograph of the missing girl was a single Post-it note bearing a large question mark and a little to the right, a photo of Shaun Collins. While his absences from home and past record counted against him, they had nothing concrete. Nothing to uphold a conviction.

'Sarge.'

Minshull nodded at Ellis. 'Did you talk to the FLO at the Perry house?'

'I did. She said Shaun Collins has been back only a few times since he came in to see us. Only ever for a couple of hours to get a change of clothes, but he stayed overnight after the press conference because Ms Perry was unwell. But she said a neighbour reported them fighting most of that night. Terrible racket, apparently. Their youngest two bawling and Collins yelling his head off at Ms Perry.'

'What do we know about Hannah's biological father?'

Ellis shrugged. 'Not a lot. He was never named on the birth certificate and Ashleigh told the FLO it was a one-night stand.'

'But Collins is the father of Ruby and Lily?'

'Yeah.'

'Poor kids. Has Mr Collins or Ms Perry given any reason for him being away?'

Ellis shook his head. 'Although Ashleigh Perry mentioned his work took him away a lot. When the FLO mentioned it to Collins, though, he claimed he only worked locally. A five-mile radius.'

'Doing what?'

'Building work, he said. For a mate. FLO reckons he does a bit of everything. She said he'd talked about doing some electrical repairs and the odd stint of plastering.'

'Do we know who the builder mate is? If not, find out. We need to pin down his movements. His staying at his mother's seems odd to me. Why not be at home when your kids and missus need you?'

'I couldn't do it. There was one thing, Sarge. Ashleigh Perry told the FLO that Shaun Collins has lived on the Parkhall Estate for seven and a half years.'

Minshull stared at his colleague. 'Six months before Cooper went missing.'

The young DC flushed, his revelation clearly a source of great pride. 'Exactly. And Matthew's family had all lived on the estate for years. Everyone knew them, so Shaun must have, too.'

Minshull clamped a hand on Ellis's shoulder. 'Excellent work. Go back to the interviews CID conducted for the Cooper murder. See if Collins was ever questioned.'

'Yes, Sarge.'

It could be coincidence, but this information felt significant.

'Thank you. Kate, any more from Hannah's schoolteacher?'

'Not really. Just backing up what she'd said to the social services when she requested their help. She didn't want to talk when pressed further, much like the people on the estate we've spoken to. She's definitely not Mr Collins' biggest fan.'

'Doesn't take a genius to work that out,' Minshull said, giving Bennett an apologetic grin when she glared at him. 'Sorry.'

'So you should be.'

'Maybe call her back and ask if Hannah had ever mentioned her stepdad being away for long periods of time.'

'I might see if I can go over to her house to speak to her. She's a bit curt on the phone.'

'Do that. Thanks, Kate.' Minshull turned back to the board, hoping to spot something they had missed. So much about Shaun Collins irked him and his repeated absences from the family home and apparent lack of support for Hannah's mother and siblings did nothing to lessen that.

He turned to Lanehan. 'Steph, see what you can find out about Collins' work history. See if anyone was named as an employer in any of his court case notes.'

'Will do.'

'Thanks. Thanks everyone. Let's keep going.' Silently, Minshull willed them to find the lead they so desperately needed.

'You really think he's a suspect?' Lanehan asked.

'I think it would be wise to rule him out as soon as we can.'

'Maybe Dr Lael should stalk him. See if his fag packets talk to her,' Les Evans muttered, his head low but his voice clear enough for everyone to hear.

'Yeah, maybe we should go through the family's bins too, eh? You can do that for me, can't you, Les?'

But even as Minshull was mocking his colleague, an idea was forming. Might Cora be able to throw some light on the man? Could it work? If they got her close enough to him to hear... well, whatever it was she could hear? He still wasn't sure he fully understood her ability. Maybe this would kill two birds with one stone: prove that someone's belongings could talk to her and uncover information Shaun Collins didn't want them to know.

How they were going to make that happen was another thing entirely.

Chapter Thirty-Five

Cora

Cora shifted in the seat of the unmarked police car. Her palms were beaded with sweat, her stomach lined with grit.

'Are you clear about what to do?' Minshull asked, his uncertainty as visible as the furrows in his brow.

'Watch for anything he discards and note what I hear.' She repeated his words as an unfamiliar mantra. 'But what if he doesn't throw anything away?'

'Then don't worry about it. We're just trying this as an experiment.'

An experiment. She'd heard that too many times lately and it was beginning to grate. 'Right.'

'Call me when you get anything. If I don't hear from you, I'll see you back at the station. Do you have money for the bus if you need it?'

'Yes, *Dad*.' It was a brave stab at humour and seemed to take Minshull by surprise.

He stared at her, with the smallest hint of a smile. 'So. Good luck? I'll wait for your call.'

Cora smiled as she walked around the corner to Cleeve Street, where the man from the photograph Minshull had shown her was sitting in a café eating a late breakfast. Her joke had been as much an attempt to take her mind off what she was about to do, as it was to admonish Minshull. She liked that she'd wrong-footed him. It was good to have the upper hand for once.

But all lightness in her spirits dissolved as soon as her hand pressed against the scratched steel handle of the café door. Now the real test began. Could she even do this?

Cora walked in, expecting the customers within to turn and face her like patrons of a Wild West saloon bar. But the radio played on and the only head that bobbed up to acknowledge her entry was that of the shaven-headed man behind the counter.

'What y'avin', gal?'

'Bacon roll, please. And tea.'

He grinned and she noticed he had a front tooth missing. 'Grab a seat and I'll bring it over.'

The man from the photograph was hunched over a crumpled copy of the *Daily Call*, a few tables away from her. It was too far away to hear discarded voices yet but from her vantage point she could see anything he might leave. Several empty sugar packets by his tea-stained mug immediately caught her eye. They could be useful – provided they were his. The half-scrunched serviette beside his plate might tell her something too. The café owner didn't seem particularly interested in clearing tables: a more fastidious worker might have scuppered Cora's plans. She found a dog-eared copy of the *Argus* and pushed away the woman's voice bemoaning the length of the post office queue drifting up from it as she turned the pages.

That's the last time I go in there on a marnin'. Ridiculous, it was…

From time to time, she stole glances at Hannah's stepfather. He had an air of prickliness around him, as if hedgehog spines protruded from the dirty white T-shirt across his back. She sensed he wanted space, his body language warding off any unwanted attention. Minshull had told her little about the man, other than that he'd been a bit touchy when they talked to him and they thought his belongings might speak more than he'd done. Was he a suspect? Minshull hadn't definitively answered her question this morning. The possibility sat awkwardly on her shoulders. Did police suspect the family first? She'd seen it as a storyline in the crime dramas her mother used to love watching, but did that happen in real life?

What am I doing?

Cora was amazed at where she was. She was the unlikeliest spy in the world – if the man turned to look at her now he'd rumble her straight away. Daniel would be livid about the police asking her to do this. Especially when he heard it had been Rob's idea.

If she told him…

Lately any mention of Minshull's name seemed to chill the space between her and Daniel and she wasn't exactly sure why. Surely he couldn't be jealous of Rob, when he knew how uncertain Cora was of the detective's attitude to her? It could be because, having facilitated her being part of the investigation, he'd found himself relegated to the sidelines, reliant on Cora for updates. Perhaps aware of this, she had deferred to him for advice about how to proceed. He'd set up a video camera in her house and insisted she film a diary of her experiences, which she'd yet to start. For the sake of the study, he'd insisted, but perhaps for his sake, too.

But this wasn't on Daniel's radar. It was new, dangerous, thrilling. And Rob had instigated it. Maybe there were some things Daniel shouldn't know. If this worked, Cora could step out on her own and discover what she was really capable of.

If it worked.

Right now she was on her own with just her ability and someone else's idea. If she failed and the man realised what she was doing, who knew what might happen? She was sure Minshull wouldn't knowingly place her in danger, but he hadn't told her anything about the character of the man she was watching. What if Rob had misjudged him? How dangerous could this be?

Feeling vulnerable, she dropped her gaze to the crumpled newspaper in her hands. Usually it was full of non-sensational local news: council rows, residents up in arms about this and that, missing cats and smiling kids in school drama productions. But today almost three-quarters of its news pages were dominated by the search for Hannah. The editor, who by the look of it was also its main reporter, had penned all but one of the stories – the exception being an unaccredited report on how searches for missing persons had changed in the seven years since Matthew Cooper went missing.

Of course, the link was made between the boy who was murdered and Hannah's disappearance, just as she'd seen on every news report. Cora stared at the grainy image of the young girl and tried to match her face to the scared little voice that had screamed out of the evidence bag. She shuddered and turned the page, but her hand still rested on Hannah's photo beneath it. As if protecting her, shielding her eyes from the insinuations screaming out from the surrounding columns.

'IF HE DID IT TO MATTHEW, HE WILL DO IT TO HANNAH,' CONCERNED RESIDENT WARNS

IS THERE A SERIAL KILLER IN ST JUST?

MISSING GIRL MUM: PLEASE BRING HANNAH HOME.

The dreams were becoming more frequent now; Hannah's voice a prominent feature most nights. Daniel said it was most likely caused by Cora's brain reviewing her experience. Nothing to worry about, he'd insisted, keen to hear more of the police case instead. But a thought kept returning to her mind and it wouldn't go away: *what if I'm the only one who can help Hannah?*

It scared her to think that she had heard Hannah's voice and the struggle the child was facing but was powerless to do anything. Maybe finding information from the tattooed man in the café could help. Cora reminded herself that she was here to help Hannah. She had to stick close to the man, no matter what.

A throaty cough beside her made Cora start and look up to see the café owner grinning down. 'Nasty business, that,' he nodded at the paper.

Cora glanced across to Shaun Collins but he hadn't moved. Quickly, she turned a handful of pages to reach the relative blandness of the public notices section. 'It is.'

'Same bastard what done it last time, they reckon.'

'Hm.' *Please stop talking about it…*

He put down her flour-dusted bacon roll and a grubby-looking white mug of rust-coloured tea. 'Last thing we need in St Just. Though we did a roarin' trade from these newspaper blighters last time the papers came up.'

'I'll bet.'

'Do you know,' the man continued, uninvited, resting his stone-washed denim-clad behind on the edge of Cora's table, 'I reckon that poor young lad carkin' it saved this place when it 'appened. Sad as it was, 'course. Turned my profits right round and I pretty near got on first names with all of 'em.' He gave a wistful smile. 'Happy times.'

For the love of all things good, go away!

Shaun Collins pushed back against his pine chair with a sudden squeak and Cora thought she was going to faint. He didn't stand or turn, but the bristle in the jutting shoulder blades was unmistakable. Just at the point when Cora was ready to make her escape, the café owner took the hint and vacated her table.

The stuffy interior of the café swam as the blood drained from Cora's head and she battled to keep her breathing in check. She watched the proprietor saunter back behind the counter as a small woman with a face like thunder burst in through the plastic strip curtain covering the entrance to the kitchen and jabbed the man violently in his ribs.

'Hush your *bloody* mouth, Murdo. Don't you know nothin'?'

'What y'on about?'

'That poor gal's kin is *there*,' she hissed back, her whisper louder than a shout. 'You stupid or what?'

Cora saw a twitch in Collins' shoulder but moments passed and he didn't move again. Behind her, the not-so-subtle row ensued, the café owner's wife quickly moving on to more of her husband's failings. Cora took her mug in both hands and drank, feeling the shaking in her shoulders and wishing she could run. The tea was thick and cloying in her mouth, the heat almost unbearable, but she needed something to distract her from the rising panic.

And then, she saw it. Collins had taken a folded piece of paper from his back pocket and was stabbing at the numbers on his phone screen with a nicotine-yellow finger. He hunched further over the phone and Cora could only make out a throaty growl as he spoke, rising to a bark as he ended the call, screwing the paper into a ball and tossing it to the floor. Cora kept her eyes on it, jumping as Shaun Collins suddenly pushed back his chair with force and approached the counter. The startled café owner took a step behind his wife, eyes wide with fear.

'Can I get you anythin', fella?' he managed. 'Anythin' you like…'

'You can hush your noise,' Collins snarled back, jutting one shoulder out across the counter until his face was inches from the owner's. 'That's what I'd *like*…'

'I-I meant nuthin' by it, bor. Didn't know who you was…'

'We don't want no trouble,' his wife squeaked, even her fiery bravado quailing in the face of Collins' barely concealed rage.

'Then *stop* the *talkin'*. Or someone might stop it for ya.'

Cora dug her nails into her palms to stop herself crying out. For what felt like an age the stand-off continued, Collins silent as he held the café couple hostage with his stare. The buzz of the fly exterminator behind the counter seemed to rise in volume until it obliterated all else, a warning siren building with the pressure in the small commercial space.

And then, abruptly, it ended.

Collins stalked to the door, the rush of air in his wake making the hairs on Cora's forearms raise as she caught a waft of stale cigarette smoke and dried sweat. The security grille on the back of the door vibrated metallically as it was violently swung open – and Shaun Collins was gone.

Forcing breath into her lungs, Cora pushed her body upright and grabbed the ball of paper as the café owner's wife began to wail. She pocketed it, together with the empty sugar packet and discarded paper napkin, using the distraction as cover. Without looking at the counter, she sat back down, racing blood banging in her ears.

'I thought he was gunna hit me! And what did you do? Hide! Some bodyguard you are, Murdo Jones!'

Cora waited, forcing mouthfuls of too-salty bacon and too-thick bread roll down her throat. When she was satisfied the moment had passed and she could safely leave, she quietly settled her bill and walked out into the familiar buzz of Cleeve Street.

In the small King George V Park, ten minutes' walk from the centre of St Just, she found an unoccupied bench beneath a blossom-heavy horse chestnut tree and fished the items from her pocket.

They know.

She shivered as Shaun Collins' voice growled up at her from the sugar packets.

Someone's ratted me out.

Bastards!

The paper bore a mobile phone number and a single name in slanting letters. The ink was rutted, as though the message had been written on a textured surface. Tiny blank crosshatches ran through the ink line, fracturing it like scratches, and the pressure the writer had asserted was sufficient to push out the paper behind the letters and numbers like a reverse embossing.

'*Jack.*' Cora spoke the name under her breath, the expletive-ridden anger of Shaun Collins snarling away as she inspected the note. His words were white-hot but remained a random ranting rather than anything coherent. Perhaps Rob Minshull would be able to make something of them. She pulled out a small notebook from her bag and wrote down what she heard, baulking at some of Collins' chosen terminology. One thing stood out: the venom with which he spoke Jack's name. It was as if he was encapsulating every ounce of fury in each of the four letters. Cora had never heard so much violent rage expressed in a single word before, and it scared her.

On the bus to South Suffolk Constabulary's headquarters, Cora tried to marry the voice she'd heard from Shaun Collins' discarded objects with the terrified child's voice that haunted her. What kind of a stepfather was Collins? If what Cora sensed from Hannah's voice was correct, she seemed a gentle-hearted girl. Was she scared of him? He was understandably under pressure with his stepdaughter's disappearance, but what she'd witnessed in the café was beyond the behaviour of a man terrified for his child's safety. His sudden transformation from passive customer to threatening aggressor had shocked Cora. What must it be like to live with someone so violently unpredictable?

The thought made her nauseous. It wasn't her job to think like that, she told herself as the police headquarters swung into view and she stood, ready to disembark. She would just tell Rob Minshull what she'd heard and let him deal with it. She considered the video camera set up in her living room, waiting for her to use. Maybe she would record her reaction this time – if for no other reason than to try to make sense of everything that had happened today.

The bus jerked to a halt, the momentum causing Cora to stumble forwards. As she did so, a tumble of rubbish skidded past her feet and one word jumped out in the middle of the general rumble of voices.

JACK.

Shaken, she snapped her head around, expecting to see the man she'd stalked sitting in the seats behind her. But Shaun Collins wasn't on the bus. Trembling, she bent down to scan the jumble of discarded bus tickets, empty chocolate bar wrappers and shreds of cellophane from recently opened cigarette packets. Beneath a half-torn leaflet for a local pizza takeaway, she found it: the crumpled note she'd retrieved from beneath Shaun Collins' table. Reaching for it, her other hand slipped into her coat pocket, finding nothing but the smooth satin of the lining fabric. Now, it made sense. It must have fallen from her pocket when the bus brakes engaged.

She tried to laugh at herself for being so jumpy, but a heavy sense of unease settled over her as she hurried into the police station, refusing to leave as she waited to be admitted to CID.

Chapter Thirty-Six

Minshull

'You did *what?*'

Minshull braced himself as Anderson's face reddened.

'Guv, it worked. We have a name and a number...'

'Let me see if I understand this. You sent a civilian – a completely unprepared, untrained individual – *alone*, into a potentially dangerous situation. And you didn't think maybe that might not be particularly wise?'

'Dr Lael was brilliant. She got us what we needed on Collins.'

'I saw her leave this afternoon. The poor woman looked exhausted. This is *not* why I brought her onto this investigation.'

Minshull bristled. So Anderson was happy enough to put people into *his* investigation without consulting him but now Minshull wasn't allowed to use them? 'Guv. With respect, Dr Lael is a part of this team. She was able to give us an insight we wouldn't have acquired otherwise.'

'And what if Collins had seen her, hmm? What if he'd realised he was being stalked?'

'He didn't...'

'That's not the point! Shaun Collins is unpredictable and capable of violent behaviour. You put Dr Lael in danger, Minshull. That's unacceptable.'

There were many things Minshull could have said, but he wasn't in the mood for an all-out battle with his superior. He swallowed down the gnawing sense of injustice – a survival skill honed over many years facing greater wrath than Joel Anderson could ever unleash. 'Guv. But we got a number.'

'And?'

'No name listed with the number. Appears to be a pay-as-you-go mobile, no registered owner.'

'A burner?'

'Could be. We'll know more tomorrow. The tech team are running checks on mast data in the area, see which towers have registered the number's use.'

'Well, that could be useful. But you will not pull a stunt like this again, Minshull, do you understand?'

'Perfectly, Guv.'

Irritated, Anderson dismissed him with a curt wave of his hand. 'Go. Get out of my office.'

'Still got your nuts, Sarge?' Evans grinned, as Minshull walked back into the CID office.

'All present and correct, thanks.'

'For *now*.'

He shot a look at Les Evans, but his smile betrayed him. He was glad to be out of the firing line and a little shared camaraderie was very welcome.

'I still think we should go back to the kebab shop,' Lanehan looked up from her computer.

'Skip lunch again, did you Steph?'

'*No*, Les. Shame you didn't.'

Minshull stopped by her desk. 'For what reason?'

'The owner was very keen to get us out of there, don't you think? And when we checked the list of Hannah's schoolmates this morning we discovered Mr Faisal's youngest son is in her class.'

'That's a point,' Bennett agreed. 'I called Miss Mills to check and she seemed to think they were friends.'

'Fine. Kate, go with Steph and check it out. Let me know if you find anything useful.'

'Is Dr Lael okay?' Wheeler asked quietly, approaching Minshull with a mug of tea.

'I think so.' First Anderson and now Wheeler – had Cora been out of sorts this afternoon? He'd been so interested in what she'd found that he hadn't noticed much else. 'Did you think she wasn't?'

Dave Wheeler was more of a gentleman than he wanted anyone to realise and Minshull envied the ease with which he understood the feelings of others. He could rely on Dave for insight that few others in his team could provide. 'It shook her up, Minsh. Badly. I took her down to the canteen for a cuppa before I was happy she was calm enough to drive home.'

'What was wrong?'

'I think the – skill – she has, it knocks her about a bit. And it sounds like Collins kicked off royally. You and I know how tough that can be when you're close to it.'

Back at his desk, Minshull stared at the phone. It worried him that he'd missed something important. Cora was proving herself invaluable to the investigation – if she backed out now they would have very little left to rely upon. Steeling himself, he picked up the receiver and dialled.

'Dr Lael – Cora – it's Acting DS Minshull.'

'Oh. Hello.' She sounded tired and the image of the exhausted young woman still shaken by her experience filled Minshull's mind. He *should* have seen it.

'I just wanted to thank you for your work today. And – er – check how you are.'

There was a definite pause before she replied. 'I'm fine.'

'DC Wheeler didn't think you were.'

'Well, I am.'

He took a breath, the awkwardness of the conversation making his skin prickle. 'Listen, I'm sorry I put you in that situation. I didn't think what I might be sending you into.'

'It's okay. I agreed to it.' Her voice was quiet, robbed of the expression and spirit he'd heard before.

'All the same, I hadn't considered the danger and I should have. So I'm sorry.'

'Okay. Thank you.'

'Get some rest and I'll see you tomorrow morning, as we agreed.'

'Away from the station?'

'Yes. It would be good to talk you through where we are. Hard to do that in the office what with all the noise – from my team and...' he hesitated, summoning the appropriate words, '...anything else that might be speaking.'

On the other end of the line he thought he caught a whisper of a laugh. 'Okay. DS Minshull?'

'Yes?'

'Don't worry about me. I'll be fine.'

Would she be? It occurred to him that he hardly knew anything about Cora Lael. That had to change.

At six-thirty p.m., after hours spent combing the never-ending Op Engel files, Minshull glanced at the clock and decided to call it a day. The rest of the team had left at six, due back in at six tomorrow when they'd hear what the phone number had turned up in the data searches. Unable to settle, Minshull had kept going, hoping a quiet office might aid his search.

He had forgotten about Anderson.

Just as he was leaving his desk, Anderson's office door opened and the detective inspector walked over. This was the last thing Minshull wanted, given the frustrations of the day and his ever-present suspicion that Anderson was out for his neck.

'Ah, Minshull, glad I caught you.'

Minshull stared at his superior officer. 'Can it wait? I was just leaving…'

'Oh relax, Rob. I don't want to fight you.'

'But you're checking up on me.'

'I am not.' Anderson gave a sigh and Minshull saw how tired his boss was. 'Do you honestly think I've made it my sole aim in life to make yours a misery?'

He was joking but Minshull couldn't answer. After the dressing down Anderson had meted out earlier, he wasn't so sure. 'No, Guv.'

Anderson sat on the edge of a desk and shook his head. He said nothing, the silence making Minshull uncomfortable. Was this something they taught people in the force at a certain age, he wondered? Wherever Anderson had learned it, Minshull's father had evidently received the same training, years before.

Finally, he spoke.

'Fancy a pint?'

Minshull stared at his superior. 'What?'

'A pint, Minshull. You know, alcohol? From a *pub*.'

'Well, I—'

'Rob. This isn't an attempt to trip you up, ambush you or implicate you in any way. Believe me, I am not that devious. It's been a bastard of a day, I'm sick of fighting and I fancy a pint. I am simply asking you if you'd like to join me. And I'm paying – unless you feel that's a conflict of interest too?'

'Yes, okay.' Minshull scrabbled to pack away every prejudice Anderson had just correctly identified.

'Excellent. Let's go.'

As they emerged into the early evening sun and walked down the street from the police station, Minshull stole glances at his superior. The move was out of character, that was for certain, but could Anderson's invitation for a drink be as simple as he claimed? Minshull knew the stories of Anderson from older colleagues who remembered the lengths he would go to in order to secure the outcome he wanted. Years and experience may have mellowed him since, but did you ever really lose the instinct?

The Green Dragon was slowly filling up with locals as they entered, the portly landlord – a former DS seven years retired from the job – giving them a nod.

'Gentlemen.'

'How's business, Rog?'

Roger Sutton shrugged. 'Perked up some since the hacks descended. Keep this up and the brewery'll make me landlord of the month. What you having?'

'Two pints of Gatekeeper,' Anderson returned, not waiting to see what Minshull wanted.

Fine by me. Let's get this over with.

He'd promised himself a curry and the UEFA cup game on Sky this evening – if he was quick here he might still manage it. Kick-off was eight p.m. A surreptitious check of his watch revealed just over forty minutes to spare.

'Don't you listen to the crap the rags are printing, lad,' Roger Sutton said, as he handed Minshull his pint. 'Bollocks-pedlars, the lot of 'em. You follow your nose, just like your old man did.'

Minshull received the advice in the spirit it was intended, aware as ever of the thick thud of disappointment it caused within him. Did the whole of Suffolk subscribe to the legend of John Minshull? 'Thanks. I'll try.'

'Salt of the earth, Rog is,' Anderson said as they settled at a table near an old fireplace. 'Shocking what happened to him. Fifty-one years old, sudden heart attack and pensioned off before his feet could touch the ground. Became a copper when he was nineteen. Some golden handshake.'

'Like my old man,' Minshull offered, before his superior could refer to it. Over the years he'd learned pre-empting mentions of his father was by far the less painful option.

'Pensioned before his time, eh?'

'Retired at fifty-four. Wasn't heart trouble, but serious enough for the force to get rid.' He could still remember the day his father received news of the South Suffolk Constabulary's decision – the first time he'd ever seen his old man cry. Back then, as a teenager, he'd sworn he'd never become a policeman, having seen how the job had scarred and beaten John Minshull into a cynical, bitter, half-man. So much for *that* resolution…

Anderson picked at the frayed edges of a beer mat. 'Rog is right, you know. We can't let the press get to us. They want a result right away, good or bad – they don't care if the child is found alive or dead. If they can't find a story, they'll concoct one. And we're in the firing line because Joe Public thinks our business is all cops and robbers, like TV detectives always getting a successful outcome. They expect us to win – and when we don't, we're a target.'

'Is this meant to make me feel better?'

Anderson sighed. 'I doubt it, but I want my lame attempt noted for the record.'

'We've just got to hope the phone search turns up something.' Was he pushing his luck mentioning it now?

Anderson didn't rise to it. 'I know.'

'What about Dr Lael?'

'What about her?'

'Do you think she can actually hear all that stuff?'

'Do you?'

Minshull stared at the bubbles breaking the thick white foam layer at the top of his pint. 'I really want to. She doesn't seem the sort to make it up. But I don't know her enough to say that for certain. I can't fault her results, though. What she got for us today could be crucial.'

'It could. I think she's our edge, even if none of it will stand up in court.' Anderson leaned over his half-drained glass. 'My advice? Get to know her. As soon as you can. I've no idea if what she says is correct, but it makes me feel a heck of a sight happier knowing she thinks Hannah Perry's alive.'

'It's just – I worry we may be asking too much of her. Dave thinks it's all affecting her. And I know I got carried away with the stalking stunt. It just felt like she's our only weapon.'

'Yeah, I get that. In so many ways, we're still acting blind, Rob, I'll be honest. I don't like being here – and I've been *here* before.'

Minshull dared to look his superior in the eye and what he saw made his blood chill. Pure, ugly fear. He looked away.

'I've arranged to meet Cora tomorrow morning, away from the station. You okay with that?'

Anderson looked tired. 'Sure. Do what you have to.'

Chapter Thirty-Seven

Cora

Cora shivered in the draughty lobby of Ipswich Town Hall and wished she'd brought a coat. Outside the weather was unseasonably warm, but the marble-pillared vault in which she stood had yet to be informed, preferring instead the deep-bone chill of a mausoleum. Cora hadn't been here for years, the last time on an art trip from sixth-form college to visit an exhibition. It had been cold then, too.

Why had Minshull asked to meet her away from the station? She didn't particularly like the barely hidden scrutiny of the CID team but she was beginning to feel she had a right to be there. This was outside her comfort zone entirely.

She shifted position and tried to drum back feeling into her toes.

The smell of coffee wafted through from the café beyond the carved oak double doors to her left, but Cora resisted its siren call. It was packed in there, anyway, the rumble of loud conversation echoing out into the lobby. Across the other side of the space, identical doors revealed the bustle of a gift shop.

'Can I help?' a bright-smiled woman behind the reception desk asked. She'd been watching Cora since she'd arrived, head bobbing up over other visitors' shoulders as she assisted them.

'I'm meeting someone,' Cora replied, glancing at the LED screen behind the receptionist to check the time. Minshull had said eleven-thirty, but it was almost midday. 'He's late.'

The receptionist raised her eyes to the ornate plaster ceiling high above. 'Aren't they always? I'd say grab a seat in the café, love, but we've a tour party just arrived and it's standing room only. You're welcome to take a pew on the steps, if you need to sit?'

'Thanks.'

Cora turned to the elegant stone staircase interrupted four steps up by a marble landing leading off to the right. Perching on the edge of the third step, she checked her phone. Where was he? Her message inbox was empty. Nothing new had been sent since a text from Daniel reminding her to film her video diary, sent late last night.

Frustrated, she threw the phone back into her bag. He had five more minutes. If he didn't show by then, she was leaving.

Such a waste of time.

Her head snapped upright as a male voice barked at her. A man taking the stairs to the upper galleries hurried on and Cora retraced his steps to see a crumpled till receipt on the lobby floor. She *had* to learn to be better prepared in public places. Insignificant objects could shake her far worse when she wasn't mindful. At least the situations she was being brought into through her work with the police seemed to be easier to control. In her few visits to the CID office she had quickly identified where all the wastepaper bins were located beneath the desks in CID and had already learned to avoid DC Evans' workspace around lunchtime, when foul-voiced obscenities tumbled from his desk with every piece of litter that dropped and missed the bin.

'Cora, I'm so sorry,' Minshull called, jogging across the polished marble towards her. 'Unexpected delay at the office. Shall we?' He jabbed a thumb over his shoulder in the direction he'd just come.

'But I thought we were meeting here?' she asked, confused. 'In the café?'

'Meeting, yes. Staying, no. I noticed three journalists come in here before I did. They don't know who you are but they're already keeping tabs on me. Can't afford to talk in a place this – liable to echoes.' A glimmer of a smile passed across his face. 'Follow me. I know a different way out.'

Cora had seen detectives in TV dramas flashing their warrant cards to gain access to places but she didn't think it happened in real life. Minshull headed up to the landing on the stone steps and pulled his warrant card from his jacket pocket, nodding his thanks as the security guard beside the onward rise of the staircase opened a roped-off area leading to a narrow, wood-panelled corridor.

'I didn't know you could do that,' she said, as they passed offices and continued towards a fire exit. 'The warrant card thing.'

'Ah. Well, I have confession to make. Eric is an old school friend and he used to let me down this passage when I was in a hurry to get to work. It's quicker from the bus stop through this building than to try to go around it. I buy him a pint now and then in return.'

'Never had you down as a bent copper,' Cora said, the joke awkward on her lips.

It appeared to surprise Minshull, too, who glanced back as if he wasn't sure he'd heard her correctly. 'Right. I'm not, by the way.'

'I didn't think you— don't worry about it. Where are we going?'

'To a bookshop across the street.'

'A bookshop?' Was Minshull giving her an unwanted tour of Ipswich?

'It has a couple of tables upstairs that just about qualifies as a café. If anyone tried to follow us up there, we'd spot them immediately.' He shook his head as they crossed the street together. 'Another friend from school owns it, actually. One more misdemeanour to chalk up on my charge sheet, eh?'

The bookshop café was the smallest Cora had seen, with only two tables that had two chairs each. It was nestled in the eaves of the narrow building, with an old school teachers' desk acting as both cake display cabinet and service counter. Beneath them a cramped second-hand bookshop offered its wares from floor-to-ceiling shelves behind a single window so unassuming Cora must have walked past many times without ever realising it was there.

They were alone here, served with tea and thick slices of homemade chocolate cake by Griff, the detective's bearded hipster friend.

'Why are we meeting away from the station?' Cora's question couldn't be contained any longer. She was uncomfortable here, out of control in an unfamiliar place. The shelves had screamed at her as she'd entered the shop and it was all she could do not to fall under the weight of the voices. Thankfully, Minshull had walked ahead, missing the devastating effect the bookshop was having on his companion. In the café, all was still and Cora was finally able to breathe. But the prospect of walking out later was already twisting her gut.

Minshull sighed. 'I'm sorry, I should've explained. I think you have a great deal to bring to this case but I'm aware that being in the full gaze of the team when you have to inspect a package isn't the easiest situation – for you or them. My team are understandably sensitive right now. Everybody is working on top of everyone else and tempers are short. Not everyone agrees with your involvement. I guess you're probably aware of that already.'

It was nothing new. Cora shrugged off his concern. 'I'm used to it. Once people know about me they take a step back. I don't expect them to understand.'

'I'm sorry.' His eyes were very still as he looked at her. Cora smiled, hoping to avoid the scrutiny.

'There's no need to be. So why are we here?'

'The man you followed yesterday, Shaun Collins? Did you get any sense of Hannah from being close to him?'

'No.'

'Are you sure?'

'I'm sure. He was angry and there was something he thought someone had told people about that he didn't want them to know, but I didn't hear Hannah. Why?'

He seemed to close in on himself. 'It interests me.'

'Do you think he has something to do with it? Do you think he has Hannah?'

'We always consider family members. More often than not there's a link.'

'Is he a suspect?'

Minshull shifted. 'We have a number of lines of enquiry that concern him.'

A shiver passed over Cora as she remembered the anger she'd witnessed in the man and seen first-hand in the café. 'I wish I had heard her. But unless he had something of hers with him I wouldn't have heard her voice. Proximity to someone doesn't seem to leave any aural trace. I'm sorry.'

He nodded. 'It's okay. How strong was Hannah's voice with the second deliv—?'

'As strong as the first. Stronger, even. More adamant.' Her answer overlapped the end of his question. She had been anticipating it and it occurred to her as she answered that Rob Minshull was the only person she could share this information with who would appreciate its gravity. Daniel never really heard what she told him, his mind already weaving theories above her head. 'Do you believe me?'

For the first time she saw the beginnings of humanity in his expression, a swift glimpse behind the professional mask so carefully fixed in place. 'Yes, I do. Absolutely.'

It felt like the most momentous commendation she'd ever received and the tears that prickled her eyes were unexpected. 'Thank you.'

'I think we can use your insight more,' he said, as if voicing his thoughts. 'How would you feel about visiting Hannah's house with me?'

It was a shock. *How do I feel?* But he trusted her: that had to count for something. 'When?'

'Now.'

Chapter Thirty-Eight

Cora

'Ms Perry, thank you for seeing us,' Minshull smiled as Hannah's mother opened the door to them, her eyes appearing to see straight through them both as they walked along the cramped hallway of her home.

Cora stayed close behind Minshull, feeling like an intruder. All around her the voices of the family called out from discarded toys, piles of dirty clothes waiting for the washing machine and takeaway pizza leaflets strewn across the laminate floor. She braced herself, tuning out each voice as she did every time she visited her mother.

'Have you had something else come back?' Ashleigh Perry asked, the act of lifting her eyes to them requiring concerted effort. 'Only the news people was sayin' there'd be more.'

'Nothing yet,' Minshull replied, and Cora noted how different his voice sounded when directed at Hannah's mother: softer, more measured, lower in tone. 'We're doing everything we can to find her.'

Ashleigh Perry stared back.

'Ms Perry, can I introduce Dr Cora Lael?' Minshull said quickly. 'She's an expert assisting us with the search.'

Vacant ghost-eyes moved to Cora. 'An expert in what?'

Cora stiffened, but Minshull didn't flinch.

'She has experience in this field,' he stated. 'Valuable experience. I wondered if you would mind Cora looking at Hannah's bedroom?'

'Why?'

'There may be something she can see that we've missed. Fresh pair of eyes and all.'

'It isn't just her room,' Ashleigh said, fiddling with the sleeve of her jumper. Cora could see a misshapen peak on one cuff caused by repeated pulling and twisting. 'She shares it with her sisters. Full of stuff. I keep telling them to tidy, but…' Her voice trailed off, reminding Cora of her mother's inability to complete sentences since her father died. The house felt like theirs had in the weeks immediately following Dad's death: hollow, stifling, crowded.

'We just need a quick look.'

Ashleigh's answer was more of a sigh than a reply. 'Top of the stairs, second door on the right.'

'You go up,' Minshull said. 'I'll stay down here with Ms Perry.'

'Okay.' Cora hurried up the stairs, flinching at the verbal punches and barks of the detritus on every step.

The door to Hannah's bedroom was scratched and hanging half-off its hinges. It had no handle, an ugly rough-cut splintered hole taking its place in the fibreboard. When Cora pushed, it flagged limply back against a stack of clothes behind, its bottom scraping against the once-lilac carpet and leaving a darker purple scar. Three loud voices screamed out in multiple versions from the piles of belongings covering the floor; two significantly younger and peppered with shrieks and protestations, and there, in the midst of the cacophony, Hannah's voice: clear, reasoning, secretly hurt.

What shocked Cora most was that she recognised the little girl's voice immediately. It was the voice from her recurring nightmares, the voice yelling defiantly from the clear police evidence bags – the voice she now carried in her mind. If she had ever entertained any notions that her mind had concocted what she had heard before, they were banished now. It was Hannah Perry's voice she had heard – and was still hearing. And Hannah *had* to still be alive.

While the girl's voice was noticeably quieter than those of her younger sisters here, it still sounded animated by living breath.

Out of respect, Cora didn't touch any of the items in the crowded room. Instead, she closed her eyes and turned her head in a slow, one-hundred-and-eighty-degree sweep, focusing on the changes in the voices that followed.

'*Mu-u-u-um!*'

'*Lily, stop it!*'

'*She started it!*'

'*Mine!*'

'*He can't find it here.*'

Cora's eyes flicked open, the sudden appearance of Hannah's whispered voice dwarfing the others. She moved her head until she located it again, bending over the messy, unmade bed and staring at the top left-hand corner. Should she reach behind the faded pink headboard where the sound was strongest? Cora wanted to find what carried Hannah's urgent whisper, but Minshull had said the family were always under suspicion in missing child cases, so did that make Hannah's room a potential crime scene?

She couldn't take the risk. Better to tell Minshull and let him look for it.

Cora pulled back and her knee knocked the edge of the mattress, dislodging a teetering pile of scribbled-on paper. As the sheets tumbled over, another voice appeared.

'*You see what happens? You want it to happen again?*'

Cora froze.

A male voice.

Angry.

Threatening.

And *familiar.*

Chapter Thirty-Nine

Minshull

Minshull had never seen fear in her eyes before. Not like that. Heaven only knew what Ashleigh Perry had made of the police's expert witness practically falling down the stairs as she fled the house. Thank goodness the FLO had been waiting outside for him to brief. He only hoped that another round of endless tea coupled with Ashleigh's current state of mind would sweep away any questions about Cora.

That kind of reaction he could have done without. Kate Bennett had been right when Minshull had initially mooted the idea: it was too risky. Why hadn't he listened to her?

Now, as they sat in silence driving back to the station, he rued his decision to take Cora to the family home. It was his own fault; he'd pushed her too hard, carried away by what she'd told him. He might understand her more than before but Dr Cora Lael remained an unknown quantity.

I just hope Ashleigh Perry doesn't tell Collins' sister.

He shook his head at a red light that pulled the car up short at a junction. Siobhan Collins had been mouthing off again to any hack who would listen about the treatment of her family: this would be dynamite for her cause.

What had happened in Hannah's room to cause Cora to freak out like that? She'd refused to say anything as he'd urged her into the pool car, past his startled team gathered outside. She was still silent now. Very soon they would run out of road to talk and he was damned if he'd attempt the conversation back at the station, where anybody could be listening.

As the traffic lights changed, he quickly indicated left, swinging the car off the main St Just road into the entrance to a drive-through fast-food outlet. He noticed Cora's knuckles whiten in her lap as he parked beside a dark blue plumbers' van, obscuring the car from the view of the road.

'What did you hear?'

She didn't look at him. 'I'm not sure.'

'I think you are. *Not sure* doesn't make you fly out of a house like that.'

'I heard her voice. It's fading from her belongings but it's still there.'

'That's great. But it isn't what scared you.'

She gave a long, slow blink, confirming his suspicions.

'What did you find?'

'I didn't touch anything.'

'I never said you did.' Heart racing as he saw his reply register in her expression, he tried a different approach. 'What *would you* have touched if you could have?'

'It wasn't – I didn't...'

So there *was* something. 'Cora, talk to me. I sent you there to do a job – whatever you heard, I need to know.'

She didn't respond.

'For the family.'

Still nothing. With one shot left, he went for broke. 'For *Hannah*...'

Seeing the way her shoulders stiffened made Minshull simultaneously congratulate himself and hate his casual mention of the missing girl's name, more than aware of the bond Cora appeared to be feeling to the child. So much of his job seemed to be emotional blackmail these days – and with every instance the lingering sense of his father's satisfaction at a job well done. He didn't want to operate the way John Minshull had for all those years; methods of manipulation he had too willingly employed on his own family when it had suited him.

'I heard the man you had me follow.'

'Shaun Collins – Hannah's stepfather?'

'Yes.'

The rush of adrenaline within Minshull was quickly tempered by the swift intervention of his common sense. Much as he would love Shaun Collins to incriminate himself, he had to consider that as Ashleigh Perry's partner and father to their two youngest daughters, his presence was bound to be in the house. Even if right now he seemed keen to avoid being there.

While Cora had been upstairs, he'd quizzed Ashleigh again about her partner's whereabouts. She'd been characteristically resigned on the subject, quietly explaining that Collins had chosen to stay at his mum's. 'We're just rowin' all the time. He said he wants to give me space.'

Space? What kind of a heartless thug left his partner alone with two small children to care for when her eldest kid was missing?

'What did he say?'

'I think Hannah's hiding something from him.' Cora's pale eyes were suddenly on his, her body twisting in the passenger seat to face him. Wide and wild, the shock of her full stare threw his concentration momentarily.

'Like what?'

'I don't know. The voice came from behind the headboard in her room. Left-hand side. Like it was pressed against the wall.'

'And Collins' voice?'

She paled even more. 'From a pile of drawing paper by the bed. Same side.'

'And?'

'He was furious. Much more than he was in the café. Raving about something happening – I think it was a threat, a consequence of being disobeyed.'

'And it scared you?'

She nodded, looking over his shoulder at the dented side of the blue Transit van.

'In what way?'

'I felt it, as if it were aimed at me. Hannah's terrified of him. She's hiding something, something that might belong to him, even. She knows it's wrong. And I don't know if he found out or if it's happened before...' She shook her head again, silver drop earrings shivering against her neck. 'I don't know where this is coming from, but I feel like... I don't know.'

Fighting the urge to grab her arm, Minshull leaned closer, willing her to tell him, all instincts on high alert. 'What? What do you feel?'

She inhaled a shaky breath. 'I feel like whatever she's done – or is planning to do – is putting her in danger. That's why I had to get out of there. Because I was scared for her.'

It wasn't concrete. It couldn't stand in a court of law. Anderson would disapprove and DCI Taylor would have his hide, but it was enough to convince Minshull. They *had* to bring Shaun Collins in again – and find a way to keep him there.

And they had to find what Hannah had hidden.

Chapter Forty

Cora

'Right.' DS Minshull's hand was on the car door handle, ready to leave, but he turned back. 'And you definitely didn't touch anything?'

'Of course not. I told you.'

'Yeah, you did. Sorry.' With an apologetic smile, Minshull left the car.

The slam of the driver's door sounded louder than a prison gate, shutting Cora out from the world. She shivered in her seat. The aftermath of heard voices always shook her, but the effect of Hannah's was different entirely. It made the inside of Cora's head feel raw, as if it had been peeled and doused in saltwater. The pain was urgent, heavy, thrumming hard against her skull.

The voice had brought something else: a punch of emotion so tangibly real it could have been Cora's own. She'd had senses of it before, but nothing like this.

A splat of rain landed on the windscreen, nearly sending Cora out of her seat. *I need to calm down*, she told herself amid the still-reverberating echoes of the child's voice. *I need to master this.*

Before she joined the investigation, Daniel had suggested that she might find some evolution of her ability. 'We've studied to some extent, but always within safe parameters of what you already know. Experiencing it *out there*, with countless unknowns, may reveal elements you weren't previously aware of.'

Well, that was certainly true. With each new test of her gift, she was discovering new things. And, despite how she was feeling right now, part of her was excited to discover what else she was capable of. The previous parameters had kept her safe but also had constricted her: as if what she had experienced was all she could do. The possibility of more – however terrifying – was enticing, ultimately freeing. *If I'm going to understand my ability, I need to test it. I need to know what else I can do...*

Was her ability developing? Or was she projecting her own heightened sensitivity onto the voices in her head? Either way, it could change her involvement in the case. If Minshull thought she was unstable, he might ask her to leave. Could she walk away, now that Hannah's voice was resident in her mind?

She could see him a little way away from the car, pacing up and down the thin grass verge at the edge of the car park, head tucked against his mobile phone. He carried tension in his shoulders, his whole spine taut beneath his jacket. Was that frustration with Cora or the thrill of the chase?

Did he pity her? It didn't feel that way, certainly not like Cora had encountered with friends and family members who had seen her ability in action. Did she frustrate him? He'd been angry when they'd left Hannah's house, seething with silent fury until he'd parked here. But just before he'd left, Cora thought she'd seen a flicker of something else in his expression. Not understanding, not in the sense that Cora longed for. But recognition, maybe.

Daniel needed to know what was happening. Any changes in her ability she experienced while on this case should be logged for the study. And he would want to know, having facilitated Cora being part of the investigation. But was now the right time? He'd been so jumpy recently, the mere mention of Minshull's name making his tone harsh and his temper short.

Maybe she wouldn't say anything for now, just begin filming it in her video diary this evening and monitor her own responses over the next few days. It would give her time to think.

She *needed* time to think.

Chapter Forty-One

Bennett

Kate Bennett ended the call and stared at the team gathered around her in the unkempt front garden of Hannah Perry's house. They had arrived to meet Minshull for a briefing before being assigned interviews with some Parkhall residents who had confirmed building work Shaun Collins had done for them in the past. But Dr Lael's explosive exit from the Perry house had shocked them to the spot. The last thing Minshull had barked over his shoulder as he'd bundled the doctor into his car was to sit tight and await further instructions.

'Well?' Evans eyed her from over the top of his roll-up.

'It's totally nuts. He's lost the plot.'

'What did he say?' Was Dave Wheeler smoking? Bennett thought he'd given up years ago. She'd never smoked, but right now she could see the appeal.

'Dr Lael heard a voice in Hannah's bedroom.'

Ellis looked up at the first-floor window. 'She thinks Hannah's in there?'

'No. But something Hannah touched *spoke* to her.'

The team groaned, only Wheeler and Lanehan refusing to join in.

'Maybe it did.'

'Steph, they're grasping at straws. No way we should be relying on some psycho-babbling, self-deluded nutter to do our job for us.'

'Dr Lael's an expert,' Wheeler countered, but Evans snorted back.

'What in? Bullshit?'

'So what're we meant to do about it?'

'Go back to the room. Look where the *voice* came from.'

'All of us?'

'Apparently. So we don't miss anything,' Bennett nodded, although she didn't agree. Bad enough they were taking a charlatan's word for it. Sending the entire team to investigate was overkill.

Lanehan frowned. 'Can you get all of us in there? From what Drew was telling me there's hardly room for the bed.'

'Maybe we'll break a world record for getting in, eh, Steph?'

'Reckon we'll break something, Les…'

'Right,' Bennett said, taking control before the conversation drifted away again. This was insane but the quicker they checked the room, the quicker they could get back to the work they had come to do. 'Let's get this over with.'

'We're going to be laughed off the Parkhall,' Evans muttered, flashing a rueful grin at the astonished FLO as the team filed up to the first floor. 'Trooping up here like the bloody Keystone Cops.'

In the doorway, Bennett stopped. She'd seen the room before, but a second viewing made it no less of a shock. How were three kids meant to sleep in there? Hearing what others had said about Ashleigh Perry, Bennett was careful not to apportion blame for the family's living situation, but the cramped bedroom with its clothes-strewn floor and broken furniture made her sick to her stomach. No child should have to live like this – and no mum should have to offer it to her kids. But Bennett had seen similar in countless homes she'd visited on the Parkhall over the years. This was the worst, though. The mess. The smell of old sheets and sweat. The unmistakable stench of damp.

'Over there,' she pointed to the team, picking her way first between the piles of clothes and rubbish. Lanehan and Ellis followed, Wheeler and Evans remaining in the doorway, peering in.

Behind the headboard, Minshull had directed. *Left-hand side.* Steadying herself against the side of the bed, Bennett reached for the faded pink Dralon padded board that rested at an odd angle as if half-detached from the bed itself. There was little space between it and the wall, so she began to reach behind it, palm flat and fingers extended.

Over in the doorway, Wheeler leaned in. 'Anything?'

'There isn't a lot of room,' Bennett grimaced, pushing down as far as she could, her fingers sweeping the space for any object. She forced her shoulder up against the wall, head knocking against the clammy plasterboard, the edge of the broken chest of drawers beside the bed cutting into her hip.

'Could we pull the bed back?' Ellis asked. 'Make it easier to get behind?'

Wheeler bent down near the end of the bed, pushing aside some of the floor piles to inspect the legs. 'I wouldn't try it. Whole thing's on the *huh*. Those little 'uns can't do without their bed tonight.'

'Can you get any lower, Kate?' Lanehan asked.

'I – I don't think so.'

'That's because there's nothing there! This whole charade is a joke.'

Pressed against the wall, Bennett gritted her teeth. 'Not helpful, Les.'

'If there was something there, you would have found it. If the kid put it there, they'd've pushed it near the top. Little arms, Kate. Little body.'

'Wait a minute, that's it!' An eight-year-old could reach further down if she'd maybe climbed onto the chest of drawers instead of having to lean across it as Bennett was. Glancing at the team, she pulled her arm back. 'Drew, reckon you could get further down behind there than me?'

Ellis shrugged. 'Possibly. My arms are longer than yours.'

Quickly, they shuffled places, a strange wobbling dance as their feet waded through the thick tide of clothes on the floor. Bennett and her colleagues watched as Ellis swung his knee up onto the drawers, pivoting his weight from his back foot so that the pressure of his shoulder against the wall allowed his arm to drop down behind the headboard.

'Whereabouts do we think it is?'

'All Minsh said was left-hand side. So as far down as you can reach?'

Ellis nodded, screwing up his eyes as he concentrated. He shifted position twice, each time edging a tiny bit lower.

Bennett watched, uncertain now what she wanted to happen. She'd agreed with the team that it was a crazy idea, but what if Dr Lael was right? What if…?

'I got something! If I can just get a hold on it…'

Ellis seemed to be grappling behind the bed now. Instinctively, Bennett and Wheeler lunged for the headboard on either side of the bed, yanking it back as far as they could.

'Got it!' The young DC edged his arm out of the small space until a small bundle emerged.

Even Evans leaned in now, straining to watch. 'What you got?'

Ellis pulled a grubby white scrunchie-type hairband from round the bundle, peeling back the layers of a faded lilac T-shirt to reveal a small, black rectangular object. 'It's a notebook.'

'Pass it here.' Bennett held out her hand, but Ellis ignored it, his fingers already opening the book.

'*Bloody hell…*'

'What is it?'

Ellis looked up. 'Lists. Dates. Times. Amounts.' He held up the open pages. 'And *names*.'

'Lending book,' Evans breathed, uncharacteristically awed. 'Collins has previous for loan-sharking.'

Bennett turned to him. 'That's what you reckon this is?'

He nodded. 'Seen 'em before. Sharks record everything but it's the first thing they ditch when we get there.'

'You reckon Collins hid it?'

'Dr Lael heard Hannah's voice there, not her stepdad's,' Wheeler said.

Bennett's mind was whirring now, possibilities and theories sparking as she stared at the notebook. 'If Hannah hid it and Collins was mad enough…'

'Or someone in this book wanted revenge,' Lanehan said. 'Taking the loan shark's kid would be a great way to kick him.'

Bennett was already on the mobile, gesturing to Ellis for the notebook. This was *huge*. It could blow the case apart and everyone in the room knew it.

'Sarge, we got it. A lending notebook, we think.' She held the phone from her ear and grinned at her colleagues as Minshull's loud expletive pierced the air. 'I reckon he's happy.'

Chapter Forty-Two

Anderson

Rosalyn wouldn't approve.

Anderson thought of the lovingly made meals in the freezer at home, each one labelled with his wife's beautiful handwriting. He was a *bad* husband. The liquid dinner on the bar before him didn't fit the bill for the healthy eating kick they had been following since January; neither would the pastry-heavy pub pie that would surely follow. But the house had become too quiet in Ros's absence and this evening Anderson needed the buzz of voices to help his mind rest.

'Here she is, the hero of the hour,' the landlord grinned, wiping a pool of spilt beer from the bar.

Anderson turned to see Jan Martin from the *Argus* walking in.

'Cheers, Eddie,' she said, shrugging off her coat and dropping it in a heap on the floor as she perched on a bar stool.

'My Marnie loved seeing you on the six o'clock news. Said you had your posh London voice on.'

'Closest Jan's ever been to London is watching *EastEnders*,' laughed a ruddy-faced man leaning on the corner of the bar.

Jan shook her head. 'You should know, Sam. Only your missus told me you prefer that *Made in Chelsea* lot.'

A raucous snort of laughter went up from the gathered locals.

'Never mess with the press, bor,' Eddie smirked. 'They'll have you. Usual, is it, Janice?'

'Please, darlin'. Feel like I've earned this today.'

The barman nodded in Anderson's direction. 'You and him both, by the looks of it.'

Jan smiled. 'Hey, Joel.'

'Jan. Bit of a day, eh?'

'Yup. I'm exhausted.'

'I saw your piece on *Newsnight* last night,' Anderson ventured, observing the editor over his pint. 'Appreciate your support.'

'Well, it's become such a feeding frenzy lately, I wanted to counter it. You feel you're any closer?'

'We have some strong leads I'm confident will bear fruit. Beyond that – you know.'

Jan rolled her eyes. 'It's all right, I'm not digging.'

'You are, but I'll let it pass.'

'Well, I appreciate it. Heard anything more from Ros? I heard her mum's on the mend?'

'Hopefully back next week,' Anderson replied. *It can't come fast enough.* He'd seen enough marriages crack under the pressure of supporting the force, but he and Ros were different. They'd weathered many storms and always emerged stronger. He didn't crow about it at work – too many broken hearts there to take offence – but it was a source of great personal pride that his marriage was where he found his strength. Ros was incredible. She'd seen him at his worst, when his mind was broken and his body shattered. When all he could do was drag himself across the carpet, she met him on the floor and helped him stand. She'd borne her own pain with his – the baby she'd miscarried three weeks before Matthew Cooper's disappearance and the ectopic pregnancy that robbed her of another chance for a child and very nearly cost her life. They'd still been coming to terms with it when the Cooper case met its bloody, brutal end – and the loss of a boy they hardly knew became the catalyst for Anderson's breakdown. He hadn't been able to save their unborn child; he'd barely been able to save his wife; and now the blood of a ten-year-old boy was on his hands. It was too much to bear. But Ros had found strength from somewhere that to this day Anderson couldn't fathom. And she had breathed for them both.

He needed her to come home now. Signs of the old beast were returning – the urge to cry for no reason, when before his breakdown Anderson could count on one hand the times he'd wept; the siren call of a whisky bottle every night before bed; the slew of Post-it notes on every wall in the house, reminding him to do the simplest tasks which seemed to slip his mind. Ros was his anchor in these times – but he needed to see her, physically hold onto her, for her magic to fully work.

'I bet your place is a tip,' Jan grinned. 'If you're anything like the blokes I know. Two minutes with the woman gone and the house looks like Armageddon hit.'

'I may have a little light dusting to do before she gets back.' It was good to share a joke. Another thing he missed in his wife's absence. 'So how's everything with you?'

'Well, Lloyd's doing my head in,' she shot back, surprising Anderson with the force of her response. 'Following me round the office like a bloodhound today. Honestly, I swear that kid'll be the end of me. Wants his thirty seconds of fame. *Vicious* about us supporting the police.'

'He'd rather be accusing us?'

Jan drained her pint glass. 'Naturally. Path of least resistance, isn't it? When you're young and an idiot you want it all but you're lazy. Follow the pack and you feel like a big shot. We've all done it. Thing is, it never lasts. The long game pays in the end. Shouting the same thing with a crowd doesn't make you stand out.'

'Are you certain you can trust him?' All of a sudden, Anderson could see what Minshull had said privately to him: that Lloyd Price was a loose cannon in possession of very explosive facts. If he chose to chase the big boys with what he knew, the consequences for Hannah could be unthinkable.

'No fear there, Detective Inspector. He's an idiot, but he knows he's onto a good thing at the *Argus*. He doesn't want to move to London or have the pressure of Fleet Street. Here he can be his own little magnate and when I go, well, the job'll be his, won't it?'

'You thinking of retiring, Jan?'

'I might be, when this is over. Too hard for me at my age. Last time I just about had enough energy to cope.' She must have sensed Anderson's concern because she reached across the bar and gave his arm the lightest of pats. 'You leave Lazy Lloyd to me, Joel. He'll play by the rules, you'll see.'

–

An hour later, Anderson left the pub. He intended to catch a taxi back home, the single pint he'd planned to accompany his pie having turned into three, but when he dug into his coat pocket for his phone he remembered it was still on his desk at the station. Frank Nolan, sole cabbie in the taxi rank beside the car park, shrugged his agreement when Joel asked to go to Ipswich instead.

'Makes no difference to me. All-nighter tonight, so better driving than freezing my ass off waitin' here.'

Joel grinned from the back seat.

It was a clear night when he waved Frank off by the station entrance, a bite of frost in the air as above Ipswich, brave stars dared to shine. Anderson remembered nights spent stargazing with his father in the tiny back garden of their home in Motherwell. They would rig up an old tent his da had rescued from somewhere and wrap themselves in scratchy wool blankets Ma kept in the cupboard under the stairs to watch the meteor showers. The Leonids and the Perseids: his father's favourites. On rare occasions they saw the Northern Lights from their back garden camp, too. No chance of such a sight over Suffolk skies tonight, Anderson mused.

Was it cold where Hannah Perry was being held? The thought made him angry. And scared. Dismissing it, he hurried into the comforting warmth of the police station.

The buzz of voices echoing down the corridor from CID was louder than Anderson expected at such an hour. When he walked in, a cheer went up. Stunned, he stared at them from the open doorway.

'What's this?'

'Party, Guv.' Bennett raised a mug of what Anderson hoped was just coffee.

'Ignore her, she's had a bit of a day,' Wheeler grinned. 'We all have.'

Anderson's head swam. 'What is going on?'

He saw the team exchange glances. 'We took Dr Lael to Hannah's house.'

'You did *what*? Did I not make myself clear to you last time?'

'But we've had a significant development, Guv.'

'Then why wasn't I informed?' he demanded, knowing full well why. If Minshull had sought permission, he would have refused.

'We were going to tell you in the morning. We didn't want to bother you unless we found something.'

'Bother me? I'm supposed to be in charge, however remotely. You run everything past me, that's how it works.' He observed the suddenly dropped heads of most of his team, turning his attention to Minshull who still faced him. 'What happened?'

'Dr Lael heard Hannah's voice in her bedroom, saying she'd hidden something.'

Anderson couldn't believe what he was hearing. Making Dr Lael stalk Shaun Collins was horrific enough, but taking her to Ashleigh Perry's home? When Ms Perry knew nothing of her involvement? And when Collins' bloody sister was shooting her mouth off to any journalist who'd pay?

'I don't care! You deliberately disobeyed orders. And roped your team in, too. Have you any idea of the trouble this could cause?'

'We found a notebook, Guv. Exactly where Dr Lael said she'd heard the voice.'

The fire snatched from his belly, Anderson stared at Minshull. 'A notebook?'

'It's his.'

'Collins'?'

Minshull nodded. 'His customer list. Or, more precisely, the one hundred and two people with most reason to want to get back at him.'

Anderson scrambled to make sense of it. 'Are we talking loans?'

'Same as before, only a much larger operation,' Evans said. 'By our reckoning, if they all paid back what they owe him, Collins could afford a nice little retirement somewhere hot. Not that any of them will ever pay enough to get their names crossed off that list. Not with the interest rate he charges.'

Now Anderson was wide awake, his mind sparking with the news. 'Any names we recognise?'

'A few. Shop owners in St Just, locals from Parkhall Estate. And a teacher from Hannah's school.'

'Miss Mills?'

Wheeler gave a slow grin. 'As if we would be that lucky. One of the male Early Years teachers. According to our interviews, Hannah never had any classes with him.'

'Do we know where he is?'

'Getting hold of that information now, Guv. We'll know in the morning.'

Anderson remembered the name Cora Lael had given them. 'Any mention of *Jack*?'

'First thing I looked for. No sign yet, but there are over a hundred names in the book. Maybe he's hiding in there.' Minshull offered him a brief smile, enough to make Anderson feel they may be on the same side after all. 'We're also cross-referencing all the names in the book with people questioned or resident in St Just around the time of the Cooper murder.'

'And so far?'

'Nothing. But we'll keep going.'

'Good, good.' Anderson's mind was somewhere else entirely, running away with the possibilities Shaun Collins' notebook might present. 'It seems Dr Lael might be invaluable to the investigation after all.'

'We certainly have her to thank for this,' Wheeler said. 'I doubt we'd have found the notebook if we hadn't known where to look. It was well hidden.'

Could Hannah have been punished for taking her stepfather's loan book? Collins certainly had form for violent outbursts, judging by his list of past offences. Was this conclusive proof that he had motive to harm his own stepdaughter?

'What do you think?' he asked Minshull, wandering across the room with his young colleague as the team returned to their celebration.

'I think this proves motive. Hannah takes his notebook – evidence of the extent of his money-lending racket – and Collins goes ape. Without it, he has no power; worse still, he doesn't know into whose hands it will fall.'

'Or any one of the names in the book could have a legitimate reason to seek revenge,' Anderson said. 'A group of them, maybe?'

'It's possible.'

'But how does that tie in with Matthew Cooper?'

'It doesn't. But the Cooper case is notorious enough that an individual or group of Collins' debtors could use it to scare him with.'

'And if his loan book has gone missing and Collins doesn't know Hannah took it, does he think one of his clients has it? Maybe this *Jack*?'

Minshull observed him. 'It's possible. We don't know. But the names in that book are our best chance yet to work out who has Hannah.'

'Do you think she's dead?' It was the question Anderson feared most, but now was the time to air it.

'Cora Lael is adamant she's alive.'

'And you believe her?'

Minshull's expression didn't waiver. 'I do.'

'Then either way this notebook is golden. If we can establish Collins had cause to fear retribution, it could add to the case against Hannah's abductor. Alternatively, there are a crowd of people in this book who can shed light on Collins' character.' He turned back to the team. 'Excellent work, everyone.'

'Thinking of staying, Guv?' DC Bennett grinned.

Anderson's coat was already on the back of the nearest chair. Going home could wait. 'I am now.'

Hannah

They tried to be nice to me today. Brought me a piece of cake in a bowl with tin foil over it. To keep out the mice, They said.

I wasn't going to eat it, like the inside of the sandwiches I've pulled out and left every time because I think the meat and cheese might have poison in them. But the chocolate cake smelled so nice. I was only going to dip my finger in the squidgy icing and lick a bit, but I couldn't stop. Now my tummy feels like it's stretching, like Mum's did when Lily and Ruby were inside.

If my tummy gets too big, I might not fit in the Small Space anymore. I might not get through the little door if They open it for me. So I'm not eating anything else They bring.

Besides, Them being nice was more scary than Them yelling.

I don't like being hungry, but if I think of the Bad Thing the Fear fills my tummy up and pushes the hungry feeling away. So when They give me food, that's what I'll think of.

I don't know why the name and number book is important, but it made Shaun really angry when Mum moved it once. I thought he was going to hit her.

I pushed it so far down behind the bed so he can't find it.

But what if Ruby does? Or Lily?

What if Shaun thinks they did the Bad Thing and not me?

And what if it's already happened and that's why They put me in the Small Space?

I pull my knees up and squeeze, trying to push the Fear from my tummy. But it won't go away…

Chapter Forty-Three

Minshull

Returning to work after only a few hours of sleep was usually a chore but today nobody in CID was complaining. The discovery of Shaun Collins' notebook had rekindled a fire and Minshull could almost feel the spark of electricity as he watched his colleagues work. Even Anderson, who, judging by the dark shadows that circled his eyes, must be nursing an impressive hangover, was throwing himself wholeheartedly into the tasks at hand.

Names from the notebook were being identified and called in, the interview schedule already impressive for the morning. A team had been dispatched to the Parkhall Estate to talk to several more.

In the airless box of Interview Room 3, Minshull and Ellis sat opposite a pale-faced man in his early thirties. Even in T-shirt and jeans, you could tell Gus Weatherall was a teacher. Clearly teachers and policeman shared that trait. Minshull remembered his mother's joke, whenever he and his brothers came over for Sunday lunch: *It's like none of you knows how to look casual. You may as well be here in full uniform. Die-hard coppers the lot of you...*

'I told you, I don't know the man.'

'Your number's in his book, Mr Weatherall. Next to a rather large amount I'm guessing wasn't a Christmas present.'

Gus Weatherall's fingers tapped out panicked messages on the desk.

'I'll ask again: did Shaun Collins lend you money?'

'It wasn't supposed to be much.'

Minshull nodded at Ellis, who began to scribble notes.

'How much?'

'I needed five hundred. For my car. The engine packed up and I needed to be able to drive to school. I live out of the village in Coombe Minor; there's no bus to St Just from there. Couldn't borrow it from the bank – my credit score's shit. I didn't know what else to do.'

'So?'

The teacher hefted a sigh. 'Bloke down the pub said he knew someone. I could have the money, no questions asked, and pay it back when the school paid me next.'

'Which bloke was this?' Ellis asked, looking up from his notes.

'I dunno. Chap at the bar. Landlord knew him but I never got his name.'

'Which pub?'

'The Plough, in Coombe Minor.'

'And he put you in touch with Shaun Collins?'

'Gave me his number. We arranged to meet in the park, back of the village.'

'So, what happened when you got your next payslip?'

'I paid it back. In cash, like he'd asked.' Weatherall's tapping hand closed into an instant fist. 'But he appeared at school a week later, while the kids were out for morning break. Beckoned me over to the gate and said I still owed him.'

'How much?'

'Another five hundred. Interest, he reckoned. I told him that was ridiculous, I'd paid him everything he owed and I'd signed nothing. There was no record he'd ever lent me anything.' He shook his head. 'He went away and I thought that was it. But when I left school later, he jumped me.'

'Jumped you?'

'I got back to my car and there was a Transit parked behind, blocking it in. I could see the driver in it, so I went round to ask him to move. Next thing I know, someone punches me from behind and I'm bundled into the van.'

Ellis gave a slight cough and slid his notes across to Minshull.

Same thing said in first two interviews.

Minshull acknowledged this and turned his attention back to the teacher, who was now breathing heavily, rubbing the sweat from his brow. 'Where did he take you?'

'No idea. Looked like an industrial estate – grey units, just numbers on them, no names. Bloke with him had one of those yellow hi-vis jackets on.'

'And what happened?'

'They kicked the shit out of me. Then he said if I didn't pay him money, he'd tell the school I was being inappropriate with the kids. Said his kid went to St Bart's and everyone at the school gate would take his word over mine.' He was visibly shaking now, eyes reddening as he stared at Minshull and Ellis. 'I can't lose my job, officers. It's the only thing that matters. Collins knows that. He can't know that I talked to you, okay? That man is dangerous. If you tell him, I'll deny everything. I'll take it all back.'

–

In Anderson's office, Minshull watched his superior read Ellis's interview notes. 'This is good stuff. Excellent. And you say it was mentioned in the other interviews, Drew?'

'Every one. Les says the bloke from the newsagent's on the High Street mentioned it, too. Getting shoved in a van, driven to industrial units, beaten up and threatened.'

'Did any of the others mention the man in the jacket?'

'One did, one didn't.'

'Did they give a name?'

'Not that I'm aware of.'

Anderson nodded, patting the notes before returning them to Ellis. 'Thanks, Drew. Are you back in there now?'

Ellis checked his watch. 'At twelve. Kate and Steph are bringing in another bloke from the Parkhall.'

'I'll let you go then,' Anderson smiled as the young DC left. 'So, could the other man working with Collins be Jack?'

'It occurred to me, especially if he's then turned against him. Knowing what he knows about Collins' operations, it could be a threat.'

'Could Jack have taken Hannah?'

Minshull nodded. 'It's possible. I've asked a uniform patrol to head out to any industrial units, estates or parks within a ten-mile radius. I'll hear back from them in the morning. And I'll call The Plough in Coombe Minor, ask to speak to the landlord there and see if he recalls who spoke to Guy Weatherall.'

'Right. In the meantime, we keep going with the names in the book. Find the rest.'

'Guv.'

Minshull stood as Wheeler entered. 'Yes Dave?'

'Something interesting. One of the names in that book turns out to be a friend of ours – well, *yours*, Sarge,' he nodded at Minshull. 'Ali-Akbar Faisal.'

'The kebab shop owner?'

'The very same. The one whose kid is in Hannah Perry's class.'

'*Shit*. How much has Collins got him for?'

Wheeler grinned. 'More than his business is worth.'

'Kate and Steph went there a couple of days ago. Hang on…' Minshull walked back into the CID office, Anderson and Wheeler hot on his heels. He picked up his phone and dialled Bennett's number.

'What's up, Guv?'

'Ali-Akbar Faisal, the kebab shop owner. What did you and Steph find when you visited him again?'

'Nothing. Well, he admitted his youngest son knew Hannah. And I asked to see the curtained-off storeroom you mentioned, but there were just stacks of crisp boxes in there.'

'Okay, thanks. How are you getting on?'

'We're on our way back with Mr McLennan from the Parkhall for his interview.'

'Great. Thanks, Kate.' Minshull ended the call and he and Anderson shared a look. 'We need to bring him in but I also need a warrant, Guv. Kate and Steph didn't find anything in the room I'd asked them to check, but Mr Faisal was very protective of his premises when we visited before. I'd like to check the rest of the building.'

The fight reappeared in Anderson. 'Do it. Ask him about his kid and Hannah and find out how he got in hock to Collins. Was the school the link? Mr Weatherall? I want to know.'

'Yes, Guv.'

'And if you find anything linking him to Hannah, bring him in.'

Chapter Forty-Four

Minshull

'I don't know this man.'

'With respect, sir, I think you do.'

Mr Faisal appeared on the point of passing out, a sheen of sweat appearing across his brow as he attempted to watch every uniformed police officer in his shop. 'You can't just come into my business and do this.'

Minshull held up the search warrant like a knight's sword. *Excalibur!* He could imagine his father crowing at the sight. 'We can, Mr Faisal. How long have you owed money to Shaun Collins?'

'I *do not* know this man!' He was fiddling with the metal strap of his watch now, eyes wide. 'I keep telling you, but you don't listen!'

'We have reason to believe you do.'

Minshull saw the fear and hated it. He'd seen it too many times in his career. Ordinary people, fallen on difficult times, made prey to scumbags like Collins – unscrupulous thugs more than happy to take advantage. Nobody should live in fear, but plenty did, and always would. Every community had them. Different outfits, different social classes, same opportunist bastards willing to bully and bribe and beat their way in.

He lowered his voice. 'Mr Faisal, you have nothing to fear. I'm not accusing you or your family of anything other than the misfortune of meeting Mr Collins. If you talk to me, you talk in confidence. You have my word.'

'And you will comfort my family with this when they find my body?' Faisal hissed. 'I'm saying *nothing*.'

'Sarge.'

Minshull looked up to see Wheeler beckoning from the stairs behind the counter. Leaving the kebab shop owner fussing over the piles of stock boxes being moved in the kitchen, he followed the DC up to the room where he had watched Hannah on CCTV days ago. The boxes Bennett and Lanehan had seen in the curtained storeroom were now moved aside, the space behind them revealed. A box of children's toys and a rainbow checked rug had been placed right at the back, a small portable TV on a low table beside them. Two beanbags sagged against the wall and a pile of paper covered in exuberant felt tip pen drawings lay nearby.

He remembered Mr Faisal's determined stance as he'd ushered them in that day – and now Wheeler stood in the exact spot the shop owner had occupied. He held up a clear plastic evidence bag, the contents of which made Minshull's breath catch.

The green covered exercise book carried three words between a snowstorm of sparkly stickers that made the blood pound in his ears:

Hannah Perry – ENGLISH

Hannah

I've found something. It was hidden away and I had forgotten all about it. But after They brought my food today I found it again.

Now my heart is beating fast. Not like it has been since I've been in the Small Space, when I feel so scared it jumbles up my thoughts, but like it does when Miss Mills is picking people for a play at school. Good. Exciting.

Only this time it isn't because I'm hoping to get picked.

It's because I just found *Home*.

I've been in the Small Space for so long that Home had started to slip away from my mind, and I was worried that Mum and Lily and Ruby were going to vanish forever. My bag is all I have and I've been holding it so tightly, keeping it safe from Them. But I just unzipped it and found Home there all along.

If I lean in, the teeth of the open zip against my cheeks, and take a deep breath, there it is. *Home*. It smells like dust and our kitchen after Mum has cooked bacon; book pages and pencil shavings. I would know it even if I had a hundred smells to choose from. It's the smell I can still sniff on my school jumper when I'm sitting in Miss Mills' class. And it's here now, in the Small Space, which has never smelled of Home before.

It makes me feel better. Like I won't forget Mum and Lily and Ruby. Like I might be able to go back there some day. And even though I'm squashed up in the Small Space and still scared the mice will come and get me, I feel taller.

But Home might not stay in my bag forever. Every time I open it a bit more escapes. So I've made an important decision. I'm going to just have one sniff each day. It makes me feel excited just knowing Home is there, safe. I don't mind waiting to smell it…

Chapter Forty-Five

Minshull

'I don't know how it got there.'

'You have an exercise book from a missing child's school bag in your stockroom, Mr Faisal. Found in a hidden space clearly used by children. The missing child is the stepdaughter of a man we have reason to believe you owe money to. A considerable amount of money. Can you explain any of that to me?'

'I don't know this man. Or this child.' He was lying now, his eyebrows so high in his hairline they might as well have been a flashing *LIAR* sign over his head.

'Your youngest son is in Hannah Perry's class at school,' Minshull countered, his voice as steady as he could make it given the surge of adrenaline within. 'Their teacher Miss Mills described them as "close friends".'

'I don't... I have no...' He coughed, the stale air of the interview room unyielding.

'Would you like a glass of water, Mr Faisal?' Bennett's question was impassive, a foil to Minshull's accusation.

'I – yes, yes, thank you.'

Minshull leaned over to the voice recorder. 'Interview suspended at 14:35 for a comfort break.' He nodded at Bennett and they left the interview room.

'What do you think?' she asked, filling a paper cup from a water cooler at the end of the corridor.

'He's terrified. It's obvious he knows Shaun Collins and a heck of a sight more than he's telling us.'

'But does he have Hannah?'

'I can't see it. He's too jumpy, too unreliable. Sweating like a trouper. Even if he was just harbouring her for someone else he'd have buckled by now.'

On the journey from St Just to the station, Minshull had allowed himself a moment to consider Ali-Akbar Faisal's potential as a child abductor. But his gut told him it didn't fit. Men like Faisal were never the aggressors, however much they might fantasise themselves capable of it. They were pawns in someone else's game, easy fodder for loan sharks, too consumed by their own failure to plan the downfall of someone higher up the food chain. The person sending Hannah's belongings back was cocky, sure of themselves. They wouldn't display visible panic in interview as easily as Faisal had.

But it didn't explain the presence of the exercise book on his premises. Had Hannah been there and left it? If so, when? And why hadn't Faisal seen her? Did he even know it was there? Forensics could check the belongings already returned by Hannah's abductor for Faisal's fingerprints but Minshull was pretty sure they wouldn't find them. Maybe Cora could pick up something from the book, but was she likely to only hear Hannah's voice as it had been left there? Maybe he would ask her, but for now it mattered to get the truth out of the kebab shop owner.

Despite protesting his innocence, Faisal was running scared. They had to get him talking about Collins – and work out how Hannah's book came to be in his shop.

By the time Minshull and Bennett returned to the interview room it was clear that Mr Faisal had sought the advice of his legal counsel. A different man sat opposite them now, a man intent on clearing his name.

'I didn't tell you about owing Collins money when you and your officers visited me because I was scared. He threatened my family. I have three children, Acting Detective Sergeant, two of them under ten. What else was I supposed to do?'

'And Hannah Perry – why didn't you tell us your son was her schoolmate?'

'I don't remember seeing her in my shop. So much of my kids' lives I am unaware of…' He looked down, embarrassed. 'But my wife Majida knows the child well. She said she's been a good friend to my son. Mahir had problems with bullies but the girl stood up to them.'

'Does Collins know Hannah and your son are friends?'

'He never said. My wife has only met Hannah's mother, not him.'

'Why is there a room hidden behind boxes where we found the book?'

'It is my son's den. Sometimes when we are busy, Majida brings the kids to work. They watch TV and play there while she helps me in the kitchen.' He paused to take a drink, the cup shaking as he lifted it. 'We put the boxes in front to make it a secret den. Mahir likes that.'

'So Mahir and Hannah could have played there?'

'If they were at the shop, that's where they would be.'

'When was the last time Hannah was at your shop?'

'My solicitor just called my wife. She thinks three weeks ago, maybe?'

Minshull leant forward, tapping his notepad with his pen. 'Three weeks. The week before Hannah Perry went missing on the way home from school. When we have reason to believe she would have walked past your shop. Is it at all possible that your son saw Hannah on the day of her disappearance?'

Faisal shook his head. 'No, that's not possible. My family and I were at my uncle's funeral in Doncaster. We didn't come home until the next day. I don't know anything about the child now or where she could be.'

It was as he'd suspected. Gut instinct proved, Minshull took a breath. 'Okay. So tell me what you know about Shaun Collins...'

–

Later, at home, Minshull pushed aside his half-eaten Chinese takeaway and leaned back on his sofa. It had been a frustrating day and in less than six hours' time it would start all over again. Leads had become half-leads, promising details demoted to the growing bank of circumstantial evidence that brought them no closer to finding Hannah. He wanted so much to bring Collins in – his first instinct when the team had found the loan book – but they needed firm evidence, as much as they could gather, before that could happen. He could so easily play his hand too early and lose any advantage they might have. Meanwhile observations continued on Collins so that when the time was right, they could act swiftly and decisively.

The evidence was starting to stack up now. Faisal owed Collins a little over forty thousand pounds, escalating weekly with the crippling interest rate. The inclusion of his name in the notebook hid eighteen months of intense intimidation behind the careless scrawl. Faisal's wife had confirmed that Hannah had lent Mahir her English book to help with a homework project two weeks before she'd disappeared. Mahir Faisal was distraught at the disappearance of his friend, but knew nothing that could help the police to find her.

One glint of light in the murk of information was a list of three names Mr Faisal had given which correlated with Collins' list. Faisal was certain he could convince these debtors to come forward – if that happened, they would have enough evidence to pin a significant charge on Collins.

Minshull's mobile buzzed beside him. He wasn't even surprised to see Anderson's name on its screen.

'So?' The impatient *click-click* of Anderson's tongue on his teeth sounded down the line.

'If we can bring in the other debtors, I think we have enough to arrest Collins, at least on unlawful money lending. If he has Hannah, that might get him to talk.'

'Bring him in now. Faisal's testimony is compelling enough.'

'We need more evidence, Guv. I want to be ready when we have him.'

More clicks, followed by a grunt of concession. 'Then keep going. Bring in as many as you can. I want everyone on this, Rob. Let's nail this bastard, soon as we can.'

Chapter Forty-Six

Cora

'So, how's it going?' Rory Jeffs asked, his gaze fixed across the sun-dappled lake as if trying to make out he wasn't bothered about the answer. But Cora already knew her workmate better than that. He would have been speculating on her absence, along with everyone else in the lab.

'How's what going?' Cora replied, playing along.

'Your secret project.'

'It isn't really a secret.'

'It's not jury service, either, is it?' The sparkle in Rory's eyes as he turned to her reassured Cora he wasn't offended. 'It's fine. I won't tell anyone. I just wanted to check you were okay. Not that I miss your ugly mug at work or anything.'

'Admit it: you're pining for me.'

Rory clamped a hand to his heart. 'I've set up a shrine in the cog psych lab.'

She'd missed this: the ease between them, the chats that required no deep analysis or further explanation. It was as much a breath of fresh air as the venue for their meeting. Sitting at home, where Hannah's voice appeared to have taken up residence, was impossible.

'But I'm guessing that's not why you asked for a catch-up.'

She held up her hands. 'Rumbled. I wanted to pick your brain on something.'

'My brain? Are you sure?'

'Only yours will do. But I have to swear you to secrecy.'

Rory's face lit up. 'I'm a thirty-nine-year-old psychologist with OCD who lives with a goldfish called Cyril. Who exactly would I tell?'

Sharing the details of her ability proved easier than she'd anticipated, helped by Rory admitting he'd sneaked a look at Daniel's study proposal and stumbled upon the section detailing Cora's involvement. She hesitated before telling him about the police investigation, though. Was it right to tell anyone else?

But waiting for the next call from Rob Minshull had been purgatory. Doubts had set in and coupled with the increasingly vivid dreams of Hannah that haunted Cora every night, she had begun to question everything. Daniel would dismiss her concerns in the way he seemed to dismiss all her questions at the moment – adamant that she was doing everything she could and shouldn't push herself beyond what they'd agreed. As far as he was concerned, the dreams were immaterial as they didn't involve a voice from an object, the prime focus of the study. Talking about the dreams and worries to the small video camera standing accusingly in the corner of her living room didn't help, either.

Talking to Rory was her only option. And the moment she began, her faith in him was proved right.

'That's incredible. The potential for using that is vast.'

'It is.'

He caught her expression. 'But?'

'I want to do more. So far, what I've heard has just convinced me Hannah's alive. But helping the police find that notebook – it made me think there must be more I can use my ability for. If I can push into it, sharpen it somehow.'

'Is that possible?'

'Subconsciously I think it's already started.' She twisted on the park bench to face him. 'I've been hearing Hannah in my dreams. Every night. And each time I feel like she's telling me more.'

Rory folded his hands in his lap as a flock of swans landed noisily on the lake. 'Do you think the dreams are real?'

'I'm not sure. They *feel* real.'

He gave a shrug. 'Vivid dreams aren't uncommon during periods of high stress. And the investigation is bound to have an effect on you physically and emotionally. It isn't a stretch to imagine it affecting your subconscious processes, too.'

'I suppose. Do you think I'm mad?'

Her question earned her a grin. 'No more than the rest of us.'

'That's comforting, but it's not what I meant.'

Rory extended his elbow towards her – a gesture she'd learned was his version of a hug. 'I think you're doing something amazing. And hard. And I think your mind, with all its quirks and strange depths, is working itself daft to keep up. If you're this aware of the detail of the dreams, maybe you should consciously listen for physical details when you examine an object for the police.'

Cora was intrigued. 'How would I do that?'

'Search me. This is your crazy brain at work here, not mine.'

'Rory...'

'Okay. Next time you hear Hannah's voice, push into it. Expand the area around it, like you're pulling it into focus. Listen for clues to the size of the space Hannah is in, the shape of the walls or enclosures, maybe try and sense where the light gets in, or how she is being kept there. I'm not explaining myself well...'

'No, you're right.'

Heart pounding, Cora let her gaze drift across the park. Sound was present in many levels, layers that increased with proximity. Behind the closest noises were others the brain chose to mute, as Cora did when too many object voices were present at once. What if she reversed the process? Instead of spotlighting each voice by removing sound around it, could she bring in other layers of noise, one by one, until a sound landscape existed around the voice?

An idea struck her. 'Could we try it now?'

'What, here?'

'Yes, in the park. There's plenty of litter around I could practise with. If what you're suggesting works, I can take it with me next time I'm called in.'

Rory jumped to his feet. 'Well, what are we waiting for?'

Chapter Forty-Seven

Anderson

HANNAH: Have the police lost their way?

Community questions missing child investigation

Anderson groaned. He threw the tabloid in the bin and picked up the next one from a stack of newspapers on his desk.

THEY DON'T CARE IF HANNAH DIES

Hannah's aunt slams police silence

'Oh, for crying out loud.'

'What's that?'

Anderson held up the offending headline. 'Is Siobhan Collins on a fame kick or something? How does that support Hannah? Or her poor mum?'

Minshull offered a sympathetic smile. It was a kind gesture, but Anderson was aware that was all it was. They both knew what the tone of the headlines implied. That they were failing Hannah Perry. That they had already failed.

IS HANNAH PERRY DEAD?

Our expert's shocking verdict

'Bastards!'

'Guv?'

'…"*Statistically the chances of finding Hannah Perry alive significantly diminished once the abduction passed the first three days. I don't think she is alive,*" our expert told us. "*In cases like these it is far more probable that she was murdered some time ago…*"… What kind of expert is he?'

'It sells newspapers.'

'It's garbage.'

Minshull stared back and Anderson kicked himself for saying too much. 'It could harm the investigation,' he said, more calmly. 'Speculation doesn't help anyone.'

What he wanted to say – and scream until the power left his voice – was that every misleading, speculative, sensational headline only added weight to Hannah's abductor's cause. The more the press pushed for a body, the more likely the bastard was to oblige.

'Guv.'

He lifted his head as Minshull turned. Bennett looked pale as she entered the office. 'Another package.'

He was already on his feet. 'When?'

'Just discovered. Left on the steps of the *Argus* office in St Just High Street.'

'Another one.' Anderson looked at Minshull. 'Call Cora Lael. Tell her a squad car's on its way to her to bring her in. We need her here, now.'

Chapter Forty-Eight

Minshull

The rainbow of pencil crayons in the small clear plastic wallet looked anything but loved. Some were shorter than others, the orange pencil chewed a little on the end. The plastic wallet was peppered with dirt, as if it had been stowed beneath a school term's worth of rubbish. They were certainly well used, even if it had been some time since they'd last coloured a picture.

The note hadn't specified a deadline or location for dropping off a ransom, but it had mentioned money. Minshull stood beside Anderson opposite Cora Lael in the CID office. He could feel the fear seeping from his superior, the presence of a ransom demand sending his stress levels through the roof.

Fifty thousand pounds and Hannah comes home.

Was this the final delivery? With Matthew Cooper, the only ransom demand had been for one hundred thousand pounds, shortly before Anderson's disastrous public statement, which led tragically to the boy's murder and the body being discovered. Minshull knew what Anderson was thinking, but it felt off to him. Why half the amount, seven years later? Was the abductor changing tack? Trying to throw them off the scent? Or playing it safe to win more time in the game?

Minshull observed Cora as she took the evidence bag from him. He was used to the routine now. Her deep intake of breath, the conscious steadying of herself in the chair before she opened the bag. She looked up at him and he smiled.

'Whenever you're ready.'

Nodding, she turned back to the bag and gently pulled it open.

Everyone waited.

Cora didn't move, or flinch. She stared down into the evidence bag and said nothing. Minshull watched her, willing her reaction to appear.

But something was wrong. Cora's expression said it all. Minshull saw Anderson's frown and moved a little closer.

'Dr Lael, what can you hear?'

'I – I'm not sure. Let me try again.' She closed her eyes.

'Can you hear Hannah Perry's voice?'

Cora took a deep, shuddering breath. 'No. I can't.'

The room fell silent. Minshull's gut twisted.

'Can you hear anything?'

'I can't hear her...'

'Can you hear anything else? Anything new, different, unusual?' He was leading her and he knew it, but her lack of response unnerved him. Were they too late? Was Hannah dead?

'Wait – I think I can hear...' She screwed her eyes shut, as if trying to decipher a noise several miles away. 'I can't be sure, but I think I hear a voice. It isn't Hannah's. It's a man, I think. A light male voice. I can't make out what he's saying.'

The abductor? Hannah's murderer? Minshull swallowed his fear. 'Listen harder,' he snapped, then added more gently, 'Please. This is so important Cor— Dr Lael.' *Get a grip on yourself! You know nothing for certain yet.* 'Take your time, please.'

'I can't hear what he's saying. But it's definitely a male voice. A younger man, perhaps?'

'And you're certain you can't hear Hannah?'

'I'm certain. She isn't there.'

Anderson swore. Minshull closed his eyes.

'But I can hear tapping.'

'What kind of tapping?'

'I don't know. Like a rhythmic click or a light tap – it's pretty regular and it's obscuring what the man is saying.'

Minshull stared at her. Then, an idea hit him. 'Wait.' He grabbed a keyboard from a nearby computer. 'Does it sound like this?' He tapped his finger across the keys.

Cora's eyes sparked into life. 'That's it! That's what I can hear.'

'Typing – of course!' That was why this parcel didn't fit. The belonging inside had no discernible link to the child, despite the pack of colouring pencils being a generic item that could be found in countless schoolbags. Ashleigh Perry had given them a list of the items Hannah carried in her school bag after the first delivery had arrived and colouring pencils weren't on it. It could have been missed, of course. The tone of the note appeared to fit that of the previous delivery, but the ransom amount didn't follow the pattern of Matthew Cooper's. Typing – a sound Cora had never mentioned before – plus the absence of Hannah's voice when Cora had always described it as strong, brought Minshull to a startling conclusion.

'Kate, who called this in to report it?'

'The young reporter from the *Argus*,' Bennett replied, checking her notebook. 'Mr Lloyd Price? He was insistent you saw it immediately and wanted to come back with Steph when she went to pick it up from the newspaper office.'

'I had to use my stern voice to stop him following me to the car,' Steph grinned. 'Nasty little git.'

Lloyd Price – the reporter harbouring dreams of running with the big boys in Fleet Street. The journalist who vehemently disagreed with his editor's decision to support the police. The kid who might do anything for an exclusive…

'Dr Lael, well done,' Minshull said, hoping his smile could convey the level of gratitude he felt towards her. 'Guv, want to accompany me on this one?'

As if reading Minshull's mind Anderson was already halfway into his jacket, his smile making a welcome return. 'With pleasure.'

Chapter Forty-Nine

Minshull

'I don't know where Hannah is.'

Anderson never took his eyes from the young reporter. Didn't blink. Didn't allow a hint of expression to filter in. 'That's not really good enough, Mr Price. You have delivered two notes and belongings pertaining to an abducted child. Your fingerprints are all over them. By your own admission you've acted without the knowledge of your employer. You've made it well known that you disagree with the *Argus'* support of this investigation and your editor-in-chief has told us of your determination to make a name for yourself using this case. All things considered, it doesn't look good.'

The duty solicitor shifted position beside Lloyd Price, his gaze resolutely focused on the briefing notes.

'No comment.' If Lloyd wanted to project an image of calm he was failing on a grand scale.

'Really, Mr Price? I would have thought it entirely in your interest to assist us with this enquiry, given the severity of the charge.'

Lloyd Price turned to the duty solicitor. 'Am I being charged?' His aide's shake of the head did little to calm his panic. 'You can't keep me here, then.'

'I have a whole day to keep you here if I like,' Anderson purred. 'And believe me, I'm not going anywhere.'

In any other circumstances, Minshull would have relished the sight of the smarmy upstart being reduced to a snivelling mess in Interview Room 3. But the strong possibility that Price had tampered with evidence worried him.

'Did you tamper with the note in the first package you gave us?' Minshull asked, aware of Anderson's slight flinch of surprise.

'What?'

'Did you fabricate the first package like you have fabricated this one?'

The duty solicitor's hand shot up. Beads of sweat appeared across Lloyd Price's brow and under his eyes. Minshull steeled himself. 'I'll rephrase. But I warn you, sir, you are in a very precarious position, as Mr Anwar will no doubt confirm shortly. My advice is to talk to us. Now. Before this becomes a criminal investigation.'

The wording was his father's but his voice was his own. If their only evidence of Hannah still being alive was now in doubt, they had no time for games.

'Did you take Hannah Perry from the Easter Market in St Just?'

'No!'

'Did you assist someone else in Hannah Perry's abduction?'

'No!'

'Do you know where Hannah Perry is being held?'

'No – I've told you – I have nothing to do with it!' Price's already squeaky voice was gratingly shrill.

'Then explain to me how you have *twice* been in possession of belongings and demands purportedly from her abductors.'

His nerve gone, abandoned by his swagger, Lloyd Price burst into tears. 'I made the new package!'

'Mr Price...' Mr Anwar placed a steadying hand on his client's shoulder, but the confession was already pouring out of his client.

'But I didn't make the first one I gave you. That was genuine, I swear. It just arrived at the office and I brought it in. I have *nothing* to do with that girl's disappearance.'

'Then help me here, Mr Price. Why – when, in your professional capacity, you were well aware of the stakes of such an action – did you deliberately falsify evidence and claim it as genuine?' Every syllable of Anderson's question served body blows to the young reporter, who had sunk so low in his chair that his chin was practically on the interview room table.

'I wanted a break,' he whimpered. 'A real break that would get me out of this craphole and onto a proper paper. Jan's lost her instinct – she just toes the line for you lot so she can keep you sweet for stories after this one. But I don't want to be like her. I want to write stories that sell newspapers. I just wanted a scoop.'

'So you fabricated evidence when a child's life hangs in the balance because it wasn't exciting enough for you?'

Lloyd Price had no answer to that. His solicitor looked on impassively as the young man broke down.

Reducing the reporter to tears was little compensation for the horror facing Minshull and his superior. The absence of Hannah's voice for Cora and the odd amount quoted on the accompanying note now made sense but it was another dead end. They were no closer to finding Hannah, or identifying her abductor. Lloyd Price had cost them valuable time: what had the real perpetrator been able to do while they'd been distracted?

Chapter Fifty

Anderson

Minshull didn't have to say a word. Anderson knew exactly what he was thinking. He didn't know whether to be pleased that they finally appeared to be on the same wavelength, or annoyed that it had taken a wee shite like Lloyd Price to make it happen.

They left the interview suite as Lloyd and his solicitor followed a uniformed officer down to the custody suite for charges to be read.

'Never seen someone sob so much,' Anderson joked, holding open the door at the end of the corridor for Minshull to pass through. 'I hope he's rethinking his career choice. No way he'll survive his current gig.'

'What that could have done if we'd assumed it was legit,' Minshull began, shaking his head.

'We didn't. We had our secret weapon.'

Minshull didn't return his smile. 'All the same, we need our guard up. If faking the package occurred to Lloyd Price, others could attempt it, too.' He looked up as Wheeler jogged down the stairs to meet them.

'Sarge. Guv. Jan Martin's at the front desk.'

Anderson turned to Minshull with a weary grin. 'This should be fun.'

If it were possible to dig a trench using only the repeated forward and backward motion of purple Doc Martin-clad feet, Jan Martin would be doing so now as she paced the waiting area. She looked up as soon as Minshull and Anderson arrived, her face a picture of embarrassed apology.

'Detectives, I am *so* sorry…'

Anderson held up a hand. 'No need for you to apologise.'

'No, but there is. I can't believe Lloyd could be so stupid! Whatever possessed him? What's going to happen to him?'

'We're charging him,' Minshull said, noting the widening of Jan's eyes at the news. 'Wasting police time. Believe me, we're letting him off lightly. It could have been perverting the course of justice. He needs to be aware his actions could have sent him to prison for a long time, not to mention further endangered Hannah Perry's life. If he's lucky he'll get off with a fine. If he isn't – given the seriousness of the situation – he could end up with six months' imprisonment.'

'Idiot.' Her curls bobbed around her flushed face as she shook her head. 'If it counts for anything, Detective Sergeant, I'm disgusted with him. I just phoned his mother. She's in bits. And that poor kid – what good does it do her? I'm horrified by his behaviour. *Horrified*. And I know you've been very gracious, Joel, but I feel responsible. He's been threatening to do something stupid for weeks but I just – I thought it was all hot air. If I'd watched him…'

'The mistake was his to make, not yours to police.'

The editor bowed her head. 'Thank you.'

'Will you fire him?' Minshull asked.

'I should. But if I did that the first thing he'd do would be run to the tabloids. It's safer if I keep him within sight, at least until Hannah's found. After that, we'll see. But I'll keep him in check, I promise.'

'See you do. For everyone's sake.'

Chapter Fifty-One

Cora

Cora shuffled her feet on the CID office carpet and wished someone would let her go. Minshull and Anderson had raced down to interview the journalist from the *Argus* but the last thing Rob had asked was that she stay until it was done, in case they needed her to qualify anything she'd heard. But that had been two hours ago.

DC Bennett gave her a polite smile as she passed Rob's desk. 'Are you sure you don't want another drink?'

'No, thanks.'

'Okay. Shouldn't be too long now.'

The clock above the whiteboard confirmed it was almost five p.m. Cora was stiff from sitting on Rob's unforgiving office chair and wished she could walk a little. But there was nowhere to go. Besides, Minshull's CID colleagues already thought she was weird. Watching her wondering aimlessly around their office wouldn't help their perception of her.

The scrutiny was becoming unbearable. Cora could feel their eyes on her through monitor screens and pages of notes, could hear their true feelings from the wastepaper baskets and piles of discarded files slapped on desks around her. They were warming to her mostly, it seemed, although DC Evans' bin still growled *Mystic Meg* at her whenever she passed it. But now Rob's colleagues were fascinated, which sometimes felt worse than mistrust. She mentally relegated concerns over their opinion of her to the back of her mind and busied herself with her phone.

I have nothing to prove. I've more than justified my position here.

When she'd first opened the evidence bag to silence, Cora assumed she'd failed. She'd practised leaning into the sound in the past few days since Rory had suggested it and this had been her opportunity to put it into action. But it had worked, hadn't it? Leaning into the nothingness where she'd expected Hannah's voice to be, she'd caught the echo of sounds beyond the item. She'd heard the ambient sound of the newspaper offices which led to the journalist's plot being scuppered.

When the door opened to reveal Rob Minshull, Cora could have hugged him.

'Hey, sorry,' he said. 'Went on longer than we expected. Thanks so much for waiting. Shall we?'

Cora acknowledged the mumbled goodbyes of the detectives as she walked with Minshull from the office.

'Have you found Hannah?'

'Not yet. But you were right about the last delivery being fake. Lloyd Price confessed to everything.'

'So he doesn't know who has Hannah?'

'No. He was so scared in the interview he would have told us if he did.' He paused by the door to reception. 'He wanted his five minutes of fame, but if we'd taken his delivery as genuine it could have proved catastrophic to this investigation. I know it doesn't feel like it, but what you've given us has really helped. Look, have you eaten?'

The question came out of the blue. 'No. Not yet.'

'Neither have I. Fancy something to eat? My shout. I'll drive you back to Felixstowe and we can grab something there?'

'You don't have to.'

A smile danced at one corner of his mouth. Cora remembered thinking he was incapable of smiling when she'd first met him. The change was startling.

'I'd like to. Honestly, it's the least I can do for making you hang around. Unless – you have other plans?'

She was tired and the promise of an early night in her own bed was more than appealing. But Cora was buzzing from her involvement in Operation Seraphine today. The chance to prolong the feeling was too good to miss.

'No actually, that would be good. Thank you.'

Chapter Fifty-Two

The pub was one of the better ones Minshull had visited in Felixstowe. It had been his idea to head here rather than trying to find somewhere to eat near the police station. Not too far to head home afterwards for either of them and altogether nicer being somewhere he wouldn't be anticipating meeting one of his colleagues. It made a nice change to be able to eat a meal in peace.

It was nice to be doing *anything* normal. Since he had started to work on Hannah Perry's case, every act seemed to play out under the scrutiny of his peers, the press, his family and anyone with an opinion on 'that poor girl from St Just'.

'So, what do you do when you aren't working?' Her light green eyes observed him, the easy smile she wore so at odds with her persona in the CID office.

'Sorry?' Minshull said, caught off-guard.

Cora laughed. 'So much for light-hearted small talk. I didn't realise that was a difficult question.'

'No it's not. It's just, I—' The realisation hit Minshull as he tried to formulate an answer. *It's just that nobody has asked me before.* Not his father, not his friends, or anyone at work. He suspected his sudden promotion within the team to acting detective sergeant, rather than a more usual slow upward progression through the ranks, was partially responsible for this. The 'what do you do in your spare time' conversation was one for police training college, or long hours walking a beat. But who was he kidding? Those years had been spent so consumed by the need to pass exams and progress his career, to prove his old man wrong, that he'd missed the buddy-building everyone else seemed to be so proud of. Besides, all the people Minshull had shared these experiences with were now posted across the country. No history, no familiarity. Come in at management level and you're never one of the lads – even to those higher up the ladder than you. Lonely. Isolated. Personifying the job. That was what was expected.

'I take it you don't get much free time,' Cora said, pushing an answer into the silence where he'd failed to reply. 'Especially not with this going on.'

She was trying. He liked her for that. 'Not at the moment. How about you?'

Cora shrugged. 'I like to walk.'

'Oh? Where?'

'On the coast, mainly. I like the sea.' The smallest smile appeared. It suited her. 'It sounds really lame when you say it out loud, though.'

'I used to walk a bit too,' he admitted, feeling the tension between them lifting a little. 'Or run. I still run, sometimes.'

She nodded, her eyes scanning the darkened street beyond the window they were seated in.

The silence returned, although noticeably less spiky than before. Minshull wondered what she was thinking. 'Guitar,' he said suddenly, surprising himself as much as Cora.

'Guitar?'

'I play – or at least, I did. Got quite serious about it in my teens.'

'Were you any good?'

'I played in a couple of bands. We even had an offer – back when I was about to go to college. Local record label wanted to sign us.'

'So you could have been a rock star?' Her amusement was gentle.

'I doubt it.' He smiled, deliberately pushing away the memory of the huge row he'd endured with his father; the incandescent anger he'd swallowed in the face of John Minshull in full, furious flow...

No son of mine...

It had hurt at the time. But then the job and the career he pursued slowly took its place. He was proud of everything he had achieved and was driven to do more. But what was there for him outside of work? He hadn't dated for over a year and even before that no relationship had lasted longer than a few months. He had friends, but nobody he went out of his way to see. Why hadn't he noticed that part of his life being edged out until now?

'I'd love to play.' Her gaze was full on him, cheeks flushing.

He found himself smiling back.

Was that an invitation?

246

Chapter Fifty-Three

Cora

Cora arrived home a little after ten p.m., her spirits surprisingly high. Spending time with Rob Minshull, away from the pressure of Operation Seraphine and the CID office, had been a revelation. Minshull had seemed as surprised to be asked about his life as she had been when he'd shared it.

From the first time she'd met him, Cora had sensed something behind his professional persona, an uncertain tension she couldn't define. Tonight, he'd mentioned his father – only in passing, but enough to make pieces fall into place.

'So why the police?' she had asked.

There had been that hesitation she'd seen before, as though he didn't quite trust her for asking. But he'd answered this time. 'You could say it was the family business. My grandfather, my dad and my brothers are all in the force.'

'So it's what you always wanted to do?'

He'd smiled. 'Not initially. I resisted for a long time. Didn't want my life mapped out for me by everyone else.'

'So what changed?'

'Me. I worked a few jobs after college – office stuff, telesales, nothing I cared about. But none of it felt right. So I gave in to the inevitable and joined the force. All through my initial training I was adamant I wasn't going to stick with it but, I don't know, when I was doing the job I found I loved it. It kind of sneaked up on me and hasn't let me go.'

'My dad was thrilled when I said I wanted to be a scientist,' she'd told him. 'Not so delighted when I said I wanted to study psychology, though.'

'Did he think you'd be a quack?'

Cora remembered Bill Lael's uncharacteristic lecture about 'head doctors and psychobabblers' and smiled. 'Exactly. He was of the generation that didn't trust psychiatrists. He assumed that was the field I was interested in.'

'Was it your – um – *skill* that made you want to study psychology?'

'It was.'

He'd nodded. 'I get that. When something's a part of your life it tends to make you an expert.'

It was an observation she hadn't expected to come from him, given how careful he'd always been around her. But the couple of hours she'd spent with him over dinner had challenged her view. He wasn't standoffish, or judgemental, just careful and a thinker. While others in his team – DI Anderson, DC Evans and DC Bennett – voiced their thought processes aloud, Minshull took time to consider everything first. In that respect he reminded Cora of her father.

She made herself a mug of tea and settled down to watch a few episodes of an American sitcom she'd found on Netflix, tired but not ready to go to bed yet. She needed to unwind, to allow her brain time to process everything that had happened today. The faked parcel had unnerved her, but ultimately proved her ability.

Halfway through the second episode, Cora was jolted awake by a loud hammering on the front door. She snapped on the porch light and saw a familiar figure shadowed through the glass.

Rain soaked into Daniel's thin jacket as he glared at her from the front step. 'Finally.'

'What are you doing here? I thought someone was breaking my door down.'

'Well *maybe* if you'd given me a key to this place I wouldn't have had to knock.' He leered down at her, his pupils not quite focusing, and made to step inside the house.

Cora crossed her arms, refusing to move. 'What do you want?'

'To see you, baby… Let me in.'

'Not when you're in this state, no.'

His smile contorted into a grimace. 'This is about *him*, isn't it?'

'Who?'

'*Minshull…*' He spat out every syllable. 'Is he here? Is that what you don't want me to see? Because I *see* it, Cora. I've seen it all.'

A hot rush of sour whisky breath assaulted her face. 'You're drunk.'

'Like you care.'

'Rob Minshull is not here. Not that it's your business even if he was. I am not answerable to you, drunk or not.'

'So you'd lie to me if you had to?'

What was he talking about? Cora could feel fury shaking her body but she kept her voice calm. 'I haven't lied to you.'

'Then where were you tonight?'

'Working.'

'And then?'

'I came home.'

'Ah!' An accusing finger jabbed at her. 'Liar! You didn't come home because I waited here for two hours and I would have seen you.'

'If you'd called me I could have told you where I was. But clearly the pub was more of an attraction.'

'At least I was welcome there.'

There was no talking to him when he was in this state. 'Go home. We'll talk when you're sober.'

'Don't play the high and mighty with me. I *know*.'

'Know what?'

'I know you were with *him* tonight. Because I *saw* you!'

Cora's breath faltered, the drumming of the rain on the porch roof briefly replacing his shouts. Had he followed her? Been spying on her? 'Where?'

'The Grosvenor on Ranelagh Road. Looking very cosy from what I could see outside in the rain.'

Cora kept her head high. It was a shock but she had nothing to hide. 'We had dinner. It was late and neither of us had eaten.'

'Are you in love with him?'

'No.'

'Liar!'

'I'm not doing this, Daniel. Go home.'

'Not until you tell me the truth!'

'I *am* telling you the truth! Why would I lie?'

'Oh, I don't know, maybe because you're sleeping with him?'

'Excuse me?'

'I saw the way he was looking at you. It's the look I see every time I look at this poor, deluded sod in the mirror. You can't deny it, Cora. He's in love with you...'

'No!'

'...and you're falling for him, too!'

249

'You're being ridiculous.'

'Cornered people always say that!'

'You're drunk, you're accusing me of something I haven't done and I'm not going to stand here and listen to this. *Go home.*'

He stared at her and Cora hated the mistrust she saw in his eyes. 'So, that's all you have to say? Because don't forget why you're in this investigation, Cora. *I* put you there…'

'You don't own me…'

'Yes, I do! You're *my* discovery, *my* project – not Minshull's!'

'Your project?'

'Not like – that's not what I meant…'

'Your *project*? I'm not a lab rat, someone you can prod and poke and train to push buttons! I thought you said you loved me…'

'I do!'

'That's not what love is. I am not your possession.'

'But you'd be happy to be his!'

'Go away!' She slammed the door and leaned against it, her tears finally allowed to flow. Was that all she was to Daniel, after everything they had shared? She trusted him, had opened her heart wider to him than to anyone else in her life, but all he saw was her ability. It was all *anyone* ever saw. How could she have missed the signs?

She could hear the thud of Daniel's fists on the door and covered her ears, willing the rainstorm to drown out his drunken shouts.

Chapter Fifty-Four

Minshull

It was just after ten-thirty when Minshull arrived home, but the tiredness that had stalked him earlier in the day was strangely absent. He had enjoyed himself this evening – something he hadn't expected when he'd invited Cora Lael for a post-work meal. He couldn't remember the last time he'd done that. The pressures of the job were usually sufficient excuse to avoid people after work and retreat to the safety of his place. It was a lonely choice made less so by box sets on Netflix or hours on his Xbox. He'd always preferred his own company, anyway. Easier to control. Fewer opportunities for people to disappoint him or place demands on his time. But not this evening. That was new.

Stumbling wearily into the darkened living room of his apartment, he looked instinctively at the far corner where a time-beaten guitar case was hidden, half-obscured behind the television and curtain at the edge of the bay window. It had been years since he'd last been tempted to open it. His single act of rebellion against his father, who had long ago assumed his son had sold the contentious instrument.

Why *had* he kept it? Sentimentality? Comfort? A passive-aggressive stand against John Minshull?

Without taking off his coat, he strode across the room and pulled the guitar case from its hiding place. The creak of its hinges brought memories back, the smell of old strings and polish rushing up to greet him like long lost friends as the case revealed its treasure. The faded gold faux-fur lining had worn thin to the backing threads in places, while one end of the carrying handle that had been repaired with black gaffer tape, was now fraying at the edges. Smiling to himself, Minshull lifted his pride and joy from the case. The weight was reassuring in his hands, his fingers finding the fret board as naturally as they had always done. Familiar and strange at once, he was immediately back in his childhood bedroom, barely fifteen years old, dreaming of taking music seriously. With no clue of what lay ahead…

Cora had made him think of this. He hadn't admitted his musical ambitions to anyone in years. So why now? Why her?

The answer was simple: because she had *asked*.

He would start playing again, he decided. But then he caught sight of his workbag dumped by the sofa and his thoughts immediately went to the small, terrified girl out in the rain soaked, chilly night, still waiting to be found. Minshull carefully laid the guitar on the sofa, his hand resting on its body for a moment before he looked away. Playing could wait.

Shrugging off his coat, he headed into the open plan kitchen to grab a beer. Then he returned to the sofa and pulled a sheaf of papers and a notepad from his bag. Clearing books and the remote control from the coffee table, he ripped out several sheets of paper, writing down what evidence they had, then laying the torn pages out across the table.

Plates were spinning, lines of enquiry converging, the team pressing in. But where had all that got them?

LOAN BOOK

So far, a little over thirty individuals listed in the loan book had been identified and questioned. Of those, fifteen had agreed to make a statement. Three debtors named by Mr Faisal in his interview were being checked by DC Evans when Minshull and Cora had left the office: he would find out what Les had discovered in the morning.

COLLINS

A tracking device – known as a lump – had been covertly fitted to Shaun Collins' van and his movements were being recorded. It had just been retrieved and the data was being extracted from it. Tomorrow they would have what they needed. Minshull understood Anderson's itchiness to bring him in, but it had to be the right time. The picture they were building of his illegal money-lending activities was close to being enough, but Minshull wanted a few more confirmed statements to be certain. He couldn't afford any chance that the case could fall apart for lack of evidence. He'd requested all the family stay within St

Just for the duration of the investigation and for the moment at least, Collins was complying. But time was of the essence and Minshull wanted to get it right.

JACK

The name Cora had heard from the note Collins had discarded was still a mystery. The phone number had been traced to a single phone mast, deep in the heart of the Suffolk countryside. A map search revealed nothing but fields there, linked by a small country road. Whoever was using it must be driving specifically to that location, only activating the phone once there. But why? And was the mythical Jack the one operating the phone? If not, who owned it?

FORENSICS

The reports back from forensics on the headband and school tie had found only Hannah's DNA. The exercise book carried Mr Faisal's wife's fingerprints which she had supplied on request and smaller ones they assumed belonged to Hannah and Faisal's son Mahir. Nothing else from any other person. Clearly whoever had sent the items to police had taken care not to touch them with bare hands. Another frustrating dead end.

COOPER FILES

A third of the boxes had already been checked and so far, no links had been established between Op Seraph and the Matthew Cooper investigation. To give Les Evans his due, he was pressing on without complaint and the progress they had made through the boxes was largely down to his efforts. There was no sign Shaun Collins had been interviewed at the time – but Minshull remained hopeful that the files had more secrets to give up soon.

HANNAH

Nothing sat below the notepaper sheet bearing her name. No direct leads. Nothing concrete to suggest who may have taken her. Collins was the nearest they had to a suspect, but did being a violent loan shark make him a child abductor? Or was one of his victims seeking revenge?

Minshull sat back, his mind taking in every thread, every possibility. They were closer than before, but the gulf between them and the truth still remained.

And somewhere out in the freezing night, a little girl was waiting.

Hannah

There's a gap. It's only little. I found it when I moved a corner of the smelly cloth I'm lying on. But when They left last time and I was sure They weren't coming back, I put my fingers in the gap. And it *moved*.

Now, if I lie with my head nearest the gap, I can see outside, like a little window. I can see the daytime and the night-time and it makes me feel closer to home. The wood around the gap is all splintery and if I pull it, it crumbles like cheesecake crumbs.

I'm frightened, but finding the gap has made my heart beat in my ears, like a drum. Nobody else knows it's there. It's my secret and I won't let Them find out. There's a strip of blue plastic down by my feet and I can push the edge of the plastic over it to hide the hole. Then, when I know I'm on my own again, I carry on picking bits of crumbly wood away.

It's scary to think of getting out of the Small Space. But staying here is more frightening than anything.

Chapter Fifty-Five

Minshull

The call from his mother was a surprise, coming as he returned from his first morning run in months. Since his conversation with Cora last night, he'd been thinking of small changes he could make to rebuild the non-work side of his life. Running seemed an easy place to begin. Pounding rain-soaked streets around Ipswich as the brave pink dawn broke over the town had been the best way to start the day. It cleared his mind, chasing away the fug of the last few days. Now home and showered, he had a few hours stretching ahead of him until he was due at work and he intended to make the most of the unusual rest.

Those plans were now rapidly evaporating.

'Come for lunch,' she offered. 'I've missed seeing you.'

'I'd love to, Mum, but I'm back in the office at three.'

'But you need to eat.'

'I'll grab something here.'

'I'm making a full roast dinner. My world famous roast beef with homemade Yorkshires and those roast potatoes I know you can't get anywhere else.'

Minshull smiled against the phone. 'Mum...'

But Fran Minshull was not about to be put off. 'Roast parsnips, too. And my gravy, which, let me remind you, is officially the best gravy in Ipswich as awarded by the town WI...'

'I really can't.'

'Your dad wants to see you.'

And there it was.

He'd been waiting for the summons and had been foolish enough to think he'd escaped. Of course he hadn't. John Minshull would have been studying every development in Op Seraph from his riser-recliner throne.

'I can't.'

'One hour, Robbie. That's all I'm asking. Do it for my sanity, please.'

Emotional blackmail was a Minshull family weapon that always cut deepest when deployed by his mum.

'One hour. Then I have to go.'

–

Approaching the 1970s semi from its regimentally paved path, Minshull swallowed down the familiar rush of nerves that transported him back to his childhood; memories of walking home from school already anticipating Dad's bad moods. As John Minshull's career in the force had ended so suddenly, being pensioned off when his health failed, so his expectation for his three sons had risen – and with it the pressure placed upon their future career choices. Rob's sister had been spared, largely due to his father's misogynistic view of women's roles. Given the years spent battling his father's style of policing, Minshull couldn't help think Ellie had the better deal.

His sister met him at the door.

'Just wanted to warn you, Dad's been watching the news.'

He groaned. 'Great. How much does he know?'

Ellie smiled and put a consolatory arm around his shoulders. 'Only as much as BBC, Sky and the broadsheets are saying. He's dismissed the tabloids, of course. But you know what he's like.'

Just over the threshold, Minshull halted. 'This was a bad idea.'

'It wasn't. And you're here for Mum, remember? She's missed seeing you.'

He conceded and followed her into the too-warm hallway, the smell of roast beef sending him straight back to boyhood. This house had always represented both ends of the spectrum: pleasure and pain, hope and defeat, pride and crushing disappointment. That his parents still lived here today did nothing to change that.

His mother had settled into her new role as grandmother as easily as she had played mum, despite her grandchildren being spread across the country with his brothers Joe and Ben working for West Midlands Police and Devon and Cornwall Police respectively.

But his father was still coming to terms with leaving the force, sixteen years later, even now fooling himself that he was one phone call away from reinstatement. As his frustration grew, so his demands on his sons increased. The Minshull legacy in the force was to be upheld at all costs.

Minshull found himself fiddling with the cuff of his sweater as he walked into the living room. His father, eyes alive already, rose steadily from his armchair.

'Here he is: mysterious leader of the Hannah Perry investigation nobody ever sees. How come that oaf Anderson gets all the press conferences, hm? You want to chat to Sue Taylor about that.'

'Hi Dad.'

'Sit down. Tell me everything you know.'

Sitting on the sofa, he felt the weight of his father's expectation bearing down, heavy on his shoulders. 'You know I can't do that.'

John Minshull dismissed this with a wave of his hand and Minshull noticed the liver spots appearing on it. 'Rubbish. I'm not just anybody, Robbie. Besides, things get back to me. You know how it works.'

Of course. 'Even still…'

'I hear you've no suspects. I hear that prat Anderson isn't helping. And who would blame him? The last abduction ended his promotion prospects.' His laugh came from a place Minshull didn't ever wish to visit. 'Serves him right. Jumped-up, pompous idiot. No balls. No grit. In my day he'd never have been in that job.'

Ellie returned from the kitchen with tea for her brother. He smiled when he saw his mother had chosen his old Snoopy mug. Always the peacemaker, smoothing things over between him and his father from the warm realm of her kitchen. Minshull often wondered what it was about John Minshull that his mother still could find endearing after forty-five years; what could make her endure so much.

'Stop picking on Rob. He's not in his uniform today.'

'He's a copper. Always in uniform, always on call. You don't stop being one just because you're in civvies.'

Ellie placed her hand on her father's cardiganed shoulder. 'Enough, Dad. You know what Mum will say.'

John Minshull shrugged. 'I have a right to ask. I want to know what he plans to do about this case.'

'What I want is *not* to talk about it!' Minshull put his mug down on the teak coffee table harder than he intended to, sending a flood of pale brown liquid across the surface. 'I'm sorry…'

As usual, Ellie breezed in to calm the storm. 'Don't worry. I'll fetch a cloth. Behave, Dad. And change the subject, for heaven's sake.'

Even moving to safer discussions of golf and Ipswich Town's prospects, Minshull could still feel his father's questions gathering in the wings of each topic.

'They need direction. I'm not convinced the manager's heart is in it. Don't like seeing my team let down by indecision. If there's one thing I learned from the force it's that there's no substitute for strong leadership from the off.'

'Dad…'

'It's just an observation, son. If the team don't know where they're heading all hell will break loose.'

'They have all the direction they need, trust me.' The edge to his reply seemed to hit the spot and John Minshull sank back into his chair.

'I do hope my boys aren't arguing again. This is supposed to be a lovely family meal, not World War Three.' The arrival of Fran Minshull brought all the welcome calm Minshull remembered from childhood. She sat on the sofa arm and kissed the top of her son's head. 'My beautiful boy, dealing with all this horror. Did I tell you how very proud of you we are, Robbie? *Both* of us are. Aren't we, John?'

'Of course. He knows that.'

'Well, then.' Fran Minshull exchanged a knowing look with her son. 'The meal's ready. Come through to the dining room but leave that blessed police talk in here, if you don't mind. I might enjoy watching *Line of Duty* but I don't want it as dinner theatre today, thank you.'

–

It was a relief to get back to work, Minshull's ears still ringing with his father's unsolicited opinions. Interviews with names from Shaun Collins' notebook were continuing, the weight of evidence against him growing by the hour. There was just one thing outstanding before he could bring Shaun Collins in.

An hour later, it came, hurried into the CID office by a flush-faced Wheeler.

'We just got the results back from the lump on Shaun Collins' van.'

The team turned to watch Wheeler cross the office to Minshull's desk.

'And?'

'Well, either he's got a nasty case of localised amnesia or he's making regular trips out to Long Deighton without telling us.'

'Long Deighton?' The small town was a good twenty miles from St Just – more than a stretch to support Collins' claim during his interview that he worked no further than five miles out of St Just. 'Whereabouts?'

'The industrial estate. Units 3 and 4, to be precise.'

'Great. Ellis, get the guv.'

'Sarge.'

As his colleague raced to Anderson's office, Minshull called up a map search on his monitor and, with Wheeler by his side, entered the co-ordinates from the sheets Tech Ops had sent. The industrial unit was small; ten identical units built on former farmland a mile and a half from the town. Around it fields stretched off in all directions.

'Odd place for an industrial estate, isn't it? In the middle of farmland?'

'Happens a lot these days. Farms going out of business too far away from town to interest house developers. Shoving industrial units on the site means the land gets reused, which councils like, and the greenbelt around it isn't built on, which local people like. It's a trade-off they'll accept.'

'Have we got him?' Anderson's bark sounded behind Minshull's head.

'We know from his loan book clients that he conducts his threats on an industrial estate. When uniform did the sweep of potentials, this wasn't in the search area. Too far out.'

'Could this be it?' Anderson asked. The hope in his question mirrored Minshull's own.

'It's got to be. Any idea who owns it?'

'No, Sarge.' Wheeler leafed through the report. 'It was leased to a steel components company three years ago but they went into receivership last February, all assets liquidated. It's unoccupied, as far as we can tell.'

'Where is it?' Ellis and Bennett had joined them now, all peering at the map on screen.

'Long Deighton. Know it?'

Ellis nodded. 'One of my mates from rugby lives there.'

Minshull looked up. 'You ever passed this place?'

'No Sarge, I don't go in on that road.' Ellis held out his hand for the lump report and Wheeler passed it over. 'What about Jack's phone?'

The question caused all of the team to stare at Ellis, who turned a deep shade of tomato.

'The mast that registered Jack's phone, wasn't it near there?'

'Hang on.' Bennett raced across to her desk, sorting through files, folders and notes. 'Shit, Drew, I think you're right.'

Minshull's breath tightened in his chest. 'Give me the location of the mast.'

Bennett read out the postcode and co-ordinates. Typing them in, Minshull zoomed out from the mast's position until the cluster of rectangular units came into view.

'Bloody hell…'

'Two miles,' he breathed. 'It's two miles from the units.' Looking up at his astonished team, he jumped into action. 'Dave, Kate, get down there. Les, call Support and send them, too.'

This was the break they'd been looking for – enough to bring Collins in for illegal money lending and intimidation – but was it the key to more?

What if Jack was at Long Deighton?

What if the calls from the mobile number and Collins' repeat journeys there weren't about money lending, but kidnap?

And what if they were keeping Hannah there?

Chapter Fifty-Six

Wheeler

Rain that had threatened the skies over South Suffolk Constabulary HQ all morning finally broke as Wheeler and Bennett drove out of Ipswich. By the time they were out in open countryside, it had become a torrential downpour. In the driving seat, Bennett switched the wipers to double-speed, leaning against the steering wheel to better see the road ahead. Out here was nothing but fields and sky, with weather-bent trees guarding the road and peppering the horizon. Sheets of rain swept across the landscape in ghostly waves and behind them charcoal clouds loomed.

Ordinarily, Wheeler would have made some quip about the weather being lovely, but today the urge to lighten the mood was lost in a tumble of questions, fear and weariness. Instead, they drove in silence, the only sound the thunderous assault of water on the roof of the car. The decision had been made to visit the location of the phone mast where the Jack calls had been made first, then continue on to the Long Deighton industrial units. The journey seemed all the more daunting for the weight of expectation now attached to both locations.

At a junction with the road that continued up and over a hill, Bennett turned right, following a narrower, twistier road through a dark avenue of trees. From above it would be completely concealed from view, the trees forming a protective barrier between the fields on either side.

'Just up there,' Wheeler said, pointing to a bend ahead where the road turned sharply to the left and the trees cleared.

Bennett slowed the car and carefully guided it to a halt in the closed gateway of a barley field. 'This is it?'

Wheeler checked the co-ordinates again. 'Apparently.'

'Right.' Unclipping her seatbelt, Bennett grabbed her waterproof jacket from the back seat and put it on, pulling the hood over her head. 'Come on.'

'I could always stay in the car,' he offered.

'Could you bollocks.' The slam of her door was a full stop to his protest.

Ah well, it was worth a try.

Zipped up in a jacket never designed for the full ire of Suffolk rain, Wheeler splodged across the muddy grass verge to join his colleague. She was leaning against a weather-beaten gate squinting through the incessant downpour at the path that edged the field, rising steeply from the road.

'So, did Jack stay in his car in this lay-by to use the phone, or did he go up there?' she asked.

'The co-ordinates can't tell us that,' Wheeler said. 'Does it matter?'

Kate Bennett gave him a look that could freeze raindrops on contact. 'Yes, it matters. Why drive all the way out here to use the phone?'

'So it wouldn't be traced.'

'Except it was.'

'Move over.' Wheeler tried to ignore the rain dripping from the hood of his jacket and sneaking inside to soak his shirt as he took hold of the gate and heaved himself over it.

'What are you doing?'

Pulling his sleeve back to reveal his phone, he wiggled it at her. 'Experiment.'

It was not the weather for trudging through a soggy field, but Wheeler had a hunch that needed testing. As they'd neared the location where Jack's phone was registered, he'd been watching his phone. One bar of reception had remained in place for the last mile, apart from a brief dalliance with two bars just before they'd driven along the tree-lined section of road. By the gate, it had been back to one again. But now, as he slowly ascended the hill, two bars showed. A little further on, three.

'Three bars!' he called back down to Bennett. 'Come on.'

He watched as Bennett leaned over and unhooked the gate from its post, opening it as if she'd done it a hundred times before. She was smirking, damn it. Closing it again, she headed up to meet him.

'What?' she asked, clearly proud of herself.

'It was locked,' he insisted.

'What can I tell you, Dave? Sometimes you have to look a bit closer.'

'You can go off people, you know.'

She smirked again. 'You love me really. So you think Jack parked by the gate and walked up here?'

'The reception gets better. My guess is it's best at the top of the hill.'

Sure enough, the higher they climbed, the better the reception became. As they reached the brow of the hill, Wheeler looked out across the fields and grinned.

'And there it is.'

Bennett followed the direction he was pointing in, her smile appearing when she saw it. 'Brilliant.'

Across the ridge of the hill, a tall phone mast stood proud white against the slate-grey sky.

'I reckon he's a local if he knows that. Maybe he grew up around here. Could be worth looking into.'

Bennett nodded. 'Let's get going.'

It was a relief to get back in the car, even if the pool car's interior fan only seemed to have one setting – Arctic cold – when Bennett turned it on to clear the fogged-up windscreen.

'What do you reckon Collins has in these units?' Bennett asked as they drove.

'No idea. They didn't look big from the map.'

'Do you think he has Hannah?'

Wheeler glanced at her, noting how carefully she kept her eyes on the road. It was the question he'd asked himself repeatedly from the day Collins came in for interview. 'I'd say he had opportunity – and the location would work for keeping a kid. But I just don't know.'

'He's violent. We know he lies.'

'Don't make him a child abductor, though.' He slumped a little in his seat. Minshull and Anderson were so certain of Collins' guilt and sure, he was far from innocent of anything. But taking his own kid? And for what? One of the papers had made noises about putting up a reward for Hannah's safe return but it had yet to materialise. There had been no mention in the notes of a ransom, but there hadn't been with Matthew Cooper, not until the very last item was sent to them – the demand responsible for Anderson's angry statement that had ended in tragedy. From what Wheeler had seen of Shaun Collins, he didn't seem to be the sort to plan such a stunt. Someone who employed his fists and threats first had no need of careful criminal strategy.

Wheeler had supported Minshull and Anderson so far and he would continue to do so. Rob Minshull was a good copper, the kind the force needed. Decent, honest, not like his bastard dad, who was little more than a thug in uniform. Anderson was a good cop, too, but Wheeler worried for him. He'd lost his way before: how close was he to repeating his mistakes?

The industrial estate was as remote and incongruous as the map had suggested. You turned a corner in the road and there it was, flanked on all sides by newly ploughed fields and not much else. The original sign from the former farm still hung at the road's edge, its board swinging furiously in the storm. The usual orientation board you would expect at the entrance to an industrial estate wasn't there, meaning someone approaching would have no idea of which businesses were situated on the site.

'No cars,' Bennett said, slowing the car as it bumped and splashed over the potholed track leading to the units. 'No sign of life.'

'Looks deserted from the road, too, so no fear of anyone stumbling on it by mistake.' A ball of nerves rolled to the bottom of Wheeler's stomach. 'You could hide a kid here.'

If she was here, who was guarding her? Could it be the elusive Jack? Or was Collins cocksure enough to leave her alone?

The flash of headlights behind them made Wheeler and Bennett turn in their seats. A white Operational Support Group van was thudding over the rutted track behind them.

Bennett checked the dashboard clock. 'Five minutes early. They're good.'

Leaving the car at the edge of the gravel square that served as a car park, Wheeler and Bennett walked over to the van. The uniformed sergeant was waiting for them, five officers watching from the rear of the van.

'What we got, Dave?'

'Right. We know our person of interest, Shaun Collins, has been making regular visits here over the past week we've been monitoring his vehicle, while his stepkid's been missing. I need you to check all the units for any signs of life, or anything that could point to illegal activity. DC Bennett and I will check Units 3 and 4. If your guys can check the rest?'

'No problem.'

As the team made for the other units, Wheeler followed Bennett, glancing up at the numbers above the doors of the identical brick and steel buildings. They consisted of steel warehouses accessed by a low, single-storey brick building at the front of each one, containing office spaces and an entrance hall. Peering in through the front windows of Unit 3, Wheeler could see two empty offices, the thin red-brown carpet bearing darker patches where furniture had once stood. The floor was strewn with old sheets of paper and discarded leaflets in the left-hand office; on the right, a large stain in the centre of the carpet suggested a previous water leak. The glazed steel door at the front was locked.

'Is there another way in?' Wheeler asked, his face pressed to the window, but Bennett had already disappeared down the side of the building. When Wheeler joined her, she had managed to wedge a fire door open and was attempting to squeeze inside.

'Hold this open for me,' she puffed, shouldering the gap as she pushed her body through.

Wheeler did as he was told, heart already thumping like he'd run a mile. As his colleague slipped inside, he peered around the door.

'Can you see anything?'

'No,' her voice echoed back. 'It's empty. Just piles of blue plastic sheets and a load of old fag ends.'

'No rooms off it?'

'Nope.' Bennett's steps echoed as she made a circuit of the unit and then her face appeared in the doorway. 'Let us out and we'll look next door.'

It was the same story in the front offices of Unit 4; the front door locked and padlocked this time. But when they approached the side door, Bennett suddenly stopped, holding her hand up.

'What is it?' Wheeler hissed.

'I heard something.'

The door was ajar here, a large breezeblock wedging it open. As the detectives edged nearer, distinct noises sounded from inside.

'Let me go first,' Wheeler said.

Bennett glanced at the door. 'I can do it.'

'No. Stay behind me and if anything happens—' His skin began to prickle. '—if anything happens, yell for the others.'

For a moment, he thought she might protest. But then she stood back, allowing Wheeler to move ahead.

'If anything happens, Dave, I'll be right here to save your sorry ass.'

Despite the adrenaline pumping through him, Wheeler shot her a smile. 'That's exactly what I was hoping you'd say.' He took a breath – and stepped inside.

Chapter Fifty-Seven

Bennett

The noise was coming from the far left side of the unit. Bennett blinked as she followed Wheeler into the dark space, made darker by the ineffective corrugated plastic skylights and the rainstorm raging beyond them, the sound thunderous from inside the space. Rows of strip-lights were suspended from the steel roof, but they weren't on. From where the noise came, a single light glowed.

Wheeler pointed to the lit area and made his way towards it. Two large sheets of fibreboard had been erected against the far left corner of the building, forming a crude room. A third, larger sheet had been fixed diagonally over the top of them to make a ceiling of sorts. In the gap between the two standing board walls, light was beaming from an inspection torch suspended from the makeshift roof.

And in the light, something was moving.

Bennett saw Wheeler pull his warrant card from his jacket. He glanced back to her and she nodded.

'Police,' Wheeler announced. 'Show yourself.'

Abruptly, the noise stopped. The shadow in the torchlight froze.

'*Police*. Show yourself!'

Wheeler edged closer. Bennett followed.

And then, a figure darted out. Wheeler was knocked to the floor and before Bennett could react she was body-slammed, barely managing to stay upright as the culprit fled from the building. The last thing she saw as they ran out of the door was a flash of fluorescent yellow.

'*Shit!* Stay where you are!' she yelled, her blood rising, powering after the intruder. At the fire exit her toe caught the raised lip of the doorframe, sending her skidding forwards, but she recovered and sprinted along the side of the building.

The man was heading for the front of the estate now, edging along the narrow gap between Units 1 & 2.

'*Police!*' Bennett yelled again as she ran. 'Stay where you are!'

Her shouts alerted the support officers and the sound of running feet from all directions injected pace into her limbs. By the time the running man neared the OSG van, Bennett reached him, flinging herself at his back and gripping hold of the hi-vis jacket as they fell.

Suddenly they were surrounded, her uniformed colleagues piling around them, restraining the man until Bennett had cuffed him.

Breathing heavily, her muscles making vehement protest, she sat up, just as Wheeler skidded to a halt beside her.

'You okay?'

'Fine, you?'

On the ground, the man squirmed, held fast by strong arms. Bennett yanked the reflective strip across the back of the hi-vis up and Wheeler leaned in. Across the material, four letters had been written in permanent black ink:

JACK

–

'I ain't done nothing wrong,' Jack growled in the rear of the CID car as they drove back to the station. He was wedged between two Support officers, his jacket now folded in Wheeler's lap.

'Then why run?' Wheeler asked.

Jack muttered something and stared at his feet.

'Sorry, didn't catch that?'

'I said it's my business and none of yours.'

'Work there, do you?'

'You can't question me in the car. It don't count.'

Bennett glanced at Wheeler, who wore a wry smile.

'Pardon me. I was just making conversation, sir. Makes the journey pass faster, in my opinion.'

'He's not a chatter, Dave,' one of the officers smirked from the back seat.

'Reckon you're right, Stu. Shame. I like a good natter when I meet someone new.'

Bennett suppressed a grin. She'd worked alongside Wheeler in CID since she'd joined and he had been her mentor during those first rollercoaster months as a DC. He might like a joke and you never, under any circumstances, ribbed him for his love of Norwich City FC, but he was eminently fair and solid as a rock. She liked that about him. No matter how the team split when disagreements arose, Dave Wheeler was always on your side.

Minshull and Anderson were waiting for them in the police station car lot when they arrived, Minshull impatient for Bennett to park.

'Well?'

Bennett's heart made a bid for her boots. 'She wasn't there, Guv. We searched the whole place.'

Anderson groaned and Minshull swore, shaking his head. 'Did you find anything?'

'Boxes of illegal spirits,' Wheeler said, slamming the car door. 'A pallet full of 'em. Our fluorescent jacketed friend here was repacking them into crisp boxes.'

'What?'

'My guess is that the boxes Steph and I saw in the storeroom at the kebab shop had these in. Maybe Collins forces his debtors to sell this stuff, or palm it off on someone else.'

'Has he confirmed he works with Collins?'

Bennett shook her head. 'He clammed up the moment Dave mentioned him. But the way the colour drained from his face I'd say he knows him well.'

'Right.' Minshull kicked his aggravation at a stone beside the car. 'Let's get him in.'

—

'No comment.'

Sitting beside Minshull in the interview room, Bennett could feel the energies either side of the table. Minshull seething, every hackle raised; Jack inviting it, his bravado thinly veiling fear.

'That wasn't a question. I need your full name and date of birth for the tape, sir,' Minshull said, every syllable laced with challenge.

Jack hesitated a moment longer, then leant across the table to the recorder. 'Adam Jackson. Thirteenth of December, 1998.'

Jackson – *JACK* – no wonder they hadn't located him before.

'Thank you. Mr Jackson, do you work at the industrial estate where you were arrested?'

'No comment.'

'What do you do there?'

'No comment.'

'Do you work for yourself?'

'No comment.'

'Do you work for someone else?'

Jack yawned. 'No comment.'

'Do you work for Shaun Collins?'

A flicker. 'No comment.'

'How do you know Shaun Collins?'

'No comment.' It was mumbled, the eye contact he'd maintained with Minshull now gone.

'You don't know him.'

'No comment.'

'So when I talk to Mr Collins in the next interview, he's going to tell me he doesn't know you?'

Jack's head snapped upright.

Bennett leaned on her elbow to watch the show.

'I... No comment.'

'Because here's the thing, Mr Jackson, we think you know where Shaun Collins' stepdaughter is. Hannah Perry. You'll have seen in the news. And we think you're involved.'

'I never!'

It was as if the tiniest crack had been chipped in a dam wall, the whole structure failing instantly. Adam Jackson gripped the edge of the table as a torrent of his words gushed out.

'I got a kid. My missus is terrified to let her out of her sight because of what's happened to Han. I never took her and I don't know who did.'

'But you know Shaun Collins?'

'Does he know I'm here?' The final note of his question was little more than a squeak.

'You were working in his unit. He visits several times a week. And we know about the van and the people he brings over to the unit for... *discussions.*'

Jackson's mouth gaped.

Minshull left the statement hanging and turned to her. 'Do you have any questions, DC Bennett?'

Bennett offered the terrified man a beatific smile. Her shoulder still ached from where Jackson had crashed into it. *Just for that, I'm going to enjoy this.* 'Is this your mobile number, Mr Jackson?'

She slid a slip of paper across the table. Jackson raised his eyebrows.

'Sorry, *one* of them. We know this isn't your regular number because your phone was seized when you were arrested and the number for that is different. But we do know Mr Collins had this number, with your name, in his possession a few days ago. And we know it's only ever used to make calls from the hill on Darsham Lane, about two miles from the estate at Long Deighton where you were arrested? Not in the lay-by on the roadside where you park – the reception's rubbish there – but at the top of the field, overlooking the next valley.'

Each revelation hit home like a slap, Jackson reeling from each blow.

'I don't use that no more.'

'Where is it?'

'Gone.' He swallowed hard, jaw working overtime. 'But Collins knows more than he says. A lot more. Stuff he never tells me.'

Bennett narrowed her eyes. 'What do you know?'

'Is he going down? Proper, this time, not a caution?'

'I'm afraid we can't say…'

'Because if he is, if you make sure he is, I'll tell you what I know. He's dangerous. He don't like to be crossed. He'll attack anyone who does and he won't mind who they are. He wouldn't stop, never. Not even for a kid.'

Chapter Fifty-Eight

Minshull

He had talked. A *lot*. Adam 'Jack' Jackson confirmed that he'd been asked by Collins to offer 'security services' at the two units on the industrial estate. He'd assumed that Collins owned them and, being short of cash and job offers, had accepted.

'Most of the time it's just keeping the place free from rats, fixing leaks, that sort of thing. But Shaun started getting deliveries at his house that he said he had no room for. He's got a lock-up, back of the Parkhall, but he said it's full of building stuff so he was going to stash it at the unit.'

'We need to check his lock-up,' Anderson said, scribbling a note. 'So how did Jackson go from glorified caretaker to repacking illegal bottles of booze?'

Minshull checked his notebook. 'He says Collins threatened him. Several times. First with telling his missus that he'd been handling stolen goods and then with telling police Jackson was the importer, not Collins.'

'He threatened that kid with us?' Anderson was incredulous. 'You need some balls to do that.'

'Indeed. And then Collins roped him into scaring one of his "clients". By then, I reckon Jackson was in too deep. So he agreed.'

'He admitted beating them up?'

'Not in so many words. But we have witnesses saying he was there and we have the hi-vis jacket he was wearing when the attacks occurred.'

Anderson sat back in his chair and closed his eyes. For a moment, Minshull thought the DI had succumbed to the call of sleep. He wouldn't blame him if he had. Everyone was on the edge of exhaustion.

Then, eyes still shut, Anderson spoke.

'So does Collins have Hannah?'

'Adam Jackson doesn't know. But he thinks Collins capable.'

'That proves nothing. And it brings us no closer to *her*.'

'One thing we do know: Jackson just confirmed he was the person at the pub in Coombe Minor who suggested Collins as a money-lender to Guy Weatherall, the teacher from St Bart's. So he's in this up to his neck. If anyone's going to rat on Shaun Collins, it'll be him.'

'We need to know if Collins took her. Or if someone he intimidated did it.'

'We'll keep pushing Jackson. There was one more thing.' He glanced up at his superior. 'The last threat Collins made to Jackson was that he'd take his kid. He said he'd grab Jackson's little girl and he'd never see her again.'

Anderson sat bolt upright, staring across the desk. 'When?'

'Just over a month ago.'

'So what if that threat was a rehearsal for his plan to snatch Hannah? Is that possible?'

It seemed fantastical, but it was too close a threat to ignore. 'I'd say definitely possible.'

'Right. Keep Jackson talking – we need as much on Collins as we can get. Ask him what he knows about Collins' relationship with Hannah. Ask him straight out if he thinks Collins might have taken her. Go for broke – push him hard. And send someone to check out Collins' lock-up. See if any of the loan book names who have agreed to make a statement were forced to accept the illegal spirits and if Collins ever threatened to harm or snatch their kids. Let's find out the full extent of Mr Collins' actions and, if there's a pattern, we bring him in.'

A knock on the door made them both turn.

'Come in.'

Drew Ellis stepped into the office. And instantly Minshull knew.

'Another package.'

'When?'

'Just handed into the front desk.'

'Another item from her school bag?' Anderson asked, already on his feet.

'Worse, Guv. It's an item of clothing.'

Minshull felt his world tilt. *Shit, shit, shit.* 'Call Dr Lael. Now!'

274

Chapter Fifty-Nine

Cora

Shrouded in the clear plastic evidence bag, the faded blue cardigan looked small and helpless. Cora was aware of the stillness of the CID team as Minshull handed it to her. Even DC Evans was unusually quiet. Perhaps the headband and school tie had been easy to detach concern from. They could be easily discarded. But the cardigan suggested something darker. Everyone in the incident room knew their car windows would be iced over when they ended their shifts. Every person was now glad of the heating within the room. A small child, incarcerated, scared and now without warm clothing – the connotations were cruel and impossible to ignore.

The note, too, was darker, more threatening:

HARD TO STAY WARM WITHOUT THIS.

HOW MUCH LONGER WILL THE GAME GO ON?

NEXT TIME MIGHT BE THE LAST.

Cora took a long, slow breath. She almost didn't want to hear anything, the possibility of a child's worsening suffering too awful to consider. But she was determined to hear more this time. Glancing at Rob Minshull, she saw the same terrible hope in his eyes.

I'm ready for this, she told herself. *This time, I'm prepared.*

She'd practised pushing into the voices she heard every day since the fake package incident. Her evolving ability had proved vital then: Rob had said she'd prevented the investigation taking what could have proved a fatal wrong turn. The sounds around where the voice should have been were what had uncovered Lloyd Price's lie, proving to Cora that she was capable of more.

The dreams of Hannah were growing stronger day by day, too, and Cora had begun to wonder if pushing her ability was unlocking other, deeper psychological skills. Was it possible her mind was linking with that of the child? She'd dismissed this initially, but now she wasn't sure. The dreams troubled her, leaving an imprint on her mind that lasted long after she woke. Filming the video diary entries for Daniel had helped a little, despite her initial reluctance to film her own thoughts. Despite his drunken accusations from the other night, she was still sending the completed video diary entries back to him – for his precious study which now she suspected meant more to him than she ever would.

She'd recorded every swing of emotion, every moment of confidence and fear, so that when the study was published, other emotional synaesthetes could learn from her experience.

She would record this moment, too, whatever it brought.

Her fingers pulled open the zip-lock – and an enormous scream rushed out. As it reached a crescendo, it stopped abruptly, the interruption sudden, and then the voice returned in a haunting, sorrowful wail.

Cora experienced a strong rush of emotion as a physical blow, her right cheek stinging as if it had been burned. She reeled back and DC Bennett caught the evidence bag as it fell from her hand.

'Dr Lael?' Anderson was by her side now. 'Are you okay to continue?'

They were staring at her. Struggling to force Hannah's pitiful voice from her mind, Cora forced a smile. 'Yes.'

'What did you hear?'

'A scream. Hannah's scream. She was fighting to keep this but—' She broke off as the memory of the sudden end to the child's protest returned. As if she had been shocked into silence. *As if she had been slapped.* Then the mournful wail of a child in pain… This was worse than anyone expected. The first audible evidence of physical attack on Hannah. 'She was silenced.'

'How?' Minshull checked himself. 'Do you get a sense of what caused that?'

I don't want to say it. I don't want to be the one who brings the news… 'I think she was hit. Slapped, maybe. On her right cheek. And then she was crying, softly, as if she was scared to make too much noise.'

A snort came from Les Evans, who stalked away to the coffee machine. Cora met Minshull's stare.

'I don't know what to say. I'd ask if you were certain, but you clearly are. Do you need to step out for a while? Or sit quietly? I'm sure DI Anderson would be more than happy to lend you his office.' He turned to his superior who nodded, face pale.

'Of course.'

Regrouping, Cora declined. 'Can I have it back again? The cardigan. Just for a moment?'

'Why?'

'I want to try something. I think, now I know what I'll hear, I can press in. Move behind Hannah's voice and try to get a sense of where she is.'

Anderson and Minshull exchanged glances.

'Can you do that?'

'I think so. It's a technique I'm developing. It's what I used with the fake package, to hear further back for room sounds, echoes, that sort of thing.'

'But your reaction before...' Minshull began.

'I'll be fine,' Cora assured him, hoping she would be. 'Now I know what to expect, it won't have as much power.'

'If you're sure...' Minshull nodded at DC Bennett, who reluctantly passed the evidence bag back.

Cora took a moment to steady herself before she began.

The scream was just as strong as before, but Cora held her ground, urging her mind behind Hannah's voice. There was a reverberation of sorts around the sound, only short but there. It reminded Cora of the staccato echo of a kitchen or tiled bathroom. As she pushed further into the background, imagining the sound as a three-dimensional projection, she became aware of constricted air above it. Was the space Hannah was in smaller than standing height?

Around her, the scream, the slap and the low wail continued in a loop, but now the physical emotion and her aching cheek were fading. In their place, Cora felt a pressure across her shoulders and at the base of her spine, as if she were being bent double. Was the child stooping? Or sitting with her back against a wall? As she processed the new sensations, her entire body went cold. Goosebumps prickled her arms. Her lips, fingers and toes grew numb. It felt startlingly real, as if she had stepped into a freezing room.

She pressed harder, but nothing more emerged. Careful to exit the way she had entered, Cora reversed her journey, slowly acknowledging each layer of sound and reaching back for the next, until the scream, the slap and the wail took centre-stage once more. With her final retreat, the sound of the CID office reappeared and Cora opened her eyes.

The team were around her now, each one watching with differing levels of belief. Even DC Evans had joined them, although he kept a safe distance behind DC Ellis's tall frame.

Anderson broke the uncertain silence. 'Did you hear anything else?'

Rob Minshull flashed her an encouraging smile. It was enough.

'I think Hannah is in a small room or space. The sound of her voice has a short echo, which might mean the walls of this space are made of brick or stone, maybe even metal of some kind. It didn't sound like there was much room above her head, so I think there must be a low ceiling or roof, and I sensed that Hannah was crouching or sitting, her back against a wall in either case. And it's cold. She's cold.'

She closed the evidence bag and held it out to Minshull. He hesitated before he took it.

Around them, nobody moved.

Cora let her gaze fall to the floor.

And then Anderson spoke. 'Call the search unit. Tell Cath Atkinson we need searches of any small buildings within St Just and the immediate surrounding area. We start there, then widen the search if we find nothing. So sheds, garages, tool stores, outbuildings, lock-ups, allotment shacks – anything with restricted room where a child might be kept.'

Bennett was already hurrying across the office. 'Yes, Guv.'

Anderson made as if to say something to Cora, but his words faltered. Instead, he gave her a nod and retreated to his office.

Cora turned to Minshull. 'I hope I'm right.'

Minshull released the breath he'd held. 'I hope you are, too.'

Hannah

They hit me. My cheek still hurts where They did it.

They hit me and then They stole my cardigan.

I screamed when They were pulling it off me, but They didn't listen. There's a big red line halfway up my arm because They yanked it so hard.

When They'd gone, I got out my bag and opened it, but the Home smell is all gone. I cried until no more tears came out. And now I'm scared again, just like before.

It's cold in the Small Space. I told Them I was cold and They yelled at me again, but the door has just opened and an old red checked shirt has been thrown in. It smells bad but it's better than having nothing to go over my arms. So I'm huddling up underneath it, hoping a little bit of warmth from it will go into my arms and legs.

All my body aches. The tips of my fingers hurt from picking at the splintery wood around the gap. My thoughts are all jumbly, like I can't make them behave anymore. And I shake all the time.

Today, when They brought my cold toast and water, They were jumpy. A few times They snapped and I thought They were going to hit me again. It's like They're getting tired of keeping me. I feel sick when I think what They might do if They stop caring altogether. Mum says bad people never get better, they only ever get worse. Their angry face today was horrible. I'm scared I'll find out what *worse* looks like.

Why did They want my cardigan? Or my headband or my tie? Those things won't fit Them. They won't wear my clothes. What happens if They try to take my bag next? I pull it under the stinky red shirt and fold my arms and legs tight around it.

They are *not* having it. *No matter what.*

Chapter Sixty

Anderson

The first search of Collins' lock-up turned up nothing. It was packed with odds and ends of building supplies – bricks, lengths of guttering, bags of cement, stacks of wood off-cuts, reels of electrical wire and boxes of tiles. There wasn't enough room between them to hide anything, let alone a child.

Anderson watched the weary faces of the CID team as they observed Minshull's latest briefing. There had been such a high when Jack had been brought in, such expectation of finding the child, but the two friends Jack told them had been threatened by Collins clammed up the moment they heard his name.

He knew Minshull was taking time to get as much on Collins as possible before they brought him in, but Anderson felt the strategy risky. He would have to intervene if Minshull delayed much longer.

Searches were continuing across St Just, the gathered journalists jumping at the development after long days with nothing new to report. As usual, the bastards were twisting it to insinuate that every person in St Just was now a suspect, further undermining public trust in the police and Anderson's team. It was to be expected, of course, but it was a pain in the backside.

He worried about the time, too. Already they had indication of physical violence being used against the child, if Dr Lael was to be believed. How much of a leap might it be for Hannah's abductor to go from violence to murder?

If Collins had Hannah, bringing him in would ensure her remaining alive at least. If he didn't, bringing him in might throw light on who had sufficient cause to take his child in revenge. Anderson's patience was dangerously thin: he needed to find the child. In his mind, he afforded Minshull another twenty-four hours: if there were no significant developments after that, he would pull rank and drag Shaun Collins into custody.

He'd been back at his desk for ten minutes when Professor Daniel Gold called. Of all the people to request an audience with him today, Anderson did not expect this one.

An hour later, the professor was sitting in the visitor's chair at the other side of Anderson's desk, laptop hugged to his chest as if it were his life support. His demeanour was markedly different from the man lounging in a rural pub's armchair that Anderson remembered meeting.

'To what do I owe the honour?' he asked, not sure if he wanted to know.

'I've been studying Dr Lael's responses to the work she's been doing with you.' He paused for an audible breath. 'I'm afraid there's a problem.'

The blood rushed from Anderson's head. 'Problem?'

'I owe you an apology, DI Anderson. I thought – I truly believed Cora was ready for this level of involvement. But it's more than she can bear.'

No. No, this was not what anyone needed. Cora Lael was vital to this investigation. They had no time for problems. They needed her. 'Has Dr Lael told you this?'

The professor seemed to stumble, a thin layer of sweat visible across his brow. 'In a manner of speaking.'

'I'm sorry, Professor, but I need more than hearsay. Dr Lael's work for us has been exemplary. Ground-breaking. To lose her now would be catastrophic for this investigation.'

'I'm worried about Cora's state of mind. It's already affecting her mood, her sleep patterns. And then, of course, there are the *dreams…*'

Anderson felt the room shift beneath him. 'What dreams?'

Daniel Gold nodded, relinquishing his hold on his laptop and sliding it across the table. 'Perhaps it's better if I show you.'

Anderson watched, heart in mouth, as Daniel opened the laptop and brought up a video on the screen. 'As part of the University's study, I asked Dr Lael to keep a video diary. Her thoughts, her reactions to the various tasks she might perform for you. She posted this entry a few days ago. There are more, just like this.' He leaned forward and hit Play.

Cora's face filled the screen, pale, frightened. Completely unlike the woman he had come to know and trust.

> I'm seeing her. At night. I can see Hannah confined, terrified. And she thinks nobody can hear her. But I can hear her. It's the same dream, every night, but each time I can see a little more. I just wish I could see clues to find out where she is. I wish this wasn't all my responsibility but – but it feels like it is. I'm the only one who can hear her. It's driving me insane…

Insane. Anderson closed his eyes. 'And you said there were more entries like this?'

Daniel nodded. 'I'm so sorry. I should never have suggested she offer her services.'

Anderson swore under his breath. 'Okay. Thank you for bringing this to my attention. I'll – I'll talk to my colleagues and we'll address this with Dr Lael.'

'If it would help – I could talk to her directly? Explain my concerns, advise her to quit?'

Was the professor enjoying this? Anderson was no expert in psychology but all the energy coming from Daniel Gold felt wrong.

'No,' he said, quickly, noting the effect his word had on the professor. 'Any decision we make regarding Dr Lael's onward involvement with the investigation has to come from us. We invited her: it will be our prerogative to withdraw our offer.'

'As you wish.'

'Thank you.' Anderson stood, and offered his hand. Daniel rose to accept. 'I appreciate your concern.'

Anderson kept his expression steady until he'd escorted the professor out of the building and walked through the gate to the station car lot. Unlocking his car, he climbed into the driver's seat. He stared at the wall of South Suffolk Police's headquarters until the unremarkable lines and squares of its red bricks imprinted themselves on his vision.

Then he let out a loud moan and slammed his fists against the steering wheel.

Chapter Sixty-One

Cora

A *phone call.*

Not a meeting in person, where she could have looked into DI Anderson's eyes and deciphered the real reason why she was being taken off the case. Because he hadn't given a reason. Just a thank you, followed by a slammed door.

This can't be happening...

Cora stared at the walls of her living room, as if a million possibilities were scrawled across the white paint. Why? Why now, when they were making real progress? Hadn't she proved herself already with the notebook and the belongings?

'I'm very sorry, Dr Lael. Please don't think this is any reflection on your excellent work for us thus far.'

How could he say that? How could she possibly take it as anything other than a personal snub?

I'm Hannah's best hope! she wanted to yell. *I'm the only one that can hear her. Without me, what do you have?*

The memory of Hannah's voice from her school cardigan in the evidence bag reverberated in Cora's mind. She'd been slapped. The mournful sound of her pain still tormented Cora. Had it been too much to tell Rob that? Had she said too much?

Joel Anderson had blamed a decision taken higher up. That it was considered unwise to continue. Why? Had someone talked to the media about her? She thought of DC Evans, the only member of the CID team she knew disagreed with her presence on the investigation. Could he have complained?

She needed to talk to Rob Minshull. But he wasn't answering his phone. Frustrated, she called again. When it went to voicemail, she left a message.

'Rob, it's Cora Lael. They've taken me off the investigation and I don't know why. DI Anderson told me not to come in again. He said it isn't personal but I think something must have happened to change his mind. I wasn't lying when I told you about Hannah crying, or the slap, or where she was being held. I *heard* her, Rob! You know I did. She's terrified and whoever has her is now abusing her. There has to be something you can do. Can you talk to Anderson? Or whoever higher up has decided this? I'm so angry, so hurt...' She stopped herself. 'Just please, when you get this message can you call me? I have to talk to you.'

Ending the call, she threw her phone across the room in frustration, where it slammed against the sofa. What was she going to do? And what would she tell Daniel? The research project had reached a critical stage – surely it was imperative she remain on the investigation until its completion?

She thought of Hannah, the poor victim of someone else's agenda, now subject to everyone else's. DI Anderson needed redemption for the boy that died. Rob Minshull wanted to prove himself worthy of his promotion. The gathering media scrum around the streets of St Just and by the police headquarters in Ipswich needed a new story to fill their columns. Even Daniel needed this to give a different focus to his study.

And me? What about me?

Was she as guilty as the rest of using Hannah's abduction for her own benefit? She couldn't deny her involvement with Operation Seraphine had made her believe in herself, dare to push her ability to new levels and lift her expectations of what she could be capable of.

And still, Hannah was lost. Alone. Afraid. And now physically in pain. If Cora wasn't there to hear her voice, how would the police ever find her in time?

There had to be something she could do.

She had to think. The silence was too oppressive here. Retrieving her phone from where she'd tossed it, she found Daniel's number and dialled. He answered on the third ring, making her wonder if he had been waiting for her call.

'I need to see you.'

'Come to mine. I've work still to finish but it can wait.'

'No, not yours. I know a better place.'

A strong easterly wind thrashed at the sea, sending angry grey-green waves slamming onto the beach. Rain was not far off, the scent and salt of it strong on the wind as it buffeted Cora's face. In the noise and the threat of the oncoming storm, her mind could finally rest.

Around her, people scurried for cover, escaping to the warm shelter of Felixstowe's seafront cafés. Al's windows were already steamed over, as if shielding the customers within from the dark prospect without.

She remained on the promenade, waiting for Daniel, or the storm, whichever arrived first. Her heart still hurt, the shock of Anderson's call as much of a physical punch as if he'd delivered a real one. How dare he dismiss her?

How dare Rob?

She didn't want to believe he'd had any part in her dismissal, but his silence didn't support her, either. There had to be a way out of it. Daniel would know.

'I don't know why you thought this was a better place to meet.' Daniel arrived at her side, coat collar pulled up to his chin, black-and-white striped Trinity Hall scarf from his Cambridge University years wrapped around his neck.

'I can think here.'

'Think here? You'll be lucky to keep your head on your shoulders here when that storm hits. Come on, let's get somewhere warm.'

The coffee shop in the centre of Felixstowe wasn't the place Cora wanted to go, its noise and clamour and the voices shouting up from every table hard to find a path through. She muted each voice as best she could, leaving just the bustle of everyday business in place. Her mind felt bruised, not by the unwanted voices that surrounded her but by the questions Anderson's call had lodged in her head.

Daniel returned to the table with two cream-topped cups, one of which he set down in front of Cora.

'What's this?'

'Hot chocolate.' When his expectant smile didn't elicit response, he groaned. 'Filthy days like today demand hot chocolate. And cream. And all the marshmallows I asked them to add for you.' He brandished a spoon. 'Go on, dig in!'

She watched him commence an attack on the cream cap of his drink, thinking that he didn't seem at all disappointed about her removal from the investigation. What about the university funding, promised to run until the end of the investigation? Or the source of research data for the study cut short by her early dismissal?

Perhaps he was putting a brave face on things for her sake, she reasoned, taking a sip of her drink and baulking at the sweetness. This was the first time they had been out together since his drunken outburst and while there had been countless apologetic texts, she had expected a little more penitence. Perhaps he believed himself forgiven because she'd asked to see him.

Was he forgiven?

It didn't matter: she needed him now.

'It's good to see you,' he grinned, a narrow line of cream lining his upper lip. 'I was an idiot last time. I'd been drinking… What I said was wrong. I should have known you wouldn't be interested in the policeman. And even if I didn't know before, I do now.'

She frowned. 'How do you mean?'

'Well, his behaviour today. Or whenever it was they made the decision.'

'I don't think Rob was involved. DI Anderson said…'

'Have you called Minshull?'

'Yes. I left a message.'

'And has he replied?' The question was diamond-edged, likely to cut her whichever way she answered.

'He's in the middle of an investigation. He probably hasn't had time to think, let alone check his messages.'

'But you were part of that investigation. A vital part, if what he told you was true.'

Her tears welled, contorting her view. 'I don't know why they've taken me off the case. But I know I made a difference. It's happened so quickly, it must be a mistake.'

'I don't think it is.'

She reached across the table, grabbing his hand. 'But you can help me. You can persuade them to take me back.'

Her touch appeared to surprise him, looking down at her hand on his as if it was their first contact. 'Cora, I…'

'You made it possible for me to be part of the investigation. You persuaded Joel Anderson to let me on. He trusts you. He'll listen to you.'

When Daniel didn't reply, the fear and dread she'd battled at home since the call came flooding back, strong as the breaking waves on Felixstowe's shore.

'She could *die*, Daniel. Hannah could die if I don't find her. There *has* to be a way to get back into the investigation. I feel like I'm losing my mind not knowing what's happening, if any more of Hannah's things have been returned. Rob won't answer my calls. Joel Anderson has made it clear he won't discuss it. I have to help her, don't you see? I have to *know*…'

'No,' he said, louder than she'd expected. 'I think those bridges are burned. And maybe that's a good thing.'

'A good thing? How?'

'You haven't been sleeping. You're experiencing dreams that upset you, a clear indication that your mind is under stress.'

'No…' In the wail of her voice she heard Hannah's.

'We have enough for the study. You've more than proved your potential. We can pursue it, you and I, away from the investigation. Take our time. Discover exactly what your brain is capable of.'

'But Hannah…'

'The police will find her. And maybe, now you've found a way in for them, they'll find her faster.' His other hand closed over hers. 'What matters is us now, baby. You have to let this go.'

Chapter Sixty-Two

Anderson

The Miller's Arms was old and tired, much like Anderson felt most days. But it suited him. It was comfortable, familiar and the kind of place you could sit without some idiot trying to chat to you. Unless you wanted company, of course. This evening, Anderson wasn't sure what he wanted, other than a stiff drink followed by a decent pie and chips and a few pints more. Anything else he'd work out along the way.

He glanced at the list of unopened emails on his mobile before finding his wife's latest text message:

> Mum's carers are all sorted.
> Looks like I'm coming home! :-) R xx

Even after twenty-four years of marriage, Rosalyn Anderson still had the ability to surprise him. Smiley faces in text messages? When had she learned that? He smiled, willing her back that second. He needed her humour to lift him from the dark place he'd slipped into in her absence. Especially now the investigation had lost its greatest asset. *Idiot.* Why had he placed so much faith in Cora Lael?

'Pie, is it?' Norma, the landlady, who hadn't changed dress or hair colour since the early 1980s, grinned at him as she slid an already poured single malt across the bar. It was definitely time Ros came home.

'As ever. Thanks.'

'My pleasure, Joel. You make yourself comfy and I'll bring it over when it's done.'

As he huddled in an alcove seat, Anderson faced the truth. The darkness surrounding him now had begun two days ago. It had nothing to do with Cora Lael.

The child's cardigan did it.

Seven years ago it had been the blue school jumper Matthew Cooper's abductor had sent back to prove a point. Same school, same colour. And after that… He winced, the pain as raw now as it had been then. After that, the only item with a ransom note. The pair of shoes, scuffed and covered in mud, with the demand rolled inside.

THE GAME'S ALMOST DONE.

TIME TO PAY.

£100,000 OR MATTHEW DIES.

It was the delivery that threw the investigation into a tailspin, top brass yelling for results, the press screaming for blood. Trapped in its core, Joel Anderson had caved to pressure and his own incandescent anger, making the statement that had ended a life.

Hannah Perry's woollen garment had looked much smaller than Cooper's, but the threat was darker this time.

NEXT TIME MIGHT BE THE LAST.

Anderson was now convinced that whoever had Hannah had taken Matthew before. And if that was true, they knew the game they were playing. This was a warning – if his gut feeling was right, the next delivery would carry a ransom note.

He remembered the sleepless nights following the discovery of Matthew's body, the memory of the young boy's naked and bloodied corpse indelibly marked in his mind. What had hurt most was that the poor lad had looked so cold – not that his thin jumper could have saved him from such savagery. But the indignity he'd suffered in death, the casual dumping of his body without even a final set of clothing, seemed unimaginably inhumane.

If this was a final warning before the endgame, how long did they have?

Anderson's finger hovered over the photo of his wife smiling up from his phone screen. As he stroked the image, the phone automatically began to call her number. He almost hung up in panic, knowing she'd hear the pub sounds and guess where he was. But tonight he needed to hear her voice.

'Hi you! I was just thinking about you.'

He closed his eyes and drank in the warmth that flooded his ear. 'That's spooky.'

'Mm-hmm. Sounds noisy – busy in The Miller's, is it?' The smile in her tone was infectious.

'For a weeknight, yes. Sorry. I know you made me all those nice frozen dinners.'

'Which I never expected you to eat. You forget, Joel, I've had you for a while. Did you get my text?'

'I did. When do you reckon you'll be home?'

'Tomorrow, hopefully. Saturday afternoon at the latest. I just have to clear a few things here and then I'm on my way. Besides, watching the news, I think I might have been away too long...'

'It's fine, love.'

'It isn't. But thanks for saying it. That child has been missing for three weeks. I know what the connotations are. You need me.'

Quite without warning, emotion claimed Anderson's throat. 'It'll be good to see you, Rosie-Ro.' The mention of his private pet name for his wife almost sent him under and he closed his eyes to prevent him making an even bigger fool of himself.

He heard Ros catch her breath and knew she understood. 'I love you. I'll text when I'm on my way, okay, darling?'

Hurry home, Rosalyn. Bring my sanity back...

What worried Joel Anderson more than anything else was the ease with which tears were coming to him. For the seven months of hell he'd endured on sick leave following Matthew Cooper's murder, tears had been the constant. He couldn't stop them. He feared he'd never be able to function normally again. It had taken a year of intensive therapy and four years of weekly counselling sessions to restore him to some semblance of who he'd been before.

Op Seraph had sent him tumbling back, tears never far away. It was getting worse and the fear that history might repeat itself was growing.

He had to pull himself together. DCI Taylor was watching him like a hawk; any hint of his emotional issues would have him permanently retired from the force. He couldn't allow that to happen.

He *was* his job, like it or loathe it. The thought of going under again terrified him. Because this time, he might never return.

Chapter Sixty-Three

Cora

No missed calls from Minshull. No messages. No response to any of her attempts to call him.

And Hannah Perry still not found.

Outside the newsagent's at the end of her street, the newspaper headlines screamed at her, almost as loud as the groans and complaints from discarded litter that mid April winds blew around her feet. But in recent days, the television news channels had made Hannah less of a priority. Three weeks missing with no discernible suspects or developments pushed the story down the TV news schedules. Last night, the investigation had only warranted a brief mention four news items down. What if the news agencies decided Hannah Perry was no longer newsworthy?

There was nothing Cora could do. And it was tearing her apart. Sleep eluded her, the little she'd managed to grab haunted by images of a child reaching out to her, lost and terrified and alone. Cora was alone, too. Daniel seemed to be tiring of listening to her, always cutting her off as if what she wanted to express no longer mattered. She'd even tried to call her mother, but Sheila Lael wasn't answering her phone.

With nobody else to call, and desperately needing advice, Cora called the only other person who knew about Operation Seraphine.

Rory hurried into the café behind the University of South Suffolk, his face flushed from a dash across campus. 'I'm sorry,' he rushed, collapsing onto a chair by Cora's table. 'Staff meeting ran over. If anyone asks, you're my emergency dental appointment.'

'I bought you cake,' Cora said, as a waitress placed an enormous slice of banoffee layer cake in front of him. 'Thanks, Pat.'

'Not just any cake. The greatest layer cake in history.' Rory grinned up at the waitress. 'Marry me, Pat.'

'You only love me for my baking,' she replied, still chuckling as she returned to the kitchen.

Wrapping a serviette around the fork handle, Rory began to attack the cake. 'So,' he said between eager mouthfuls, 'if you're cracking out the edible bribes something must be up.'

'I've been removed from the investigation.'

'The police?'

She nodded.

Rory put down his fork. 'Why?'

'They won't tell me.'

'But you found stuff for them, didn't you?'

'Yes. What I heard led them to uncover significant evidence against their chief suspect. Rob – Acting DS Minshull – said so. I don't understand why they don't want me now.'

Rory listened as she recounted the events surrounding her dismissal. Any doubts she'd had about sharing details of the investigation were gone: she needed to talk about it and Rory was ready to listen.

'It's their mistake,' he said, finally.

'You think so? Because honestly, I don't know anymore.'

'Their mistake, mate. Not yours. You did what you said you would.'

'Thank you.' His confidence in her almost summoned tears. 'I just wish I understood, you know?'

Cake eaten, Rory pulled a small bottle of antibacterial hand cleanser from his pocket and began to clean his hands with the precision of a surgeon scrubbing up for an operation. 'Is there any way you could talk to someone in CID? Off the record?'

'I only have Rob's number. And he isn't returning my calls.'

'So talk to the press.'

Cora stared at him. 'I couldn't do that.'

'Why not?'

'I promised Rob…'

'Maybe Rob isn't Hannah's best option. I've seen the news. It's like the media think Hannah's a lost cause. It's been three weeks and they don't have anything to report. But if they knew she was still newsworthy… If you gave them something to reignite their interest…'

'Like what?'

'Get them to step up the search with the general public. Put up that reward several of the tabloids were saying they'd offer. That never happened, did it? Maybe if they thought they could sell papers off the back of a campaign Hannah would be headline news again.'

'It's unethical.'

'So is leaving a child with a psychopath.'

It made sense, but Cora shook the suggestion away. 'I've seen the investigation from the inside. I know how hard the team are working to find Hannah. I couldn't betray them.'

Rory sat back. 'But if it was a choice between protecting the team and saving Hannah?'

The thought made her stomach tense. She took a breath, pushing the temptation away. 'There must be another way.'

Rory flexed his newly sanitised fingers. 'Then you have to ask the universe.'

'What?'

'Ask the universe. Don't look at me like that, I mean it. In situations you can't control, you have to go to a higher power. Ask the universe for a solution.'

'And you a devotee of science...'

He shrugged. 'Doesn't hurt to have a back-up plan. Put it this way, by asking the question you subconsciously give yourself permission to look for solutions. You can't find answers if you aren't predisposed to seek them out. That's the science bit.' He leaned towards her. 'Who knows? It might help.'

It didn't matter that Rory's solution had been so left-field. Cora drove home, her spirits a little lighter. Her friend hadn't once questioned her ability, or her right to be angry with the police. His belief in her was implicit.

As the road edged towards the bright light of the Suffolk coast, Cora sent her request to the wide sky above.

Hannah

My ankle hurts. It's not light enough yet to see in the Small Space but I think there might be blood. I've tried moving my toes and they hurt, too. I want to cry, but I daren't.

They might hear.

They might come back.

I can't make Them angry again.

In the shadows I reach down and touch my sock. It feels stiff where the pain is and cracks a bit under my fingers.

I feel sick.

All I wanted to do was keep my Peppa Pig pencil case. Nanna Perry gave it to me when I started school and Nanna is in heaven now. I tried to ask Them nicely, but then They wouldn't let go so I shouted. And then I got up.

I almost got to the little wood door but then I heard the metal thing behind me. The thing that lives by the toilet bucket.

And that's when They hit my ankle.

My throat is sore from when I shouted. My ankle *really* hurts.

But I still have my bag. I didn't let Them take it.

And even though I'm scared, I've been thinking about it. They were surprised when I got up. They *wobbled*. Maybe next time I can push Them over and open the door…

Chapter Sixty-Four

Cora

'Hey love.'

'Mum? Is everything okay?'

'Everything's fine. Great, actually. Why don't you come over? It'd be lovely to see you.'

The phone call from her mum had been a surprise in itself, but her mother's calm conversation and sentences that ended properly were a shock. But Cora was completely unprepared for what she found as she walked into her childhood home.

The hall was empty and eerily silent. Its absence of noise shook Cora more than the cacophony she'd become accustomed to. She edged along the hallway as if entering a new house for the first time.

'Mum?'

'In here, lovely.'

Her voice was different, too. As though the mum of her far distant childhood memories had sneaked into the present. Disorientated by the changes, Cora peered around the living room door.

The room was bright and smelled of polish and newly vacuumed carpet. The curtains were drawn back and a vase of flowers had been arranged in the window, like Cora's grandmother used to do, in the old cut-glass vase Cora hadn't seen for years. Around the sagging green sofa and armchairs – now covered in pale cream throws – no valuation catalogues were stacked; no boxes of yelling items were balanced around the furniture. It was silent here, too, save for the soft hum of the radio playing Smooth FM.

And in the centre of it all, stood Sheila Lael. Dressed in new clothes, the old oversized hoodie and baggy leggings gone, grinning broadly.

Cora bit back tears. 'Mum – this place – *you…*'

Sheila clapped her hands and giggled like a teen. 'Ha ha! I *knew* you'd be surprised! And I didn't want to say anything until I'd done it.'

'It's – amazing. But how? When?'

'First things first, have a hug.'

A *hug*. The last time Cora had been hugged by her mother was the night they buried Bill Lael. In shock, Cora froze initially, the sensation overwhelming. Then her arms gradually found her mother as Sheila embraced her.

'I'm sorry,' Sheila rushed against her shoulder. 'I've been away for too long.' Breaking the hug, she ushered Cora to the sofa, which smelled of fabric refresher when she sat down. 'There you go, make yourself comfy. Kettle's on.'

Cora reached out and held her mum's hand. 'Mum – wait. What made this happen?'

'I just decided. Well, no, not just me. I had a bit of help. Do you remember Maureen, who used to work at the council with your dad? No, you probably don't. She was one of the secretaries in his office and a good friend to him. Anyway, turns out she's now retired and interested in antiques. Auctions, you know, actual ones. She popped round, out of the blue, to ask my advice. And the state of the place – well, I was so embarrassed. I haven't had visitors since your dad passed. It was like I hadn't realised what a state everything was in. I ended up sobbing over her, silly fool that I am, and she invited me to the St Just WI. She came to help me straighten everything up, too. Brought her two boys round and we cleared the place. All the stuff's in a storage unit now.'

Cora could hardly believe what she was hearing. 'But how did Maureen know where to find you?'

Sheila grinned and sat beside her daughter. 'That's the really funny thing. Do you remember Jan Martin, from the *Argus*? She was the one who told Maureen I was on my own now but still in the same house. How funny is that?'

The surprises just kept on coming this afternoon. Cora stared at her mum. 'That's very funny. I saw her a couple of weeks ago but I didn't think anything of it.'

'Well, there you go. Your dad had all sorts round here back in the day. Pretty sure Jan would have been one of them. Mo says Jan'll be at the meeting on Tuesday afternoon so I'm going to thank her. I'm doing a talk for them on antiques – me, talking in front of a crowd! Your dad would have laughed himself daft about that.'

As Sheila bustled into the kitchen, still chattering away, a swell of excitement rose in Cora. Rob had said not to talk to the press. Rory disagreed. For two days she had thought of nothing else but Hannah and how best to reach her. And now Jan Martin – the sole voice of reason in the media scrum to condemn South Suffolk Police – had brought about a change in her mother that Cora had worried she might never see. She had a lot to thank Jan for.

Rory had said if she were meant to talk to the press an opportunity would present itself. Cora wasn't certain she shared his belief in the universe but it seemed like she was being handed the chance she had secretly hoped for.

'How about I come with you?' she asked, before she could think better of it. 'I'd love to hear your talk.'

Sheila placed the teapot on the newly polished coffee table. 'Would you? Oh sweetheart, that would be wonderful! I'm so nervous. It would be great to see another friendly face on the front row. I can't remember the last time we went out together.'

Smiling up at her mum – her brave, utterly changed mum who was daring to rebuild her life – Cora knew her course was set.

Chapter Sixty-Five

Anderson

Blood.

It was visible across the bright yellow fabric of the child's pencil case, a darkly menacing smear marring the smiling face of the cartoon pig.

Anderson couldn't take his eyes off it as Minshull held up the evidence bag containing the latest delivery. The last delivery, if the pattern from Matthew Cooper's abduction was being followed. A flash of more blood, from slashes in young skin, assaulted his mind. *Not this time*, he repeated. *Not this child*.

'Check the blood type against Hannah Perry's,' Minshull said. DC Wheeler nodded and took it with conscious reverence. All around him, Anderson saw the shock and fear of his team. They all knew what this meant. The note accompanying the pencil case left no doubt:

SO HERE WE ARE AGAIN.

AND THIS IS HOW IT ENDS.

£100,000 IN THE BLUE SKIP BEHIND THE GARAGES, LEONARD ROAD.

TELL THE PRESS YOU'RE CONFIDENT OF FINDING HER. EXACT WORDS.

THE DAY YOU SAY THAT, LEAVE THE MONEY AT NOON.

DON'T LET ME DOWN THIS TIME.

The long-dreaded demand for money – but it was the location that chilled Anderson's blood.

'Leonard Road. That's on the Parkhall Estate, close to the Perrys' house.' Bennett looked at Minshull. 'It has to be Collins.'

'It's the same road mentioned in Matthew's final note. Last time it was a litter bin: this time a skip. But it's too close to be a coincidence. We have to bring Collins in.' Anderson wished he couldn't hear fear in his voice.

Minshull stepped in. 'But if he has Hannah, what happens to her?'

'A damn sight less than if she remains with him.' Anderson jabbed a thumb in the direction Wheeler had gone. 'We know his lock-up turned up nothing. Could Hannah have been there at any point but moved somewhere else?'

'I doubt it, it was packed,' Lanehan said. 'And he knows we searched it now because of the warrant.' Lanehan softened her voice. 'I'm sorry, Sarge, I think it's a dead end.'

'He could be working with someone.'

'We have Adam Jackson in custody, Rob, Collins' only known associate. If anyone got the thankless task of watching a stolen kid, Jackson would be first in line. But there was no sign at the Long Deighton industrial estate and I don't think they would have chosen the lock-up, even if there had been room to get in it – too many people around on the estate at all hours. Someone would have heard her.'

'But what if there's someone else?' Minshull refused to let it go. 'I've seen cases like this before – family members concocting abductions for the reward money. Someone is always assisting them.'

'Is that what you think this is?' Bennett asked Minshull.

Anderson turned, revelation illuminating his expression. 'That's it, isn't it? The link? Collins loves money. He'll do whatever he can to get it, threaten whoever he needs to – and we know he threatened to take Adam Jackson's kids if he didn't comply. He has opportunity, he has motive and now we know he has *form*.'

'Then why only include a ransom note in the last delivery?'

Anderson's body thrummed with an energy he'd not felt in weeks – years, even. 'For the news story. For the theatre. This whole abduction is a way to get money. Maybe he thought the rumoured reward in the tabloids would happen and he could cash in. That happened for Matthew, too, only it was a broadsheet mooting the idea, just to sell papers. There was no need for ransom notes with each of Hannah's belongings because it wasn't the game. But the last one, the big finish, that's where he could put his demand for what he'd wanted all along.'

'Did Collins kill Matthew Cooper?' Bennett was watching both of them now, her gaze flicking between them.

'If he did, he blames you.'

Anderson stared at Minshull. 'How do you know?'

'You denied him his payout with Matthew. Made him dispose of the problem.' He seemed to disgust himself with his chosen words. He shook his head as if trying to dislodge them from his skin. '*Don't let me down*. He wants his plan to succeed this time. He wants to win.'

It was time. They'd waited long enough. Steel resolve coursing down his spine, Anderson made the call.

'Arrest Collins. Bring him in.'

'On what charge?'

'Unlawful money lending. We have more than enough evidence to support it. And suspicion of abduction. Once he's in and interviewed, we can present to CPS and ask for the charges to be actioned. There's enough to convince them now.'

Bennett glanced at Minshull. 'But shouldn't we go straight for abduction?'

'We level the money-lending charge at him first. Make him think he has a lesser charge to face if he confesses to taking the kid.'

'Exactly.' Anderson smiled at Minshull. At last they were united. 'And then he'll tell us where Hannah is.'

Chapter Sixty-Six

Cora

'So you're going to see Jan?'

Cora looked at Daniel as they sat on a sun-warmed bench on the lush grassy park across the road from Daniel's home on the outskirts of Ipswich. April sunshine had finally broken the curse of wet weather that had ushered in the month.

'I want to sound her out, at least. She's supported the police all along and I think she might know how we could help them regain public support. I don't want to jeopardise the investigation, only find Hannah.'

Daniel smiled. 'I think it will help you,' he soothed. 'And Hannah. The police don't seem keen to find her alive. At least if the media up the pressure, it might just push them into action.'

'That's what I'm hoping. It's Rob I feel let down by the most,' she admitted, brushing a fly from her face as if dismissing the detective.

'Are you okay?' he asked, as gently as he could.

She turned to him. 'Not really.'

'I hate seeing you like this. Come here.'

Cora rested her head against his shoulder, curling herself into him and he rested his cheek against the crown of her head, the contact warm and comforting.

'Maybe we should get away for a while?' he murmured into her hair. 'I could wangle cover for a long weekend in the May half-term break, or maybe we could head off for a few weeks in the summer? Now you aren't so worried about leaving your mum it's the perfect time to escape.'

'I'd like that,' she replied, struck by a sudden need to be away from it all, from the dreams and Hannah's voice, Rob and Anderson and the constant concern. She was tired – bone-tired – her body aching for rest. In this small moment, she wanted it more than anything.

'Somewhere warm,' Daniel continued, the game catching his imagination. 'Or remote. Definitely remote.'

'Mmm, and quiet...' She closed her eyes, her head growing heavy against his shoulder.

'I'd go anywhere for you, Cora.'

She smiled as his voice began to drift away.

'This is what matters. It's who we are, Cora. It's all we need to be. This is why you needed to leave the case. It was making you ill, pulling us apart. I should never have put you in that situation. I'm so glad I got you out.'

Suddenly awake, Cora scrambled out from under him. The heels of her boots dug ugly divots into the grass as she stumbled to her feet.

'What did you say?'

'What are you doing? Come back and snuggle me, you crazy lady.'

'*What* did you just say?'

Daniel laughed, nerves flickering at the edge of his voice. 'I said I'm glad we're happy again...'

'How did you "get me out"?'

'What are you talking about? Sit down. You were falling asleep just then. You're adorable when you sleep.'

She ignored his outstretched arms, backing away. 'You said something to them. To Anderson. To Rob.'

'What? You're being ridiculous.'

'You're lying. It was your fault I had to leave...'

'Look, just calm down, okay?'

But it was too late. Truth crashed around her, shattering the illusion, revealing who Daniel Gold truly was. 'You're *lying*. I can see it all over your face. What did you say, Daniel?'

'This really isn't worth getting upset over.'

'*Upset?* Do you have any idea what you've done?'

'I saw how ill it made you, how it took over your life. And I knew we'd made a mistake.'

'So you had me removed from the case?'

'I told them I was concerned about you. I said it was affecting your sleep, your wellbeing – neither of which you can deny.'

'The case is affecting everyone in the team,' she countered, staring him down. 'Why should I be any different? I want to find Hannah, just like they do. *That's* what I was losing sleep over.'

'You were in a dangerous situation. We don't know how this could affect your state of mind. You said in the video diary that you were doubting what you were hearing...'

Cora's mouth fell open.

It all made sense.

When she spoke, her voice was low, measured, utterly cold. 'You showed him the video.'

'Cora, look...'

'Nobody was supposed to see that but us. You said it was private, a personal record. Why did you show it to the police?'

Now Daniel was standing too, reaching out for her. 'To get you out, okay? You'd become too involved. And I'm sorry, Cora, but when I saw such a change in you – not to mention your growing dependence on a man you hardly know – it was the only sensible course of action. As your partner, I was worried. As your professor I was downright terrified. You think I could sit by and watch that happen to the woman I love? Absolutely not! I love you, Cora. I did what I had to.'

'So it had nothing to do with my wellbeing. This was all about your petty jealousy.'

'No! I didn't say that. I said...'

'You *said*, "my growing dependence on a man I hardly knew". Not Hannah's voice, not the investigation. You did all this because you're jealous of Rob Minshull.'

He jutted out his chin like an unrepentant child. 'Maybe I am. Maybe I didn't enjoy watching my girlfriend, who claims to love me, fawning all over another man.'

'Fawning? I was helping him to find a missing child!'

'And what did you expect would happen when you found her? That the two of you would be swept up by the euphoria of the moment? That Minshull would fall for you?'

'What? No!'

'I think you did. I think that's what you wanted. And the more he needed you, the more you wanted him. Let's just get away, like we agreed, and—'

'I'm not going anywhere with you! I am *done*, Daniel.'

'Don't say that. Come here...'

He tried to grab her hand, but she shoved him away.

'Cora, stop! Where are you going?'

'Away from you!' she yelled over her shoulder as she began to walk away.

'Don't be like that. Let's talk about it… *Cora!*'

But she didn't stop. She didn't turn back. She was done: with the study, with the lies – and with Daniel. She got into her car, started the engine and slammed her foot on the accelerator.

–

Everything she had believed was wrong.

Daniel had lied, Anderson had chosen to believe him and Rob had betrayed her with his silence.

Well, no more.

As she drove, Cora's anger gave way to a different emotion. Hope.

Now she knew the truth, they *had* to listen. Daniel must have tampered with the video diary to make her look unstable. If they discounted that, everything she had done for Operation Seraphine had furthered the investigation. She'd helped them locate Shaun Collins' notebook and had established that Hannah was still alive. Without her, what did they have? Most importantly, what hope did Hannah have?

Rob Minshull wasn't answering his phone again, so Cora left one message and ended her subsequent calls before they went to voicemail. Clearly, she was going to have to do this in person. He couldn't ignore the truth if he saw it staring back at him.

On the radio, the dance music ended and a news bulletin began.

'Police leading the search for the missing Suffolk school-girl Hannah Perry have today arrested a man on suspicion of abduction. The 37-year-old, believed to be Shaun Collins, the partner of Hannah's mother, was arrested this morning at an address on the Parkhall Estate in St Just. Alex Haynes reports.

'It's over three weeks since eight-year-old Hannah Perry went missing on her way home from school for the Easter break. Despite a widespread police search and tireless efforts of the local community, the St Just school-girl has yet to be found. While South Suffolk Police are refusing to confirm the identity of the man arrested, he has been named locally as Shaun Collins, stepfather of the missing girl.

'Hannah's mother, Ashleigh Perry, has not been implicated in Hannah's abduction.

'This is a significant development, in an investigation dogged by criticism and the spectre of Matthew Cooper, the ten-year-old abducted and murdered in St Just seven years ago. Meanwhile, the family of Shaun Collins are vehemently denying his involvement, accusing the police of a witch-hunt. While Hannah Perry remains missing, hopes this evening are growing in this small Suffolk village that we will soon know where she is. Or what has happened to her...'

No! This couldn't be happening! If they arrested Collins, what would happen to Hannah? What if he refused to tell them where she was? Someone had to speak for the child – and now Cora knew Daniel had lied to Anderson, she had to be back on the team.

Turning the car around in the next pub car park she came to, Cora headed for the road into the town centre – and South Suffolk Police HQ.

Chapter Sixty-Seven

Minshull

By the time the end of Minshull's shift arrived he was more than ready to leave. It had been a long day, not helped by the news of Shaun Collins' arrest leaking and a very public fracas on the front steps of South Suffolk Police HQ after Shaun Collins' sister Siobhan and a gang of placard-waving supporters blocked the entrance for an hour. Things had turned ugly when the television cameras arrived and several protestors had been arrested. Dave Wheeler had been caught in the fray and was now nursing an impressive black eye for his trouble.

Of course, Collins' arrest had dominated the news all day, incurring the wrath of DCI Taylor, which Anderson did his best to deflect. But the episode had made the CID team jumpy. Minshull had ordered in bacon sandwiches and, later, pizza in an attempt to boost morale, but he couldn't help feeling both were hollow gestures.

The press were gunning for them, of course. Siobhan Collins, too, screaming blue murder because they'd arrested her poor sweet innocent thug of a brother. Anderson seemed resigned to it all, relieved at least to see Collins safely incarcerated. But what if Collins refused to reveal where Hannah was? Nobody on the CID team wanted Anderson to go through what he'd endured over Matthew Cooper. Already whispers about his state of mind were passing between them.

Collins was in the custody cells, where Minshull and Anderson had decided he'd stay overnight to let him sweat. At five o'clock tomorrow morning, he would meet his brief and at seven they would start to question him. Minshull hoped he would give up Hannah's location quickly if he believed he'd only face the lesser charge of unlawful money lending instead of abduction.

Minshull worried about Hannah, wherever she was tonight. But at least with Collins in custody, she would endure no more violence.

It still smarted that Cora was off the investigation, days after the decision had been made. It had been done quietly, supposedly, but as was usual with this kind of response, everyone knew. To the CID team's credit, they weren't talking openly about it, but Minshull suspected they were discussing the decision privately. They had her to thank for bringing them Collins, after all. He just wished she could have seen it.

Meanwhile, the missed call notifications and waiting messages in his voicemail were growing in number. He couldn't bring himself to reply, or listen to her messages. The decision had been made over his head: what help could he be to her? He didn't like it, but it was no longer his responsibility. Better a clean break than a messy post-mortem of events.

'You off, Sarge?' Drew Ellis gave a tired smile as Minshull met him in the corridor.

'I am. Just going to grab a few hours' kip then I'll be back. How's Mr Collins liking our custody suite?'

'Oh he's loving it, I heard. Going to give us a glowing review on TripAdvisor.'

'Well, let's hope he tells us something tomorrow.'

'Yeah. Um, for what it's worth, Sarge, I don't think Dr Lael faked that stuff.'

Minshull faced his colleague. 'Neither do I. But appearances can be deceptive. All that matters now is finding Hannah – alive or dead.'

He turned and punched the double doors open, giving the desk sergeant an apologetic wave as he passed. He wished he hadn't let his gym membership lapse this year. A punch-bag might be therapeutic right now. He should have said something to Cora. Should have listened to her messages. But he couldn't let it take his eyes off the ball.

The car park was almost empty, bathed in an unearthly orange glow from the streetlights. A takeaway, a bath and bed. Maybe a bottle of beer to help him sleep. That was all he wanted tonight.

But as he neared his car, a figure on the car park stopped him in his tracks.

He saw her before she saw him, but his attempt to turn back caught her attention.

'Rob! Wait!'

She was running towards him now, that haunted look he'd seen in the professor's video now staring back at him in person. Why had he believed she wouldn't pursue him if he failed to respond to her calls? He'd been so sure...

'Cora, you need to go.'

'*No*. Not until you listen.'

He resisted the urge to hurry back to his car. This needed to be dealt with now, a firm line drawn. 'I have listened. Repeatedly. You need to let this go. The decision's been made and I couldn't change it if I wanted to.'

She stopped dead, inches from him; cheeks flushed from her race across the car park and pale green eyes trained on him like sniper sights. 'Are you saying you agree with them?'

'I think it's for the best...'

'You of all people should know what's really going on here. I thought we were friends. I *thought* you understood.'

'Believe me, I'm trying to. You're not making it easy.'

She blinked. 'You think I'm mad.' It wasn't a question, but the hurt in her expression dared him to reply.

'I think you need to give yourself a break.' Was she unhinged? He didn't want to believe it, even if her current behaviour screamed that she might be. He took a step closer, edging his way around the question. 'What you found for us – what you *heard* – it's made all the difference. We're so much closer to finding Hannah because of your help. So please, rest easy in that. I appreciate your help more than you know...'

'You think I'm mad. You think I've become obsessed and my judgement is impaired.'

'I – no...'

'Doesn't it seem odd to you that we were making such progress right before Daniel – my *ex*-boyfriend now, by the way – came to you with that video?'

How did she know about that? His face must have betrayed his surprise because she let out a hollow laugh.

'Obviously not. I can't believe you didn't see what he was doing. He was jealous of us, Rob. He thought we were having an affair... And I know how crazy that sounds. He told me.'

'When?'

'This afternoon. I'd been keeping a private video diary as part of our research project. I think he edited it to look like I was losing my mind.'

Had the video been doctored? Minshull tried to take his mind back to viewing the footage in Anderson's office, but it was hard to remember any obvious edit points. Cora clearly wasn't in a secure frame of mind: to accuse her senior professor and allegedly former partner could be a spectacular work of paranoia. Had there ever been cause for anyone to assume he and Cora were more than colleagues? Given her unkempt, wild appearance this evening, it was difficult to believe she was fully in control.

And yet, there *had* been a moment when he'd felt a shift in their relationship. He'd dismissed it soon afterwards, but it had been there. If he'd been aware of it, who was to say the professor hadn't seen it too?

The thought made him uncomfortable. As did the distinct possibility that his colleagues might see him talking to Cora. He had to put a stop to this now, however shaky his reasons for doing so.

'We have to think of what's best for Hannah,' he stated, hoping it was authoritative enough to make her hear him. He thought of the bloodstained pencil case, of how easy it would be to get her to listen to it for signs of Hannah still being alive... No, he couldn't do that. *Look at her, she isn't reliable...* 'The decision is out of my hands. I'm sorry – truly sorry, Cora. You can't be part of this anymore.'

'But if you have Collins, who is looking for Hannah?'

'That's no longer your concern.'

'But it is! I'm involved. Let me back on the team and I'll help you find her.'

'Cora, you can't be here...'

'I can *still* hear her!'

He began to back away. 'You only think you can,' he said, hating every word. 'It feels real, but it can't be.'

'You said you believed me...'

'I did. I *do*. But the dreams and the theories outside of her actual belongings – they are just hearsay. They mean nothing – not to the police, at least. You've got to let this go.'

She shook her head, tears burgeoning. 'No – *no* – you have to listen to me. You have to let me help...'

'You have to leave it to us now. We know what we're doing.'

'But you can't *hear* her!'

'Stop this and *go home*, Cora. Please. We can't talk anymore.'
He was shaking as he walked away.

Chapter Sixty-Eight

Cora

Cora stared at the orange car park lights as heavy rain slowly turned them into a thousand diamond trails across her car windscreen. She'd watched Minshull drive away and the car park slowly emptying. Now, she was the only one left.

Everyone had gone. Nobody on her side. And the age-old ache of being an outsider had returned.

I'm shaking.

She was chilled to her core, but not by the temperature around her. Rob's final dismissal of her had frozen her from the inside out. The jacket she'd pulled from the back seat hung limply over her shoulders now but made little difference.

He thinks I'm insane.

Despite the bleakness of her position, she'd clung on to threadbare hopes that Rob might still believe her. They had shared so much in such a short space of time: didn't that count for anything? She'd thought they'd shared a connection – not the kind that Daniel had supposedly seen, but an understanding she would never share with the professor. Daniel could never understand what being an outsider felt like, because he wasn't ever outside of anything. He was 'one of the boys' and always would be.

Rob was different. Part of a team in body but emotionally excluded from all that should give him. Cora had sensed it from their first meeting and the few clues he'd shared since revealed a man passionate about succeeding but trapped by doubt that his father's legacy was all anyone else saw. He was wholly outside while giving every appearance of belonging. Nobody understood that like Cora did.

She had hoped the truth about the video diary would make him believe her. But he thought she was a charlatan, just like Anderson, the CID team and every other person who had ever known about her ability. The world belonged to those who fitted in, who assimilated without awkward corners or rough edges. Being bombarded by invisible voices disqualified Cora from seamlessly slotting into society. Always had, always would. With the look of pity she'd seen in Rob's eyes tonight, her last hopes of an ally had died.

All I've done is make things worse.

Even if she did find vital information about Hannah now, Rob wouldn't listen. By coming here tonight she had hammered the final nail into her credibility. How hadn't she considered this before it was too late? If she was Hannah's only hope – as she'd led herself to believe – she had just signed the child's death warrant.

Utterly broken, she leant her head against the steering wheel and sobbed.

Hannah

I've got a secret – a new one. Better than the Home smell! Finding it has made me smile so much it hurt my face to hide it when They brought me a cheese sandwich earlier.

I found it by accident. I was hugging my bag, wishing the Home smell was still inside it, when my cold fingers found the zip on the front pocket. Why hadn't I looked in there before? Because inside there was still a little bit of Home smell – and something else, too. Chocolate! Right in the bottom of the pocket, down where the crumbs are. The lovely little chocolate chicks and bunnies the nice man in the bunny costume at the Easter Market gave me!

They're wrapped in foil with pictures on them and the colours make my heart beat like I'm running a big race. Everything in the Small Space has been dark and dull, but the chicks and bunnies are like finding bits of rainbow hidden in my bag. They taste good, too.

Now, even though I'm still squashed up in the Small Space and my ankle still hurts, I feel taller. And the Tall Feeling has helped me make a plan. There are ten chocolate shapes. So I'm going to eat one each time the Small Space gets light. The splintery gap and the crack in the glass behind me are just wide enough to push the pieces of foil wrapper through, so They won't find them.

Eating the chocolate makes me feel better. Stronger, like I can run when I have to. And having a secret again makes the scary feeling go away, just like it did when I found the Home smell.

They don't know about the secret chocolates. But I do…

Chapter Sixty-Nine

Cora

'And so, that's that. Thank you for listening. If you have any questions, please ask. I hope you all go home now and find Rembrandts in your loft.'

Sheila Lael blushed as the village hall rang with applause.

Cora squeezed her hand when she sat down, but in truth she'd hardly heard a word. Tiredness dragged at every muscle in her body but she'd been determined to come to the WI meeting this afternoon. She'd spotted Jan Martin walking in late, as the chairwoman Margaret Mitchell was introducing her mother, and hadn't been able to take her eyes off her.

Her last conversation with Rob had galvanised her resolve. Collins was still in custody, the news reports confirming police had been granted more time to question him. Too much time for Hannah to be alone. Her voice still entreated Cora at night, growing fainter as if losing hope was pulling her from reach. Cora had to do something.

The police didn't want her anymore.

Rob Minshull had refused to help.

But the universe had provided a solution.

As soon as the meeting was officially closed, Cora moved to the back of the hall, praying the newspaper editor wouldn't leave before refreshments were served. Thankfully, she saw Jan joining the queue and hurried over to stand behind her.

Jan's smile was broad and warm as she turned around. 'Lovely to see your mum again. Her talk was excellent.'

'She knows her stuff, doesn't she?' Cora replied, taking a cup and saucer from the stack. 'It's so good to see her out. She hasn't done much since Dad...'

Jan nodded. 'I understand. Lost my dad a few years ago. It makes you want to hide from the world for a while.'

'Tea or coffee, ladies?' The lady behind the refreshment table asked, her broad smile beaming towards them like a beacon.

'Tea, please, Cynthia,' Jan replied. 'Cora?'

'Same, thanks.'

'Ladies after my own heart,' Cynthia chuckled, pouring tea from an enormous ancient enamel teapot. 'Lovely to see you, Janice. I wasn't sure if you'd be here today. You must be exhausted with all that horrible business.'

Jan gave a rueful smile. 'Occupational hazard, I'm afraid.'

'I'll bet. Been most impressive to see you on the news every night, though. And standing up for those poor police officers when nobody else is. Before you know it they'll be headhunting you, mark my words. And rightly so. You should be on Sky News with that lovely Dermot Murni-bloke, not hidden away here in St Just.'

Jan rolled her eyes but flushed a little with the compliment. 'I don't know about that. But thank you.'

'Ooh, Janice, I've been meaning to pick your brains about publicity for our summer fair,' an older lady called, hurrying to Jan's side and linking an arm through hers. 'Can I steal you?'

With a helpless grin at Cora, Jan was ushered away. Her chance to speak to the journalist gone, Cora reluctantly returned to the rows of chairs, where her mother was timidly nodding in the middle of a conversation with three other WI members. She held her teacup like a porcelain shield, knuckles whitening where they gripped the handle.

'Ah, Cora dear. We were just saying to your mum that she should take up public speaking. She's very good.'

'Oh, I don't think I could—'

'Knows her stuff, too. My Sid wants to ask you about ashtrays, Sheila.' The woman pulled a face. 'He's obsessed with them. Got hundreds of the things gathering dust in his shed. I'm hoping you'll tell us we're sitting on a goldmine, my love, otherwise I'll be ordering a skip.'

'Well perhaps if you ring me this week we can arrange something,' Sheila mumbled, relief flooding her expression when her answer was enough to pacify her interrogators and send them scurrying away to hound someone else. 'I thought they'd never leave.'

'You did so well, Mum. It will get easier.'

'I know. It's just taking time to get used to people in person again.'

'One step at a time.'

'Only way to do it.' Steeling herself, Sheila patted Cora's arm. 'So, what are your plans for the rest of the day? Are you seeing Daniel?'

'Not today.' Cora bristled at his name but didn't let Sheila see. Her mother didn't need to know about him yet. There would be time, when Hannah was found and this was all over. 'I think I might just head home. I could do with a quiet evening.'

'You do that. Have a little stroll by the sea. There's a lot to be said for being alone sometimes.'

Cora had never been more alone than she was at that moment.

The WI members were beginning to disperse, the village hall slowly emptying, its echoes deepening as fewer voices sounded. Sheila gathered her belongings together as Cora fetched their coats from the rack by the door.

'There's your coat, Mum.'

'Thanks love. Oh no,' Sheila said, picking up a stack of antique price guides. 'Jan forgot these.'

'I'm sure she'll have them next time,' Cora said, keen to get going.

'She wanted them today. And the auction she was talking about is happening on Friday.'

Cora recognised the look of panic in her mother's eyes. Order was paramount in the brave new world Sheila was discovering outside her own four walls. Any shift sent her into uncertain territory – and the last thing Cora wanted was for her mum to retreat again. 'Okay, why don't I drop these off at the *Argus* office for her on my way home?'

Sheila immediately brightened. 'Would you? Oh love, that would set my mind at rest. You don't mind?'

'Not at all.' An idea was fizzing in Cora's brain – the unexpected diversion presenting a perfect opportunity. She took the books and kissed her mother. 'Will you be okay getting home?'

Sheila nodded. 'I'll be fine. Margaret and June have invited me for a coffee at that new place on the park. I think I might go.'

In the car, driving into the centre of the village, Cora smiled. The change in Sheila was remarkable. She owed Jan Martin a great deal of thanks. She would tell her when she delivered the books. It would be a perfect opener to what she really wanted to say...

Guilt stabbed her conscience as the first houses of the town came into view. Cora steeled herself against it. She had made her decision: this was the only way.

Rob had said talking to the press could harm the investigation. But the thought of Hannah, alone while her abductor was in custody, was too much to bear.

She couldn't let Hannah become the next victim. Whatever Rob, Anderson and the CID team thought, she *had* to find the girl. They were linked by the voice she heard. Hannah was everywhere, in everything, as if her voice was stalking Cora. She was beginning to doubt her own hold on reality but Hannah's voice and the thought of the child confined, terrified and alone wouldn't leave. She had been chosen for this. She had to find her.

Jan Martin would know what was happening. Rory had said as much the last time they'd spoken. *Journalists always know more than they let on...* If Rob wouldn't tell her, maybe the newspaper editor would. She'd been on every news programme lately, the undisputed star expert in the missing child case. Jan had to know what was happening and how to turn the media's attention back to finding Hannah.

Rob had insisted that nobody on the team should talk to the press. But Cora was no longer on the team, Rob wasn't taking her calls and Hannah was still missing.

Nothing mattered now but bringing Hannah home.

Parking her car in the small car park off St Bart's Street, Cora's mind was set. She was going to talk to Jan.

Chapter Seventy

Minshull

'I'm going to ask again, Mr Collins, just so I'm certain you understand where we're at. Did you take Hannah Perry and hide her somewhere?'

Collins had begun the interview by eyeballing Minshull at every opportunity; his right eyebrow cocked just enough to imply he didn't care. Now, hours later, he was lounging back in his chair, the hood of his grey sweatshirt pulled over his eyes. 'No comment.'

'Because I think you did. I think you abducted your partner's child as a means of obtaining money, either from a reward or a ransom.'

Across the table Collins' solicitor, Elliot Jenkins, made furious notes, an incredulous shake of his head greeting every accusation Minshull made. Not that he had a hope of getting to him. It didn't matter how long they remained in Interview Room 2, Minshull wasn't letting up.

Calmly, he took the ransom note in its plastic evidence bag from his folder, and slid it across the table. '..."One hundred thousand pounds, in the blue skip behind the garages on Leonard Road..." Bit close to your gaff, isn't it?'

'No comment.'

'And in a skip, too. Classy.'

Collins snorted and leaned further back into his hood.

'Exactly the same location as the ransom note for Matthew Cooper, seven years ago. Not a skip, though, that time. A litter bin. Bit more genteel, although I'm guessing that was burned out years ago.' He caught Bennett's smile beside him.

'With respect, Acting DS Minshull, my client is not here to discuss a previous case.'

'A previous case with startling similarities to this one...'

Jenkins glared over the top of his designer frames. Minshull raised a hand.

'I'll rephrase. One hundred thousand pounds. It's still a lot of money these days. You like money, don't you, Shaun? I mean, we all do. But you like it a bit more than most.'

'Unless you have evidence...'

Minshull eyeballed the solicitor. 'Actually, Mr Jenkins, we do.' He nodded at Bennett, who pulled out a stack of papers from her file, placing them one by one across the table. 'Twenty-eight sworn statements from people you extorted money from.'

Inside the hood, Minshull saw the whites of Collins' eyes increase.

'I'm sorry, people you *lent* money *to*, unlawfully, then threatened to ensure they kept paying.'

Jenkins slammed his pen on the table. 'This is ridiculous. You have no evidence my client was connected to any of these individuals.'

'Every one of these people are listed in this book.' He placed another bag containing the loan book in front of Collins. It was opened at a page revealing the list of names, dates and sums of money. Collins leaned forward. Even Jenkins closed his own notebook and bent to inspect it. 'It was found in your partner's house.'

Bennett glanced at Minshull and he nodded her in.

'So far, we've traced half of the names contained in this book. There are one hundred and three entries. And twenty-eight have stated that they borrowed money from you, then were taken, by you, to an industrial unit out in the countryside, assaulted and threatened. They say you had another man with you assisting in their assaults. Can you tell us anything about that?'

Collins glanced at his solicitor, but didn't reply.

'The industrial unit is part of a small estate built on former farmland just outside Long Deighton,' Minshull continued, selecting a printed map from his notes and offering it to Jenkins, who passed it to Collins. 'You go there quite a lot, don't you, Mr Collins?'

'I fail to see how that's relevant.'

'We did a check on your client's van.' He slid the warrant across the table for the solicitor to see. 'Eight visits over twelve days. Much further from St Just than you told us you worked.' He paused, letting it sink in, watching the shift in body language of Collins and his solicitor. 'And twenty-eight people can attest that you are familiar with this place. Oh,' he paused, relishing the killer blow, 'sorry, twenty-nine. Adam Jackson – Jack, to anyone who knows him. He's admitted to working for you, taking delivery of quantities of illegal spirits that your debtors were forced to buy, participating in intimidation and assault, the whole shebang. He also told us you threatened to snatch his kids if he didn't comply.'

'I didn't take Han!'

'Mr Collins, I—'

Collins was out of his seat now, bearing down on Minshull. 'No! Enough of this shit. You can point at me all you want for this, but taking the kid? That's not possible!'

'Sit down, Mr Collins.'

'You've got it wrong! Someone still has her!'

'Sit down, sir.'

Collins thumped back in his seat, his chest pumping. 'I need a break.'

'In a moment.'

'No. Now. I need to talk to my lawyer.'

Minshull glanced at Jenkins, who was blinking fast behind his expensive glasses. 'Okay. Interview suspended at four fifteen p.m.'

–

'How did he take the news?' Anderson was at the door of the CID office when Minshull and Bennett returned.

'He's talking to his solicitor,' Minshull replied, secretly enjoying the delight on his superior's face. 'We'll be back there in an hour or so.'

'Any joy on Hannah?'

'He was adamant he doesn't have her,' Bennett said, accepting a mug of coffee from Wheeler who was fussing around them. 'Thanks, *Mum*.'

'Less of your cheek, thank you. I'm just doing my bit for the brave soldiers battling away in Interview 2.'

Wheeler passed a coffee to Minshull, who gulped half down in one go. The hot liquid stung his throat but it felt good. He felt good. The pieces were falling into place and they'd penetrated Collins' defences. Even if he came back with No Comments after consulting Jenkins, he was rattled. Now they had a chance to make him crack.

'Right, where are we at with the rest of the list?'

'Still going through them,' Evans said, rubbing at the small of his back. 'Three more are coming in tomorrow to talk to us.'

Minshull nodded. 'Excellent. I know it's a slog, Les, but we'll get there.'

At the desk beside Evans, Ellis raised his hand. 'Guv, there is one thing. The FLO over at Hannah's house called. She was talking to Hannah's mum and Ms Perry mentioned about meeting Collins for the first time.'

'Are we interested in their torrid love story, Drew?' Evans snorted.

'You might be, actually. So, we know he moved to the Parkhall Estate seven and half years ago, six months before Matthew Cooper went missing. Turns out he moved to St Just from Bury St Edmunds.'

'With his mum and sister?'

'No. They didn't come across until the following year when a council house became free. Collins would have been living alone at the time Matthew disappeared.'

'When did Ashleigh Perry meet him?'

'Six years ago. He did some building work on the house next door and they got chatting. Within a month he'd moved in.'

Minshull took it in. Links were made in his mind, threads almost meeting but falling frustratingly short. 'Thank you. Find out everything you can about it, please. Why did he move? Did he leave anyone behind? Who did he work for? Does he still have ties to Bury? What was he doing there before he came to St Just?' He looked around the room. 'Good work, everyone. Let's keep it up.'

—

Before he was due back in interview, Minshull headed down to the car park to collect his notebook from his car. The fresh air was a blessed relief from the overzealous heating in the building, which had inexplicably decided to work just as spring removed the need for it. He paused to fill his lungs, then walked back to the building.

'Minsh.'

He looked up to see Wheeler leaning by the wall. 'You move fast, mate. You back on the marathon training?'

'Not much chance of that while this all goes on.' Wheeler blew out a cloud of fruit-scented white smoke then clicked his vape shut. 'I wanted a word. Off the record.'

Minshull stopped walking. 'Oh?'

'I just wanted to check – as a mate – that you know what you're doing. Framing Collins as chief suspect.'

Of all the people in CID, Dave Wheeler was the last person Minshull expected to question Shaun Collins' guilt. 'Yes I do. The evidence is there... Do I take it you don't agree?'

'It's not that – he's guilty as hell of the money lending, the assaults. We've got him by the nuts for that. I just think we should be careful on the rest.' He stuffed his hands in his pockets, scuffing at the grey concrete path with the toe of his polished shoe. Minshull hadn't seen him so self-conscious before and it didn't suit him. Everything Dave Wheeler did was front and centre, the man was as transparent as glass and as happy in his own skin as anyone Minshull had ever known. He envied it, the ease with which Wheeler appeared to live. This was new, alien. A warning sign...

'Meaning?'

'Last time – with Matthew Cooper – Joel was convinced Matthew's mother's boyfriend had taken him, possibly murdered him and tried to cover it up with the abduction and ransom story. There were other possible leads I felt he dismissed too quickly. I said it to him at the time, but he was under so much pressure from above for results that he just didn't listen.'

Minshull had heard that. But Matthew Cooper's killer had never been found – and might now be the one holding Hannah. And Collins had both motive and opportunity, perhaps for both cases. 'All the evidence points to Collins, Dave.'

'Yes but that's just it, Minsh. Does it? Maybe it does because you and Joel have convinced yourselves Collins is guilty. Was he even around at the time of Matthew Cooper's murder?'

'You heard what Ashleigh Perry told the FLO. Collins has lived on Parkhall for seven and a half years. It's possible.'

'Possible, yes. But Kate moved to St Just seven years ago, too, days before Matthew Cooper disappeared. Drew was at school six years above him and his younger brother was in the same Cub Pack as Matthew when the kid went missing. Have you investigated all of them as potential suspects?'

'Don't be ridiculous. It isn't like that at all.'

'Isn't it? Tell me, what's the difference?' He kicked at the ground. 'I've held my tongue till now because I believe you and Joel are great coppers. If anyone can find this poor kid, you can. But I can't just stand by and watch you make the exact same mistake Joel did. Every minute you focus on incriminating Collins for this, you lose in investigating others. Now Collins is a git, no denying that. I hate the attitude he has to his stepkid. But does that make him a premeditated killer?'

Minshull didn't want to hear this, not now they were so close to charging Collins. Everything pointed to him: the book Cora had helped them uncover, the people listed in it who had agreed to give statements. Even Adam Jackson throwing him under the bus. If he was innocent, why intimidate anyone who could vouch for him? He hadn't considered the families of the people he'd extorted money from, and he'd blatantly threatened the family of Jackson, his accomplice in the crime; why then develop a conscience about using his own stepdaughter to get what he wanted?

It all made sense.

Didn't it?

'I know what I'm doing,' he replied firmly. 'And so does Joel.'

Wheeler threw his hands up in defeat. 'Whatever. I said what I wanted to. Just be careful, okay? Remember it's a child's life you're playing with. A child who is still bloody well out there.'

Minshull watched his colleague slouch away. Overhead the sky began to darken.

Chapter Seventy-One

Cora

Cora gave the encampment of journalists a wide berth as she entered the High Street. They had set up residence around the small parking area by the Meatcross, usually reserved for traders' vehicles when the markets were on, and looked intent on remaining there for the foreseeable future.

'Bloody rabble,' said an elderly lady with a bright floral shopping trolley as she passed Cora. 'I preferred the gypsies moving in. At least they were polite and tidied up after themselves last time they came.'

The mood in St Just seemed to match the pensioner's as Cora walked quickly towards the *Argus* offices. Groups of local people gathered to voice their complaints, many annoyed by the attitude of the press pack. Their disdain sang from the litter bins and pavements, too, and Cora switched her focus to muting the voices behind the hum of late afternoon traffic. She needed to concentrate on the task at hand, to push aside the nerves that had gripped her since she'd decided to make the journey here. The antique price guides she carried were dragging weights as she walked, as if they were a portent of the guilt that might burden her after talking to Jan Martin.

I have no choice, she told herself again. *Hannah deserves to be found...*

Reaching the newspaper office, she rang the bell and waited. Her face looked small and pale reflected in the glass door and she instantly thought of Hannah. They were inextricably linked and she could hear the child now, calling out for her help. Her reflection muddied for a second and she realised another person was standing behind the door, opening it.

'Can I help?' the young man asked.

Cora smiled. 'I hope so. I have some things for Jan Martin. From my mum. She was supposed to take them from the WI meeting today but she forgot... Is she in?'

The man didn't smile. 'Sorry. She's gone home for a rest. Sky News are supposed to be interviewing her at six-thirty and she wanted a break before then.'

'Oh. I see. I don't suppose you have her address, do you? My mum was adamant she needed these today.' She indicated the heavy books in her arms without showing him the covers. She had come this far and if she didn't talk to Jan now she might lose her nerve.

The man seemed to sag, as if the very act of conversation were too much. 'Yeah, okay. Hang on a minute and I'll get it for you.'

Cora waited, her heart in her mouth. Was he taking the chance to check with his boss while she was on the doorstep? What happened if Jan told him not to bother? She would never find an excuse as plausible as this to obtain an audience with her.

A moment later, he returned, handing her a folded piece of paper. 'I've put the address on there. She might be asleep so make sure you knock loudly.' For the first time, Cora detected a glint of amusement in his eyes.

'Thank you – um…'

'Lloyd. Lloyd Price.'

Cora remembered her conversation with Minshull the night she'd determined the pack of coloured pencils was a fake. Lloyd must still be kicking himself after such an embarrassment. She gave him a bright smile. 'I'm Cora Lael. Thank you so much for your help.'

Turning quickly, the information she'd hoped for held tightly against her, Cora headed back to her car.

Chapter Seventy-Two

Minshull

'Sarge.' Bennett's usual grin was absent as she beckoned Minshull over.

Leaving his team, Minshull joined her. 'What's up?'

'Development. Control had a call from a resident on the Parkhall Estate in St Just, about twenty minutes ago. Thinks a kid is locked in a garage.'

Minshull stared at the report on screen. 'Where?'

'Rickard Street.'

Rickard Street. A row of scruffy lock-up garages Minshull was well aware of. There had been the odd instance of stolen goods being stashed in the squat buildings, far too small to accommodate modern cars, but that wasn't what was making Minshull's head swim now. There had been crank calls already since the news of Hannah's disappearance broke – around twenty by current count. People were concerned, people wanted to do something to help, some people just wanted their five minutes of notoriety. But since Cora Lael's suggestion that Hannah was in a small, confined space, any report regarding garages, sheds or outbuildings had to be taken seriously.

'Was Rickard Street checked by uniform in the small building searches?'

'The garages were on the list but there's no record of them being checked yet.'

Minshull let out a groan. 'Why were they missed? Bloody hell! Are they sending a patrol out now?'

'We should go,' Lanehan said suddenly, standing from the desk she'd been assigned.

Minshull turned. 'Why?'

'I saw the report come in and checked who the garage is registered to.' She stabbed her finger at her screen. 'Siobhan Collins.'

'Shaun's sister?'

Lanehan nodded. 'So I tried calling Ms Collins, to ask her to open it for the officers. No joy from her mobile, so I called her home. But get this: her mum answered and said Siobhan's not been there for a couple of days.'

Minshull's heart kicked into gear. 'How many?'

'Not since the protest.'

'The night we brought her brother in.'

'Exactly. And Maddie Grove, the FLO over at the Perry house, said Siobhan's not been there, either. It might be a coincidence, but it looks to me like she's gone to ground.'

'Or gone to look after her niece while Collins is here.' All along, Minshull had assumed Collins was working alone, the arrest of Adam Jackson seeming to suggest his only potential accomplice was out of the picture. With Siobhan being so openly vocal in her criticism of the investigation, it made no sense that she should disappear now. Unless Hannah was closer than anyone thought – in a lock-up garage at the edge of the estate, disastrously missed in the search of small buildings. A lock-up owned by her aunt...

–

'Should we tell the guv'nor?' Bennett asked, breaking into a jog to keep up with Minshull as he sprinted from the office.

'No,' Minshull shot back, but when he reached the double doors to the stairwell he paused, eager hand pressed against the fingerprint-smeared steel doorplate. Anderson should know. They needed a team to go there, now. *He's not Dad*, Minshull scolded himself. *It's not a competition.* 'Hang on, yes, tell him. Ask for Support to meet us there so we can break in. I'll head straight over – he can follow as soon as he's able.'

Leaving Bennett to deliver the news, Minshull headed for the car park and a dark blue pool car. As usual it was low on petrol and filthy outside and in. But there was enough to get him to the Parkhall Estate – and if he found Hannah there Support could tow him back for all he cared. His palms were slick with sweat on the steering wheel, the vinyl slithering beneath his skin. Could this be it?

The elderly man was watching from the window of his bland council semi, peering around a grubby net curtain, when Minshull pulled up outside. As he left his car, the curtain fell back across the glass and the peering eyes reappeared through a chain-restrained crack in the front door. People here were fearful of strangers at the best of times; prowling journalists and waves of police in recent days were bound to have added to the mistrust of anyone they didn't know. The door remained barely ajar as Minshull knocked against the yellowing uPVC.

'Yes?' the old man barked.

Minshull attempted a smile. 'Mr Williamson?'

'Yes?'

He passed his warrant card through the narrow gap. 'Acting Detective Sergeant Rob Minshull, sir. I understand you called the police regarding a sound in a lock-up?'

The door slammed shut and Minshull could hear the chain being yanked back. The old man was struggling into a dark green anorak when the door opened again, practically knocking Minshull from the doorstep as he bustled out. 'I'll show you.'

They walked down a cracked flagstone path to the pavement and turned sharply left to head up a small alleyway between the crumbling back fences of neighbouring gardens, past part-worn verges of overgrown grass and overhanging brambles that reached out to grab their trouser legs. The alleyway ended with a dark arch of ivy-tangled hawthorn, emerging into the short cul-de-sac row of six garages. Their bright red doors had been faded by many summers, chipped by winters and mottled with crudely painted-over graffiti tags. A faint smell of urine and rotting rubbish punctured the air.

'There,' Mr Williamson pointed, indicating the third door. 'I was walking my dog this morning and I heard it.'

'What did it sound like?' Minshull asked, approaching the door and pressing his ear against the dusty steel.

'Like a kid. Crying. Do you think it's her? The missing girl?' His voice cracked a little, the elastic cord of his anorak hood winding around anxious bony fingers. 'I wouldn't have called otherwise, but my wife said – well, if you did nothing and it *was* – you know – you'd never forgive yourself…'

Minshull listened again, willing any sound to meet his ear. 'You did the right thing, sir.' He should wait for uniform and Support to arrive – but the old man's words rang out in his mind. 'Hello?' he said, tapping the door, which shuddered against his hand. He listened. *Nothing.* 'Hello? Is anyone there?'

'I definitely heard it, officer.'

'I'm sure you did, sir. Let me just listen, okay?' Minshull pressed his ear against the door, flakes of ancient paint brushing his cheek as he did so. The old man started to speak again, but stopped when Minshull raised a finger to his lips.

And then he heard it – a small wail coming from inside. His pulse quickened as he tapped against the locked door. 'Hello? Can you hear me?'

Another wail, louder this time.

'It's the police,' he called back, willing back-up to arrive *now*. 'Stay where you are. We've come to help.'

The wail came again – and Minshull's blood ran cold. It sounded like a child. A terrified, incarcerated child…

Without warning, his last conversation with Cora returned to his mind. Her fear, the conviction in her eyes he'd dismissed as fantasy, *those* words – '*She's alone, she's curled up somewhere small and she's terrified…*' And the voicemails – increasingly urgent and crazed. He'd started to ignore them, stopping short of blocking her number entirely. Part of him still wanted to believe her, to think that she was telling the truth. But even if the video diary had been faked, as she'd claimed, her desperate pleas and insistence to his face that she still heard Hannah's voice had confirmed his worst fears.

But what if she was right?

His mobile buzzed again. Stepping back from the lock-up, he walked a few paces away. 'Minshull.'

'What *exactly* did you think you were doing, going there without a team?' Anderson's fury bit against Minshull's ear.

'How far away are you, Guv?'

'We're parking. Where are you?'

'Take the alley beside number forty-two. The lock-ups are at the end.'

'Heading there now.' His breath became puffs as the pounding of feet sounded down the line. 'I'm not happy, Rob.'

Minshull turned to the elderly man. 'My team will be here shortly. Thanks for calling us.'

Understanding his cue, Mr Williamson nodded and hurried away. A moment later, five uniformed support officers bearing lock-cutters and a battering ram emerged from the alley, led by a very red-faced detective inspector and trailed by a much fresher-faced Kate Bennett.

'Number Three,' Minshull said, beckoning the team over.

'What do you think?'

'Definitely someone in there, Guv. No coherent verbal response but definitely distress.'

'And it's Collins' sister's?'

'According to Steph.'

They stepped back as the team moved in, lopping off the padlock with ease but battling with the locked handle, which quickly proved surprisingly sturdy for its age. Minshull, Anderson and Bennett watched from a distance, exchanging a look when the pitiful cry came again.

'Just get in,' Anderson commanded. 'Do what you have to.'

'And if it isn't her?' Minshull looked at his superior.

Anderson's jaw was set. 'We'll deal with that if it happens.'

Chapter Seventy-Three

Cora

A faint mist of drizzle smeared the windscreen as Cora drove into the wide driveway leading to Jan's farm. The ageing windscreen wipers creaked and scraped across the glass in response, the ugly sound jarring her nerves. She parked by a pile of rusting machinery being slowly reclaimed by grass and weeds and sat back against the unforgiving fabric of her car seat.

Am I doing the right thing?

She'd ignored the question on the journey here but now, in the sudden silence as the engine cut, it returned. Rob Minshull and his team were still looking for Hannah, doing everything they could to find her. She remembered his words from their last heated exchange: 'You have to leave it to us now. We know what we're doing.'

But what if they didn't?

They'd misjudged Matthew Cooper's abduction. What if they failed Hannah, too?

I have to know.

It was the only solution, the only hope Cora had of finding peace. She *had* to break cover and risk everything she'd promised Rob she'd protect from the press. If it meant finding Hannah alive, it was worth the betrayal.

Hurrying through the dampness of the farm courtyard, Cora pushed her doubts aside. She edged around Jan's battered Range Rover and rapped loudly on the newly repainted front door.

When it opened, Jan's look of surprise quickly softened into a smile. She wiped soapsuds from her hand with a tea towel and offered it to Cora. 'Cora, this is an unexpected pleasure.'

'I'm sorry, Lloyd at the *Argus* gave me your address. I hope you don't mind.' Cora held up the antiques guides. 'You forgot these. Mum was worried you'd need them.'

'Oh. Right you are – she needn't have worried.'

There was a pause that felt like an invitation – but the words dried up on Cora's tongue before they could fly.

'It was kind of you to drive out here to bring them. I'm sorry we didn't get much of a chance to chat...' Jan's brown eyes narrowed a little and Cora's courage shrank back. 'Your mum said she thought you'd had a rough time lately?'

Did she know already? If she had sources within the police, as Rob had intimated, was Jan well aware of Cora's involvement? 'A little. But I'm fine. How are you holding up with all this attention?'

Jan shrugged as she tucked the tea towel under her arm and accepted the books from Cora. 'It is what it is. Hopefully it'll be over soon. That's what everyone wants now.'

'Well, you've done an amazing job.'

'I appreciate that, thanks.' Jan shifted in the doorway. 'Look, I don't have long before I need to go out, but the kettle's just boiled if you fancy a chat?'

It was the opportunity she'd been waiting for. Gratefully, Cora followed Jan into the farmhouse.

Chapter Seventy-Four

Minshull

'Break it down!' Minshull yelled.

The sound from inside the garage was almost constant now, a banshee cry that spurred on the efforts of the rescue team.

'Stand back from the door!' a uniformed officer shouted – and the sound from within ceased.

The first swing of the persuader cracked against the metal door, steel buckling beneath the blow. The handle, which had put up such a valiant fight against them, inverted in on itself as the second blow came. Shouts of instruction and encouragement sounded from the team as they worked as one, jamming their combined weight behind the ram.

Minshull and Anderson were beside them now, ready. They said nothing, but Minshull could barely breathe. Four weeks of fruitless searching, frustrating dead ends, hearsay, cranks and useless leads had taken its toll on all of them; for Minshull this was the moment he'd clung on to fading hope for.

A fifth blow sent the handle shearing through the steel, leaving a gaping wound. Six pairs of hands united to wrench the garage door up and overhead as the ageing mechanism groaned in defeat. Stunned by the success, the team paused in the gap to survey floor-to-ceiling stacks of greying cardboard boxes. Pushing through the stationary bodies, Minshull called out.

'Hannah! Are you there? Can you hear me?'

From deep within the shadows a faint wail sounded, summoning movement from Support. Minshull led them through the cardboard maze, blinking in the gloom as he neared the back of the garage.

'Hi, Hannah, it's the police. Where are you?'

The cry came from the far left of the space, behind a tall metal shelving unit almost against the back wall. Heart hammering in his ears, Minshull tore away at the final box barriers. He could hear the support officers behind him and Anderson hot on his heels, hopes and fatigue and fear combining to pull them all towards the shadows and the unearthly distress.

Just a few more steps…

Almost there…

'Hannah?'

And then a heavy weight shoved hard against his shin, followed by a shower of stinging barbs as Minshull lost his footing and fell, sharply slamming his shoulder and head against dust-thick concrete. Lights flooded his vision as he went down – then blackness descended.

Chapter Seventy-Five

Cora

Cora walked slowly back to her car, the weight of conscience heavy on her head. She'd maintained a smile as they'd walked out together, but as soon as Jan climbed into the Range Rover, Cora turned away, fighting tears.

Regret was all she had now. It was done.

Jan had been kind, but it didn't help Cora. The whole thing had left her feeling cold. She'd expected it to lift the weight from her shoulders, to finally bring her some peace, but this was worse than before.

It hadn't been easy to find a moment in their small talk to speak. After all, it wasn't the kind of thing you casually mentioned. And then the gap had arrived, the opportunity had presented itself... and everything had gone wrong.

'I trusted the investigation. I was proud to be part of it. And I know significant breakthroughs happened while I was there that I helped bring into being.'

'I know you can't tell me what,' Jan had smiled, scribbling strange unreadable shorthand on a reporter's notepad, jagged hieroglyphs across the curling-edged page, 'but did things change when these breakthroughs occurred?'

'I thought we were all on the same page. But then the focus seemed to shift. It became about pursuing one single theory, to the exclusion of everything else.'

'And that theory wasn't locating Hannah.'

That was when she should have stopped. But as Cora spoke, the hurt and betrayal finally granted a voice, it all came out.

'What I'm concerned about – what scares me – is that saving Hannah has become something secondary to nailing their prime suspect. It's like they've lost the drive to look for her. I felt I was increasingly the only voice in that team speaking for Hannah. And I'm not there anymore.'

Too late, she'd seen interest register in the journalist's eyes. 'You're saying Hannah is no longer a priority?'

'I don't know.'

'But you said you don't see the drive to find her like it was at the beginning?'

'Honestly, I feel like they aren't expecting to find Hannah alive. Like they're convinced it's Matthew Cooper all over again and they're expecting a body.'

That was when she knew she'd made a mistake. At least she'd managed to brake before mentioning her ability. But that was little comfort now. She'd done the one thing she'd sworn she never would: she'd betrayed any confidence Minshull still had in her.

Jan didn't know any more than she'd already reported, of that Cora was now certain. The new information Cora had brought was probably what Jan had been praying for. What would the next headlines be?

LOCAL POLICE LOSING CONFIDENCE IN
THEIR OWN INVESTIGATION... WHO WILL
FIND HANNAH NOW? FORMER POLICE
EXPERT ASKS...

More speculation, more accusation – and no closer to finding Hannah. What if Hannah's captor was Matthew Cooper's killer? What if they thought the police were losing interest in finding Hannah alive?

What have I done?

Cora watched Jan's Range Rover pulling out of the farmyard, her last chance to help Hannah leaving with it. There was nothing more she could do for the child, even if Hannah's voice refused to let her go. So, where did it leave her now?

She couldn't take back what she'd said, or seal the Pandora's box she had just given Jan the keys to open. She had to think of something else. But what?

She could try to talk to Rob again, or maybe appeal to DI Anderson's better judgement. If she repeated that Daniel's motives had been far from professional, perhaps they would reconsider. But then they thought she was unhinged already: haranguing them wouldn't support her case for sanity. Trying to convince somebody you weren't mad by desperately hounding them wasn't a particularly sane course of action. She had left Rob too many voicemail messages already. And if Jan printed what Cora had said, then all hope of rejoining the investigation was gone.

But Hannah was still out there. Who would speak for her now?

Cora bit back tears as she crossed the farm courtyard. Around her, the wind had picked up strength and her hair flapped about her face as if beating sense into her. A skitter of old hay and rubbish danced past on a gust of wind, swirling around her feet.

Mine – said a voice.

Hannah's voice.

Cora froze…

Chapter Seventy-Six

Minshull

'A *cat*.'

'Sarge.'

Minshull sat back against a stack of boxes and batted away the hand of a PC who was hell-bent on inspecting the wound to his forehead. 'I'm *fine*.'

He wanted to return his brow to the concrete, repeatedly, until the last vestige of stupid hope was battered out of his head. It had sounded like a child crying – how could he have been so mistaken?

'Rob, mate, we all thought the same.' Anderson bent over him like a benevolent referee after a bad tackle. 'It sounded like a kid.'

'But a *cat*, Guv.'

'I know.'

By the look of his colleagues, everyone felt foolish. That didn't make him feel better. He struggled to his feet, the angry jab of pain in his shoulder nothing compared to the fury within.

A gaggle of people, most with phones held aloft, had gathered at the end of the alleyway, gawping at the five police offers it had taken to demolish a garage door and rescue a stray cat.

Brilliant.

It wouldn't take long for news to spread and they'd be a laughing stock within the hour. Worse still, every one of the Parkhall Estate witnesses knew *exactly* whose lock-up it was. If they were wrong about Hannah's aunt being complicit in her abduction, it would play right into the media's grubby hands. *Victimisation*, he imagined the headlines screaming. *Going after that poor kid's aunt instead of finding the scum that took her…*

Deflated, Minshull walked into the street, the pretence of being busy on his phone a convenient way to avoid eye contact with anybody. He stared at the screen. Two new missed calls. Both from Cora.

He tried to ignore the thought that Cora could have prevented this mistake if she'd still been on the case. Everyone had been right about her, he told himself. *You got too involved, let your guard down.* He ignored his phone. There was no point calling her back.

'What now, Sarge?' At least Bennett had the decency to assume Minshull knew.

'Back to the station. Regroup.'

'Take the car and head back, Kate,' Anderson said, handing her the keys. 'I'll drive Rob and we'll follow you back.'

'I'm fine,' Minshull insisted irritably, as his phone buzzed again.

'You've had a bump to the head, sunshine. No way I'm letting you drive until it's been properly checked.'

'But Collins...'

'Kate can continue, she has your notes. Take Evans in. He deserves a treat.'

'Guv,' Bennett smiled. 'Don't worry, Minsh. We've got this.'

Knocked out by a terrified cat, replaced in the interview he'd worked hard to lead and now babysat by his boss. It was turning into one hell of a day.

Chapter Seventy-Seven

Minshull

'You're in demand,' Anderson said, nodding at Minshull's vibrating phone. 'Aren't you going to answer that?'

Minshull glanced at the caller ID and his heart hit the ground harder than his head had earlier. 'No. Let's just get back in the car, Guv.'

'Could be important.' Anderson's smile faded when Minshull turned the screen to face him. '*Still?*'

'I don't even know what to say to her.'

'The professor reckoned she was mentally fragile.'

Minshull shrugged but didn't reply. Cora may have been telling the truth about the professor's manipulation of her video diary, but the constant messages made him doubt how much control of her emotions she still had. It was too much to consider with every other concern battling for his attention. They needed Collins to confess and reveal where Hannah was. And they needed to locate Siobhan, to ascertain definitively whether she was aiding her brother or not. He didn't have time to waste on wondering whether Cora Lael should still be on the team, however much he owed her for Collins being in custody.

'Have you listened to her messages?'

'Not for a while.' *Not since she ambushed me in the car park...*

Anderson looked over to the team who were trying to fend off amused questions from a group of residents. 'Maybe you should. Can't be any more insane than our efforts here this afternoon.'

'I give it two hours tops before the press gets wind of this. So much for boosting our media image. So what's the plan now, Guv?'

'Head back. Press Collins for a confession.'

'And Hannah?'

Anderson groaned. 'We pray we aren't too late.'

Chapter Seventy-Eight

Cora

She was mistaken. She had to be.

There was no way Hannah's voice would be here.

Cora slapped a hand to her forehead, the sudden jolt causing a sharp ache to claim her brow. Maybe Daniel had been right when he'd said her preoccupation with the missing girl was becoming an unhealthy obsession. It *had* to be a mistake.

Another gust of wind butted the back of her legs like an unseen animal nudging her away from the farmyard, a shower of tiny, metallic scraps scuttling across the rough earth road.

It's my secret...

This time, Cora knew. Bending down, she scooped up a handful of the colourful foil scraps – and winced as five identical versions of Hannah Perry's voice sounded at once. The force of the quintet was such a punch to her gut that she almost dropped the scraps that bore the sound. Where had they come from? Why would these foil pieces be here? And how had Hannah's voice become attached to them?

One thing was certain: Hannah was close – and alive.

Cora had to find her.

But where should she look? After a glance towards the end of the drive to the farm to confirm the journalist had gone, Cora looked about her. The farmyard was old and hadn't seen livestock for many years. Several smaller outbuildings framed the perimeter, their foundations bearing age-old manure stains, their windows cracked and paint peeling from their scuffed doors. If Hannah was here, could she be in one of these?

The entrance of the barn was half-obscured by a large block of wood that looked like it had been a door in a former life and now lay on its side across the space. It took several attempts for Cora to nudge it away with her hip, the last one tilting the barrier just enough for her to squeeze through. Inside, it was dusty and dark. Shafts of pale light braved gaps in the corrugated iron roof and pooled on great rusting hulks of farm machinery. The whole place stank of damp and neglect. Jan might have inherited her home from her father but he had clearly failed to pass on any passion for maintaining it.

Cora squinted against the dusty gloom to make out shadows around the periphery. There didn't appear to be any doorways, concealed or otherwise, here. Certainly no anteroom that a young child might be locked inside. She wondered if she should call Hannah's name – but would that terrify the missing girl into silence? Deciding against it, she held her focus on the tin foil pieces on her palm.

Where are you? she asked.

Silence stared stubbornly back.

This wasn't the place. Her voice wasn't here. Heading outside, Cora retraced her steps. The wind had dropped suddenly and she couldn't remember exactly which direction it had blown from. If she could pinpoint that, she'd know where to look next...

Fighting the urge to run in any direction, she made herself stand still, willing her skin to find the breeze. Waves of Hannah's whispers danced around her, almost drowned out by the heavy beat of her heart.

Where are *you?*

My secret... Mine...

And then, the beginnings of a wind gust appeared, causing the hairs on her forearms to rise. She closed her eyes as another rush of Hannah's words engulfed her, trying to focus through the sound to the wind that carried them.

Suddenly she knew.

Homing in on the direction of the breeze, she blinked against the light of the farmyard and hurried between two rusting tractor carcasses shrouded in tarpaulins. Behind, she saw a thin earth path passing between the barn and another, older-looking outbuilding that might once have been a pigsty. It was barely six feet tall at the apex of its steeply pitched brick roof, a wedge of chipboard partially obscuring a roughly made entrance. A solitary glass pane in one side was cracked and seemed to have a double board fixed across it from the inside, blue plastic sheeting flapping through the small gap in the glass.

And beneath it, tangled in a muddy scrub of grass where the outbuilding met the ground, a tiny collection of shiny foil scraps...

Pressing her head to the makeshift window, Cora listened, and then called through the cracked glass.

'Hannah? Are you there?'

She could hear no actual sound but the sense of Hannah's voice was cacophonous here. She *had* to be inside.

Cora called again, hoping the child could hear her. 'Hannah, my name is Cora and I'm a friend. I'm going to get you out and take you home. I promise.'

Should you promise a child something so bold?

There would be time for considering that later. Cora had to reach Hannah.

'I'm going to try to get to you, okay? Don't be scared.' She reached for the board across the entrance, then froze.

In the distance, the low growl of an engine grew nearer. Was Jan returning? Breath held, she crouched low, the sour earth at her feet rising around her boots, seeping up over the toes and sucking her heels. She listened, willing the sound to pass by. She looked up in time to see the unmistakable outline of a light aircraft making its progress across the cloud-crowded sky.

Next time, it could be a car. The shot of fear propelled her into action. She grabbed the chipboard and heaved with all her strength, surprised when it swung back against her right hand on a single nail. Pushing past a veil of blue plastic sheeting, Cora ducked inside.

'Hannah?'

Within the cramped brick exterior of the pigsty, Cora heard a small scratching noise. She pictured rats living in the dank shadows and instantly gagged. The smell of damp and ancient manure was over-whelming, the stench increasing as she moved further inside. There wasn't enough room to stand and only four solid brick walls visible. Where could a child hide here? There was no sign of the cracked window she'd seen from the outside – there had to be another section of the building concealed from view. Cora edged towards the furthest wall. As she moved to the back of the building, her foot clattered against an upended metal pail.

YOU LITTLE BITCH!

The sudden yell of Jan's voice physically propelled Cora to the opposite wall. She squinted against the darkness, expecting to see Jan Martin standing over the entrance, but no body blocked the light. It was only when a small, barely discernible whimper sounded from the far left of the building that Cora realised she'd heard an object's voice first, but a real voice second. Hannah was here – extremely close – and terrified…

She can't see me now…

'Hannah, don't be scared. My name is Cora and I'm a friend…'

In the semi-darkness, Cora slapped her hands against the dirt-caked walls and began to scratch at brick and paint to find a hidden entrance. Hundred-year-old dung and dust pushed beneath her fingernails as she searched the walls, her head swimming in the physical and audible presence of the child who had haunted her dreams for weeks.

'I'm going to find you, Hannah – hang in there.'

Reaching the end gable, she heard a tiny sob beside her and, moving her hands down, felt a small door secured with a rusted slide bolt.

STAY IN THERE!

Jan's voice screamed as Cora touched the bolt, a blast of intense anger catching her cheek as the emotion of the slap had before. The fixture seemed to ebb and flow as Cora's tears welled but she pressed on, pushing past the voice and the emotion as her fingers pulled and slipped and scratched at the stubborn metal, determined to shift the barrier.

The sobs were becoming louder as she fought with the lock, then a crack sounded, followed by the sharp groan of old wood against brick as the door finally surrendered.

And Cora found herself face to face with the girl whose voice had sought her out.

The child clung to a dirty tartan work shirt draped pathetically over her blueing limbs, eyes wild with fear.

'I'm a friend,' Cora rushed. 'Hannah – are you Hannah Perry?'

The child's gaping mouth moved in response and Cora noticed dried blood on the cracked skin of her bottom lip.

'Are you hurt?'

Terror-stricken blue eyes blinked back. And then, the voice Cora already knew came from Hannah's trembling lips. 'My ankle hurts.'

'What happened?'

'They did it.'

Had someone else been here, too, helping Jan? 'Who?'

'The newspaper lady. She hurt it when I wouldn't give her my pencil case.'

A pencil case? It must have been delivered after she'd been dismissed. She was glad she hadn't seen it. The thought that the case might have been used against Hannah as a weapon was more than she could bear.

Not wanting to frighten the child any more than she already was, Cora edged closer, lowering her voice to a warm murmur, willing reassurance and comfort into every syllable. 'I know you're scared. But you're going to be okay if you trust me, all right?'

Was this what Jan had promised Hannah on the day she'd abducted her? How could anyone plan to take a child? And had Jan lured Matthew Cooper with the same promises? How could the woman who had been such a good friend to her mother in recent days have calmly returned home to terrorise and abuse a young girl? The thought made Cora physically sick. 'Do you trust me?'

Hannah blinked, then lowered the makeshift blanket and held out her arms like a baby. Cora didn't hesitate. She scrambled into the cramped space and pulled the child tight to her, wrapping her in the folds of her jacket and leaning her cheek against the dirt-matted, sour-smelling blonde crown.

'It's okay,' she promised, meaning every word. 'I'm going to get you out of here. Can you walk?'

'I don't think so...'

'Don't worry. I'll carry you. My car is just outside – it's not far.' She paused. 'Do you trust me?'

Hannah's frantic nod against Cora's chest was all the confirmation she needed.

Chapter Seventy-Nine

Minshull

In the car speeding away from the scene of South Suffolk Constabulary's latest embarrassment, Minshull's thoughts were a tangle. He'd been so certain they were about to find Hannah Perry. That the lock-up belonged to Collins' sister had made the possibility even more delicious.

They may have hit a dead end, but it wasn't the end of the connection. Collins knew more about his stepkid than he was letting on. There was still every reason to suppose he knew where she was. While he'd been in custody, his sister had been gone for long enough to move Hannah – maybe even stow the cat in his lock-up to distract police attention, or make further mockery of the investigation.

'We'll get him,' Anderson said from the driver's seat, as if Minshull's train of thought had been broadcast through the pool car's radio. 'Maybe not for the child. But for the money lending and the assault and the intimidation.'

'None of that helps Hannah.'

'I know. But it'll stop him terrorising the neighbourhood. It's something.'

Was that what the investigation had come down to? Snatching tiny points in a game they couldn't win?

Minshull glared at his mobile screen, as if the vital piece of evidence they were missing might appear upon it.

5 missed calls – Cora Lael

This was totally out of hand. He had to put an end to it. Selecting his voicemail, he listened to the most recent message:

'Rob, it's Cora. I don't care what you think of me, but you have to listen to this. I've found Hannah Perry. She's in an outbuilding at Jan Martin's place. The editor from The Argus. It's called Light Hill Farm. Hannah's hurt but she's alive. She's alive, Rob, just like I told you. But I'm scared Jan's coming back. I'm going to get her out...'

In shock, Minshull slammed his hand against the dashboard; the pool car swerving as Anderson narrowly avoided hitting the kerb.

'What the...?'

'Turn *around*!' he yelled.

'What are you talking about?'

'I said, *turn around* Guv! Cora's found Hannah.'

Anderson jammed on the brakes, causing the car behind to swerve, blaring its horn. 'Where?'

Minshull braced himself. He could hear the desperation in Anderson's question, knew exactly the impact his answer would have. The person Joel Anderson least expected, and worse still: the person he'd considered an ally since Matthew Cooper disappeared.

'Light Hill Farm.'

He heard the air rush from his superior in one long expletive.

Chapter Eighty

Cora

Cora edged to the entrance of the pigsty, every sense on high alert. Being united with the child had finally silenced the voice that had inhabited Cora's head for weeks and the absence of it within her left a discomforting void. The young girl in her arms felt fragile and far lighter than a child of her age should have been. Had Jan bothered to feed her? She could feel the jut of Hannah's ribs against her as the child's wraithlike arms clung to her neck.

'The lady might see us,' she whispered, close to Cora's ear. 'I don't want her to be angry again.'

'She isn't here,' Cora replied, checking every shadow and movement in the farmyard just to make sure. She didn't know how long Jan might be gone for and didn't want to be there when she returned. Hannah's terror at the mention of Jan was enough to tell her that. 'Okay, let's go.'

'Wait! My bag!'

'You don't need it, sweetheart. We have to go.'

Hannah's pale features scrunched into a stubborn frown. 'No – I *need* it! I want my bag!' Her hands gripped Cora's shoulder, small nails like pins digging into her skin.

Cora was tempted to rush to her car regardless, but Hannah's panic was raising the sound of her voice to a dangerous level. Poor kid, it had been her only connection to home for the past four weeks – a connection Jan Martin had been only too happy to abuse. Of course she needed her belongings. They were all she had.

'Okay, okay, we'll get it. But we have to be quick and you have to whisper, all right?'

The child nodded.

Ignoring every survival instinct telling her to run, Cora turned back into the darkness of the pigsty...

348

Chapter Eighty-One

Minshull

'I need all units to Light Hill Farm, off Bardell Way close to Evernam. Suspect may be in attendance with Hannah Perry and Dr Cora Lael. Status unknown. We have Support following but need more. Over.'

'Confirmed, Sarge. We'll do our best. Out.' The police radio crackled its reply but brought no comfort. The end game was here, without any of them prepared to face it.

If only I'd listened to her...

Minshull kept his eyes on the road but as he called for back-up tension was sparking from Anderson beside him. They were less than a mile away but it was still too far. As Anderson threw the car around the right-angled bends of the country road, Minshull prayed no farm vehicles awaited them ahead. He had replayed the message more times than he'd counted and now his head buzzed with Cora's voice.

I've found Hannah. But I'm scared Jan's coming back...

'How long has it been?' he asked Anderson.

'She left the last message fifteen minutes ago.'

Fifteen minutes. Too long.

'What if...?'

'I don't know, kid.' For the first time, Minshull could hear fear in Anderson's voice. 'We had no timeframe with Matthew. But if she's spooked, or if she finds Cora and the child...'

He didn't need to finish the sentence. The danger was unavoidable.

'Jan Martin,' Minshull growled. 'Jan *bloody* Martin. How did we miss that?'

'She was an ally to us before. And a personal friend.' Anderson shook his head. 'I thought having one member of the press on our side was a gift.'

'She was lying, Guv.'

'I know that. What I don't get is why. And why do it again?'

'Fame? Notoriety?'

'But why leave seven years between them?'

'Enough time to pass suspicion? Or find the right victim? Seven years sounds like a Hollywood plotline.'

'I should have seen it.' Anderson butted his forehead against the fog of the driver's door window. 'She's my wife's friend, for crying out loud! Into every story locally as long as I've known her. How did she think she could do this undetected?'

'Because she *did*?' Minshull flinched as the words delivered a blow to his superior. A direct hit his father would have applauded. He shuddered. 'Sorry, Guv.'

'No. Say it. It's the truth. We suspected everyone else but her. Everyone *male*.'

Truth clung to the stifled air between them. It had been too easy to assume the child's aggressor was male. Minshull's heart hit the footwell of the car. It had been too easy to assume Shaun Collins was the prime suspect. Cora had been right about that. Dave Wheeler too. He'd become obsessed. How had his judgement become so clouded? And now not only Hannah's life was in danger, but Cora's too…

'We assumed male because it fit the narrative. Because every media outlet framed the culprit as he or him.' Anderson's train of thought was flooding out of his mouth, an audible stream of consciousness. 'We assumed male because we assumed sexual motive. It's been true before. Although no evidence of that on Matthew's body.'

'Guv, we all made the mistake. Collins—'

Anderson interrupted, '—is a nasty piece of shit and guilty of much more than he'll ever stand trial for. But in this case, wrongly accused. Though without it, we wouldn't have broken his money-lending racket. Don't beat yourself up, Minshull. Collins made himself a suspect by his behaviour. A loving stepfather wouldn't block our investigation like that. Even a toerag one.'

'If anything happens to her…' He wasn't speaking about Hannah now. Horrified at hearing his own voice betraying his thoughts, Minshull gripped the sides of the passenger seat until his hands hurt.

'We'll get them out.'

'What's Jan's motive? Could it still be predatory?'

'Possibly. Or a bid for attention.'

'Murder for attention?'

'Unless murder wasn't the intent. The note on Cooper's body...' Anderson broke off.

'Said we made her do it,' Minshull finished. 'How did we make her resort to murder?'

'By ignoring the game. By refusing to play. By pushing for results.'

Have we ignored the game here?

Minshull felt the ground shift beneath them as the car bumped across the rutted country lane. He glanced at the dashboard clock.

Twenty minutes since Cora called. Had they run out of time?

Chapter Eighty-Two

Jan

She hadn't meant to kill the boy.

She'd been pushed into it – just as she was being pushed now. The press wanted a rescue or a body. If what Cora had said was true, a rescue was looking less likely. Perhaps the police wanted a body now. Nice, clean, over.

She shifted gear, her anger crunching the transition.

What annoyed her most was the messiness of it all. If they had just followed her plan it would have turned out beautifully. A sweet innocent kid goes missing, a TV drama-worthy seven years after a bloody murder too similar to ignore. The police and community search tirelessly for the child. An evil game of cat-and-mouse ensues between the child-snatcher and the hero cops. A significant amount of ransom money is demanded. But at the eleventh hour, just as all hope seems lost, the lead investigator cracks the code, rescues the kid with no ransom being paid and returns triumphant to the waiting village.

And throughout the entire ordeal, one small town journalist never gives up hope...

It was never about the money. It was all part of the show.

Her plan had been so simple. Why did they have to make it so hard?

She imagined her father's mocking voice over her shoulder, as if the old bastard was condemning her from the back seat.

Best laid plans, eh girlie? Never thought you could do it. No skills, no finesse.

The best day of her life had been the day she'd found her father's broken and bloodied body, crushed by an overturned tractor in the far field. Douglas Martin had been a monster, terrorising his only daughter who he blamed for the death of his wife. How could a seven-year-old have prevented her mother's suicide? *Women were weak*, he'd insisted. And he'd set about beating the weakness out of her.

He'd made her kill a piglet once, laughing at her clumsy attempts to slit its throat. *You'll never be good enough at killing*, he'd said. *You don't have the nerve…*

Except she had, hadn't she?

And now she would have to again.

The reports after – the grieving family and a community in shock – would be little compensation for another failed plan. Within a week of the funeral, they would forget her again. Her four weeks of fame over. Some other tragedy would summon the press pack away from St Just and she would be left behind, one more by-line in a fading history.

In a way, it would be a relief. The seven years since Matthew's disappearance had seen the news become an omnipresent beast, constantly consuming current affairs, greedily demanding more and more. It was exhausting. Seven years ago, rolling news and social media were in their infancy and it was easier to drip-feed information. Now, every man and his dog was a media expert. She'd given up trying to follow the #findHannah hashtag on Twitter after it had quickly turned from concerned attempts to locate the child to gruesome predictions of her fate. What gave these people the right to comment? Did they know St Just, or the missing girl? What did they care what happened other than to spout their prejudice and bile over another tragedy their voyeuristic timelines flagged up?

Her only hope of continuing the interest was to copycat the murder. A prophecy fulfilled, another life stolen, with the murderer still at large, the story still tantalisingly unfinished. But that grated with her. Not the killing – this time she was mentally ready, where the first time had been borne out of panic. It was that she was being forced to replay her mistake, her ultimate failure, on a world stage she'd worked so bloody hard to win a place on.

She'd killed the boy because to *not* go through with it meant her father would have been right about her weakness. She'd embellished the death – the slashes, the note – to create the greatest impact. Riding the resulting shockwave was exhilarating and it had lasted longer than she'd expected. She'd even involved herself in the aftermath faced by Joel Anderson, investing hours of time collecting every delicious detail of his trauma.

There had been some remorse. Rosalyn Anderson was the closest thing to a sister she'd ever had and she felt some guilt for the years of pain she'd caused her husband.

That was why she'd taken Hannah. When she'd spotted the young girl wandering alone at the Easter Market while Jan handed out yellow *Argus* balloons in front of the newspaper offices it had been a gift. Blonde hair, blue eyes, a pretty face in a school uniform – the perfect symbol of innocence and absolute catnip to her colleagues in the national press. A girl represented greater danger: the public were only too aware of attacks on young women. The stakes were higher with a younger, female child.

That had been her mistake with Matthew: by ten years old boys were less cute, assumed to be tougher than girls that age would be.

Persuading Hannah to follow her through the empty newspaper office to her waiting vehicle at the rear car park had been the easiest thing – so simple she'd had to bite her lip to stop herself laughing out loud. The child had been too preoccupied by an odd-looking balloon animal dog she'd been given at a nearby stall to question where Jan was taking her. It was perfect: a second chance to get it right – both the plan for herself and redemption for Anderson for losing Matthew. He was supposed to follow the clues and at the eleventh hour, before the ransom was delivered, receive an anonymous tip-off that Hannah was in a shed in the grounds of St Just Church, where Jan would have placed her the moment Anderson spoke the words detailed in the ransom note. She had planned it all. Why had Anderson been sidetracked again?

Stupid, *stupid* police! Hadn't she given Anderson every clue about how the game should be played this time? Nobody could accuse her of not being compassionate.

I don't think they're taking it seriously enough. I don't think they believe they'll find Hannah…

Cora Lael's words buzzed about Jan's head like a cloud of angry midges. At least she'd believed Jan could do something. If only everyone else had that faith. It was almost enough to make her want to step up the game, to take it to the next level instead of straight to checkmate.

But the child was becoming a problem. Matthew Cooper stopped trying to fight back soon enough. A bit of shouting, some threats and a day without food was enough to scare him into silence. But not Hannah Perry.

At first it had seemed she would be simpler than the boy. She was younger, easier to frighten – or so Jan had thought. But in the last week she'd changed. Started fighting to keep her things. Refusing food. Trying to run. The girl was smart – and Jan had begun to worry she'd try to find a way out. She hadn't wanted to break her ankle, but what alternative did she have? It kept her from running – but Jan hadn't reckoned on it birthing a new defiance in the child's eyes. She'd seen it every time she'd taken food or water in. No words, but a look that screamed louder than a siren.

It was like seeing her father's eyes blinking in the child's face. Judging her. Exposing her failings. That couldn't go on.

The press wanted a horrific end. The machine demanded it. *The perfect angel meeting a violent, bloody death.* There was only one option left.

She'd have to miss the Sky News interview. But it was a small price to pay. A bigger, bloodier exclusive was on its way, one that would eclipse all that had gone before it.

Slamming her foot on the brake, Jan braced as the Range Rover skidded on the narrow country road. She punched her hand hard against the steering wheel, her yell dislodging a cloud of jackdaws from their treetop perches. The pain in her knuckles and the commotion overhead were penance for the act she was about to commit. To do what was necessary required anger – the kind that abandoned reason and forged ahead into oblivion.

Jamming the gearstick into reverse, she turned back for Light Hill Farm – and the darkness that awaited her there.

Chapter Eighty-Three

Cora

It was a momentary lapse of judgement but Cora knew it could be about to cost her everything.

Reaching the entrance of the outbuilding for the second time, Hannah clutching her school bag as if it were her life support, Cora heard the rumble of an approaching vehicle and knew it was too late to run. The last sight of her own car was swamped by the dark grey shadow of Jan's Range Rover. The sudden silence as the engine cut was followed by the slam of the vehicle's door.

It sounded like a death knell.

Panicked, Cora looked around the area in which she and Hannah crouched, seeking any sign that there could be another way out. But it was hopeless: the closest building was the barn and to get inside would mean running straight out into Jan's sight. All Cora could hope for now was that Jan wasn't heading for Hannah. If she went into the house there was a possibility they could escape.

She weighed up her options: run directly to the car, head for the nearer shelter of the barn, or remain where they were. As she would have to run past the kitchen window, the fastest route to her car was out of the question. The barn was an option, but from her earlier visit she knew its empty interior offered nowhere for them to hide. If Jan looked in there, they would be found. But if they stayed where they were, they were sitting ducks.

Sweat began to bead Cora's brow and slip between her shoulder blades.

Think, Cora!

There had to be another option. But what?

In a single, heart-stopping moment, Cora watched Jan turn towards them. Instinctively she pulled Hannah closer, her hand cradling the shivering child's head, and willed their bodies to meld into the crumbling brickwork of the pigsty. Every breath sounded louder than a thunder crack, her heart beating out of her chest. Against her, Hannah whimpered. Cora shushed the child through gritted teeth. Her peripheral vision revealed there was nowhere to run.

If Jan comes this way…

Cora struggled to focus through rising panic, this time her head only filled with conflicting versions of her own voice.

If Jan comes this way, I could stay still and hope she hasn't seen us… Or I could make a run for it.

Would the newspaper editor outrun her? Cora was sure of her own ability to run, but carrying a child over uneven ground and avoiding obstacles would slow her considerably. Jan could be faster than her frame suggested – after all, she had overpowered Hannah and, if what Rob and Joel Anderson had suggested were true, she had killed before.

Jan's face was flushed, her brow knotted into an ugly frown. The sight sickened Cora, as if the journalist had finally shed her skin, revealing the monster beneath. She was looking right at them. Had she seen Cora, realised what she was doing?

And then, the awful realisation hit her. Her car was still parked outside the farmhouse in plain sight. Jan *had* to know she was still here. How had she overlooked such an obvious fact? If Cora could see her car, so could Jan.

And then, Jan spoke. 'Cora? Where are you?'

The crash of her heartbeat in her ears, the voices of her conscience screaming for attention and the faint sob of the child against her chest almost drowned out Jan's words. But there was no mistaking the anger sparking from them, the dark threat contained within the question. All she could do was watch Jan open the boot of her vehicle and place something long wrapped in a buff travel rug on its roof. As it landed one edge of the rug fell back to reveal two dark grey metal barrels.

A shotgun?

Cora couldn't move, frozen in the farmyard mud by intense fear as she saw Jan leave the gun on the Range Rover's roof and start walking towards her. In vain she hoped it was a coincidence: that Jan hadn't seen them after all.

But it was hopeless. Jan knew they were there and it was only a matter of time until she found them. Everything within her screamed to run, but Cora held her nerve, the precious prize in her arms too valuable to risk.

Think! There has to be another way to get Hannah out!

But it was too late. Jan's eyebrows rose as she stopped walking.

'Cora…?'

Cora said nothing.

'What are you doing?' Her voice was icily calm, the question as threatening as a wielded sabre.

'I'm taking Hannah home.' Cora could hear fear fraying the edges of her words. But as soon as she said them, a new strength fired within her.

'You found her? Oh thank goodness! Put her in my car and we'll drive her home together.' Jan's smile clashed with soulless eyes, a jaw set in anger.

'No. I'm taking her home.'

Jan didn't move. Cora's calf muscles twitched, as if under starter's orders.

'I can't let you do that. This is *my* responsibility. I broke the story.'

'And I will make sure the police let you finish it.' Cora kicked herself for the slip. Why had she mentioned the police?

'*I don't think the police care about Hannah anymore,*' Jan replied slowly, repeating Cora's words from less than an hour ago. '*I think they've given up…*'

Thinking on her feet, Cora forced a smile. 'Then let's prove them wrong, shall we?'

'You and I both know it's too late for that. Give Hannah to me and you can go home.'

'No. Hannah's coming with me.'

Jan looked up at the darkening sky and sighed. 'Just – do what I say, Cora. Trust me, I know what I'm doing. It's the best possible outcome for everybody.'

She really believes this…

Jan's cool rationale was shocking. How could she think her actions were justifiable?

'Think of the story,' Cora rushed, resisting the shiver of dread as Jan's stare fell back on her. 'Think of the headlines: LOCAL JOURN-ALIST SAVES HANNAH. The ultimate scoop. You would be asso-ciated with the good news story for years. It could make you.'

'Good news? Do you think people remember good news?' Jan's wild curls danced around her head like a thundercloud as she spoke. 'Tell me, which historic news events are people still talking about now, hmm? 9-11, the London bombings, disasters, wars, murders. The happy stories are sidelined to the back pages then fall out of the news altogether. People feel good about themselves, then forget. We don't forget tragedy. We're programmed for bad news and hour after hour of analysis of how bad the news really is. *That's* what the public wants now. Ever more lurid, sickening headlines to feed their need for negativity.'

'I disagree.'

'You would. Psychologists, psychiatrists, therapists, you're all the same. Selling some happy-clappy version of life to line your pockets and fool us into believing human existence isn't the mean, vicious bitch it really is.' She started to walk towards her and Cora's body contracted. 'You want to know the biggest irony? Without the bad news we report you'd be out of a job. *We* feed the need, *you* feed the guilt.'

'I'm taking Hannah home.'

'Give her to me.'

Hannah's fingernails bit into the skin of Cora's neck as she clung tighter. 'No!'

'She's *mine…*'

Incensed, Cora pushed all her anger into her reply. '*Not* this child!'

Jan yelled and made a sudden lunge for Hannah. Instinctively, Cora kicked out, catching the journalist hard in the stomach. She heard the rush of wind leave her lungs as Jan's body crumpled in pain, the hands that had been reaching for the child turning to grip her own body. As she fell, her forehead smashed hard against the scratched metal fender of the farm tractor and the last thing Cora saw before she looked towards her escape route was a dark slick of blood smeared across it as Jan slumped to the ground…

Hannah

The Nice Lady is scared. I can feel it like steam rising from her.

But she is holding me like only Nanna Jo used to, like I'm the very last sweet in the tin.

They aren't moving anymore. The silver metal is covered in dark red sticky blood where Their head hit it. I don't want to see the blood, but now I can't stop looking. There's a *lot* of blood. It's dripping off the end of the metal onto Their head where They lie on the floor.

Are They dead?

I lean in as close as I can to Nice Lady's body, holding on tight. I haven't wanted anyone to die ever, not even Lily's gerbil that bit me and made my hand bleed. But I let out a secret wish that They are dead. I want Them to be dead so I can go home.

Nice Lady is shaking now. She has been staring at Them on the ground for a long time and I'm scared she's forgotten she was taking me away from here.

'I want to go home,' I try to say, but my voice is just a squeak when it comes out. Instead, tears stream from my eyes and I just put my head against the softness of Nice Lady's scarf. Through my tears I can see tiny silver stars shimmering in the pale blue material.

Nice Lady shudders. 'Come on,' she says. Her voice sounds like she's been jumping on a trampoline – wobbly and out of breath. 'Let's get out of here.'

The silver stars dance in front of my eyes as Nice Lady starts to run...

Chapter Eighty-Four

Minshull

The Victorian brick buildings of Light Hill Farm loomed into view, starkly red against the darkening grey sky. Minshull scanned the farm-yard for any sign of life as he and Anderson jumped from the car, the support unit van screeching in behind them.

'Guv?'

Anderson indicated the lead officer talk to Minshull.

'Sarge?'

'Somewhere here. Approach with caution.'

'There!'

Across the farmyard a figure appeared, running. Anderson held up his hand. The figure was carrying something – a bundle with a bright yellow rucksack.

'Wait!' he yelled. 'She has the child!'

'Cora! Over here!' Minshull shouted as the woman lifted her head and changed direction.

From over Cora's shoulder a second figure appeared, smaller and less steady, but unmistakably Jan Martin. She walked slowly, weaving a little as if drunk. Cora was making headway, almost within view of safety. Behind her, the newspaper editor was shaking her head, dragging something with effort in her right hand. As Cora neared the police cordon, Jan yanked the object to her shoulder and Minshull realised with sickening horror what it was.

Chapter Eighty-Five

Cora

Cora ran, the fear and anger and injustice of recent days becoming fuel for her limbs. The child whimpering in her arms was final, irrefutable proof that her voices were real. Nobody could doubt her now; better yet, she no longer doubted herself.

There had been times in the darkest, starkest hours of the night, reeling from another dream of Hannah, when Cora had believed she was reaching the edge of her sanity. When Minshull had dismissed her, she'd battled the possibility he was right.

But not now.

She had been heading for her car but was suddenly aware of lights ahead – bodies and movement at the fringes of the farmland. Too many to be anything else. A flood of relief engulfed her as she saw the familiar figure of Rob Minshull rise from behind a vehicle parked across the road to block it.

He'd got her messages. He *believed* her.

'We're okay,' she urged into Hannah's hair, injecting another burst of power into her speed. 'The police are here. We're safe.'

She was almost there, moments away from the end of her ordeal. She was stronger, braver, her ability finally proven. She was justified, for the first time in her life. Her lungs were on fire, her body screaming in protest, but she felt alive and part of something real. She *belonged*. Hannah dared to lift her head and Cora wanted to yell in triumph. Two lost souls, running home...

Minshull was close enough for her to see his expression now. Relief and apology radiated from him and all Cora wanted to do was to deliver the child into his arms. Like she'd promised. Like she'd always known she would. His smile reached out to her as he beckoned her on. Behind him DI Anderson stepped out, the pronounced folds of his forehead smoothing as she ran closer.

Rob reached his hand out to her…

…and everything changed.

In a heartbeat his smile was gone, eyes widening as his face fell. He yelled something that Cora couldn't hear above her own breath and she saw Joel Anderson grab his shoulders. In slow motion they fell to the ground as behind her the air exploded. A huge force hit Cora's back, twisting her around towards the farmhouse. Disorientated but desperate to keep running, she kicked out against the mud rising up to claim her and forced her body onwards. Rob and Anderson had dropped from view but she knew they were there, waiting for her. Waiting for Hannah. She had to reach them.

Her legs skidded and she wrapped her arms tighter around the child as she struggled to keep her balance. From a place far away she thought she heard Rob call her name. Hannah screamed in her arms as another enormous blow lifted Cora's feet off the ground.

And then she was falling, the world around her stretching and contracting, the dank greyness of the farm giving way to blood-red mist and deep, all-consuming darkness.

Her last thought before she surrendered to nothingness was to hold the child high, the crack of just her own head against unforgiving earth confirming she had succeeded in protecting Hannah from the fall.

'You're safe,' she said, her voice slow and dreamlike. '*Safe*…'

It was the word she'd dreamed of saying: a promise to herself, to the child, to Rob, that was now reality. With the word came a flood of peace, as if its four letters formed a key to unlock the rest Cora had sought all her life. The ground swelled and rose and her eyes blinked in the brightness of the car headlights.

So close now…

The shouts around her – or were they within? – began receding into fathomless, velvet silence. A warm, welcoming absence of noise engulfed her, pulling her deeper. She sensed the voices leave and didn't wish them to return.

Her task complete, Cora let go.

Chapter Eighty-Six

Minshull

The coffee from the machine in the hospital ward was worse than DC Wheeler's. Minshull drank it anyway, the events of the past twenty-four hours requiring caffeine in whatever form he could find. Anderson paced the other side of the narrow hospital corridor, his shoes squeaking on the pale green linoleum.

'Time?' He barked.

Minshull checked his watch. 'Five minutes since you last asked.'

'Cute. Try that again and I'll tell DCI Taylor to demote you to uniform.' He glared at the door to the room where Jan Martin was. 'What are they doing in there?'

'Obs. The sister said we can talk to her when the consultant's finished his visit.'

Anderson muttered under his breath, but Minshull could see his mind working. Any relief he may have felt at finding the child had been all but obliterated by the end game. Minshull sensed it, too. Hannah may be safely tucked into a children's ward bed, her mother by her side, but the revelation of her abductor – and more than likely Matthew Cooper's murderer – had shaken him to the core.

The official statement would be issued within the next hour, they had been informed, DCI Taylor no doubt relishing the job of delivering news of Hannah's rescue to a hungry press pack. A day ago, Minshull and Anderson would have fought over the right to tell the world Hannah Perry was alive and safe. But not now.

That was the reality though, wasn't it? Nobody came out of a case like this unchanged, unscathed. Anderson might rest easy knowing Hannah hadn't suffered the same fate as Matthew Cooper, but could he be content knowing his wife's close friend had been playing him for a fool for so many years? Hannah might have had a tearful reunion with her mum, but what would the long-term effects of four weeks of incarceration and intimidation be?

Shaun Collins was facing charges of illegal money lending, intimidation and assault. His sister, who had been laying low on the advice of the tabloid newspaper she'd sold a tell-all story to, would face no charge, but her precious pay cheque for her story had vanished the moment Hannah had been found alive. Nobody wanted Siobhan Collins' opinion now.

And what about Cora Lael?

He couldn't shake the image of her being tossed to the ground by the impact of the shotgun blasts, her smile becoming shock and determination and then resignation as she fell, still holding Hannah out to them...

'Rob.'

Anderson had moved to his side and his hand was on his shoulder. The gesture was so unexpected and heartfelt that Minshull had to blink back tears. A fatherly gesture – only nothing like his own father would ever have shown his sons.

'Yes, Guv.'

'We can go in now.'

Minshull was shown into the room first, but he could almost feel the white-hot anger of his superior burning through his back. In the middle of the room, Jan Martin lay in bed, her head heavily bandaged and a drip attached by cannula to her right hand. Behind her, a small grey box pulsed with her heartbeat.

The stern-faced nurse checking her notes beside the journalist nodded at them.

'Keep it short please, gentlemen. She needs rest.'

'She needs something...' Anderson stopped. Even he was no match for the steely-eyed sister. 'All we need is ten minutes.'

'I'll just be the other side of the door,' she replied, a warning delivered with clinical proficiency.

Jan's eyelids flickered as Minshull and Anderson approached. There were a million things Minshull wanted to say to her, but they needed her to talk as much as possible. He gave a small cough and Jan opened her eyes.

'To what do I owe the honour?' she croaked, her voice raspy and slowed by sedation.

'Why did you abduct Hannah Perry?' Anderson's reply was cold as steel.

Her eyes slid to his. 'Really, Joel? You're starting with that?'

Anderson didn't flinch. 'Why did you abduct Hannah Perry?'

'You can't question me in a hospital bed. No lawyer present, no recording of our conversation? I would have expected you of all people to know that, Joel.'

'Consider this a visit from a good friend, then. Why did you abduct Hannah Perry?'

Bloodshot eyes narrowed. 'No comment.'

The heart monitor continued its steady *blip... blip...*

'Did you take Matthew Cooper seven years ago?' Minshull asked, the barely contained fury of his superior beside him prickling his own skin. 'Did you take him, send his belongings back to police with demands and finally murder him?'

'No comment.'

So much for getting her to talk.

He changed tack. She wasn't getting away by playing dumb. 'Hannah's okay, by the way. The child you abducted. She's going to be fine. She's a fighter.'

Jan's flinch was tiny but Minshull caught it.

'I don't know what you thought you'd achieve, Jan, but if you wanted to break the kid I'm afraid you failed. Hannah Perry won.'

She closed her eyes, the spikes of the heart monitor quickening. 'Go away. I'm tired.'

'You're tired? What about that child? What about her family – the community – *my officers* – who you've put through hell? You think any of us have slept?'

What was Anderson doing? Minshull laid a hand on the hospital bed, a physical block between his superior and the journalist. 'Why, Jan?'

Her eyes remained resolutely shut. 'You're the detective. You work it out.'

Anderson leaned as close as he could, his voice a hissed whisper. 'Better start writing your defence story, Janice. Make it a good one. Because we're going to make sure we throw everything at you.'

A slow, thin-lipped smile spread across Jan Martin's pale features like an ugly oil slick. 'Say hi to Ros for me, Joel. Give her my love.'

It took all of Minshull's strength to wrestle Anderson out of the room.

'She was never going to confess,' he offered, when Anderson had calmed down enough to be coherent. 'Even though she knew it was over.'

'I didn't want her to confess – not to that. We have her on that. I just wanted to look her in the eye and understand. My wife and I – oh what the hell, Rob, you know it already. I almost lost everything because of *that* woman. Years of counselling, of being too scared of my own mind, of trying to hold shattered glass together in the face of the force. You hear people talking about being on the brink – well, I was so far over it I saw the abyss. I almost didn't come back.'

Minshull didn't know how to reply. How were you supposed to respond to that?

'I just wanted to know why.'

'You might never know that, Guv.'

The DI and the Acting DS observed one another across the bright hospital corridor.

'How are you doing, Minshull?'

He didn't have an answer. Not one that he could put into words yet. He hoped his shrug would suffice.

'It's not been easy, I know. I appreciate you coming in but you could take some leave – if you need it.'

'No need, Guv.'

Anderson's stare drilled into him. 'But Cora—?'

He didn't want to hear her name. Not yet. 'Not now, please. It's too soon...'

He didn't need to say any more. Anderson understood. 'There's no hurry, kid. Whenever you're ready.'

Eight Months Later

Chapter Eighty-Seven

Cora

The oncoming storm churned the sea into slate-green waves that broke across the yellow shingle spit. Torcross, at the head of Slapton Sands in South Devon, was a tourist haven in the summer but now, with Christmas just weeks away, it was a place only the hardiest walker would brave.

But Cora liked it here.

Her lunch break, such as it was at the small, thatch-roofed beach café, had been extended today due to the lack of customers. Mac, the retired Scottish fire-fighter turned café owner, had handed her coffee in her favourite mug and told her to take her time. 'I know you like this weather, you crazy woman. Go. Make the most of it. If we get a rush, I'll yell.'

Staring out to sea, Cora took a deep breath as peace flooded her body. There were no ghosts here, only nature and its own symphony. It had been the right decision to move from Suffolk to this wild, impossibly beautiful place, if only to allow herself time to heal. Sheila had already visited, thrilled her daughter was making her own way in the world, just as she herself was still learning to do.

'You're a difficult woman to track down,' said a voice.

She recognised it immediately.

Cora's eyes remained on the steady roll of mossy waves edging lengthways up the wide shingle beach. 'But you did.'

'Were you expecting me to?'

'No.' She looked at Rob Minshull, a little disconcerted by how unsurprised she was to find him there.

Minshull drew his collar closer to his chin with one hand as the icy December wind bit at his face, and took a sip from the takeaway coffee cup he held in the other. 'Bit bleak here, isn't it? Even for you.'

'I like it.' Her answer was curt and she dropped her head as soon as she'd said it. 'I came here on holiday once when I was five. We rented a caravan,' – she pointed a gloved hand towards a flat patch of land alongside the lea, next to the road that straddled the gap between freshwater lake and the ocean – 'over there. The park is long gone now, but I have happy memories of it.'

She remembered the scene in the heat of a South Devon summer, almost twenty-five years ago; and the carefree child she had been, playing by the sea, before the shock of her gift had assaulted her. Before any of it.

Cora was sad for what had been lost, but her grief lay concealed, sarcophagus-tight, beneath layers of time. She drew the yellow striped mug to her lips, inhaling the sweet tang of caffeine and sugar, soothing in its immediacy. This was what mattered now: the senses of the present. There were no adverse voices here.

'I wanted to give you this.' He took a white envelope from the inner pocket of his brown cord jacket and held it out to her. 'The final verdict of the Jan Martin case. And a letter I think you'll like.'

Cora hesitated, the mere mention of Jan's name enough to shake the equilibrium she had spent so many months fighting to reclaim. She winced as the injury in her shoulder smarted and an image of her assailant flashed across her mind. Her pale eyes sought reassurance in his.

'You could have posted it.'

'No, I couldn't.' His smile was genuine. 'Take it, Cora.'

The envelope contained two items: a single sheet of printed white paper and a smaller, pale pink envelope with childlike handwriting, decorated with holographic puppy stickers. Opting to open this first, Cora's apprehension lifted like morning mist when she read the neatly written message:

> *Dear Cora*
>
> *Thank you for coming to get me. I was scared but you made me safe.*
>
> *Mum wants you to come for tea soon to say thank you properly.*
>
> *You can meet my new dog Amber when you come!*
>
> *Lots of love*
>
> *Hannah xx*

'How is she?'

'Good. Her ankle healed well. She's being counselled, of course, but she's making progress. She's back at school and, bar a few nightmares, her mum says she's getting back to normal. Her stepdad's off the scene permanently now, which helps.' He paused, scrutinising her for any sign of emotion. 'She talks about you a great deal.'

Cora acknowledged this with a silent nod, the thought of Hannah unharmed and reunited with her mum far better than the peace she had discovered since moving here. Breath tight in her chest, she turned her attention to the verdict:

> Janet Martin, journalist, 51, found guilty on all counts of: the manslaughter of Matthew Cooper, 10, child abduction with intent to cause harm, perverting the course of justice, blackmail and the attempted murders of Woman A, 29, and Hannah Perry, 8.
>
> Special commendation is given for the bravery of Woman A, but an enquiry is to be held into the policy of allowing non-standard experts to assist in future South Suffolk Constabulary investigations...

'Non-standard?' Cora laughed, the sting of its implication smarting. 'Is that what they're calling me now? I must add that to the list.'

'The judge and the CPS feel it was irresponsible of us to place a civilian in danger. They have a point.'

Cora laughed again, but this time she wasn't smiling. 'If I hadn't done what I did, when I did, the outcome could have been very different.'

'Hey, nobody's arguing. But we had no right to ask that of you. *I* had no right...' His words trailed off as he kicked up a shower of pebbles with the toe of his boot.

She could stay angry with him for the rest of her life. But where was the peace in that? 'If you came here for forgiveness then you already have it.'

'That's not why I'm here.'

'Oh.' It was her turn to stare at the beach. 'How long?'

'Fifteen years.'

'That's nothing! She killed Matthew Cooper. She would have killed Hannah...'

'I know. But her counsel claimed diminished responsibility.'

'And the jury bought that?'

'It didn't harm her case.'

'It's a joke.'

'Tell me about it.' He changed tack. 'How's the shoulder?'

'Painful.'

'I thought it might be. Did the doctors say how long before it heals?'

She shook away irritation at being questioned. 'Months, maybe. But there will be physio and they're hopeful the damage won't be permanent.'

'Cora, I—'

'Why did you come?'

Her question momentarily threw him. 'I think you know…'

She stared at him. 'No. I'm not sure I do.'

He stared back, clearly not convinced. 'We've been through a lot, you and I…'

'Which is over now.'

'Is it?'

She looked away. 'Hannah is safe. Jan can't hurt anyone else. And my *non-standard* services are no longer required. There's nothing more.'

'I think there is. And I think we should talk.'

Cora's pale eyes rounded on him. 'Talk about what? About how you took Daniel Gold's word over mine? About how you didn't listen to me when you needed to? About how you dropped me like a stone the moment it suited you?'

His smile was barely perceptible. 'I thought you said I was forgiven.'

'You are! You always were…' She let out a groan of frustration. 'I came here to be away from the voices, to be *quiet*…'

'To hide, I know.'

'No, not to hide. To start again.'

He took a step towards her. 'And that's why I had to come.'

'Go *home*, Rob.'

He turned his face towards the waves, blinking as sprays of salt hit his skin on the increasing breeze. 'What are you doing to occupy yourself here?'

'I'm working at the café.' She nodded in the direction of the cottage beyond the breakwater. 'I bake.'

'And it's good money?'

'It's enough.'

'Has—' Minshull hesitated. 'I don't suppose you've heard from Daniel?'

She laughed, despite herself. 'What do you think?'

'Fair enough.'

Dark clouds, rain-heavy, were beginning to roll in from the sea and a noticeable change in the waves was already underway. Cora finished her coffee and wrapped her arms about her body. Minshull stared at the dregs in the bottom of his paper cup, as if trying to plan his next move.

'There's a storm on the way,' she said suddenly, surprising herself as much as Minshull. 'The beach won't be the best place to stay soon.' It wasn't much of a lifeline but it was the best she could afford. For all her anger at his unheralded arrival, she found comfort in him being here. It was time to hear what he'd come to say.

'So, what's this café like?' Minshull asked.

She took a breath. The salt air stung her lungs with its freshness. 'Why don't you come and see?'

Minshull smiled back and began to walk slowly towards the sea wall. Cora tipped the dregs of her coffee onto the shingle beach and followed. As Minshull reached the concrete steps, he paused deliberately, screwed up his paper cup and discarded it in the wooden litter bin before sprinting up to the promenade.

Cora stopped by the bin as a strong voice spoke. Staring down, her pale eyes widened in surprise. She lifted her head and watched Minshull striding towards the beach café, the revelation still reverberating in her mind.

Then, with the smallest smile playing on her lips, she began to ascend the steps after him.

A letter from M.J. White

Dear Reader

This is a story ten years in the making. A story I never thought I'd have the chance to share. Welcome to the first book in my debut crime series. You're about to meet characters that have been hanging about in my head since 2012 – I hope they behave on the page for you!

I have loved crime fiction for many years as a reader, and police procedurals the most. Reading books by my writing heroes such as Ian Rankin, Ann Cleeves, Mari Hannah, Val McDermid and Stuart MacBride inspired me so much and made me wonder if one day I could follow in their footsteps. This story began as a dare to myself. I noticed that the short stories I was writing were always noticeably darker than my published novels – and that got me thinking: could I write a darker story of novel length?

Dr Cora Lael's story began on a trip to Suffolk in 2012. I was there to see my fourth novel, *When I Fall in Love*, being printed at Clay's in Bungay and decided to stay overnight in Lowestoft, being a landlocked Midlander who will take any opportunity to see the sea. It was late October and freezing cold, blowing a gale and magnificently gloomy when I arrived. A thick mist obscured the sea from view completely when I ventured onto South Beach – but that's where Cora arrived. I imagined her walking out of the mist and instantly knew I wanted to tell her story. I spent the next two years trying to discover what that story was. And then came eight year-old Hannah Perry, taken in broad daylight from a tiny Suffolk village…

Writing about a missing child was a challenge, made more so when my daughter Flo arrived and I understood the fear of anything happening to her. But I wanted to celebrate the deep resilience of children in the middle of such horror and show you Hannah's story in her own words, as Cora, Rob, Anderson and the CID team from

South Suffolk Constabulary fight to find her. I wanted to show how individuals and communities are affected by a terrifying event and how the media can twist a local tragedy into a national debate.

I loved creating the community of St Just and the members of the police team working so hard to find Hannah. Most of all, I loved developing Cora's unique ability. Emotional synaesthesia doesn't exist, but it is inspired by the lived experience of people with real-life, sensory-based synaesthesia. The mind is incredible and the way it can adapt and develop through a range of neurological divergences is amazing. Cora's story is of someone daring to see what she *can* do, rather than be 'othered' by the things society perceives she can't. I hope her journey to push her ability is inspiring.

I hope you enjoy reading Cora's first case – I am already writing the second book in the series for Hera Books, which is due to follow later in 2022. I am thrilled to be finally sharing Cora, Rob, Anderson and Hannah with you!

If you enjoy this book, let me know! You can get in touch via Twitter, Instagram, Facebook and YouTube and also on my weekly Facebook Live show, Fab Night In Chatty Thing (where I first read extracts from this book and, encouraged by the reaction from my viewers, sent it out to publishers) – it takes place every Wednesday at 8pm and I'd love to see you there. And if you fancy leaving a review or, better still, telling people about this book, I would be over the moon!

Thank you for your support of me and my stories. I am beyond proud to write them for you and, trust me, there are more to come! Cora's next case promises to be even darker than this…

Happy reading!

Brightest wishes

Miranda x

www.twitter.com/wurdsmyth
www.instagram.com/wurdsmyth
www.facebook.com/MirandaDickinsonAuthor
www.youtube.com/mirandawurdy
www.miranda-dickinson.com

Acknowledgments

Dear Reader

I wanted to tell you this story for ten years. Despite setbacks, doubts and rejections, it refused to go away and now I am proud to share *The Secret Voices* with you.

So many people have believed in this story over the years and kept it alive. Huge thanks to my brilliant agent, Hannah Ferguson, for her endless faith in me and willingness to keep pushing doors for my writing. I am thrilled that Hera Books wanted this story and am delighted to work with the awesome Keshini Naidoo to bring Cora, Rob, Anderson and Hannah to the page. Thanks for believing in me and seeing what this book could be. My sincere thanks to Jennie Ayres for wise, insightful copyedits and Vicki Vrint for proofreading.

Massive thanks to PC Steve Franklin for his advice and guidance on police procedure and also for giving me valuable insight into life as a police officer. Any mistakes in procedural details of this book are mine alone.

Huge thanks to the amazing Dreamers – Al, Sherri, Stephen and Catherine – who first heard this story in 2014 and have supported it all the way. Big love to AG Smith and Claire Smith for being constant cheerleaders, and gorgeous author chums CL Taylor, Rachael Lucas, Anna Mansell, Kim Curran, Jo Quinn, Kate Harrison, Tamsyn Murray, Rowan Coleman, Julie Cohen and Ian Wilfred for their support and love. Thanks to Andrew Wille for wise words and belief in me. Thanks too to the lovely viewers of my Facebook Live show, *Fab Night In Chatty Thing*, for loving this story when I read extracts of it and encouraging me to get it published. Look! We did it!

Sincere thanks to amazing authors Mari Hannah, Emma Kavanagh, Clare Mackintosh, Steve Cavanagh, Luca Veste, Dorothy Koomson and Mel Sherratt for offering advice, help, wisdom and support over the years as I worked on this book. I am in awe of you all and you continue to inspire me.

Big love to Pat Elliott, who loved this story years ago. Hope you like your cameo in the café Cora and Rory visit! And much love to my Mum and fantastic in-laws Phil and Jo White, for always being awesome. As always, my love and thanks to my lovely Bob and fantastic Flo – you are the reason for everything. I love you to the moon and back and twice around the stars xx

Sometimes the stories that refuse to leave are the ones worth telling. I hope you enjoy *The Secret Voices* – I wrote it for you.

Brightest wishes,

Miranda x

Book Soundtrack Playlist

When I start to write a novel, I compile a playlist of music that fits the atmosphere and emotion of the story I want to create. I play it every time I work on the story, from initial draft to finished book, and it helps me to maintain focus on the story. Here is the book soundtrack for *The Secret Voices*. Enjoy!

SKYWORLD – Two Steps from Hell – *SkyWorld*

I FOUND – Amber Run – *Pilot EP*

YOU FROM ME – Bailey Tsuke – *Laid Bare EP*

WAY DOWN WE GO – KALEO – *A/B*

SNOW ANGELS – Two Steps from Hell & Thomas Bergersen – *Unleashed*

THRU THE GLASS – Thirteen Senses – *The Invitation*

RUNNING HOME – Reuben Halsey feat. Miranda Dickinson – *Eucalyptus Tree*

IF YOU CAN HEAR ME – Ben Rector – *The Walking in Between*

SOMETHING BETTER CHANGE – Seabird – *Troubled Days*

SEE ME NOW – Ryan Keen – *Focus EP*

DEEP FOREST – Neal Schon – *Beyond the Thunder*

HEAR ME – Imagine Dragons – *Hear Me EP*

SOMEWHERE – Within Temptation – *The Silent Force*

ARCHANGEL – Two Steps from Hell – *Archangel*

EXONERATION – Michael Price & Nicholas Hill – *Emotional Cinema*

FOLLOW YOU HOME – Robby Earle – *Lifted*